The Angel Seedlings

Vincent Redgrave

ISBN-979-8-88627-638-1

Printed in the United States of America

CONTENTS

Table of Contents

Dedication

A heartfelt thanks to my close friends for listening to my insane ideas and then reading various iterations. Good readers and meaningful critics are hard to find, and even harder to keep. The lure of coffee and alcohol should not be underestimated.

A further thanks to those same beautiful souls for not calling the authorities and having me carted off to a padded room. In no particular order of preference, color, creed, ability, or persuasion: Randy, Heather, Jeanneane, Martin, Darlene. Thanks to my editor, Craig Bourne, for his patience and invaluable insight.

To anyone who has ever made a mistake or two - at least you can say that you lived.

For those of you reading the dedication I can assure you that the best is yet to come. Stay tuned.

CHAPTER ONE

Spring 2021.

"Let them praise the name of the Lord; for he commanded and they were created."

The words floated in the air as if they were part of a dream. When she opened her eyes, the shadowy figure's gaze looked back at her, and then, too late, she realized it was real. Time was missing. Laughter had ceased. Fear ruled, and her resolve instantly evaporated.

"Our creator has shown me the way," the figure assured. "You will be re-made."

"No." Strangely, she understood. As easily as her resolve had evaporated, hope abandoned her.

"Don't be afraid." The voice was genuinely wrapped in warm empathy, matching the accompanying kindness of the bright gaze.

The bedroom was eerily quiet. Silence gripped the air, banishing sound.

A solitary candle glowed from the back of the bedroom on top of the antique chest of drawers. The open curtains showed that darkness had overtaken the landscape, and only a wispy radiance from the partial moon forced its way through the ground floor windows. The candle provided a soft illumination, struggling in the form of high flickering shadows against the brilliant white painted walls. Selected modern art pieces hung in careful precision alongside the hand-selected furniture, where each piece complimented the next in color, texture, and fabric. Money had been well-spent on presenting a coordinated feast for the eye in every room, with each teasing the observer to the next offering. Now the offerings were changed with resounding finality. Money could not buy the things which were left unseen. The modern condo had lost its appeal where the chic spectacle acted as a conjurer's cloak to hide the tragedy underneath the elegant façade. None of it mattered. She knew it. The figure knew it.

The beautiful young woman on the bed coughed, and a white sticky froth oozed from her purple lips. "Please!" Her plea was labored. Her brunette hair was neatly styled and adorned with a white silk rose, where the loose curls were meticulously parted on the side of her head. Two thin straps dropped from her broad shoulders to the vintage white silk chemise that hugged her body – a fanciful item she'd never purchased or previously possessed. It was handmade and had been brought here for the auspicious occasion. The breast and neckline were decorated with intricately-patterned lace, matching the same above the knee. It was a garment fit for a glorious honeymoon, with its plunging backline loosely tied over the small of her back and a slit to the hip up the right-hand side. Her fingernails were manicured and freshly painted with a decorative floral rose on each index finger.

The young woman's facial expressions changed with each passing second, unsure how she came to be this way or why her uncooperative body could not rise from the bed. These were not her things, but she was in her bedroom. Confusion accompanied the fear.

Above her, the hooded figure remained concealed within the shadows – the candle's small flame was not enough to display all the features. She could only make out the slender eyebrows and the sincere tenderness of the watchful eyes.

The figure understood the opulent surroundings were to impress would-be visitors. The elements displayed a particular type of lifestyle, and they were simply props, no different than an actor readying for a performance.

The hooded figure softly stated, "Once this is stripped away, there's an emptiness of spirit, emptiness of love, and a void that desperately desires human connectivity. It's these awful failures that have brought us together. I see it no differently than I see the real you. The slow spiral of your degradation is over." The figure took hold of her hands and whispered, "It is for the best. I'm going to help you."

The young woman, adorned in white silk, looked into the light brown eyes that gazed lovingly at her. She tried to move from the bed, but her limbs betrayed the signals from her brain. "I don't understand." She choked on the words, and her tongue became numb, useless, an unresponsive piece of flesh inside her mouth. Tears leaked down her face onto the pillow. A latex-gloved hand reached up and wiped away the soft tears.

"Soon, everything will be okay," the voice tenderly encouraged her. There was a definitive belief in the statement, reflected in the satisfying glow from the adoring gaze.

The young woman pressed her eyelids tightly shut and tried to roll herself off the bed. Typically she was strong and entirely in control of her faculties and all facets of her life. She partially recognized the soft eyes – a recent familiarity. Kindness and understanding had been exchanged. "Why?" She struggled to push out the single word. She thrashed her body to shake herself from this mess. Nothing obeyed. Only gathering cloudiness to her thoughts prevailed with a sudden recognition of invasive clarity–a moment of pure startling terror.

Earlier, the wine they'd shared over dinner, the chatter, laughter, and even some flirtation made no sense. She was lying helplessly on her bed, dressed in a silk nightgown. Drugged, for sure. She reminded herself she was Daphne Montclair, the physically powerful owner of Dynamo Fitness Wear. She was one of Northern California's leading young entrepreneurs, a millennial millionaire, and a highly recognizable Instagram celebrity and influencer. Daphne was in charge of her life; her female followers adored her and many male admirers too. She would not go down without a fight. Summoning all her willpower, she gave everything she had to rise up and rid herself of the shadowy specter.

"The angels are calling you," the voice hummed. "Save your strength."

Daphne's efforts were in vain. The hopelessness that descended upon her was compounded with crushing regret. There were many things she'd wished had turned out differently. In her recent life, compromises had been made that tainted the fabric of her mortal soul. Her conscience had pricked her each time, yet she'd ignored the signs. The lure of money, and the increase in her profile, were too great to resist. Now the worry folded within, and she was unable to make amends. Daphne's vision was impaired, and she had to blink hard to initiate focus. Her limp arms and legs hadn't moved an inch. The sympathetic eyes watching her showed that they pitied her struggle. As she sniffed the air, something light and familiar pleasantly entered her nostrils.

"Frankincense. For your transition. You have such beautiful skin. What you're feeling is simply your humanity dissolving. Greater things await you."

Daphne shivered, unable to recall any of it, but the thought of being stripped naked and vulnerable in someone else's hands was too much. She cursed herself for the shame of being exposed in front of a stranger. It was an irrational thought under the circumstances, yet her mind toyed with her by repeating a series of defenseless images. She could not recall whether or not a violation had taken place. It was better not to know.

The smiling eyes from above aggregated the idiotic humiliation and served only to fast-track Daphne to the inevitable. "My lungs."

The gloved hand squeezed her fingers tight. "You are closer to God than to life. Let it all go." The figure nodded its admiration of Daphne's surrender. "Soon, you'll be complete. No one can hurt you anymore. Not even yourself."

"Why?" Daphne gargled as parts of her body lost feeling, and others twitched and fluttered, signaling that her organs were fast shutting down.

"You've always been lonely. You said so." The hands squeezed tighter, and the pretty eyes showed compassion. "Your pain will be gone. It's a time to rejoice. I promised you I'd never let you die alone."

Daphne's sorrow should have made her cry, but her body no longer functioned as it should, and all she could do was stare in disbelief. Her eyelids were heavy. Daphne felt like she was drifting to sleep, and the faintest sound in her ears was of someone humming a soft tune. She marginally recognized the soulful hymn that lightly brushed her ears.

Panic ensued as her airwaves struggled to receive enough oxygen, and an irregular heartbeat barely pumped blood around her dying body. Her jaw slackened, and she could no longer prevent her mouth from falling wide open, and all the while, the shadowy figure hummed the tune. A latex glove wiped away the thickening white spittle that oozed from her mouth, making sure none of it spilled onto the straps of the delicate nightgown. Finally, Daphne's heart could not take the strain– her eyes fractionally opened before closing for the final time.

The figure touched Daphne's chest, feeling the heart reach its beautiful end. The shared surge of oncoming death bonded them for eternity. "My sweet girl. I hope I'll see you again one day."

The figure looked out the windows across the open fields and sighed with satisfaction. It was a picture-postcard evening, with the rows of leafy trees that lined the distant main road and, beyond, the glistening surface of the ocean. The westside of Santa Rosa in Northern California provided extensive miles of uninterrupted views over the Pacific Ocean. It was an exquisite pathway for Daphne to enter a new spiritual life, surrounded by the things she loved and accompanied by someone who deservedly loved her. The love given was pure, and as she passed over, there was no sadness, only thanks to the Almighty. The figure carefully turned Daphne onto her side and lay next to her, with its right arm folded over Daphne's body. It cradled her as though she were a beloved sister. Loving contentment enveloped the figure. "My sweet Daphne. When my time comes, I hope that it's serenely beautiful just like yours."

They remained snuggling for several minutes to help with the journey and ensure the soul knew it was safe to proceed towards the light. There was no more need for unnecessary self-doubt, manipulation, or misery. This was a gift that few people would ever be able to appreciate. The figure had often considered its mortality and had hoped that a generous individual would provide the same level of comfort one day. And so it would be a life well-lived.

Minutes later, the figure busily prepared to take Daphne to her final resting place – a peaceful location, meticulously selected. A fitting and respectful end. The figure tidied away the syringe and other items. The backpack was secured and taken through the adjoining doorway into the underground parking and placed in the back of Daphne's car. On the way through the condo, the figure removed the small gilt-edged frame that showed the smiling Daphne, a picture taken on a trip to the south of France in 2018. The figure kissed the picture with love. "Now, you can smile again," the figure proposed. It was a keepsake, not for the macabre or evil, but a loving reminder of the kindness supporting Daphne's transformation.

Daphne's picture would accompany the others at home on the sideboard. Those timeless photographed smiles were a pearly symphonic thanks for seeing them into the next life. Each one was a treasured moment of their time together, and each held a heartfelt memory.

"We are so fortunate."

Moving the body would be a struggle, but the figure was strong, and there was no other way. It was a long drive that they would take in the dead of night, and an even more arduous journey on foot, into the thick of the forest. Transporting Daphne's body through two miles of dense woodland from the nearest road would be impossible for some. The figure had scoped out the terrain and calculated Daphne's body could be steadily taken to the burial site, which was already prepared. Daphne would be at peace, surrounded by the nature she loved so much. Such a blessing to have someone to care for you as much in death as in life.

With Daphne's body safely wrapped in the body bag, she was gently placed in the trunk of her car for the final journey to begin – a four-hour drive into the northern tip of California's Redwood Forest. It would be dawn when Daphne was laid to rest in the soft earth, and the light would burst through the gaps in the overhead canopy to illuminate her. The figure had seen the reflections of golden light from the leaves and how the sun's rays penetrated the ground. It would provide a showcase for Daphne's ascendency.

"Oh my God." The voice cracked open as the vision ignited. "Daphne, do you hear them? The angels are singing. They're coming for you." The image, along with the heavenly score, brought uncontrollable tears. "Daphne, it's perfect. Now you will grow into God's loving arms."

Daphne's blossoming into a servant of the Lord was indeed something special, and a quiet celebration would be held in her honor.

The figure thought ahead and smiled. "Don't worry, my beauties; I will soon help the rest of you. We'll all have our wings." The angelic vision was a toe-curling prospect.

Lainey Stewart leaned forward, slowly touching her toes. Her hamstrings tightened, and the stretch locked the backs of her knees. She held the position for a few seconds with her head caressing her shins like she was a ballerina. Her flexibility wasn't quite to the same high standard of a few short years ago, but good enough and way better than most. Body fluidity and physical strength were paramount in Lainey's world. From within herself, she demanded physical power to match the high levels of her cognitive skills and her ambitions.

The windows in her exercise room ran the entire wall length, providing a beautiful natural morning light that radiated throughout the space. She breathed in gratitude and slowly exhaled love to the world. "What a day," she sighed. In front of her were rows of dumbbells, a squat rack, weight benches, a pull-down machine, and a full rack of loose weights. Behind her were her two beloved hi-tech running machines.

The exercise room was one of many different functional rooms within the six thousand square foot home. The modern design and technical features within the structure rivaled that of anything a hundred miles further south in the technology belt of northern California. Every feature inside could be controlled from either a remote or her cell phone. A massage table accompanied an indoor sauna and spa and built-in surround sound for fully absorbed healing frequencies to soothe and repair – something much needed in the competitive world Lainey occupied.

Outside, the waterfall flowed into the swimming pool and rippled outward to the infinity view. Beyond was the secluded grotto, set around surgically manicured gardens and terraces leading into the woods on the north of the property. To the south were open fields with extensive views that provided the sumptuous landscapes overlooking Cock Robin Island and out to the horizon of the Pacific Ocean. Beyond the immediate gardens were twelve acres of property that included a small vineyard, a small lake with a hidden Gothic folly, and a non-denominational shrine for meditation. The house was situated four miles south of Eureka and set on the side of a steep hill. Everything was done with precision and maintained to Lainey's meticulous instruction. Keeping her surroundings with the right level of appeal took thoughtful consideration, an eye for detail, and strict follow-up on those assigned to keep it in order.

Life in the small town of Eureka, California, was hardly the bustling world of San Francisco or that of the tech giant boroughs scattered throughout northern California. Still, for Lainey, it was the comfort of the town in which she was raised and one where she felt safe. At least, as safe as she could be, given what had transpired.

There'd been many offers and temptations to draw her business south. Still, Eureka presented all she needed or wanted and an opportunity to give something back to her local community in the form of steady, well-paid employment. It benefited from allowing Brian and her to employ people familiar to them. It is a win for their business to have trustworthy, motivated, and dedicated people.

Lainey started her day with her favorite exercise on her state-of-the-art treadmill. She straightened her torso and raised her arms high above her head, giving a full stretch to her long limbs. Her five-foot-eight-inch frame was strong and toned, and at thirty-three, Lainey was in excellent physical condition. Her psychological condition had room for considerable improvement, but with each passing day, she seemed marginally better than the preceding one. The image of being under the woodland earth, soaked in sweat, and the associated panic, blitzed through her mind. "Urgh!" Lainey snarled and shook her body to rid herself of the imposing thought. It was a memory yet to be fully extinguished. She needed immediate control, and the best way to get that was to run.

Running was Lainey's passion, and ever since she took up track in middle school, she'd never looked back. From there, she got into triathlons and eventually into trail running. In addition to pushing her lungs to the limit, Lainey loved to test all her muscles. Her photographs adorned many fitness magazines and those in the entrepreneurial world. At one time, it seemed like photoshoots were the only thing she was doing. Thankfully, she was no longer in the news headlines, particularly for the reasons she most wished to forget. Lainey focused all of her efforts solely on the fitness business to occupy her mind and her time. Her business was equally as strong as her body, but other elements of her life had fallen by the wayside. Running left all her worries behind. It was more than a passion – it was an obsession. It had been ten years since Lainey failed to qualify for the US track team in the 10K trials.

At the time, she was so sickened by failure, primarily because of the one-tenth-of-a-second difference that had meant she had to stay at home. For months afterward, she'd been too distraught to train correctly. By the time the next opportunity came around, Lainey and Brian's business had taken off, and her chance to try again was lost. That didn't stop Lainey from asking herself what might have been. She'd pictured herself on the winner's rostrum a thousand times. Finally, four years later, her track times were good enough for her to have qualified. The retrospect pained her, and yet she looked back anyway.

She tightened the pink band around her ponytail and pulled her long dark hair through to ensure there was no need to adjust it once she started running. Interruptions were not appreciated when she was in her flow and happy place. Her leggings, sports bra, and running sneakers were all part of her brand, with the signature logo of three small triangles connected within the shape of a heart. The symbolic components of 4D Fitness: Mind, Body, Effort, and Heart.

Lainey stepped onto the treadmill and slid her bio-card reader into the slot. The curved twelve-foot long, eight-foot-high wrap-around digital screen sprang immediately to life. The display personally welcomed her alongside the 4D Fitness logo. Every time Lainey saw it, she was filled with pride. Lainey worked harder than most, pushing her body to keep herself looking and feeling fit, and she applied the same level of focus to driving the sales, marketing, and development of their product. As co-owner and CEO of 4D Fitness, she was once the face of the business to the public. However, since the unspoken incident a year earlier, Lainey entertained only a handful of media interviews inside her home. Her husband, Brian, had taken over the role of all public-facing events, regularly traveling the globe to expand their growing empire. Yet, behind the scenes, Lainey was the one driving hard. Their digitally enhanced treadmill was like nothing else on the market, and they intended to capitalize before the competition picked up the baton.

She tapped the keys on the digital display to select a local run through the tall pinewoods in Prairie Creek, just a few miles north of where they lived. Four years earlier, while running through those woods, she and Brian first produced the concept of their business. The wrap-around screen showed the beginning of the trail, where the undulating dirt track led deep inside the ancient forest. Wherever her eyes tracked on the massive screen, the software adjusted the three-dimensional view accordingly in real-time. On the central portion of the screen, Lainey could see how many times she'd run this course, her best time, average time, if anyone else in some part of the world was on the course, and how fast they were tracking. There were 173 people across the US and 64 other people jogging on their 4D treadmill along this same trail. They were currently in their home or an expensive gym and enjoying the same three-dimensional technology.

In Osaka, Japan, a guy was just two minutes ahead of her. Lainey referenced his fastest time and figured she might be able to catch his avatar further along the trail. She guessed it must be midnight on the other side of the world and wondered why he ran so late. Perhaps he was like her and couldn't sleep properly, or maybe it was the only way he could wind down after a hard day's work. No matter, she was determined to beat him.

She selected the start button, and the treadmill lifted six inches as it wound up to the pace she'd input. As the 3D track twisted through the trees, the treadmill reacted as it pivoted up, down, left to right with synchronized variations. It was a high-priced toy for those who wished to run in the comfort of their home, but they could feel as if they were anywhere on one of the twenty-five courses digitally mapped around the globe. The sounds of the forest filled the room, including the birds in the trees, the rustling of leaves in the wind, and the crack of a falling branch. Lainey preferred not to listen to music, as she liked the complete surround-sound feel of the outdoors. Instead, she quickly settled into a steady rhythm.

Getting investors for such an expensive piece of equipment had not been easy, and many people had told her and Brian to forget the idea, but she refused to quit. Lainey pushed Brian to the breaking point on many occasions, but it had been worth it, and he admitted the struggle had made him a better businessman. When the money came and the prototype was developed, the public offering followed. Lainey and Brian unleashed a marketing campaign to avid runners worldwide, especially those who could not run outdoors due to harsh weather conditions for a few months each year. Their product was the perfect antidote. Many buyers were elderly, wealthy people with no interest in running but simply liked to walk through the three-dimensional landscapes that transported them to different areas of the planet. All of the courses were set in perfect sunlit conditions, giving the feel of a pleasant walk or run through the chosen woodland or scenic hillside landscape. The 3D surround-screen downloaded constant updates and improved the clarity of each course anytime someone physically ran the real thing and uploaded their GoPro data.

Pre-launch sales went through the roof, making Lainey and Brian millionaires before a single combination set was shipped to eagerly awaiting customers. Over ten thousand units were sold in the first six months, forcing them to engage with a second factory to keep up with demand, and a further thirty thousand units were sold in less than three years. Besides the showcase equipment, they also sold every piece of known complimentary running wear.

The sales of leggings, shorts, vests, tops, hoodies, socks, underwear, and sneakers far outsold any technology packages. Soon, they would launch an offer to those who couldn't afford the whole technology package in a single purchase, and buyers' could make monthly payments. At eighteen thousand dollars for the complete setup, they needed to extend credit for those who couldn't afford a one-time payment. Data indicated that thousands more units would be sold along with their merchandise.

In the early days, when Lainey became the poster girl of new fitness startups, the media loved her as much as she loved the limelight. Her interviews were forthright, and her attitude was all about getting people off their couches and get going. Sections of the media criticized her and Brian over the cost of their product, but, as Lainey had laid out, the product was guaranteed for ten years, with free servicing. Over that time, it worked out to about half the price of a fancy cup of coffee per day to stay fit. Lainey quickly realized that the throw-away statement had enormous value. She refined it and became the much-used tagline to promote 4D Fitness innovation: "Get your life moving for half the price of a coffee per day!" Upscale gyms and executive offices were placing orders. Users were hooked, and the reviews were great.

Lainey was forced to reduce her media exposure. However, she provided the occasional live update via Facebook from her home, and she made sure that those who purchased their products could see that she was fit and strong, as well as could be expected. Only last week, she had Running International magazine in her home to provide updates on 4D Fitness as a global brand leader. Lainey was all too happy to show off their latest designs. Although she kept herself in great shape, her message was resolute in getting up, dusting herself off, and making an effort. It wasn't about a specific look but more of an attitude to never give up, no matter the circumstances. The message was genuine and an integral piece of the mindset that 4D Fitness supporters rallied around. Even though Lainey certainly did, the mantra wasn't about having a bikini beach body; it was effortful consistent determination. Still, their users cared about feeling connected to nature and one another via their loyal online community. Lainey's personal story was the ultimate comeback, and dusting herself off proved to be the single biggest challenge of her life. Their online family had nothing but outpourings of best wishes and love that had rallied her through the darkest of times. The online comments were 99% positive, and Lainey needed them. Lainey needed her online family, Brian, and especially running to keep her sanity, in that order.

Some ran to compete, and Lainey was right up there with her personal best times. Lainey and Brian had initiated their annual online competition with prizes given for the fastest times. The primary purpose of the competitions was to build a digital community and one that supported all those who took part, no matter what their level of achievement. Lainey and Brian worked hard to get the culture dialed in, and their subscribers happily followed along. People of all ages were celebrated within the digital network. The partnerships and online community were highly involved in helping to update the technologies and to ensure that they got the best out of what they'd paid for. It was a win for the business and the owners alike. The owner's community continually recorded their real-life trail experiences and digitally fed the data to enhance the product. 4D Fitness had a willing army of runners and walkers sending their video data. There was also the option to run side-by-side or walk on the trails and chat about whatever you desired as the users observed nature.

Lainey's feet pounded hard on the treadmill. Within a few minutes, she was catching the man in Osaka. Her screen popped up a message asking if she wished to receive the message he'd sent from Japan. Lainey accepted, and the technology provided the translation: You move fast. I wave as you pass by. Lainey used the voice-activated system to reply: "I'll wave, too." The 4D Fitness users loved these types of small interactions between people worldwide. The system gave users a choice to partake or ignore. Their data showed that nearly 98 % of subscribers would connect with a wave from their avatar or some other form of communication. A true virtual community of incalculable value!

Lainey's blue-gray eyes focused on the track ahead, and her feet expertly adjusted to the fractional undulations of the moving treadmill. This was where she felt strongest, as each foot landed with precision in seamless synchronicity through her calves, thighs, and hips, with her arms punching purposefully through the air. In this space, Lainey felt powerful, just like she used to in her everyday life. All she had to do was translate this level of belief into the rest of her waking day and continue the momentum. Unfortunately, her confidence had been shattered by events from a year ago and getting herself mentally fit was damn near impossible.

A sweat-induced thirty minutes into her run, she passed her Japanese subscriber and followed the trails through dense woodland to open fern-filled meadows and back into the shade of the tall trees. She mopped her forehead with the white towel, draped it over the handrail, and kicked on. The digital display made the user believe they were in the thickness of the trees where the sunlight barely pierced the forest floor on either side. The track went up a slight incline, and to Lainey's right, she noticed movement between the trees. It was something significant, not a deer. A person. It was the briefest glimpse, but enough to be sure.

The digital feeds were built from multiple ground-based data sets, archived, and seamlessly pulled together. There were no live feeds used. 4D Fitness had a strict policy of digitally removing people from all the trail runs. The movement was less than a second and off the trail, but nothing escaped her. The track swung ninety degrees left, and the view was lost. Lainey noted the time; she would have her team edit the feeds. The figure appeared at the thirty-two-minute mark. With all the constant data uplinks, there would be slight variations in the landscape to each side, where a deer might come into view that didn't exist in previous versions or a raccoon scurrying across the track.

This was the first time she'd ever seen a person on their trails. All uploaded GoPro views were carefully edited to prevent any privacy concerns. This was a bad miss from 4D Fitness. There was no view of anyone's face, and the movement was only a split-second, but still an elementary glitch on the part of their technical review team. It was this lax attention where Lainey became upset with Brian. He was great at marketing and promoting the brand but hopeless with fine detail, especially details that mattered. The programmers should have caught this, and so should Brian. He was supposed to review every update for all community members. Brian was too trusting. After two weeks of promoting the brand in Japan, South Korea, and Hong Kong, he would return home tomorrow. There was no sense in her reaching out to him right now. "Son of a bitch," she said to herself.

Lainey completed her run and saw that it was only thirteen seconds outside her personal best for that trail. She double-checked that she'd recorded the session. Lainey could review places to improve and see where she witnessed the figure in the trees. She wiped her face with the towel and tossed it in the basket. A quick shower, and she would be ready to review the latest sales trends.

As she stripped to get in the shower, Lainey called Phil in tech services. She explained what she'd seen and demanded they drop what they were doing and fix it. Phil got right to it. He was a good guy, but Lainey was pissed that they had allowed it to slip through.

Lainey and Brian had recently hired a new technical director, and Lainey would ensure their new recruit would eliminate these basic errors.

The mystery figure could have been someone illegally camping in the forest. California had lost thousands of acres of woodland to fires in the last few years, and no one could get overnight permits to camp out in what was left of the great redwoods.

"Bastards," Lainey angrily exclaimed as her fingers tightened into fists. Selfish people jeopardized the entire forest. "Dumb." Her annoyance recycled towards her team that had missed the detail. Lainey couldn't get it from her head. "What the hell? Why did we not see it? Why would some idiot have strayed fifty feet from the designated walking trails, knowing it was forbidden to trample through the forest floor and destroy the ecosystem. So stupid," she said of both the trespasser and her team.

She rinsed off and pulled on some fresh 4D clothing. Video conferences throughout the day meant she needed to be presentable, and her new employee would soon join her. She finished with her hair, pulling the long dark semi-curls over one shoulder. Her eyes were clear, and her liner was good. With the video camera calls, she didn't want to risk looking anything less than her best in case someone decided to leak excerpts to the press. It had happened before, not long after her recovery. There was nothing worse than feeling less than your best and having the whole world see you looking like shit into the bargain. Silly betrayals were personally bad for Lainey. Although she could get over that, the potential damage to her beloved brand was not as easy to recover. She and Brian had to present a picture of health and fitness. Months earlier, Brian got himself photographed drunk in a restaurant in Paris, and plenty of online trolls had jumped on it to use against them. It was the pernicious nature of people, especially those online, who so readily wanted to destroy anything they could latch onto versus trying to build something. The online world made it easy for cowards to extol their fake sense of virtue. Lainey despised those who chose to rise at the expense of someone else. Lainey understood it all too well, given her previous unwanted news headline coverage. Something she equally detested.

Photographs of Lainey connected to life support, with tubes hanging from every part of her, once circulated online. It was a cruel and deliberate invasion of her privacy in her most desperate time. "My tits are all over the internet!" Her complaint to Brian made him laugh, and Lainey chased him with the floor Swiffer until he apologized. The originator of that particular transgression was sued and their employer. The settlement had yet to be reached, but Lainey announced any settlement awarded would go to support the Special Olympics.

Some good may come from the cruelty that others have inflicted. Lainey was not one to be wasteful and leveraged that particular frustration within herself, vowing to come back stronger. Everyone loved a Phoenix rising from the ashes, particularly when the fire was not of her own making.

For now, she pushed away from the emotional remnants of places she wasn't prepared to go. Her dreams took care of the facts she couldn't forget, often drawing her into whimpering nightmares and cold sweats. Lainey did whatever she could to avoid going there if she didn't need to think about it. Therapy had done little to extinguish the terror associated with the events that led to her being hospitalized and only rekindled a series of haunting, jumbled flashbacks. Lainey quit therapy after a few weeks, having tried multiple therapists. It only served to re-imprint pieces of her memory that she had decided were better suited to be locked deep inside. She'd found that burying those things, and tossing away the key, was more effective than reclining on her leather couch. Unlocking the neural pathways that rekindled the events were unwanted reconnections. "Enough," she told herself.

4D Fitness needed her in the driving seat and solely concentrated on her tasks. However, Lainey knew she needed the business more than she dared to admit.

The buzzer from the large iron gates sounded. Lainey observed the white BMW and the nervous young female's face staring into the camera through her phone. "Hi," was all Lainey said.

"Oh, hi, yes, this is Veva. Veva Unwin. I'm your new senior technical development director. I was told to join you here for the conference calls today."

Lainey recognized the bob-styled, straight black hair, and light green eyes, against the sharp-cheeked features of the woman staring into the camera. She'd interviewed Veva via Zoom and had a copy of her resume in her home office. Veva was a great acquisition to the 4D Fitness team. "Come on in." Lainey pressed the remote, and the massive gates opened at the end of the winding driveway.

"Thank you," came the overly enthusiastic reply.

15

Lainey wanted anyone new to their business to spend a few days at the house so that she could get a good feel of their capabilities and if they would be a good fit for the team. Brian said it was a risk, due to the pandemic, but Lainey dismissed the notion. "I want to know what we're paying for," Lainey insisted. Brian knew better than to argue.

"Let's see what we have here," Lainey remarked as the BMW moved towards the house.

CHAPTER TWO

Veva pulled her car up to the front of the house, next to the gleaming Bentley. She grabbed her leather satchel, laptop, and linen bag that held her homemade lunch. She was careful not to tread on the flowerbeds that bloomed with a myriad of late spring colors. Gazing up at the ultra-modern house, with its sleek lines and carefully blended exterior textures, it appeared more imposing than it had from the road. Up close, the clever design led the eyes towards the central, double-sized front doorway. One side was decorated with strips of redwood, the other with a light gray concrete finish, and above, a dark gray stainless-steel canopy. The minimalist exterior was offset with interesting inlays, and one corner of the house had a bay-fronted glass sitting room. It was evident that fitness technology paid well.

Veva was excited to join an organization with a great product and plenty of scope for additions and improvements and get to work closely with the iconic figure of Lainey Stewart.

Veva straightened her knee-length black skirt, shouldered her bag, and rang the front doorbell. The long buzz on the lock opened the door a couple of inches, and she stepped inside the open hallway. The ceiling was thirty feet above her head, and light poured in from the two overhead skylights. "Hi," she called out with her friendliest tone.

It had been unexpected to be invited to the main house so soon after joining 4D Fitness. Colorful artwork strategically lined the wall, enticing her to explore further. Veva tepidly came to the end of the hallway, where it opened out into the massive reception room and the dining kitchen beyond. "Hi there." Her voice echoed in the enormous house.

The entire ground floor was one continuous open space, with different sections delineated by the furniture, fireplace, and décor. Everything was coordinated with colors and textures from one area to the next and far-reaching views from the back windows. "Hi," she called again.

"Hi, I'm Lainey," said the voice from behind, startling Veva.

Her lunch box slipped from her shoulder and dropped into the fold of her elbow as she clumsily tried to shake Lainey's extended hand. "Hi, I'm…"

"Veva. I know who you are," Lainey abruptly answered. "You wouldn't be here otherwise."

Veva was momentarily lost for words. Her new boss's unfriendly delivery was at odds with her friendly smile. "Thanks for inviting me," she finally said.

"I hope you're as good as your resume suggested and what your first week has indicated."

"I hope so too," Veva stammered.

"How was your first week at head office?"

"Interesting and useful," Veva replied.

"Two words covering all manner of sins," Lainey suggested. "You've already made quite an impact. Our resolution was already the best in the business, but now it's even better." Lainey looked around as if someone might be watching them. She leaned forward and whispered, "Did you get lucky with that suggestion, or did you figure it out?" She intently studied Veva.

"Both. It was only a 2% difference."

"A noticeable percentage," Lainey corrected. "Our users' feedback showed us they have noticed, and we didn't announce anything about the upgrade. I told Brian our active-matrix organic lighting system was underpowered. You proved me right. There are dozens of tech companies in California who promise everything and deliver with considerable underwhelming monotony. We'll never be one of those," Lainey told her.

"I'm just happy to help in any way I can. I'm looking forward to improving the design and the integration."

"Be careful what you ask for. Thank you, the immersive feel you helped improve is way better, but we need more."

"Not quite perfect, but close?" Veva offered.

"Nothing is ever perfect," Lainey countered. "And we've got an issue with editing new data uploads. I found an unforgivable mistake this morning. I'll show it to you later."

Lainey observed Veva's athletic body. "How tall are you?"

"Five foot seven."

"Is that why you wear those flat shoes?" Lainey pointed at Veva's scuffed and plain footwear.

"No. They're comfortable."

"Oh." Lainey's tone indicated some amusement.

Veva presented herself like some girl who was never kissed in high school and didn't get asked to the prom. Her black skirt was made from cheap material, which accumulated lint at an alarming rate. Her white blouse was frumpy, with a strange ruff around the neck, like a grandmother would wear. Her hair was straight and pulled tight to her head. Her eyes had some soft liner, and her lips a pinkish gloss. Her face was pretty but presented as if she wished to be invisible. Protruding below her skirt were two highly toned calves, and above the knee, a formed muscle tone that Lainey could see had been worked hard. Veva had just turned twenty-nine and had impressed her employers wherever she'd worked. She was a young star on the rise in a tech-filled state. Still, Lainey sighed as Veva dressed like she was seventy.

"Did you bring your own lunch?" she asked, pointing at the box hanging from Veva's arm.

"Yeah. I only eat organic. As much as I can, I wasn't sure what the day would look like."

Lainey took the bag from her. "Here, I'll put it in the fridge."

"How cute," she observed the picture of two fairies playing on the side of the lunch box. She walked ahead into the white open kitchen. "We have a busy day. We have a few calls with tech support, visual development, and creative design. All video conferences."

"Good. Then I can put faces to names. I haven't met everyone yet." Veva followed Lainey into the kitchen. As much as Veva soaked in the grandeur of the showcase house, her eyes fell on Lainey's shapely rear end. Veva became lost in the thought as though Lainey's rear was formed from the expert hands of a Renaissance sculpture. Little wonder she adorned the covers of every fitness and tech magazine. From every angle, Lainey's formidably athletic look matched her aura. It was intimidating and impressive. Veva's quiet confidence in her physique took a dip as Lainey put her lunch box in the fridge.

Lainey held the fridge door wide open to display the contents. "We have plenty of fresh fruits and vegetables here, so help yourself. All organic, you'll be pleased to know. Fresh coffee over there and filtered water here. It's not like I'm sending out for pizza five nights a week." Lainey patted her flat stomach.

"I see that," Veva replied, instantly blushing and biting her lip. It was impossible not to notice Lainey's overwhelming presence. Her chest stuck out at a right angle to her tiny waist, the curvature beneath her leggings was solidly formed, and the penetration in her stare was unnerving. When Lainey turned around, Veva dipped her head and pretended to look at the mosaic-tiled floor.

Lainey gave her new employee a quizzical look. "Let's get you situated and familiarized with the layout."

Veva told herself to avoid any more dumb comments and not stare at her new boss. Veva imagined Lainey could read her thoughts and hoped to God that she was wrong. Instead, Lainey kindly explained the layout and how things worked. Veva politely nodded. Lainey's explanations were plainly spoken and matter of fact. It was bad enough being the new girl in the company, but it was weirdly uncomfortable being in the Stewart's home.

"Have you got all that?" Lainey asked.

"Sure," Veva lied. Her stomach was tied in knots, and it was damn near impossible to prevent her mind from drifting. She could barely breathe, and each time she caught Lainey's eye, it filled her with a sense of being second-best. Lainey Stewart had built a successful fitness empire. Everyone knew who she was, and now, Veva was in Lainey's home! Veva's armpits were soaked in sweat, and she wanted to take off her jacket, but she was afraid the damp stains on her shirt would make her look foolish.

"Follow me," Lainey said.

Veva was given a quick tour, feeling like she was on one of those TV shows that showcased houses of the rich and famous. After using the restroom, she joined Lainey in the sizeable upstairs office at the front of the house. She had her own desk a few feet from her boss. She felt like a small girl, sitting close to the teacher's desk for being naughty. She was not herself, feeling like she had so much to say, but nothing came from her dry lips. Lainey dominated everything, even though she was helpful and amiable.

"You can move your desk anywhere you want," Lainey said. "From the window, you can see the woods on one side and the ocean on the other."

"I will," Veva replied, rising from her seat. The minor distraction was welcomed. "How come you don't take advantage of the view?"

Lainey's glare suggested disbelief that Veva didn't know the reason why. "The outdoors isn't my thing these days."

"I'm sorry. I was only…"

"No, it's okay. It's fine. I'll help you move the desk."

They lifted the glass top desk from either side and placed it at an angle so that Veva could take in most of the view without blocking the light or Lainey's distant view from the other side of the room.

Lainey moved swiftly away from the window. "There, now you're all settled. If I need to know what's going on out there, I can ask you what it looks like."

"I'm good at describing things. I didn't mean anything before." Veva humbly offered.

"I know—just one of those things. One day I'll greet you at the door? Have you connected to the Wi-Fi yet?" Lainey asked as she breezed past the awkward conversation.

"I'll give it a try," Veva replied as she slid into her seat. She kept her head down and fired some sly glances at her boss. She hadn't meant to be thoughtless or rude. Everyone on the Northwest coast knew Lainey Stewart hadn't left her home for a year. Lainey's ordeal shocked all of California and made headlines across the country. Veva cursed under her breath at having placed herself in an uncomfortable position. She didn't want to ruin the decent early impressions she'd made with her efforts on the OLED upgrade.

Curved screen technology had never really caught on for regular family TV viewing. Still, the extensive wrap-around version for the treadmill was perfectly suited to make the user believe they were moving through an outdoor landscape. "Like a personal Imax for those training at home," Lainey had famously described it. Likewise, Veva loved the technology and was excited about her chance to improve its application.

Lainey clicked the remote for the flatscreen on the wall and prepared for the first conference call. She had Veva pull her chair and laptop next to her, so they shared Lainey's desk for a short while. "I'll introduce you to everyone and give you a minute to introduce yourself. Some of them will be wondering who you are and why you're here in the house with me. Tongues are always wagging," she warned.

"You know what they say about wagging tongues," Veva suggested.

Lainey stared at her new acquisition but didn't ask for the answer.

"I'll open up the call." Lainey talked first at the video conference and handed it across to Veva. She made a less than inspiring self-introduction. Lainey watched the reactions from her team, who clearly wondered why the new girl was at the big house. Veva's reputation was high, and Lainey's teams were full of competitive individuals, an edge which she liked, although some were too quick to throw their colleagues under the bus and reverse back over them for good measure. Lainey demanded excellence and endeavor in all things and liked aggression, although it was not easy to keep that in check. Most of the meeting's participants were around the conference table in the main office on the northern tip of Eureka. It was attached to the small assembly factory seven miles north of Lainey's house, but it may as well have been in another country. Her fear of the outdoors hadn't improved, and Lainey hadn't set foot inside their head office for over twelve months.

Three of those on the call worked from home. Lainey wasn't sure those working from home were as highly motivated as they might be, and their dress attire wasn't in keeping with business casual or wearing the company's 4D apparel. Some individually tailored email reminders would sharpen them up. Since COVID had long since been through Eureka, Lainey and Brian had allowed those with medical vulnerabilities to work from home until the vaccinations were completed. Thankfully, things were returning to normal for most people. However, Lainey wasn't sure if she'd ever return to the office. COVID was the least of her worries. She had no idea if she was capable of mixing into regular society. At present, she was a classic prisoner in her own home.

Ironically, the epidemic had been great for 4D business. People were locked out of their regular gyms, and millions working from home had gone stir crazy, leading to increased sales. It wasn't the ideal way to expand, but certainly a positive step for the business.

The late morning and afternoon rolled by quickly. Veva showed herself to be efficient in whatever Lainey asked for. Unfortunately, their conversation over lunch in the kitchen lacked flow, and Lainey had to keep asking questions of Veva to get anything from her. She put it down to nerves and hoped her newest team member would relax so that they could have a normal conversation. At least Veva wasn't cocky. There was only room for one oversized ego in her house. As stumbling as Veva's company appeared to be, the truth was that Lainey enjoyed having someone with her, and especially not someone kissing her boots or simply trying to impress.

Veva worked away in the corner most of the day, and just after five p.m., Lainey declared, "Veva, it's time you were heading home. Brian will be home from Japan in the morning, so I need to clean away all my stuff from the ensuite bathroom. I can be as messy as I like when he's away, but he hates things being disorderly. You know how it is – all the stuff us girls need to stay looking beautiful."

"Some of us need it more than others," Veva replied, with her glance briefly catching Lainey's.

"Thanks. You underestimate yourself," Lainey suggested. "C'mon, I'll walk downstairs with you."

They exchanged light chatter about the conference calls before Veva took her empty lunchbox, linen bag, and laptop. Lainey stayed in the reception area as Veva went along the hallway. "Close the door on the way out. I can see if it's locked properly on my app. I'll see you back here on Wednesday."

"Oh, okay," Veva sounded surprised.

"I would have had you work from here tomorrow, but I haven't seen Brian for two weeks," Lainey said, pulling her lips to one side of her face.

Veva nodded at the insinuation. "Gotcha. See you Wednesday." She closed the massive door, checked that it was locked, and got into her car. She sorted her things, started the engine, looked up at the house, and was surprised to see Lainey standing near the front window. She gave her a solitary wave, which Lainey returned.

Veva drove down the winding driveway, waited for the gates to open, and followed the winding road before joining the main coastal highway heading north towards Eureka.

Lainey's suggestive remark about her husband played with Veva's imagination. Brian Stewart was a handsome man, a former personal fitness trainer, who still looked the part. In her first week at head office, Veva heard some female colleagues gossiping about him and how sexy his glutes looked through tight work trousers. Veva had yet to meet him, but she looked forward to it. However, it was Lainey who had caught her eye. She was stunning, to the point where Veva could barely converse with her.

Lainey had insinuated that she and Brian needed some space, as they would be getting down to it on his return. Veva's thighs flexed and tightened as she shuffled in her seat, picturing Lainey stripping seductively from the ultra-tight leggings and the workout vest. Veva couldn't help herself, and she let the thought play itself out, with the handsome Brian removed from the picture. Veva found herself biting her bottom lip and tightly sucking air through her teeth. With one hand on the steering wheel, she pulled up her skirt, and her fingers stretched her panties to one side. She envisioned Lainey's skintight material dropping to the floor, revealing her firm thighs, perfect ass, and rounded breasts.

Veva's fingers toyed with her wet lips, teasing herself and letting her fingertips wander slowly to her most sensitive part. Once she began to rub, the moistness soon covered her fingers, and she slammed her spare foot into the angled footrest to prevent her body from lifting out of the seat. There was a slight swerve and correction on the wheel as her playful fingers pressed harder, and her circular rubbing increased.

She pictured Lainey crawling seductively onto the bed and beckoning her to approach. The fantasy was crystal clear. She was going to cum hard. The pulse passed through into her abdomen as her body lurched forward, and she crashed backward into the seat. The vision of the smiling Lainey tantalized her, stroking her hands over her firm breasts, with her nipples fully alert.

"Oh fuck!" Veva cried out as she climaxed. Quickly, she used both hands to gain complete control of the car. Some of her juices were on the steering wheel. It would easily clean. Veva hadn't expected such a visceral reaction to seeing Lainey up close but suspected it would trigger something. "Exquisite," Veva panted, trying to catch her breath. She was grateful not to be at the house tomorrow, as Lainey's intuition was ultra-sharp. Veva straightened her underwear and pulled the skirt back to her knees.

"Lainey Stewart!" she gasped.

CHAPTER THREE

July 10th, 1996

Aunt Lucy read aloud from the tiny remembrance card in her hand: "Into God's hands, delivered by angels, forever to reside in his glory. Emilia Hurst July 1st, 1966, to July 7th, 1996." She studied the laminated card with the floral-patterned edges. "At least she made it to thirty." She looked to her older sister, expecting a comment, but Aunt Carm stayed quiet, her eyes falling on the sorrowful figure of Ginny.

The little girl kicked the backs of her heels against the wooden chair, mournfully staring at the carpet. Everyone had been so kind to her, but she was afraid now that her mom was gone.

"Are you absolutely sure about this?" Aunt Lucy sharply asked.

"Yeah, quit asking," Aunt Carm replied. Aunt Lucy gave her that look she hated. Aunt Carm strained herself not to lose it. "You've already got three kids, so… you've got enough to contend with. Little Ginny's no trouble. Are you, my little angel?" Aunt Carm pretended to nibble Ginny's ear, and she ruffled her hair.

The little one began to cry.

"Hey now, what's the matter?" Aunt Carm asked. "You and I are going to be just fine." She put her arm around the sniffling girl and squeezed her.

"I'm no trouble, but I know nobody wants me," Ginny sobbed.

"That's not true," Aunt Carm assured her. "I want you, and Aunt Lucy wants you to go live with her. Much more fun with me, huh? Besides, we're Hursts, and we stick together."

"I heard Grandma Priscilla say I was a burden," Ginny quietly sniffed.

Aunt Carm gave Grandma Priscilla the death stare. "Well, sometimes Grandma doesn't know what she's talking about. I love you, and you love me, and that's all we need. So we'll show silly old Grandma."

Grandma Priscilla frowned, "All I said was…"

"You said enough," Aunt Carm cut her off.

Little Ginny was inconsolable. "Is mommy in heaven yet?"

"Of course, she is," Aunt Lucy quickly replied.

"But she's over there," Ginny pointed to the open coffin by the fireplace.

"The angels already took your mommy's soul, and she's in heaven, looking down on us all right now," Grandma Priscilla explained. Her wrinkled old face softened. "All good souls go straight to heaven if they earned it. All those prayers you said have made sure of it."

"Are you sure?" Ginny asked through bloodshot eyes.

"Course, I'm sure," Grandma Priscilla replied. "That's just a dead body over there."

Aunt Carm swept Ginny up into her arms. "She's only four, for God's sake," she scolded the surprised Priscilla. She cradled Ginny over her shoulder. "Your mommy was an angel in human form, and now she's with the angels above. Aunt Lucy was right – Mommy's in heaven. Never mind Grandma, she's just grumpy because we're not mourning for her. She wanted to go first, so we'd fuss over her."

"I'm the one who lost a daughter," Priscilla complained.

"You can't lose what you never had," Aunt Carm grimaced. Priscilla opened her mouth, but Aunt Carm silently dared her to say another word. "C'mon, Ginny, let's go out back and look up at the stars and say hi to your mommy. She'd like that." Aunt Carm shook her head at those gathered in the room, letting them know she'd swing for anyone who said another word. She carried Ginny outside.

Aunt Lucy and Grandma Priscilla exchanged a look that confirmed their shared doubts. But, despite their protests, Aunt Carm was adamant that she would follow her dear sister's wishes and take little Ginny to live with her.

The outer door closed, leaving Aunt Carm and Ginny out of earshot.

"That child needs to be in a good Christian home – not with whatever she's got going on," Grandma Priscilla stated.

"She won't change her mind, you know her."

"Ginny should be with me," Grandma Priscilla insisted.

"That's enough," Aunt Lucy groaned.

"That child needs to be brought up properly," Priscilla persisted.

They watched Aunt Carm and little Ginny outback, pointing at the night sky.

"You'll see," Grandma Priscilla warned.

"Not today, please," Aunt Lucy sounded exhausted. "Not today."

The Present Day:

Brian Stewart ran his fingers across his lips, feeling like they were glued together, as he waited for the gates to swing open. He would play nice, but his mouth had run dry, and his hands were sweating. Brian was glad to be done with the traveling, but there was little else to look forward to. He wanted to be a calm, understanding, sympathetic husband, and all the things he imagined a good partner should be to the wife he loved. But instead, his love for Lainey was slowly crushing him, and its weight bore down on his strong shoulders, threatening to snap his spine. He'd lost all self-respect because of the number of times he'd considered leaving his wife. The last few months had been intolerable, and he felt like a loser for not being able to do anything to bring Lainey back. He'd almost completely lost her over a year ago, and he was thankful she was alive. But parts of her were still missing, and Lainey was unwilling to get the help she needed. "They can't fix me! They're making me worse," she complained.

The trauma his wife had been through, and the ongoing issues left Brian isolated. His wife had been through hell, and he felt like a dick for having the nerve to complain, but it had affected him, too. Brian was unsure if she'd ever again be anything like her old self, and he wondered if he, too, was permanently changed. Over the last twelve months, the events had taken him to places where he disliked himself for the way he thought. His outward behavior was well-mannered and well-intentioned, but he was knotted in self-loathing and edging closer to despair. He never imagined being apart from Lainey, but the recent, awful truth was that he no longer knew how to be with her.

Brian wanted revenge on whoever was responsible for her condition. The thief who stole his once loving wife had fractured their once-solid marriage.

In his quieter moments, Brian terrified himself with the darkest thoughts of revenge on the world that allowed it to happen. Lainey was abrasive at times, but she'd never done anything to deserve what happened to her. It was shameful that he had not protected his loving wife. Brian learned that shame carried a heavier burden than any of life's negative bombardments. The shame brought guilt, and it festered into much worse, where it felt like the responsibility was determined to flatten him, like some gravitational succubus. He resented the fact he was not the man he thought he was or should be.

"C'mon, Brian." He tapped his hands to either side of his face as he pulled up outside their lavish home. Lainey's Bentley was parked to the right – a place it had occupied for months on end. It was only moved whenever the car detailing guys came to clean it. She had insisted it not be kept in the adjacent garage so that it would be a reminder for her to get outside and use it – something that made Brian roll his eyes in frustration. He parked his Jaguar I-Pace next to the flower beds. The lush green of the stepped terraces that separated the blooming flower beds caught his eye in the morning sun. "We are so fortunate," he thought as he admired the view.

He turned, looked up at their designer house, and his brief moment of joy evaporated. The house was an architectural marvel, yet it had lost its sheen and welcome. He was tired of asking himself how in this most beautiful of places and a dream they'd built together, could it have become cold, lifeless, and…he let the thoughts slide. Going there again wasn't helping. He was afraid that if he allowed those thoughts to ulcerate more than a few moments, he'd never walk through the front door again. Only his devotion and loyalty to Lainey led him to raise his hand, where his finger was scanned, and the front door clicked open. "Be nice," he whispered to himself.

He wheeled his suitcase down the hallway into the main body of the house and looked around. He recognized the furniture and artwork as theirs, including some of the things he'd picked out, although most of the touches were Lainey's. It was familiar to the point where he barely noticed any of it like it had become second nature, but all of it was laden with the same barren echo as if walking into the faceless void of a large chain hotel anywhere in the world. Of course, staying in hotels around the globe wasn't a bad thing, but Brian's idea of fun traveling was only if Lainey was with him – at least the old Lainey – and yet, at the moment, anywhere was better than here. His recent lived experience was like being in the belly of the whale, where he'd volunteered to be swallowed whole, and there was no chance of escape.

His instinct urged him to turn around, get back in the car, and go. The internal signals were loud and desperate. What sort of a useless husband and human being would he consider himself if he gave up on the woman he loved? Lainey would never give up on him. Never. Her determination for life, love, and improvement was too strong. Stronger than his. Her resilience was unmatched, a quality he admired in her and one he could only aspire to emanate. Lainey was tougher than he was in many respects. Lainey and Brian liked competition, but he was at the point where it might be one hurdle too many, and the finishing line was beyond his reach.

The sickly vibration in the base of his abdomen refused to go away, a nasty physiological reminder that the smile he presented to his wife was a sham. Brian was clinging on to something without understanding exactly why – thinking it would be easier to let go and freefall into a different unknown.

"C'mon, Brian," he reminded himself. The thought of a sterile house, a marriage the same, and the prospect of it all continuing in the same vein made him angry. It was embedded deep enough that he'd gone beyond images of creating mayhem and taking vengeance. Instead, Brian's imagination pushed him into places where destruction was bland and suffering was inconvenient. He'd thought long and hard that if the universe were controlled by forces unknown, he wanted vengeance on the guiding hands – to hack them off and stick their useless hands down their throats. But, for a man who looked like he had everything, he would rather have nothing if it would prevent him from going to places that most people couldn't even conceive existed. He'd learned the tortured mind was a dangerous place and one he could easily unleash against his fellow man.

Brian left his case against the wall, not wishing to clutter the room, and dropped his laptop bag on top, leaning it against the handle. He walked into the large open kitchen and fixed himself a coffee, using the barista's espresso machine on the white-surfaced counter. The open dining kitchen was clean and organized, with a modern go-getter texture to the surface materials in a synthesized combination. It looked like the archetypal advertisement for the successful young businessperson, sipping their favorite beverage and smiling as the aroma perfectly made its way to their nostrils. This was a place for those who had it together, going about their day before the rest of the world arrived at their desk jobs. As the machine hissed and sputtered, he knew the sound would alert Lainey to his arrival. She heard every sound at night since the incident as though her survival instincts had been permanently kicked into a higher gear.

He took the hot drink and sat alone at the breakfast bar. Next to him were five empty white leather stools. He was living in what the TV advertisements presented as the American dream. This was the place everybody aspired to wake up to. A vision of something with endless possibilities for the day and life. Brian reflected that he'd felt the same way living in the house the first few months. The initial excitement it had generated when he came down the stairs would cause goosebumps all over his flesh. The dream had spiraled into a nightmare. It seemed so long ago, but it was only two years since they'd moved in. He longed for that same vigor to pump through his veins and for he and Lainey to feel the same way. Unfortunately, however, sitting alone in the pristine space offered zero satisfaction.

"Brian?" Lainey's voice came from somewhere up on the open landing.

"Down here," he cheerily replied, making an effort. "I wasn't sure if you were up yet. Didn't want to wake you." Previously he would have returned her words with some sweet sentiment, like calling her sweetheart, babe, or darling. She liked those little terms of endearment, but the words of affection were firmly trapped. Any attempt to be openly loving with his speech would be a betrayal of sorts.

Lainey came down the sweeping staircase, her body covered in a mauve silk dressing gown and her hair tied up in a messy bun. It was only six a.m., and she wore no makeup, but still, she looked akin to his vision of absolute beauty. If this had been before her incident, Brian would have gone straight upstairs and joined her under the sheets. In Brian's estimation, another option was stolen away, and a good reason to be resentful. He watched her approach. Lainey's skin tone had a slight olive tint so that people often mistook her for someone with Italian or Middle Eastern roots. Her light blue-gray eyes were in contrast to her jet-black hair. Her penetrating eyes held the onlooker's gaze. Brian imagined that Lainey's appearance would have made her a desirable target for the highest powers as a queen in ancient times. Brian witnessed business associates being immediately intimidated by her, sometimes for good reason. Others simply melted – men especially, and women too. The Lainey effect was not to be underestimated.

"How was it?" she asked, kissing him on the cheek and laying an arm partially around his neck.

"Good. We've got some work to do in Hong Kong, with their ever-changing customs rules, but other than that, I think we'll see more business coming. They've got millions of people packed tight into small living spaces, both an advantage and a disadvantage." Brian placed his hand over the back of Lainey's and gently patted her skin before she removed her arm.

"Breakfast? I feel like eggs," she said.

"Sure, thanks." The conversation should have been more. Brian wished to embrace his wife fully. Instead, he stayed rooted to the high stool and watched her whisk some eggs in a bowl. It was painful not to get what he needed from her or give her what she deserved. There was a strange barrier between them, like liquid glass, where only a sporadic meaningful touch or word might get through to the opposite side. A stalemate was held, with unspoken rules, where neither fully dared to venture into the no-man's land, fearful of drowning in isolation. Brian instinctively knew that if he took Lainey in his arms and expressed his love and desire for her, it would send her shrinking away to the corner of the room, and he'd never have the chance to bring her back. He hated the rejection as much as she hated having to pull away – something they'd learned the hard way in the last twelve months.

Their conversation was bland, about the details of his trip and what she was doing with the development team. All were necessary concerning business, but the conversation that really mattered couldn't occur.

"We have the new girl settling in," Lainey explained. "Veva." She noted Brian recoiled at the name. "Yeah, Veva with a V and an E. I told her to return here tomorrow after you've had a chance to acclimatize after your trip."

"She was here?"

"All day, yesterday. She's the one who fixed our resolution issue. A timid thing, but I like her."

"I remember her from the video interviews." His observation lacked enthusiasm. "She could have come here today if you wanted her to. I'm going to shower, catch up on email, and head up to the office. One of us should put in an appearance."

Lainey raised a single eyebrow as she stirred at the scrambled eggs in the pan.

"I didn't mean…you know."

"I know."

Brian quickly changed the subject. "I got to run along the trail we have in Arashiyama, Japan. The bamboo forest was spectacular. It didn't take long to get through it, but every step was worth it. I ran the loop, went over the Katsura River, along the old Sagano railway line, and circled back through the forest. The colors were amazing," Brian went on to enthusiastically describe the Acers.

"Have you uploaded the data into our mainframe yet?"

"Not yet. Tonight. I got to run it a second time a couple of days later, but my camera failed to record."

"Maybe we can watch it together in bed tonight on your laptop," Lainey suggested. "I'd love to see the colors and hear your thoughts. It will look amazing through our 4D."

"Sounds good," Brian flatly replied. He was hoping for a different kind of entertainment in bed tonight—any night. They'd fought so many times in the last few months that he couldn't risk talking about intimacy. Only three times in the past year had they shared their bodies, and on two occasions, they'd stopped, with Lainey hysterically bawling and wailing uncontrollably. She'd sworn that nobody had sexually touched her during her incident, and the medical examination backed her theory, but her recollection was incomprehensible, and something profoundly affected her.

Brian missed the feel of his wife on his skin, and she disclosed the same loss. Some nights they lightly cuddled, but it was rare. Lainey remained aggressive in her work and fitness regime, but her sexuality was diminished to nothing. It was like she had no trust in Brian, and it hurt. Losing that connectivity was tough on both of them. Lainey tried to explain that she felt perfectly safe with Brian. Lainey loved him, and she found him sexually attractive, but the incident had removed parts of her ability to trust, robbing her of the possibility of sharing herself with him, and she didn't know why.

The therapy hadn't yielded anything nor suggested a remedy for the issue. Lainey was once a fierce and passionate lover with verbal sexuality that equaled her physical presence. Brian longed to have her whisper those sweet profanities, to spur him into giving every ounce of his body. He shook himself from the sexual daydream. She was only six feet away, but it was like they were in different cities. "Let's get to bed early. I'd like to feel you next to me." Brian knew he was pushing it.

"Okay," she replied, dishing out the eggs. Lainey sat next to him at the counter, and they ate in silence for a minute. She tapped him on the shoulder and looked into his worried light brown eyes. "Thank you." Her voice broke, and her eyes showed a rare sign of tears. The shakiness in her voice agitated her, and she immediately cleared her throat.

He put an arm around her shoulder and pulled her head, so it nestled under his chin. "For what?"

"Everything. I know you've thought about…I know you've thought about it." Lainey said.

"Everybody goes through some shit. We're having our turn." Brian kissed the top of her knotted head. "We'll be okay."

The words did nothing to convince them that they would make it through together. All he knew was that he loved his wife as well as any man, could, and he'd do anything for her. He'd already done everything he knew possible, and nothing seemed to help. There was nothing worse than a helpless man who meant well but ran into a brick wall at every turn. Everything before them seemed an unhappy choice. Brian expended the limits of his intellectual capacity and reasoned he was at the point of emotional exhaustion. He knew that Lainey truly suffered, and he repeatedly chastised himself for daring to consider giving up. Everyone had their limits, and he was sure he'd gone beyond the things that could break him. But, it was more than that – he was long since broken. Lainey was no longer herself, and he was much less of the man, the husband, the lover, the companion he'd once been. It was like infection had poisoned their union, and no amount of ointments, medicines, or magic spells could stop it from spreading.

He'd met Lainey ten years ago when they were finishing college. He was one week older than her. Then, they were wide-eyed and full of determination about every subject under the sun. Now the steam had evaporated into the ether, and there was no way to build back the pressure. Their chemistry was so strong in the preceding ten years that the present situation was unimaginable. They didn't always agree on a strategy or a go-forward plan, but they remained committed and inseparable. They'd lain in bed on many a star-filled night at college and swore they'd always be together. They were the dreams of youth that were yet to be corrupted by the interference of the real world.

Things change fast in life, often without either party being at fault or knowing how to stem the spread of lethargy. It was only ten years ago, yet they reminisced about that time as if it were forty years ago. They were smart, intellectual people who found themselves strangely balanced on the cusp of indifference. They exchanged their commitment and love for one another, despite their difficulties. It was a small comfort, but it made the reality more painful. They were only a few short steps away from resentment, and then they'd be finished. Recognition of the fact was of little value, as they could not move the needle to fix their issues.

Lainey released from his grip and patted her palm on his thigh. She shook her head and sighed with exasperation to the point of a growl. Then, in her dutiful homage to 4D Fitness, she said, "Time to put our game faces on."

Brian swiveled away to keep Lainey from seeing the tears rolling from his face. "I'll unpack." He hacked loudly and took his case upstairs. "Leave the kitchen. I'll clean it up. Thanks for breakfast."

Lainey watched him disappear as she placed the dishes in the sink. His body language, his smile, and his every inflection were a struggle. Life without Brian would be unthinkable.

Lainey texted Veva, and told her that she could come back today, and work from the house. Veva instantly texted back 'okay.'

Lainey stared the other way and looked blankly through the glass sliding doors over the patio and beyond the swimming pool. Every angle, inside and outside their house, indicated that they were people who had everything anyone could ever want. The internal and external views were filled with misleading inferences. Lainey and Brian's perspective had become accustomed to a horizon filled with desperation – a flat earth scenario where they were destined to slide off the edge into oblivion.

Lainey sat at the breakfast bar and sipped her drink. She thought about going after him, but she knew it would end in a fight. Brian's frustration was like an electric charge that applied static to every surface. She'd always been good at finding inspiration when needed and fixing things. Lainey swung her legs, turning a full circle on her stool – while inspiration remained silent.

CHAPTER FOUR

Lainey finished her meditation. The house was calm, and there was relief now that Brian had gone to the main office. He placed a small sticky note on the side of her dresser that read: Have a great day. I love you. XX. Lainey's immediate reaction to it felt cold, as though the ink on the paper held no meaning. It was sweet and thoughtful of him, but how she read it made it appear forced, like a token offering. "I'm such an ungrateful bitch."

She wasn't the type of woman easily persuaded to think everything was okay with a bunch of flowers. She trusted her instincts, and they screamed back at her. Lainey listened to what her body was saying and went upstairs to check Brian's suitcase. It seemed overly paranoid, but she could have sympathized with him if he'd packed his bags and left. Mostly, however, she would've throttled him.

She found his unpacked case in the walk-in closet. If Brian had decided he was going anywhere, he was going without any of his clothes. There was a slight twinge of guilt for not believing his sweet note. Lainey didn't want to lose him, and she was sure he felt the same. He said he loved her, and her senses knew he meant it. However, Brian's eyes gave away his intentions. He could not disguise his love for her or their marriage's strain on him. Thankfully, that was one thing he couldn't hide. She glanced at their wedding photograph beside the bed. "I'll fucking kill you if you leave."

She was about to get on the treadmill when an unexpected name appeared on her cellphone. She answered. "Hi."

"Hi Lainey, this is Detective Steve Strahan. How are you this morning?"

"Good. Is everything okay?"

"Yeah, fine," he melodically replied. "I was in the neighborhood and wanted to pay you a quick visit. There are some questions I wanted to ask you. I know – it's been a while – and I'm the last guy you want to be talking to. Any chance I can swing by? What's your schedule look like today?"

Lainey was unusually flustered. His delivery was pitch-perfect, like he was about to tenderly sing a love song, but she knew Strahan wouldn't simply be in the area. Her neighborhood was full of reclusive millionaires and not the kind who took visits from a homicide detective without alerting everyone for ten square miles. "I don't know. I've got meetings and things." She used her spare hand to bring up her schedule on her tablet.

"That's what you get for being a high-flying executive," he remarked. "I can make any time today workable. The sooner, the better."

"Are you sure everything's okay?"

"Absolutely. Just some routine questions to complete parts of your case file. Your case will stay open as we continue to look for the perpetrator. But, unfortunately, we don't have any new leads."

"Then what do you need me for?" she asked with suspicion.

"As I said, routine questions. When did you say you were free?"

"I didn't. My first meeting is at 10.30 this morning."

Before Lainey could add any color, Detective Strahan was already talking. "That's great. I'll swing by now. It should only take a few minutes. I'm right down the street."

"I don't know…" Lainey pondered, trying to find an excuse.

"Better to get me out of the way and get the rest of your day just where you want it, don't you think? Then it will be like it never happened," Strahan said with conviction.

It was over three months since anyone from Eureka Police had contacted her. Immediately, Lainey was filled with anxiety. "I guess I could…"

"Excellent," Strahan cut in. "I'll be with you in five minutes."

The line went dead. Strahan was always so Zen-like in his delivery and rarely pushy. She knew there was more to this than routine questions. He could have asked her over the phone. Hopefully, they'd gotten a breakthrough and were close to finding the person responsible for turning her life upside down. There were no indications why Lainey had been targeted by her attacker, nor the exact purpose, except murder. Lainey couldn't leave her house, knowing her attacker was still out there. The local and national news made sure everyone, including her attacker, knew she'd survived.

The buzzer from the gate sounded like a train horn, and Lainey's bones nearly jumped clean through her skin. The security camera showed Veva's mop of black hair sticking out of her car window. "Hi, Lainey, it's me, Veva." Lainey pressed the buzzer to open the gates and texted Veva that the front door was unlocked and to come straight in.

As Veva drove through the gates, a Ford Taurus came right behind her and followed her. In her rear mirror, Veva saw the fair-haired man driving it. She noticed the searchlight folded back next to the side mirror, signaling it was a plain-clothes cop. Veva guessed it had something to do with the unsolved case. Once parked, she didn't hang around, quickly gathering her things with her double lunchbox over her shoulder and headed through the main door.

"Lainey, I think there's a cop behind me. He followed me in through the gate. I didn't let him in."

"It's okay. I'm expecting him," Lainey cut off the panicked Veva. Lainey buzzed her front door, using her cellphone to open it again. "Said he has some routine questions for me," she said, uncertainly pulling her thick lips across her face. "Would you mind going upstairs to the office, and I'll speak with him down here."

"Of course," Veva nervously looked around as she heard the front open. She moved swiftly past Lainey and placed the lunchboxes in the fridge. "I brought us both lunch," she said, hurrying toward the stairs.

"Thank you." Lainey looked at Veva's horrible brown sandals, a pink turtleneck shirt, and tight black trousers showing her entire panty line. She shook her head and considered telling her new technical director that she dressed like a grandma.

Detective Strahan approached with an outstretched hand. "Lainey, thanks for making the time for me." As they shook hands, he glanced at the figure of Veva hurrying up the staircase.

"That's Veva. My new tech guru and working lunch buddy," Lainey explained.

Veva waved an unenthusiastic hand toward the detective, keeping her head down as she ascended the last few steps, disappearing through the office doorway.

"I have an upstairs office," Lainey said.

"I suppose you'd have to, in your line of business. So how is the tech fitness world?"

"Fine. Can I get you a coffee? I just made myself one."

"Thanks, that would be great." Strahan pointed at the coffeemaker. "See, you have the real deal. It looks like you could open your own store."

"Brian's the coffee connoisseur, and he insisted we have the best. He's very particular...when it comes to coffee."

"A man of impeccable taste. I'll take mine with milk and sugar. It's pretty much my only vice – taking sugar in my coffee." His speech was metered in an easy flow.

"So, how can I help you, detective?" she asked as she made him a drink. Strahan looked up towards the open landing. Lainey saw his concern and offered, "You can't hear our conversation from up there, and anyway, Veva's desk is over by the front windows."

Detective Strahan nodded his understanding. "How are you doing?"

Lainey extended the palms of her hands toward the open house; "I'm still stuck in this designer palace on the hill." Her smile was filled with sarcasm.

"Sorry to hear that. If you're going to be stuck somewhere, there are worse places for it to be. I know we haven't spoken for a while. Have you heard anything from any reporters or anyone lately?"

"About what specifically?"

"About your case, or anything similar."

"No. Similar case?" Lainey passed him the coffee and slid the milk and sugar with a spoon in front of him. "There's no way you just swung by here without reason." The friendliness dissipated from her tone. "You're busy – I'm busy. Can we cut to the chase?"

Strahan's eyes flickered upward toward the open landing space before he answered. "Have you ever had any contact with anyone other than me about your case since we last spoke?"

"No, I already said that. What is it you really want?" Lainey tightened her fluffy bathrobe around her waist. Her eyes blazed with a determination to get to it.

Strahan was used to her abrupt approach. Anger flushed her cheeks with deep crimson; her shoulders were pushed back, and she firmly adjusted her ponytail without taking her gaze from him. "What I'm about to relay to you is highly confidential and not to be shared with anyone. Not even Brian. I know if you give me your word, you'll keep it." Strahan raised a single eyebrow.

"Tell me."

"We're keeping it out of the news as long as we can, but it will soon go viral, like everything else these days. We've discovered a body in Oregon. In the woods near Shellburg."

"Shellburg and Stassel Falls?" Lainey exclaimed.

"The same. You know them?"

"You know I do. It's a running trail on our digital platform."

"Yes. I already checked," Strahan cut her off. "One of the running trails offered on your 4D Fitness treadmill."

"Oh no," Lainey grumbled as she ran her hands through her hair and re-tied the elasticized knot. She could already imagine the negative publicity. "Was the body close to the trail?" She snatched her robe tightly over her chest, suddenly feeling cold.

"Within fifty feet." Strahan checked towards the upstairs with his mid-blue eyes scrutinizing the length of the upper landing. "The signatures are the same as yours. The news will break within a day or two."

Just inside the office doorway, Veva was leaning against the frame. She couldn't help listening to their conversation. The voices indicated they were coming from the kitchen, so there was no chance of her being caught snooping. She pushed her ear closer to the gap where the door hinged to the frame, not wanting to miss anything.

"We have a deceased female, as yet unidentified. I'm working with my colleagues in Oregon, and I'll drive up there later today. Unfortunately, again, this information cannot be shared. Has anyone contacted you – at all?"

"No," Lainey angrily repeated, shaking her head. She placed her coffee back on the countertop as her hands uncontrollably shook. "He's still out there."

"You said he?" Strahan asked.

Lainey gave the detective a hollow stare. Strahan was five feet ten inches, had an average build, a slender waist, and inquisitively kind eyes. His short fair hair made him appear much younger than his forty years. His nose was crooked like he'd lost a hard fight when he was younger, and on either cheek were scattered half a dozen freckles. His lips were thick, and his voice was practiced for calm – more suited to someone crooning in a smokey late-night jazz club than police work.

His jacket looked too big for him, and his hands looked soft like he'd never worked at manual labor. With his calming presence, if he weren't a homicide detective, he'd have made a great clinical psychologist. His demeanor was carefully manufactured to draw out information and make the recipient feel like they were talking with an old friend about the weather. He was designed for this purpose, but Lainey still wanted to smash him in the face.

"I'm not sure if it was a man or a woman. I presume a man. Aren't most murderers men?"

"Typically. What makes you think it was a man?"

"I don't know. I don't remember anything. I was drugged!" Lainey raised her voice. "You came here to ask me that?"

"No. I came here to see if anyone had reached out to you."

"Why would they?"

"The deceased was dressed in the same vintage silk dressing gown as you were. She also had a white silk rose in her hands, and her fingernails were manicured; you get the picture."

Lainey's legs were suddenly useless, and she collapsed onto one of the high stools as she slumped forward with her head in her hands. "What happened to her?"

42

"We don't know yet. The body was discovered earlier this morning. Someone was walking their dog. The dog ran off the trail and started digging."

"Whoever she is, she didn't put herself in the ground," Lainey scoffed like it was Strahan's fault.

"Like I said, we don't have details, and we're keeping it from the press as long as possible. But, once word gets out – and it will – people will want to talk to you."

"I don't have anything to say to those bloodsuckers."

"Good. Is there anything else, any other detail that has returned to you since we last spoke?"

"Nothing. And I don't want to go back to any of it. Life's hard enough without reimprinting myself with the stress. You could relate if you'd woken up inside your own shallow grave." Her words were spiked with venom, and her fingers trembled as she ran them through her hair.

"There's nothing you can tell me?" Strahan probed as if he were doubtful.

Lainey snapped her head up from the kitchen counter and watched him methodically stirring at his coffee. She seriously thought about pouring it over his head.

"Yeah, there is something: When people are clinically dead for a few minutes, you've heard, they report that, before being brought back to life, they saw a brilliant, white light oozing love, and they had no fear of death – well, I've died once, and I can tell you I saw no light, no dark, no welcoming hands of angels. When I awoke, all I had was this visceral fear inside and outside on every part of me, and through my skin," Lainey ran her hands down her torso. "It's still on me. Absolute dread. Nothing was welcoming about death. Have you ever known pure fear, Detective Strahan?"

"Not as you describe it." He took a sip of the drink. "You said no welcoming hands of angels. I didn't know you were religious?"

"I'm not."

"Curious phrase to use."

"I probably heard it somewhere. A movie or something. I don't know?"

Strahan crossed his legs in a perfectly relaxed pose like all he was missing was a Sunday newspaper. "Early indications would suggest it's the same person that took you. Except for this time, they completed their fantasy."

"Why a fantasy?" Lainey asked.

Upstairs hidden in the office doorway, Veva openly wept, having listened to Lainey's description. She felt a pure sorrow, hearing that her new boss had gone through such a Godless outcome when death was imminent. The thought of a dying person filled only with fear broke Veva's heart, and she prayed for Lainey's emptiness to be resolved.

Strahan leaned forward, their faces only two feet apart. "There was a lot of planning and care taken. Somebody was completing a vision of some sort. It could be symbolic in a religious sense. We don't know." Strahan extended a hand and softly touched Lainey's forearm. "We'll catch them. We always do."

"How long was the body in the ground?"

"We haven't gotten the details, but the early estimate is three months … could be longer." Strahan removed his hand from her arm and looked sheepish that his touch was too long. "I understand you've no wish to look back, but Lainey, you're my only witness to what could be a serial killer. Anything you have locked away inside of you could help save lives. All we know from your description was someone with light brown eyes and dark eyebrows, wearing a hooded top."

"Please don't." Lainey screwed her eyes tight shut and raised the palm of her hand toward him, signaling him to stop. "I can't."

Strahan sat upright, took his contact card from inside his jacket, and slid it across the table. "Lainey, I know you're hurting, and you haven't left your house since you came from the hospital. Please, I'm asking. Call me, or email me, and I'll see you. You can do this."

"I didn't see anything. I can't help you."

"I think you can try. We've all seen and done things we should never witness. I can attest to that."

"Really," she remarked with disbelief.

"I'm a homicide detective. I have to meditate twice a day just to be able to stay in this job." He rolled his eyes to emphasize the point.

His inflection made Lainey laugh and fight hard against her body's insistence to cry. She nodded and swished a dismissive hand through the air at him. "Please leave."

"Thank you, Lainey. I need your help." He walked toward the front door. "Great coffee. Call me, please." His emphasis was on the word, please.

Lainey crumpled on the kitchen counter and propped her face in her open palms, resting her elbows on the surface. "Oh, God."

She should text Brian and have him call her. A glance at her phone showed it was only eight in the morning. She blew out the air from her lungs and thought about what to do. He'd only been at work for an hour. There was no point in asking him to come home. There was nothing to be done. Anyway, she had Veva upstairs with her all day. The idea of being alone in the house felt lonely - unsafe. Lainey checked via her phone that the front door had locked correctly, and she scanned each of the security camera feeds. Everything was clear. A straightforward conversation pushed her from a strong alpha female into a little girl who was terrified of what might be hiding in the bedroom closet.

"Fucker!" she exclaimed.

She wanted to be done with all this nonsense, and now it was starting again. People had been on virtual lockdown for a year with COVID-19, but Lainey had her own set of reasons for isolation. It was a different virus that wholly owned her, and even now, her infection remained. Another uncontrollable twist in her path was maddening beyond belief. Lainey despised not having control. "Double fucker!"

Upstairs in the office, Veva rushed to her desk and started her laptop. She wiped her face using a tissue to dab under her eyes. Lainey's agitation was understandable and scary. She wafted her hands in front of her face to dry off her eyelashes and pretend she'd been busy working.

Outside the house, Detective Strahan looked around the grounds and took note of the license plate on Veva's car. He gazed over the fields and out toward the vast ocean. "Damn, I wish I'd have thought of 4D treadmills." The slight motion from the window above caught his eye, and he saw Veva ducking from sight. He stayed still to see if she would reappear. Nothing happened, and he drove away. His boss had left a voicemail, asking him to drop into Eureka's Police Headquarters in the old downtown area. Strahan would need all his karmic reserves to get through it and hopefully, this time, find some evidence that led to the killer. He had searched online to locate Shellburg Falls, a seven-hour drive, which meant he'd have to spend a few days there to assist the local Oregon team.

From the first moment, over a year ago, when Detective Strahan was given Lainey's case, he had the strongest inclination it would never be straightforward. Rumors circulated that it was the work of rival tech companies who tried to take Lainey out and make it look like the work of some lone nutjob. Strahan never bought into any of the conspiracies. The work carried out was too careful and considerate. Nevertheless, he was sure that Lainey's attempted killing was the work of someone who would try again, and now his forecast had come to fruition. Not something he wanted to be right about, but more of a gut feeling that the killer would try again. In Oregon, the young woman's body showed that the killer had not made the same mistake that allowed Lainey to survive.

Lainey cleaned her face and decided she'd run later in the day. She popped her head into the office, ensuring Veva was okay before taking a quick shower.

"Veva, can you join the portfolio expansion call in two minutes. Sign on with my credentials and let everyone know you're there because I asked you to be."

"Sure. Anything specific you want me to take note about?"

"Yeah, everything that's important."

Veva politely smiled. A minute later, she heard a door slam somewhere down the landing. She did as Lainey asked, taking copious notes on the call.

It was half an hour later when Lainey appeared in the office, with her long-wet hair draped over one shoulder, still wearing the fluffy white robe, only this time, her upper chest was no longer covered by a t-shirt, and her long bare legs were on display. Veva turned her head, not wishing to stare.

"How did it go?"

"Fine. I made notes."

"Okay, bring your notes, and come with me." Lainey walked into her bedroom, and Veva dutifully followed. Lainey signaled Veva to sit on the bench seat by the small dresser with the attached vanity mirror. "You're not someone who's prudish or who cares if we do things a little different around here?"

"No." Veva cleared her throat as Lainey towel-dried her long hair.

"Good. We try to keep things informal, even in our workspace. A bit different here in the house, of course. It's not like we've had the entire office out here—only two people in the last year. What happens at the big house stays at the big house. You know what I mean."

"I get it." Veva's gaze flitted between Lainey and the carpet beneath her feet.

"Take me through your notes. We have a follow-up call later this afternoon."

"Sure." Veva read out her notes and who said what. In the mirror, she saw Lainey pull a pair of invisible underwear up her smooth legs before sliding into a pair of 4D leggings. Lainey turned her back and dropped the robe, pulling the sports bra over her head and wrestling it in place. Veva read aloud which potential trails could be added to their portfolio, particularly the one in the Cleveland National Forest near San Diego County.

"Hang on, what was that again?" Lainey asked. She approached Veva and took the notebook from her to read it. "I've told them before about this shit. We have to include some more remote trails into our technology. People like to experience something a little different. It's good for everyone. It doesn't matter if it's a popular destination or not – that's the point. So we use our technology to put these unknown trails inside people's homes," Lainey complained.

Veva kept her head down, with Lainey's bare midriff only six inches from her face. She got the light scent of Lainey's deodorant, and the body wash she'd used on her skin. A yummy combination.

She gave Veva back her notepad. "Your handwriting is impeccable. You practiced when you were younger, didn't you?"

"Yes. I have lots of compliments on it," Veva proudly said, raising her head, watching Lainey's fit body as she pulled on a light zip top.

Veva ducked back into her notes, relaying the rest of the meeting's discussion. Lainey sat next to Veva while she fixed her face in the mirror. Their upper thighs were pressed together. Although Veva could feel herself becoming extraordinarily hot, Lainey didn't seem to care. Instead, Lainey continued to ask questions as she applied mascara and lip-gloss.

"Nice job," Lainey observed on Veva's detailed recap. "Okay, let's get ourselves a quick organic juice blend and get back to it." Lainey led the way down into the kitchen, with Veva following behind.

"If you're working from here, you can dress casually. Do you have any of our 4D clothing line?"

"Not yet," Veva confessed. "I will do. I work out a lot at home. There's a kickboxing gym in town I'm going to join."

"Regular little Gym rat, aren't we?" Lainey prodded. "I can tell by your body you work out."

Veva blushed. "Really?"

"I'm a fitness freak too, so I can tell," Lainey noted Veva's cute embarrassment. "You should show off those curves you've worked so hard on. Why not?"

"I'm not sure…" Veva shrugged her shoulders.

"I am. Do you always wear granny pants?"

"What? I don't…" Veva looked down at herself.

Lainey chuckled. "How tall are you in heels?"

"Depends on the heel, but sometimes nearly six feet."

"You should wear some the next time you're at head office." She quickly threw some fruit and veggies in the juicer and made them a smoothie. They had an in-depth discussion on different workouts and what made them feel most elevated. Lainey listened carefully as Veva opened up a bit. Not as dull as Lainey had first supposed. It turned out that the mousey Veva had a lot of knowledge about the fitness industry and detailed knowledge of physiology and the body's workings.

They returned upstairs, this time to the office. Before commencing more meetings, Veva opened the door to the patio and stepped outside.

"Oh, my God, it is so beautiful," she gushed, extending her arms and soaking in the sun. She looked around, expecting Lainey to join her, but her new boss stayed a couple of feet inside the doorway.

"I don't," Lainey pointed outside.

"I'm sorry," Veva began to head back inside.

"No," Lainey held out her hand for Veva to stay on the balcony. "You go ahead. I can feel the heat from here. I'll enjoy it vicariously through you."

"I didn't realize," Veva fussed.

"No problem. I know it doesn't make any sense … not even to me. Go ahead."

"I wish you could join me," Veva pointed north out of Lainey's line of sight. "The sun's rays are reflecting off the tops of the trees, and it looks like a massive rolling green ocean as if it's moving."

"Describe everything for me." Lainey watched the side of Veva's face, with her wide childish grin, basking in the sun and acting as if she'd never seen a view before. Lainey was slightly envious of Veva's ability to take immense pleasure from it.

"It's like the dancing forest is telling the ocean that it, too, knows how to shimmer, and the ocean is responding. One shows pale green, and the other responds with pale blue. It's like they're working together in perfect union to show us how amazing our world is. The birds sing along and serenade what God provided for us." Veva gave Lainey an assured smile. "Can you step closer and see part of what I'm describing?" She stretched out her arm and wiggled her fingers.

Lainey inched closer to the doorway and strained her neck but remained firmly inside the home office. "Yes, it is breathtaking. I didn't have you down as a believer. So few tech people are."

Veva turned and, with a white-toothed broad smile, declared, "How can you not believe in divinity when we have all this?" She opened her hands as if she were on a TV game show, displaying the star prize. "None of this an accident," Veva enthusiastically declared as she slowly turned her face towards the sun.

"You might have a point."

"God has a plan for all of us. Is there no way you can?" she spoke softly, encouraging Lainey onto the small balcony. "I'll make sure you're okay."

Lainey shook her head. "No. Not today. One day. Thank you for asking."

"I feel guilty for not being able to share it with you, and it being your house and all."

"Your description was good enough." Lainey paid her a compliment and gave Veva a slight bow, which Veva returned with a curtsy. "C'mon, let's finish up. I still need to run today. I want to be ready for Brian when he gets home."

"Oh, I see," Veva replied, her voice full of innuendo and an impish grin.

"If only," Lainey sighed. "I've got way more problems than not getting outside. Just between us girls, I can't get anything inside either, if you know what I mean."

"I'm sorry. That must be hard on you both," Veva sympathetically added.

"It is. Not having…never mind. Back to work." Lainey didn't know Veva well enough to go further. In time, she might become a girlfriend. Something Lainey had missed out on for some time. She only had two real girlfriends – both were married with kids, and since Covid hit, she'd only seen them twice in over a year. Lainey's focus was on the business and, more recently, simply trying to get through each day. She missed girl time.

They spent the afternoon in more meetings before Veva packed away her things to head to Eureka.

Lainey was suitably impressed with her new director. They'd sourced Veva from a hiring agency, and they were paying top dollar for her compared to people in similar positions. Still, Veva's resume, working with some of the California tech giants, was impressive, and it already showed. Neither Brian nor Lainey were awestruck by Veva's online interview, but they'd agreed to press ahead based on her knowledge of the digital world on which their empire was founded. Veva departed mid-afternoon to attend a face-to-face meeting at their head office. "Strange little mouse," Lainey remarked as she watched Veva drive away.

Momentarily, Lainey pushed aside all other thoughts and considered what to say to Brian when he came home. The silence was ripping them into irreplaceable pieces. Detective Strahan wanted her to reach inside for things she wasn't sure she possessed. The brief glimpses she recalled were terrifying microcosms as if tempting death to take a permanent hold on her.

"Memory is a cruel mistress," Lainey sighed.

CHAPTER FIVE

Brian offered to pick up dinner on the way home, and Lainey chose sushi, so long as the rolls were fresh and he didn't order fried tempura.

When he readied himself for work earlier that morning, Lainey had watched him dry himself after his shower. His slender body was fit, with a tight waist and broad shoulders. He wasn't a classically handsome man but rugged, with his long, straight nose, square chin, and bright brown eyes. Those soft kind eyes made her melt – until the incident had left her frozen. Lainey knew that a man like Brian, fit, active, intelligent, persistent, and a millionaire, could easily be targeted by other women, especially when traveling alone in foreign countries. She was sure he hadn't strayed off the path, but she didn't believe that could hold out forever. His sex drive was healthy, and his physical enthusiasm in the bedroom was always impressive. His equipment was average, but his effort and willingness to please her made up any shortfall. Brian was a most committed lover, and she was sure he had much more to give. She wanted to accommodate him, but intimacy with her devoted husband somehow exposed her, and each time they tried, Lainey came crashing down. It made her appear feeble, and she couldn't bear that. Worse was that Lainey could not describe why it manifested that way. Lainey was rarely short of words to describe anything, but in terms of her marital relations, she was at a loss to explain why it was that whenever Brian got close, she imploded as if somehow violated.

"Maybe tonight?" she told herself, not really believing that she could. Brian was wearing his tight black briefs with a white waistband that made him look like a private male revue dancer. He'd retained the fit body from his days as a personal trainer. "Just try." She pushed out the words, hoping her body would take action. Lainey was determined to find a way back into Brian's loving arms. But each time she tried, the flashbacks were vivid, always the same, and the fear was real, like a physical reaction, draining the strength from her body. Finally, she shook her head and grunted in disgust at her frailty. "How can I have done all this, but I can't shake off this other shit? Argh!"

She was distracted by the unlisted number calling her cell.

"Hi, Lainey, it's Veva," the voice said.

"Is everything okay?"

"Yeah. I forgot to ask before I left if you wanted me to join you at the house tomorrow."

"Haven't said anything different, have I?"

"No."

"Then I'll see you here at eight in the morning. How did you get my number?"

"Brian, your husband, was in the office when I got there and introduced himself. He gave me your number and said it was okay to call you."

"Tell him I said thanks. Anything else?"

"No."

"I'll see you tomorrow." Lainey dropped the call and saved Veva's number to her contacts. She'd been unnecessarily curt and had nothing against Veva; in fact, she quite liked her. Nevertheless, her situation made her increasingly glum. From the open landing, she looked around the house. "This will not be my prison," she told the house, hoping to serve it notice.

Lainey skipped down the stairs and grabbed an apple. She gave thought to the mysterious figure she had spotted on her run and fired an email to tech services, making sure they'd fixed the footage from Prairie Creek. "Frickin' weirdos," she complained.

Lainey had scrabbled in the dirt inside the thick of the forest a year earlier. After the incident, she'd scrubbed under her fingernails for two months to remove the dirt she was convinced remained there. The ritual caused her to bleed from her fingertips for weeks on end.

Veva called again. "Yeah?"

"I'm bringing my lunch with me again. Would you like some? It's all organic, chicken and vegetables with my own Meyer lemon dressing."

"That's very sweet of you. I'd like that, thank you."

"Okay. Cool."

"Anything else?"

"Brian said he's heading out to pick up sushi for you guys."

"Tell him to get a move on. Thanks."

"Will do. Bye." This time Veva hung up the call.

Lainey frowned at the phone. She resolved to accept some form of kindness and not be so bitchy about it. Also, to be more civil to her new director.

An hour later, Brian came home, and they shared the fresh sushi rolls. Lainey cleared everything away while he went upstairs to take a run. Lainey took off her 4D workout clothes and slipped into a silky nightie. Nothing too sexy, but interesting enough to be noticed beyond her usual shirt and what Brian referred to as her college-girl cotton panties. She sat upright in the bed when Brian strode into the room, his chest heaving from the run.

"Which trail did you take?"

"The Aliso Summit trail and all the way out to the ocean. Our sunset resolution looks unbelievable," he replied, pulling off his shirt and shorts.

He was about to head to the shower. "No. Come here," Lainey beckoned.

"I'm all sweaty."

"I like you that way," she felt a quiver in her voice.

Brian shrugged, removed his socks, and kept on his tight briefs as he climbed in next to her. Lainey had her laptop resting on her thighs. Her skin bristled with a mixture of excitement and dread. Brian pressed his boiling hot body against hers. Lainey gave him a lame smile, which he returned.

"What are we looking at?" he asked.

"I took your download from your GoPro and uploaded it already. I thought you could take me through the monuments and things you saw in Japan."

"Sure. You look nice." He ran a hand over the smooth fabric by her hip and traced his finger over the tiny thong underneath.

53

"Kiss me," she abruptly said.

"You sure?"

"Do it." Lainey pushed the laptop away from her knees. Brian placed one hand on her face and softly pressed his lips to hers. Lainey purred as his sumptuous full lips dampened hers and slowly glided on her. She responded and turned her upper body to meet him as the kiss intensified. His left hand slid over her abdomen and slowly stroked the material covering her thighs. Lainey instinctively parted her legs, encouraging him to probe wherever he pleased. His touch against her, and the heat of his body, were electric. The smell of his fresh sweat rose to her nostrils, and she dug her nails into his skin as he slipped his tongue inside her mouth, and she eagerly responded.

His left hand pulled up her nightdress, and his fingers dipped under her briefs, touching the skin above her crotch, teasing up and down. She swung her knees apart, fully opening herself to him. His tongue flicked suggestively, reminding her of his oral skills and a clear indication of what he'd willingly give. He felt good to her; she was okay and had somehow managed to let go. She wanted him to lick her all over like he used to and make her shudder. His light touch around her crotch was divine, and she adjusted her hips, giving him full access. His lips moved over her neck, into her clavicle, right onto the spot she liked that sent her head backward, and shivers ran through her toes. Her breath turned into short sharp spurts, and he tantalized every inch of her skin. She reached over and fumbled at his swollen crotch. His briefs stretched out under the pressure of his bulge. Her hand stroked his proud erection, forcing him to moan.

"Oh, Lainey," he longingly whispered before he began suckling on her alert nipples.

Still, she had no thoughts other than Brian taking her and feeling him inside. She missed him. His left hand pulled down one side of her thong, and his fingers drew closer to her lips. She had retained her appointments for her waxing lady to be at the house only days earlier, and she was glad to maintain appearances in all parts of her body if only to make herself feel as normal as she could. His teeth pinched at her nipples with a precision bite, driving her to pull his erection from his briefs and stroke it. It had been three months at least since they'd tried anything, and this was way more than the odd peck they'd exchanged in that time.

"I want you inside me," she gasped in his ear.

"Let me taste you," he replied, and his head dropped down over her stomach. He kissed and licked his way from her navel to the tops of her inner thighs, working his way on either side of her soaking lips.

Lainey pulled at his hair as he slipped lower, teasing her, and finally, his tongue was on her. Her thighs flinched; her muscles clenched as if she'd never been touched before. He made small, satisfying noises as he moved that skillful tongue up and down and then lapped at her sweet spot. She gripped his hair tight, grunting loudly. His hands removed her underwear and discarded them at the end of the bed as he feasted on her. Lainey moved the cushions so she lay flat on her back. His attentions were delicious, and his rhythm heavenly. Lainey opened her eyes and looked at the ceiling as she fully relaxed into Brian's oral gift.

The briefest, awful flash came to her mind just as Brian picked up the pace. She told herself no. Her body tightened. For a microsecond, she saw the eyes that once looked down on her – she was alone, helpless, afraid, as though she was there again. Her body jolted, and she was terrified. Another flashback – the warm light brown eyes gazed upon her once more. She tried to push it away, but she looked down and saw his eyes over her crotch – soft, willing, and an intense light brown.

"No. No!" Lainey cried as she used her hands to push his head away from her crotch. She scuttled backward on the bed and nestled into the pillows. "No. I'm sorry, I'm sorry," she called out, with her body suddenly shaking.

"Lainey, it's me. It's only me," Brian said as he came alongside her and carefully placed his hands on the back of her shoulders. "It's okay. I'm here with you. No one else is here," he softly assured her.

"I'm sorry. I thought…"

"It's okay." He kissed the back of her head, cuddling her trembling body. "It's okay."

"Oh, Brian," she wailed, folding into him. "I don't know what to…" Lainey was humiliated. She'd led him on, only to let him down once more. In her eyes, failure was unforgivable.

"It's okay, Babe." He gently kissed her neck. "I've got you." Brian tightened his arms around his distressed wife. He made sure his quickly dying erection wasn't pressed against her. There was nothing he could do. Words were no use. He stroked the skin across her heaving shoulders and tried to reassure her.

Neither of them said it, but they both knew it was far from okay.

It was a full minute before Lainey spoke. "I thought I could." Lainey held out a shaking fist in front of her face. "I thought I was okay. I want you; I do. It's just…I don't know."

"Me too," he replied. "Let's talk about it soon, when we're ready. Not now. No judgment, no promises, or anything like that. But let's get it all out, Lainey. We have to be open and honest, no matter what. I love you, and I want to support you. Even if we can't produce any resolutions, it doesn't matter, but we have to go through it. We can face anything together. We have to throw down what we're both holding inside."

"I don't deserve you," she sniffed, feeling sorry for herself.

"You're right," he joked, causing her to blow snot from her nose. "We're a team, always have been. There's nothing we should keep from each other, no matter if one of us feels hurt by it. We swore we'd always be honest."

"I know you're disappointed in me," she wiped her face on the silk nightgown.

"I'm disappointed for both of us. But, it's us – not just you or me. Of course, I want to be connected physically to my beautiful wife, but I want you to be healthy and feel good."

"I do, right until we get, you know, and then these stupid images just appear in my head. Then, it's like I'm there again – seeing those eyes. I keep seeing them looking down at me."

"Oh, my poor baby," he nuzzled her.

Lainey yanked her body away from him and headed into the restroom. "I need to wash my face. It's not you – you know that." Her meaningful stare demanded a response.

"I know."

They held each other's gaze until Lainey went into the bathroom, closed the door, and ran the hot water. She splashed her face and neck and stared at her reflection. Lainey hated residual fear's cruel stamp on her. Lainey's energy drained as she leaned on the sink, and her limbs could barely support her. She made a dab with a fresh towel, and wearily she walked back into the bedroom, avoiding looking directly at Brian. He was a decent man. Sometimes mean, especially when challenged, and Lainey challenged him a lot. She'd seen the change in him, and none of it was good. She dropped the silk nightgown and pulled on some comfy cotton pants and a t-shirt. She slid under the single sheet and felt for his hands. He switched off the lamp and spooned her with his leading arm over her body. Lainey played with his fingers before they interlocked hands.

The room was silent. The white walls with bright artwork usually held magic in the dim light from the partially open blinds, but tonight it offered nothing. Not even Lainey's precious artwork could provide a spark of inspiration. Instead, their latest intimate failure dragged her mood downward.

Lainey had never been one for tears or emotional outbursts. Her reactions to events were typically controlled and sparse. But, understandably, in the last year, everything changed. The room's silence was broken by the sound of Lainey quietly sobbing.

Brian knew the only thing to do was for him to hold her. That spluttering from her throat repeatedly stabbed at his aching heart, filling him with a horrid discomfort. Nothing came closer to genuinely frightening Brian than the awful sound of his despairing wife. Patiently he held her, feeling her body's spasms, each in violation of the promise he once made to protect her. Their position was unbearable.

Fortune and a certain level of fame were all good, but there was nothing their millions could do to buy them peace of mind.

CHAPTER SIX

Brian kissed Lainey's cheek, told her that he loved her, and ate breakfast alone before heading to work. Lainey waited for him to go before getting up. She still felt awful about last night. It was humiliation blended with anger. Communication was unwelcome.

Before her first appointment, Lainey got on the treadmill and selected the course through the bamboo forest Brian had run in Japan. Arashiyama was beautiful; walking through it would be a better way to appreciate all it had to offer. Forty-two people were logged in simultaneously on the same course. From Lainey's specially formatted screen, she could see there were currently over three thousand people worldwide running or walking on their technical miracle. It gave her shivers just thinking about it, and she needed something to make her feel good. By the early evening, that number would be anywhere from twelve to twenty thousand people running one of the many trails they offered. The number of owners grew, and the community got stronger. Lainey dismissed the irony that she and Brian connected thousands worldwide but couldn't figure a way to connect themselves.

She scanned the Tenryuji Temple before engaging the treadmill into action. The prominent pagoda-style Buddhist place of worship was pristine, next to a man-made lake, and the sun reflected the image onto the water's surface. Jogging down the pathway and turning the corner, Lainey was met with the towering bamboo on either side and the track through the forest, lined with tall grass reeds. She was quickly on pace and winding her way through the depth of splintered light shaded by the sparse overhead green canopy. It was only a few minutes into her run when she spotted a figure off to the right in the trees. It startled her, and she almost tripped, gripping the safety rails of the treadmill to steady herself. "What the fuck?"

She quickly regained her rhythm. That was the second time someone had appeared on two different trails within three days. She'd not had the chance to go back and look at the footage from the Redwoods in Prairie Creek, but she'd been assured it was taken care of. Lainey decided to forego her first online meeting to look at her run and compare it to the California trail.

She completed one circuit through the Japanese bamboo forest and looped back on the abandoned railway line, cutting her run short, and switching off the treadmill. Lainey was determined to find the source data and learn why her team had missed another digital edit. There was the added mystery of why a similar-looking figure had suddenly appeared in two different places. She quickly wiped down with a towel and went to her desk to replay her trail runs. Lainey used her top-level passcode to enter the archives. She selected the California data, forwarded it to the twenty-four-minute mark, and froze the screen. There was the crouched figure in the Redwoods. She set the level of play speed to ten percent of normal and watched in slow-motion. Someone in a dark blue hoodie knelt on the ground and hunched over. Only part of the right arm was visible, and there was a slight movement like the hand was doing something. The thought struck her that it was some pervert jerking off in the woods. "Eew," she retched.

On the other side of her screen, she froze the image of her earlier run in Japan. The figure was wearing a dark blue hoodie and partially hunched over. "What on earth are they doing?" she asked herself. She rewound at slow speed and watched both again. There was no view of anyone's face. "This is stupid," she hissed at her team's failure to delete both incidents. Lainey didn't want their thousands of happy customers freaked out by seeing weirdos in the woods. Tech services were going to get an earful. It wasn't good enough!

None of which solved the issue of what these people were doing. Each snapshot was less than 1.2 seconds long and not enough time to know what they were doing. Lainey thought it was too much of a coincidence – the timing, the dark blue hoodie. Could it be the same person was in California and then Japan? It seemed unlikely, but Brian had just returned from the far East, so it was possible.

"What are you doing?" she asked the mysterious figures. Lainey tried several Google searches about Japanese rituals involving people praying in the woods. She learned about forest bathing and considered it an excellent idea, and if circumstances were different, she would have gone outside to try it.

As it was, Lainey was resigned to the mercy of severe agoraphobia; the diagnosis had been made shortly after she was released from the hospital. Once she'd returned to her home, she had never left. Her therapies were conducted inside her house, and all her subsequent business dealings were managed via the internet. Despite paying top dollar to three different psychologists, she had not been able to find the courage to go outside or be able to use one of their four separate balconies or the rear deck with extensive views over the hills. Lainey stared towards the gothic folly. "Fucker," she hissed through clenched teeth.

Lainey hated being beaten by anything, especially her own psyche. It was a loss she'd not come to terms with. She was an outdoor runner of the highest caliber and now reduced to this thing, barely able to stand in the doorway. It sickened her stomach to think she was anything less than strong. The emails and comments of support on their website she received were most welcome, all wishing her well. Lainey desired a return to everyday life for herself and her devoted online following.

She left Phil a voicemail, telling him to remove the figure from the Japanese trail. Then, she switched off both screens and wandered to the front of the house. Lainey looked at the distant tree line from the office window that shadowed the main coastal highway. It was so distant; it felt like she was passing by in a rocket ship, with no way of setting foot on the ground.

Lainey's emotions rippled from sadness to anger and back again. She'd fought hard, worked hard, trained hard, loved hard, and for it to end, withering away inside her designer house on the hill was too much to digest. "No way." The mesmerizing distant views hurt her – they were within easy reach, but they were presently untouchable.

The sadness returned, taking over with aplomb as it mirrored her relationship with Brian. She wanted to love him, feel him, and reach out, but he seemed outside her grasp. Lainey was tempted to hide under the bed covers whenever she witnessed that vacant look in his eyes. His light brown pupils had retained their kindness, but the special glint was gone. The small touches whenever he passed by her were only a memory. Ever since they had first dated and subsequently married, Brian always pinched her behind or caressed her cheeks around the house or when no one was looking. Now, Brian's hands hadn't touched her rear end for months, and she knew he was holding back because of how she felt. He didn't want to rock her boat for fear of sinking her to the bottom. She wanted his small touches, but if he touched her in these ways, the expectation could grow into something Lainey was unable to provide. Normality had become a mirage. The small things mattered. She patted her hands on her behind and averted her eyes from the outside view. "I'm going to fucking win," she snarled.

Detective Strahan entered the two-story concrete building on C Street. The police department was at the corner of an intersection, looking more like an abandoned burger joint than a center for criminal investigation. There was nothing friendly about the interior, which matched the drab exterior. Money was tight, and no expense was ever spared to make Eureka Police headquarters look pretty.

He went upstairs, across the worn-out carpet on the second floor, and toward the corner office of his captain. He assumed his orders would be to play nice with their Oregon colleagues. Strahan was adept at playing friendly. Though his style was much different from most of his fellow detectives, and his laid-back approach seemed too casual, he got results. Strahan's technique hadn't endeared him with his colleagues, but he worked equally as hard as anyone. Strahan believed in treating all people with dignity and respect, no matter the circumstances. Something much easier in theory than practice, given some of the desperate people he came into contact with.

His captain saw him approaching through the glass window and waved him to enter. Strahan hadn't seen the tall, slender woman in a green wool jacket, partially reclined on the small sofa. She was tucked into the corner and greeted him with an overly big smile.

"Hi." Her firm grip met his extended hand. Her fingers were long and bony. "Detective Strahan."

"Detective Hurst," she replied, taking a long look at him.

Strahan sat on the single chair by his captain's desk.

"Detective Hurst is out of Albany, Oregon," the captain explained. "She was down here on vacation until this morning."

"Cut short by a day," she added.

"You were vacationing here?" Strahan asked.

"Yeah, I was fishing. I like to catch things." The deadpan look in her eyes matched her tone as her dull pupils lingered on him.

Strahan returned her gaze. She winked at him and vigorously chewed on some gum.

Detective Hurst was in her late fifties, with visible stress lines around her eyes and the corners of her mouth. Her shoulder-length hair was a bleached-blonde mess, as though she'd done it herself one night in the kitchen, with the lights off. She was five-foot-eight, with bony wrists sticking out from the end of her sleeves. Her brown leather shoes were scuffed. Her jacket appeared too tight, surprising given how gaunt her stick-limbed body appeared. Her beige trousers were stretched tight over two long thighs. Her pupils were dark, virtually jet-black, and her eyes were narrow with pale skin. A slight touch of mascara was the only sign of any makeup. Her jaw quickly rotated as she chewed on gum with the attitude of a petulant schoolkid, waiting outside the principal's office. All the while, she never took her eyes off Strahan. He gave her a polite smile and blinked slowly. Detective Hurst had a familiarity, but he couldn't place her.

"Detective Hurst has been assigned the flower-girl case in Shellburg Falls," The captain stated.

"Shouldn't it fall to Salem and not Albany?"

"I guess I'm just lucky," Hurst interrupted. "Salem's not going to touch that shit. They have resource issues, and they know better. I got the call at four a.m. this morning."

"Give Detective Hurst everything we have," the captain said.

"So, you want me to partner with Detective Hurst?"

"You and me, handsome," she replied, cutting off the unamused captain.

"That's what I said, didn't I," the captain huffed as if bored with the whole conversation. "Get your shit together. You're going north with Hurst."

"Why so quick?" Strahan asked.

The captain gave Detective Hurst the nod to proceed.

"We think there's more than the one we just found and the near-miss with Lainey Stewart."

"Near miss?" Strahan inferred it was an understatement.

"Your girl here in Eureka, Mrs. Stewart, had a calling card marked "one of seven." The body we have in Stassel Falls, Shellburg, is marked number "two of seven," carrying the same business card with a floral motif that says, "Let them praise the name of the Lord.""

"We never gave that data to the media."

"I just told her," the captain complained.

"If the notation is correct, we can expect five more bodies to be buried somewhere. So saddle up, cowboy, we're taking a road trip," Hurst cheerily announced. "I want to speak with Lainey Stewart before we leave."

"No way," Strahan quickly replied. "I just interviewed her, and she's in no condition for any of us right now."

"Then we can leave tomorrow after I speak with her," Detective Hurst insisted.

Strahan turned his attention back to the captain and waited for his orders.

The captain's face was unhappier than ever. "You'll support Detective Hurst in her…"

"Support?"

"Yes, support. She has the dead body – we don't. So it's her investigation until we hear differently." The captain looked past him to Detective Hurst. "Tell us what you need, and we'll do what we can."

"Told you I was lucky," Hurst smiled.

"Mrs. Stewart has been locked in her castle for a year, and we're not bringing her down here for questioning, so figure it out. We don't need any crap from the media." The captain went back to reading his emails.

"And me?" Strahan asked.

"Pack your scented candles, your yoga mat, your eight-armed Buddha, or whatever you need, and help Detective Hurst." The captain never looked at Strahan as he tapped his fingers on the keyboard.

Strahan gave Hurst a courteous smile. She winked at him again. "Looks like I'm all yours," he said.

"Knew I'd land something special on this trip. If you take me through whatever you have that's not in the Lainey Stewart file – like your thoughts, and I'll share what I've got so far from the team in Shellburg."

"Why don't I take you through what we have in the file before that?"

"I already read it this morning," she said, taking a copy from her shoulder bag. "I have no life, Detective Strahan, other than a few fishing days each year. What about you?"

"Outside of having this kind of fun, I do yoga and make sure I'm at one with source energy."

Detective Hurst looked at the captain with a straight smile. "I love this guy." She cupped a hand to one side of her mouth, pretending her voice wouldn't carry beyond the captain, "I bet we fall in love on this case, and detective Strahan asks me to marry him."

"He could use a wife," the captain said, suddenly perking up.

"So, could I," Hurst agreed with a knowing arc in her slender eyebrows. She uncrossed her legs and chewed hard on the gum, returning her dark-eyed gaze to Strahan. "Don't sweat it, Detective. I know I'm hard to resist."

"So, I see," he glibly replied, inferring the opposite.

Detective Hurst's insinuation of needing a wife jogged Strahan's memory. He recognized detective Hurst from the news reports from back in 2016. She was the one who'd infamously had an affair with a female suspect who'd been acquitted of murder. An Albany housewife was accused of killing her abusive husband until a court found her not guilty. Detective Hurst was the arresting officer assigned to prosecute the case, who subsequently finished up in a lesbian relationship with the accused once the woman was freed. It caused a significant stir in the news and accusations from the deceased's family that Detective Hurst and Albany Police were corrupt and hadn't looked at the facts correctly.

The case was reinvestigated, and Hurst and the Albany Police were found to have presented all they could. The housewife remained free and went about her life, and Detective Hurst got on with her policing. Strahan recalled seeing Detective Hurst being interviewed on local television and saying, "I'm having a relationship with a woman who was found innocent of any crime, so where's the crime in being with an innocent woman?" The latter part of that phrase was repeated many times and adopted as a meme by the Northwest Lesbian community. T-shirts were printed with the slogan, "Where's the crime in being with an innocent woman?" Strahan was aware Detective Hurst had earned herself quite a reputation as a ballbuster. Working with someone of the opposite style to his was a tricky prospect.

Strahan glanced over his shoulder into the main office and saw the sly smiles from his colleagues. Inside his head, he called for calm. Obviously, everyone knew who Hurst was, even if they didn't know exactly why she was there. It wouldn't be long before they figured it out. He could hear echoes of the crap he'd take and be labeled Detective Hurst's new bitch. Detective Strahan took a deep breath and imagined a protective light around his body that made him impervious to negative energy. He breathed out slowly, showering Hurst in a loving light, and envisioned a productive working partnership.

"You're too pretty to fight crime. Are you gay?" Detective Hurst asked him.

Strahan's bubble burst without a pop. His captain showed a rare sign of amused interest.

Strahan measured his words, "Thanks for noticing my beauty as a human being. I consider myself as someone who loves all people."

"Bisexual, huh?" she prodded.

"No. If I had time to find a partner, which I don't, then she would be someone with a similar outlook as myself."

"Fuck me sideways. He means a hippie," the captain explained.

"We should light a joss stick and pray that we find you a wife before losing those good looks. But, like me, not everyone can stay pretty this long," Hurst chewed faster than ever. She returned the file copies to her bag.

Strahan noticed the zipper on Detective Hurst's beige pants was unfastened, and her white laced underwear was on display. "Is that an offer?" he said, pointing toward her fly. "Or are you equally desperate to find a wife?" Strahan had to press back, or she'd become unbearable.

"No wonder I'm so popular this morning," she chuckled, zipping herself up. "You see, we're a team already. I'll show you mine if you show me yours?" she suggested as she rose from the sofa. "Shall we?" she pointed to the door.

In her flat shoes, she was as tall as Strahan. Her wiry body had good posture, a straight back, broad shoulders, and a confident stance. He wondered if she was an athlete in her youth. They shook hands again, but she didn't attempt cracking his knuckles this time.

"We'll use my office." He invited her to follow him.

As they walked through the main office, all eyes were on them. Detective Hurst smiled at those immediately around them. "Everybody's so nicely dressed," Hurst observed. "Makes me think I need to find a Macy's, just to fit in here."

"Are there any of them left?"

"I've no idea. Get most of my clothes at Outdoor world."

"You'd never guess."

"I like you, Detective Strahan," she said, deliberately making her response loud enough for those within thirty feet to hear it.

"Namaste," he replied.

CHAPTER SEVEN

Lainey was in Brian's face before he had dropped his satchel on the countertop.

"How many times do I need to intervene? The creation team keeps ruling places out because they're remote! We get way more traction with remote places. I'm sick of saying it."

"I'm sick of hearing it," Brian snapped as he poured himself a glass of water.

Lainey was in no mood for excuses. "And we had another person fully pixelated off to the side of a trail, this time in Japan. Two in a week! You're supposed to be in charge of it. Do your job, and I won't have to step in."

"You'd step in any way so that you can tell me or anyone who has to listen how they permanently suck. You like it too much." Brian turned his back on her and drank the water.

"That's what you think I am?" Lainey frothed at the mouth, talking to his back.

"I don't know what you are." He turned and placed his glass on the counter. The dark circles under his eyes gave away his exhaustion. The tightness of his jawline showed Brian wasn't in the mood.

Lainey had been stalking around their home all day like a caged animal. "You think being me is easy?"

"No. And it's not easy being the husband of the darling of 4D Fitness Tech."

That remark had Lainey spoiling for a fight. "I never said it would be easy. You knew what I was like before we were married. Finding myself half-dead in the woods wasn't part of the master plan."

"We're doing okay as a business. Perhaps you could lighten up a little."

"You sound like you don't know me. But, I won't ease back on my desire to succeed."

"I can promise you that you've repeatedly made it clear." Brian's chest released a heavy sigh.

Lainey bared her teeth. "And you've made your case abundantly clear." She could have left it there, but she was going all in. His eyes gave away that he was ready to let go – some fire at last. Lainey needed to hear him say it. "Either way, sort out your team, please. I'm tired of it."

"And I'm tired too, Lainey."

"Tired of what exactly?"

"All of this shit."

"Really?" Her voice sharply taunted.

"Yes, Really! Tired of you interfering and tired of hearing that you're tired. Guess what? I'm tired of this … this pretense! Tired of the constant bullshit and rejection. Fuck!" Brian threw the rest of the water down the sink, took his laptop bag, and headed for the stairs.

"I haven't finished rejecting you," Lainey angrily called after him. He ignored the barb and wearily climbed the stairs. "Why should I? I haven't finished rejecting myself," she added. She watched him disappear into their bedroom as he made a pathetic point to slam the door. Lainey paced up and down, slapping her fist into the palm of her hand. She was tempted to go after him and tell him what Detective Strahan had shared with her. Instead, she found herself growling like a threatened dog. She was in the mood to bite someone, and Brian had better watch it, or she'd rip his legs off. It could quickly escalate if she pursued the argument, which was a minor annoyance. It was rare that Brian had gone after her since her near-death incident. His inferences told Lainey what he was thinking. No wonder. The toll on them was too heavy.

She picked up an apple and bit down on it, chewing hard as she talked herself down. It was a good thing he'd released some of the pressure. Then again, they talked all the time about disclosing their feelings. If he'd felt that way for some time, he should have said something before now instead of being an asshole.

Lainey felt the vibration of her phone against her thigh. She pulled it from the tailor-made pocket on her 4D workout pants. The text was from Veva. Lainey, I wanted to let you know you're all over the news. Sorry. I didn't want you to get surprised. Veva. Lainey switched on the 70-inch flatscreen TV and switched to the local news. "Oh, no." The report was all about the murdered woman in Oregon, linked with Lainey's case. A glance at her cell phone showed the new case, and her old case was trending everywhere. She texted a thank you back to Veva.

Their bedroom door opened, and then the door to the exercise room slammed shut—Brian's way of letting her know to stay away.

"Fudgesicle," she grunted. Lainey listened to the news report. The Oregon Police believed it was directly linked to Lainey's case. She walked to the expansive front windows and looked towards the gates, expecting to see cars and news crews gathered. For weeks when she was first released from the hospital, reporters were caught on the house's grounds and trying to take her photographs through the windows. "Frickin' vultures," she muttered. Lainey was momentarily surprised by how long she could tolerate being up against the window. Veva had almost tempted her outside the other day. A positive.

Lainey went upstairs and heard Brian's footsteps bashing away on the treadmill. She paused before entering. Lainey and Brian had had their share of fights, but they were good at letting go of things and sleeping with a clear conscience. She entered the room and walked up alongside him, having to squeeze herself between the frame of the treadmill and the wrap-around screen.

"I need to let you know something about my old case."

Brian kept running, his focus straight ahead. "I already know. You're in the news again."

"Why didn't you say something?"

"I found out sixty seconds ago."

"You were checking the news while you're running?"

"No. Veva texted me so that I wouldn't be surprised."

"I didn't know she had your number."

"I gave it to her. She's here in the house with you, and I was … never mind."

"I suppose she's cute, in a timid way," Lainey couldn't help herself.

Brian glanced sideways, showing he didn't appreciate the comment.

"So, what do you think?"

"About the news, or about Veva being cute."

"Let's start with the news." Lainey waited, and he said nothing. Only silence. "Brian! People are being killed, and you're acting like you don't care. I could be next!"

"People get killed all the time."

"Don't fuck with me, Brian!"

"I don't know what to think about it." Instead, Brian focused on his run.

Lainey watched the trail he was on and recognized it as the rugged coastal track outside Marseille, France, at the Parc National Des Calanques. The rocky terrain and ocean views were spectacular enough to distract her for a few seconds.

Brian's ignoring her wasn't going to work. Lainey reached over and hit the red stop button that slowly halted the treadmill, and the whole unit dropped several inches into its resting place, and the trail paused.

Brian averted her gaze, took his face towel, and wiped his brow, despite not having formed any sweat. His body language indicated he was about to leave the room.

"You're seriously going to walk away and say nothing?" Lainey skirted around him.

"I think we've said enough for one day."

"Brian, I'm asking you for your opinion, and you're walking away."

"No, Lainey, you asked me a question, and I gave you my answer. I'm walking away before we say anything we regret. Leave it."

"You don't have an opinion that my face is all over the news?" she asked, folding her arms across her chest and heading him off before he could get into their master bathroom.

He rolled his eyes and turned his head away from her. Lainey poked her finger in his chest. "Truth or nothing at all. We agreed, remember."

"How can I forget?" He went to move around her, but she blocked the way. His kindly eyes narrowed with intention.

"Uh huh," she insisted, poking his chest.

Brian knew that he'd better give her something, or she wouldn't budge. His full lips tightened, and his cheek muscles flexed as he snorted through his nostrils. "The truth? The truth is, Lainey, I don't know what to do. I want my wife back. Shit! I don't want this permanent tension between us. I want you to get some professional help that will make a difference. I want you to feel safe and well. Happiness would be a fucking amazing bonus. And I don't know how to do any of that! That's the truth. Have you heard enough?"

Her eyes flitted around as she read every micro-movement of his teeth-clenching delivery. "What else?" Lainey sensed he was holding back. She was having none of it and poked his chest again. "C'mon, Brian."

"What else?" he stood closer, so their faces were six inches apart. "I'm scared for the both of us – every day. This murder thing is going to explode again. I'm scared for your safety. I'm scared because I couldn't keep you from harm before, and I don't know if I can prevent God-knows-what from happening again! I'm scared you'll disappear so far inside yourself that you won't be able to claw your way out. And most of all, I'm scared that a small part of me doesn't care. Is this what you wanted to hear?" His face was bright red.

Lainey studied him and nodded her appreciation. Brian's angry words filled her with absolute serenity. She unfolded her arms, placed a hand on the top of each of his arms, and leaned forward, gently kissing his face. "That's better. Go take a shower," she said and opened the door to the bathroom. "I'm scared, too." She told the confused-looking Brian.

She smiled as he walked past her, and he switched on the water. He yanked off his clothing, throwing them on the tiled floor, and stepped into the flow of hot water. Lainey picked up his dirty clothes and put them in the laundry basket before putting his running shoes on the rack in the walk-in closet. He'd said what she needed to hear, and a weight lifted from her. It wasn't like she welcomed his message, but it was a relief that it was out there. Now they were being honest. Lainey could deal with what was known. "I'm going downstairs to fix us some dinner. Don't be too long."

Lainey knew Brian better than he knew himself, and she left him to simmer under the hot water. It always took Brian longer to wind down than her. She thought it was the same with most men – that they needed longer to cool off – and women could rationalize much faster. All those indentations to the male pride required the gentle touch to tap out the kinks and make them flow again or, failing that, Lainey would beat it out of him.

Lainey hummed a tune to herself in the kitchen as she cut up the veggies and re-heated some chicken breasts. There was a level of contentment found in the truth. It wasn't like the issues had gone away, but now she understood their true depth, and that was something.

Brian joined her, dressed in gray shorts and his blue hoodie, zipped up halfway to his chest. Sitting quietly at the end of the worktop, he watched Lainey fix dinner.

"Veva brought me some of her Meyer Lemon dressing and left it here. I'll sprinkle some on the salad. It's quite delicious," Lainey spoke as if they'd not had a single ugly word between them. As she put the side plates on the counter, she puckered her lips towards Brian and touched them to his before withdrawing two inches. She held the puckered pose and waited for him to meet her halfway. He touched his lips to hers with the briefest contact. "Nah-ah," she murmured and waited again. She made a smooching sound with her lips. This time Brian placed his lips on hers and left them on her for a few seconds. "More like it," she said and went about carving the chicken.

"Detective Strahan came here this morning, not long after you left for work. I had nothing new to say to him. Said he needs me to dig deeper and help save lives."

"I read the news report on my phone after I showered. Do you think you can?"

"I don't know." Lainey waved the knife in the air as she gave it more thought. "I know I have to try."

"What can I do?"

"Love me."

"I'm doing that as best I can."

"Don't give up on me."

"I don't know how to."

"Likewise," she said. "If you do, let me know, and I'll stick this knife in your eye."

Dinner was a talkative affair, although the conversation was quiet, controlled, and matter-of-fact. Lainey left a voicemail for Detective Strahan, saying she would see him tomorrow if he had time. He later texted back, asking for eight in the morning. Brian offered to cancel the trip he had planned to Europe. There were new trails to be run and recorded and sales meetings with potential new distributors. Lainey refused and said business must continue to be pushed. She appreciated his willingness to stay home, but she was secure in the house.

"Not like I'm going anywhere, anytime soon. I'm not brave enough yet. There's a therapist in San Francisco with whom I can connect online and see how it goes. I owe it to myself, you, and everyone I used to spend time with. I have to face the world - it's spent enough time facing me."

They talked late into the night about the possibility of hiring twenty-four-hour security for the grounds, especially since the killer might come back or the media might try once more to gain illegal access. Lainey said she'd think about it. She explained if they had someone patrolling outside it would mean she could no longer wander around downstairs in her booty shorts in the warm weather. Brian suggested she do it deliberately, and then security men would work for free!

He also added his admiration for her work ethic to keep her body in peak condition and her drive in the business. He recognized her efforts in attempting to hold their marriage together. Lainey well received his compliments. When they settled in bed, it was like nothing had ever happened. Both acknowledged there was much more to do in repairing their connectivity, and each swore to make further efforts. Finally, they exchanged a sweet kiss and said goodnight.

In the lobby of the grubby hotel, Strahan approached his new colleague.

"No flowers, Steve?" Detective Hurst ribbed him.

"I never told you my first name." He stood awkwardly in the middle of the refreshment area, with all eyes on him. Detective Hurst was wearing the same clothes she had on the previous day.

She caught his recognition. "Your name was on the reports we looked at yesterday. I'm not a Detective for nothing, you know. And yes, I'm in the same clothes as yesterday. Thank you for noticing. A girl likes a man who pays attention. I was down here fishing, not policing. I think you should know that I did change my underwear. Would you like to see?" Hurst feigned as if she was going to unzip the front of her trousers.

Strahan raised a cautionary hand. "I'll take your word for it." His eyes caught some of the hotel guests looking nervously at him.

"No coffee and no flowers, huh? It's no wonder you're single." Hurst made sure her voice was heard.

"I never said I was single."

"You didn't have to."

Hurst followed him across the parking lot to his car. It was only a few minutes' drive to the Stewart's residence. Hurst gave some insight into the reports that Strahan had walked her through the previous day. Her commentary was concise, accurate, and in many parts, word for word. Strahan spent part of his evening looking up Detective Carmilla Hurst's record. Aside from the affair with a former suspect in a murder case and subsequent 'lesbian scandal,' her police record was as good as anyone's, with a detection rate as formidable as her mouth.

74

"To recap, Lainey Stewart is fragile. If we lean on her, we could lose her altogether."

"I'll be as delicate as the silk flower in the victim's hand," Hurst replied.

"Are you always like this?"

"No. Sometimes I'm an absolute nightmare."

"Only sometimes?"

Detective Hurst gave him a friendly pat on the arm. "We're going to do just fine, me and you, Strahan. I reckon we can solve anything thrown our way with your looks and my charm."

"How about we start with this one and find the killer before the body count increases. I'd settle for that."

"Touché, Detective. I'm not as barbaric as whatever you've heard or read about me. Well, not all the time," Hurst laughed at her joke. "I know you've already done your research."

"How do you know that?"

"Because I researched you, and I know you're meticulous, like me. Don't worry; I can be softly-softly when I need to be."

"We'll need to be." Strahan turned into the lane toward the massive, gated entrance.

"Oh, I'm going to enjoy this," Hurst observed, looking up at the house on the hill.

Strahan's facial reflexes gave away his tension. They stopped by the keypad, and he pressed the intercom. There was no verbal exchange as the gate opened. Strahan gave a brief smile toward the camera, assuming Lainey was watching. He'd not warned her about Detective Hurst accompanying him and was unsure about Lainey's reaction.

"All this from pimped-out treadmills," Hurst commented as the car drove up through the levels of manicured grounds and parked at the front of the house.

"Most of their revenue comes from selling their apparel and running shoes. They've got their own brand."

"You don't say. Wonder if we can score some free merchandise?" Hurst's comments were partly true but also designed to provoke a response. "I've only seen her on the front of magazines in the grocery store. Is she as hot in real life as she is in those photoshoots?"

"We're here asking her for help solving a murder, or possibly a series of murders," Strahan flatly replied.

"I know that, but I need some inspiration and some new sneakers." Hurst was out of the car and looking around the front of the house before Strahan could unfasten his seatbelt.

He stopped the engine, checked that his notepad was inside his jacket, and jumped out. Hurst was up against the building, with her long fingers feeling at one of the windows. As he came alongside, she pointed out. "These windows have a tint built into them to reduce UV light coming into the house. You can't even feel it. A metal oxide and these are triple glazed."

"You're an expert on windows."

"More of an expert in violent burglaries. Very efficient for maintaining air conditioning temperatures. Not to be underestimated."

"That's good to know," Strahan produced a rare frown.

"I should be charging you for this kind of information."

They stood side by side in the central doorway. Hurst poked her finger on the doorbell and listened to the pleasant chime inside the house.

"She already knows we're here," Strahan whispered.

"She does now." Detective Hurst swiveled her torso toward Strahan and straightened the lapel on his jacket, patting it down with an attentive hand like she was his mother. "You look lovely."

A sharp click followed a loud buzz, and the front door opened.

"She can't come to the front door," Strahan said.

"Good thing we're not delivering pizza."

Strahan led the way into the reception area. Lainey was off to the side in the kitchen.

"Over here," she called out. "Coffee?"

"Yeah, thanks. Lainey, I have with me Detective Hurst from Albany in Oregon. We're partnering on the new case and your old one."

Detective Hurst marched toward Lainey with a broad smile and extended her hand. As they shook, Hurst wrapped a second hand over Lainey's. "Lainey, so nice to meet you. Heard a lot of great things about you. I want you to know Detective Strahan, and I want to be as little an inconvenience to you as possible." Hurst removed one hand but kept the other on Lainey's as she gestured a finger around in the air. "What a beautiful home you have here. I was just admiring the energy-saving windows you have."

"Thanks. It helps with the heating bills," Lainey replied, slightly confused.

Hurst finally let go of Lainey. "Can I give you a hand with the coffee?"

"It's okay. How do you take yours?"

"Smooth and white, with a little sweetness," Hurst's reply hinted at mischief.

Strahan approached the countertop and felt obliged to step into the conversation. "Lainey, after we spoke yesterday morning is when Detective Hurst and I became assigned together."

Hurst cupped her long fingers to her mouth and whispered loudly to Lainey, "What he's not telling us is that I'm the lead detective, and he's assigned to help me. Men and their pride, huh?" Hurst knowingly rolled her eyes. "I've told him not to worry – I'll look after him."

Strahan disliked how Hurst feigned to muscle him out by forming a female alliance against him, even if it could be useful. He'd spent many hours alongside Lainey and her husband and had built a trusting relationship with them. He did not want to see that come crashing down in the space of a single coffee. As he was about to push his way back in, Hurst slyly signaled him for calm, and just in the nick of time, she returned to her charm offensive.

"Detective Strahan has kindly brought me up to speed on your case. His insight was critical in enabling me to become familiar with the details," Hurst told Lainey. "I've been assigned the case in Shellburg, Oregon. I was only down here to do some fishing."

"You fish?" Lainey asked.

"Yeah, but I never catch what I'm looking for, at least not in the rivers and lakes," Hurst flickered her eyebrows up and down.

"Then you'll know I don't recall much about what happened to me," Lainey said as she handed them a coffee. She pushed milk and sugar to the middle of the granite-topped surface.

"Do you have honey?" Hurst asked.

Lainey turned around and reached up into one of the cupboards.

"Thanks," Hurst said, squeezing some into her cup. "I know Detective Strahan told you what's happening in Oregon, or at least as much as we can say for now. Have you considered regression therapy under hypnosis? It's perfectly safe and won't leave any emotional or psychological scars. Quite the opposite." Hurst served milk and sugar into Strahan's coffee. "I only use the top experts."

"I thought about it, but I'm worried about what I might find back there," Lainey said.

"I understand. Many of my witnesses have used it and myself. Never had anyone come out worse than they went in, including me."

Her statement caused Strahan to give her a quizzical look.

Detective Hurst continued, "Lainey, we need your help. Even one tiny recollection from you could make a difference. A piece of jewelry, a detail of a hand or tattoo, anything."

"I don't know." Lainey chewed on her lip.

"I swear to you, I've used it myself, and it works. Perfectly safe. I've been a female Detective for twenty-five years and the only one in my area. So trust me; I needed something safe and workable."

Lainey answered the beep on her phone, and a buzzer sounded in the reception area. "Excuse me, it's my tech director." Lainey turned her back on the two detectives. "Come on up, the door is open," she called as she pressed the button to open the gates. "She offered to collect my dry cleaning on her way here."

"Good to have good people around you," Hurst said. "I really believe the sessions can help you clear residual negative trapped thoughts and emotions. There may just be something to help us in the bargain."

Hurst stopped talking. Strahan stayed quiet as they held their attention on Lainey.

Lainey sipped at her drink, taking her time as she gave it some thought. "What if I can't remember anything useful?"

"Then no harm done," Hurst replied. "You'll be fully regressed and have cleared any negative energy within you at a cellular level."

Veva bustled through the door with a bag over each shoulder and half a dozen hanging garments over each arm. She saw the two detectives, dipped her head, and went straight for the stairs. Nobody saw her until she was already halfway up. "I'll put these in your room," she called out, scurrying away with the dry cleaning.

Strahan watched Veva disappear and trained his sights back on Lainey. Hurst only caught sight of Veva from the rear.

Hurst gave Lainey a quizzical pair of raised eyebrows, waiting for an answer.

"She's shy and new," Lainey explained Veva's avoidance. She put down her drink and sucked in a sharp gasp of air as she leaned on the counter, stretched out her calves, then slowly pushed out her glutes while lowering her head toward the counter. She came back up, and pushed her arms high above her head, with her top raising above her waistband, showing part of her hard, flat stomach. The two detectives remained silent. Lainey finished the extension of her limbs and leaned her elbows on the counter before putting the mug back to her lips. "I'll do it, but it will have to be here in my house, and I want to know who it will be in advance and exactly what they're going to do. I need to check their credentials."

"Wise words. Checking credentials is important," Hurst agreed.

Strahan gave a single celebratory clap of his hands. "Good stuff."

Hurst walked to the counter's edge and took Lainey's hand in hers. Then, with a much-softened expression, she looked deep into Lainey's eyes. "Thank you. You'll be perfectly safe, and you might help save lives."

"Thank you, Lainey," Strahan added.

"I like a woman with courage," Hurst said.

Lainey didn't know where the surge of emotion came from as she found herself hugging Detective Hurst, and the long fingers of the senior detective patted Lainey on the small of her back. Lainey didn't shed any tears, but, without warning, she felt elated and robust. Then, sheepishly, she moved away from the female detective and nodded to confirm she was in.

"We'll be in touch with you tomorrow," Hurst said. She drank half her coffee and looked at the massive open-space living room beyond the modern kitchen. "Mind if I walk through there and look outback? Not every day I get to see a designer place like this."

"Sure. I'll give you a tour of the inside," Lainey offered.

Hurst left her bag on the counter and gave a sly smile to Strahan. Strahan never flinched and stayed put. The two women walked away, chatting about décor, furniture, and the artwork on the walls. Strahan shook his head at his partner's brassy but effective display.

Strahan's attention was directed to the landing, catching a glimpse of Veva's dark hair as she ducked into the office. He fixed his gaze upward for a couple of minutes while Hurst was busy working her magic as she and Lainey moved to the other side of the house. Getting Lainey to cooperate was more than he could have done. Unfortunately, there was no sign of Veva reappearing.

Lainey and Detective Hurst came back into the kitchen, chatting as if they were old friends.

"You want to see the upstairs?" Lainey asked.

"Some other time. Thanks for asking. We'll let you get on with your day," Hurst replied.

The detectives thanked Lainey for her time and got back in their car.

Lainey watched out the front window as they pulled away and placed both hands firmly on her queasy abdomen. Agreeing to help was the right thing to do, but all the same, it didn't stop her from feeling like she wanted to throw up. If she didn't try to help, the guilt would be unbearable, and Lainey had enough to contend with. On the other hand, maybe Detective Hurst was right, and nothing bad would come of it.

As they drove through the gates, Hurst declared, "That wasn't too bad, was it?"

"No, nice job."

"Did you see the cameltoe on Lainey Stewart? Jesus of Nazareth! I almost climaxed when she stretched out that ass," Hurst pronounced, blowing out her cheeks.

"Good to have you back," Strahan sarcastically replied.

"I know you saw it and thought about it, too. But, phew! I bet her pussy tastes like a thousand-dollar bill."

"Would you like me to put that in the report?"

"Lighten up, Strahan. You need to get laid. You're pretty, but you're not my type. Now Lainey Stewart, on the other hand. She'd look good on my boat in a bright yellow bikini, serving me cold beers while I'm fishing. It makes me moist thinking about it."

"She is a nice lady."

"Don't pretend you haven't thought about it. I don't care who you are or your preference; she's everyone's type."

"I have to drive to Shellburg with you?"

"Think how I feel," Hurst adjusted her crotch. "I'll be dreaming about that cameltoe the whole way."

CHAPTER EIGHT

The bedroom was lit by a single candle that thinly textured the darkest corners of the room. The figure was curled in a fetal ball in the middle of the bed. The hood was raised, and, in the shadows, only the bright brown eyes were visible. Its body rocked gently forward and back, inspecting the framed pictures in its gloved hands. The index finger lovingly traced a line across the brilliant smiles once filled with life and vitality. The figure saw past the smiles. "There's a falsehood in photographs, even for you - you beautiful souls. My precious beauties, don't worry; I will keep my promise."

Time had been invested in seeing the depth of hurt these beautiful young women experienced when they were alive. It was hurtful to know the truth and yet liberating in some sense. There was a freedom in getting to the ugliness and rooting it out. From there, decisions could be made to the benefit of everyone. Only the figure appreciated what they were going through underneath the headlines, the nice cars, fancy clothes, the accolades, and financial rewards. Those things portrayed a flimsy material covering without substance, without meaning. The truth was concealed from the public view but not from the figure.

The figure did its homework on each of the young women. Some of them were rewarded with the gift of absolute love. One had dared to reject the loving gift. Lainey Stewart. She had not fully accepted deliverance, and that was hurtful. It showed a level of ingratitude, and a lack of appreciation for the time, effort, and compassion shown to her. It was pure love at the heart of seeking to help facilitate her transformation. The figure was disappointed but knew some people weren't ready to face the stark reality of the hollow existence on which they drifted. "You're pretending all is fine when I see you overflowing with pain." These young women were only successful in deluding themselves, believing they were leading a meaningful existence but were merely trading fragments of their souls for some temporary exaltation.

Taking their lives was a mercy, but that was simply a bonus compared to what else they were being given. They were being gifted the wings to rise upwards to the heavens. None of them would feel the rejection, the shame, the humiliation, or suffering anymore. Only the figure's studious investment of time and love could empathize with their plight. It, too, had suffered rejection that led to eternal despondency. It was good to remove uncertainty and suffering – a true blessing. It was something the figure had been ordained to do. A promise was made in the eyes of God, and it must be kept. There would come a time when the figure would reap the rewards, and it, too, would have the opportunity to ascend.

The figure adored their beautiful smiles – not the flimsy poses for social media. Now, they were smiling in grace at their elevation. Those transformed were radiant, befitting a worthwhile memory and justifying the efforts. "I haven't forgotten you all. Please don't forget me. I think of you all every day. Mommy promised the angels would welcome me if I sent you with peace and loving-kindness. So I will send you more. Now you can smile for all eternity."

The thought of having God's angels waiting in the heavens with a fanfare welcome was exciting beyond imagination, and the figure doubled over in excitable pain. To join the chorus of God's angels would be worth everything and even better to have sent ahead those who'd be joyously waiting. It was too much to bear.

The figure wiped its eyes and looked at the framed picture of Lainey. "I won't let you down again." The gloved hand stroked the picture. The frame was one it had taken from Lainey's house over a year ago. The photographs of the chosen ones that the figure had helped on their unique journey took pride of place on the side cabinet. It had been a risk to bring back the picture frame of Kumi Shinnabe from Japan inside the suitcase, but respect and love had to be continually paid. Kumi was with her sisters in heaven and removed from the agonies of life.

It was fitting that they were honored in the right way, with their brilliant lifeforce entirely on display. The figure placed the four frames side by side on the cabinet. Each had a special place; each was looked upon daily and always cherished, like members of a close family. Behind the four frames was a picture of mommy. The one who started the whole thing and who received the most honor. God took her at such a young age, but she went with gratitude and grace. She showed the path to spending eternity with God and continuing his work.

"I've kept my promise. I love you." A tender kiss was given to the smiling face in the photograph and placed again behind the four smiling girls. The figure had no framed self-portrait to join them, feeling unworthy and not yet ready. There was much work to be done. The Lord God had made the world in seven days, but this was not a mission with such a time constraint. Sacrifices of the right kind were necessary through careful and thoughtful consideration.

The ancients sacrificed seven oxen and seven rams, given in thanks for what was granted. These beautiful sacrifices were to honor God, add to his heavenly army, and pave the way to join in his divine glory. The sprinkling of oils was once used seven times to consecrate the altar to God. Now it was the sprinkling of seven young lives in service to God. Each one was delicately treated and given to the earth from where they could grow their wings, nurtured by what God intended. A perfect cycle of death and rebirth.

"Soon, I'll be with you," the soft voice promised.

Brian sat at his desk and fired off a couple of emails to their European vendors, asking for improvement plans and deadlines on their delivery capabilities and any follow-up maintenance for the units and displays. It was hard to focus. Jet lag and a general lag in his energy dragged him down. He wanted Lainey and him to be like they once were, and he wanted her respect. She never pronounced it out loud, but her loss of admiration for him deafeningly filled their home.

He half-heartedly scrolled through the rest of his emails. With an endless digital parade of problems, he questioned why he was putting himself through this. Work was a grind, and his home life even harder. "What's the point?" he lamented.

He stopped scrolling when he came across the email titled: Watch Me Carefully. Brian opened it, and there was a link to an unknown video platform. It looked like spam or a spyware trap until he read the capitalized sentence: IF YOU WANT TO KNOW WHERE LAINEY'S MISSING ENGAGEMENT RING IS HIDDEN, CLICK TO FIND OUT.

He almost slipped from his chair as the shock sucked the strength from his limbs. It had never been disclosed that Lainey's engagement ring had been taken. Brian had bought it for her in Oxnard. Lainey's wedding ring had not been taken, so theft was never thought to be the motive. It was assumed that the killer had kept it as a memento. Brian looked into the main office in case anyone was playing a prank. He quickly dismissed the idea. Only Lainey, Brian, and Detective Strahan knew about the missing ring. He clicked on the link, which immediately took him to a foreign server, where the background language appeared to be Russian. He checked the firewall, and his internet spyware blockers were active. He pressed play.

The shaky video showed someone walking through a dense forest, along a twisting dirt pathway and using a head-mounted GoPro. The person stopped beside the fallen redwood, one that was cut through to allow visitors to access the track. Brian knew this trail. The video tracked to the right, off the path, and through the undergrowth, before stopping in a small clearing, where the tall redwoods were fifty feet apart. The sun's light penetrated through the foliage, partially illuminating the ground. The camera moved backward and stopped against a tree trunk. Slowly it moved ten paces forward, and the angle dropped low as if the person had knelt. The soil was darker and raised, surrounded by sparse grass. Brian guessed the darkened mound was twelve inches high and six feet long. A leather-gloved hand placed a small cross made from tied clusters of deergrass on the mound's edge.

"What the fuck is this?" he asked himself. The video stopped before he could get any further, and the words appeared on the screen. YOU KNOW THE PLACE. THIS VIDEO WILL BE GONE ONE MINUTE AFTER YOU VIEW IT.

Brian quickly reset the video to the beginning. "You know the place; you know the place," he repeated. The whole thing was ninety seconds long. "Oh, shit!" Brian realized this was filmed in Prairie Creek woods, just a few miles north of Eureka. He'd seen the fallen tree when using the 4D Fitness module. Only a couple of years ago, the tree came down in a heavy storm. He tried to find a way to download the footage and make a copy, but the server didn't give him those options. Brian reached for his cellphone to record the video. Unfortunately, his jacket pocket was empty! "Aargh," he gasped.

Shooting from his desk, he ran into the conference room. His phone was on the table where he'd attended the last meeting. In his haste, he scattered the laser pointer and control for the TV onto the floor. Ignoring the bemused looks from his colleagues, he dashed across the office and back into his chair. Quickly he opened the link on his screen and used his phone to record. Less than eight seconds into the video, it fizzled from view.

"Bastard!" he exclaimed. "The email." It had come with an anonymous link to the video. Brian went back to his emails, and it was gone. "What?" No sign of it in his deleted or spam folders. He knew for sure that he'd not touched it. Whoever sent this knew what they were doing. He picked up the internal phone and called tech services.

"Hey Phil, it's me. Listen, I accidentally deleted an email, and I can't seem to recover it. Can you log remotely into my machine and pull back anything that came to my inbox this morning? I need the last one I opened."

"Sure. Give me two minutes. I'll text you when I'm done. Logging in now."

"Thanks."

Phil took over his screen and quickly dug around into the emails. Brian ground his teeth. He checked that his cell phone had recorded a few seconds of the video. He noted that he had failed to capture the URL at the top of the page. He considered going to the police, but to show them what? He had nothing.

'All done.' came Phil's text. The email with the video link was still missing. He was about to call Phil again and then stopped. What was he going to explain? That someone knew Lainey's ring was stolen, and they'd sent a weird video placing a cross in the dirt at Prairie Creek? People would think he'd lost his mind. However, a quick check of his schedule showed three one-hour-long meetings for the next phase of adding more trails to the portfolio. He could easily catch up with all of these.

Brian had his running gear in the back of the car. He canceled himself from the rest of the day's meetings. Prairie Creek State Park was only forty-five minutes away, and in his beloved new Jaguar, less than that.

There was only one way to know if it was genuine. If it were some sort of ruse, then only he would be its victim. No way could he tell Lainey. She was strung out enough already, and putting additional strain on his wife was unthinkable. He was not impulsive by nature, yet something pulled him onward. Brian engaged the drive and raced from the parking lot. Within a minute, he was on his way up the 101 Coast Highway to the Redwoods. He'd not been able to do a damn thing to help Lainey through her ordeal, and in the back of his mind, if there was a chance he could recover her beloved silver ring with inlaid diamonds, it might go some way to giving her some comfort, and for once make himself look useful.

Brian had never been a hero – far from it. Brian followed his instincts, ignoring the thumping in his chest and the twist in his gut. He could be walking into the hands of whoever tried to kill his wife, but he had to know the answer. If he couldn't retrieve her ring and salvage some respect from his wife, at least he might discover if he had any courage.

After Lainey finished her first conference call, she had a spark of something indescribably good. The industrious Veva was busy at her corner desk. "Hey Veva, want to see something really cool?"

"Like what?" Veva replied, with her face wrinkled in slight suspicion.

"C'mon, follow me," Lainey playfully teased and left the room. She walked down the landing and into the vast exercise room. She inserted her bio-card into one of the two side-by-side 4D treadmills and selected the special menu. Only she, Brian, and Phil from tech services had this level of access.

"I can't believe you have two of these! And what's that menu? I don't have one like that," Veva pointed out.

"I know. You will, in time, if you're good," Lainey further teased. She selected another menu. "And here we have our new trails."

Veva stepped forward with her mouth wide open and the whites of her eyes showing. "You've got Pontcysyllte in Wales! That's it!" Veva excitedly shouted, with her finger pointing at the picture among the selection options.

"How did you know that?" Lainey sounded deflated.

"I've seen YouTube videos of people running through the woods and over the aqueduct. I've always wanted to go there."

"Well, Brian did a few months ago. The river is called the Dee. We put out a note for video volunteers, and more than sixty people showed up to do the run, and we compiled the data. Very accommodating, those Brits. It just needs a couple of tweaks, which you'll be working on next week."

Veva had her fingers in her mouth. "Oh my God, I can't wait. When will it be available for public use?"

"As soon as you finish with the resolutions and Brian approves it."

"Can I see?"

"Only if you run it," Lainey offered an open hand toward the treadmill.

"I don't have my gym clothes with me."

"Bad luck."

"I can run barefoot," Veva said, taking off her flat leather shoes.

"I'm not having you run in your clothes and be all sweaty in my office. Not happening," Lainey pointed tantalizingly at the screen. "Just us girls," she waved her finger at Veva's clothing. Lainey pressed the Start button and immediately froze the view at the beginning of the run. "It's right there."

Veva's eyes nearly popped from her head at the suggestion to strip. She looked at the screen and huffed at the view in front of her. Lainey's goading was a test of wits and how far Veva was prepared to go. The location was near the top of Veva's bucket list, and it was in glorious three-dimensional display, only six feet away. "I'm not sure."

"No problem. You can see it in a few weeks when we're finished with development," Lainey sounded bored and motioned to switch it off.

"Okay, okay," Veva protested. "But don't tell anyone."

"And get myself sued for having a half-naked staff member in my house?" Lainey said.

Veva grimaced. She didn't like the way the carrot was dangled. Then, in a rush of blood, she quickly unfastened her black trousers, stepped out of them, and whipped off her jacket and white blouse.

"No granny pants today," Lainey smirked.

Veva ignored to comment, hopped onto the treadmill and hit the start button, where she was immediately immersed in the trail. Within seconds, her bare feet briskly rotated with her downward pressure, airy and light, as she skipped along, increasing the cadence of the treadmill.

Lainey leaned over and turned up the speed to the next level. Veva never flinched. She breathed hard as she powered her arms through the air. Lainey nodded with admiration at Veva's determined style. Veva's body was tight, muscular, and clearly, one that spent hours training and running. She wore white full-back panties with a pink bow on the front with a matching bra. Her glutes were solid as she ran, and her thighs honed. Her breasts were small, a B cup at best, but in keeping with her body shape.

Lainey strained her neck to look outside to make sure Brian hadn't decided to return home for any reason. It would be challenging to explain Veva running in her underwear - and Veva's body was hot. Lainey's inability to satisfy Brian meant there was no way he could be allowed to view the surprise package. Lainey moved behind Veva, looking at her smooth-skinned back and the lovely arch from her spine into her butt, with the elastic of her underwear cutting into her cute cheeks. From the front, Lainey saw Veva had a small dark pubic spread visible through the ultra-thin fabric at the front of her underwear, indicating Veva was partially trimmed to some degree. She wasn't the mousey geek she appeared to be.

"How is it?"

"Awesome," Veva puffed, coming through the tree line onto the top of the ancient aqueduct.

"It's over two hundred years old. They used to transport coal and limestone over it."

Veva increased her speed as the sweat formed on her brow.

"Looking good," Lainey encouraged with a touch of envy. The wrap-around screen convinced the visual receptors that they were actually in North Wales, with Veva rushing across the impressive wrought iron structure. Lainey was impressed with Veva's body and her tenacity. It gave new dimensions to what she'd learned of Veva since spending some time together. On the surface, she was unassuming and almost unnoticeable, but she got things done and had a real competitive spirit. Lainey decided she liked her new employee.

Once Veva ran towards the village, Lainey called a halt to proceedings. "If you bring your running clothes tomorrow, then after work, you can run the whole thing. That way, you can see what we need to improve."

"It's perfect," Veva puffed as the treadmill wound to a stop. "Brian and his team did an amazing job."

"First time for everything." Lainey handed Veva her clothes. "Would you like to shower?"

Suddenly she looked embarrassed, standing around in her underwear. "No, thank you." Veva covered herself with a handful of clothes.

"I already looked," Lainey loudly whispered. "Don't worry. I won't tell the tech team you're quite the little sex-kitten."

"I'm very private." Veva breathlessly pulled on her trousers and buttoned her blouse.

"At least go and use some of my deodorant. I can't abide foul smells. Remember what happens in the big house…"

"I hope so," Veva said as she put her shoes back on.

"Cute undies. Where did you get them?"

"From a little store in Eugene. I shop online with them."

"Eugene in Oregon?"

"Yeah. I used to live around there when I was little."

"Full of surprises, aren't we? Shall we have some lunch? I have fresh salmon and salad."

"Sure," Veva waited for Lainey to go first.

Over lunch, they talked rapid-fire about the new offerings 4D Fitness was about to launch. Lainey was enthused about having a VIP access menu, where users could pay an additional monthly fee and access a whole other bank of trails worldwide. Her idea was to keep adding to the general menu but save the spectacular ones for an additional $30 monthly fee. Veva liked the idea but cautioned that VIP access should include at least twenty additional trails, ready to go. Lainey and Brian had thought a dozen, but after listening to Veva, she agreed twenty was a good number. More trails would be needed and quickly.

"That'll keep the tech team and me busy," Veva smiled.

"I'd better check that Brian's passport is good for a long while," Lainey thought aloud. She twisted her full lips.

"Shame you can't go, too," Veva replied.

"You're right."

"It might help if a tech team member went on some trips," Veva said. "They could pre-run and advise on what to capture or avoid. That way, there would be less editing, and it would make integration easier."

Lainey rubbed her fingers over her chin. "Hmmm…" She looked closely at Veva. "That's not a bad idea. Plus, we could avoid the debacle like we had in Sweden. Ugh"

"I heard about that." Veva tried not to laugh. "All that data lost on one failed laptop."

"Not funny." Lainey playfully swatted her assistant's arm. "Brian wasted three days, all that expense, and the time of the runners. He had to go back there six months later and do it again once the winter snow had melted."

Veva leaned forward, snickering into the hands covering her face.

"Just for that, I'm sending you overseas," Lainey threatened.

"Me?"

"Yes. You."

"But I've only just started working here."

"And we're paying you top dollar to sit around in my house when we could make better use of you out in the field. Yes. You should go. It's settled."

"It is?"

"Yes."

"Aah!" Veva leaped from her stool and hugged Lainey. "I can't wait…" she immediately let go. "Sorry. Do you mean it?"

"Every word. Is your passport current?"

"It is. It still has four years left on it."

"Pack your mail order undies and running gear; you're going to Europe next week."

Veva stamped her feet on the tiled floor, and short jabbed her arms in the air as if shadowboxing. A stifled squeal forced its way from her throat, and she bobbed back and forth, shaking her flapper-style hair.

"I'll speak to Brian when he gets home."

"Will he be okay with it?"

"I'm sure. Brian's been saying forever that he needs assistance on the foreign trips. Besides helping with the promotions, you can directly interact with users and receive their feedback. Much better when someone shows us something in person than through our satisfaction surveys. You can work remotely on technical improvements from foreign time zones."

"I can't wait." Veva's wide-eyed shock was loaded with genuine excitement like she'd won the star prize in a competition.

"Glad to leave me already?" Lainey prodded.

"No. I love it here," Veva coughed and then dialed down the rest of her response. "You've been very kind to allow me into your home and get me up to speed on everything."

"Not quite everything," Lainey cryptically replied.

CHAPTER NINE

October 1, 1996

"Aunt Carm, look, look," Ginny excitedly exclaimed.

"Oh, well, well. I'll be darned." Aunt Carm crouched to inspect the first sign of the white flowering on the stalk. Ginny curled sideways into Aunt Carm's safe hands. Aunt Carm held her tightly and loved her.

"When I read the book, it said these angel orchids are impossible to grow here. They're supposed to flower in July. You must have green fingers," Aunt Carm inspected Ginny's fingers and tickled her.

"Soon, they'll be like real angels and fly away," Ginny suggested.

"One step at a time," Aunt Carm replied. "Let's give them a little more water. The book said they like moisture as the monsoon season approaches."

"What's a monsoon?"

"It's like a time of year when it rains for weeks and weeks. But, don't worry, it doesn't happen here in Albany, or we'd be building an ark."

"When our angels are fully grown, can we help them get to heaven?" Ginny asked.

Aunt Carm kissed her little forehead. "Let's see how they grow, and then we'll figure it out. We have to be very careful and not touch them. They're sensitive to light, water, air, and especially to the wandering hands of five-year-old girls."

Ginny giggled and tucked herself further into Aunt Carm's body. "I'll be careful." Suddenly she started to sniffle. "Do you think mommy would like them?"

Aunt Carm pulled her little one tight and turned her head away so Ginny couldn't see the tears in her eyes. "She'd be so proud of you. All these little pots, some angel seedlings, some sun, and a whole lot of love. You see what love can grow?"

"I guess," sniffed the tiny voice.

Aunt Carm surveyed the pots and plants that Ginny had insisted they spend time on. Most were in bloom and gave the small yard some needed color against the gray concrete walls. "I can't believe you got orchids to grow here. Pretty impressive for someone who can't get dressed for bed by herself." She squeezed on the little love in her arms and covered her in kisses.

"Can we see them again tomorrow?" Ginny asked.

"I'm on shift tomorrow and the day after, so that it will be Saturday. So you'll be at the sitters for a couple of nights. Then we can see what we have. Something to look forward to, huh?"

Ginny didn't reply but dropped her head into Aunt Carm's shoulder and rested there. Aunt Carm gently rocked Ginny in her arms. "Growing Angel Orchids in Albany. We should let somebody know and get your picture in the paper."

"Angel seedlings," Ginny smilingly repeated.

The Present Day:

Brian parked his car at the edge of the dirt lot and counted four other vehicles. Ahead, the dark soil track led into the mighty forest, where it quickly vanished from sight amongst the dense trees. Brian knew that whoever sent the email was someone with a high level of technical expertise. He thought about the movies he'd seen, where the protagonist walked towards something potentially dangerous while the viewer willed them to turn back or get help.

Sitting in his car, Brian acknowledged it was a spectacularly bad idea but too compelling not to proceed. Lainey's ring must be there, or why bother with a video. He had considered that if he found it and returned it to her, he'd have a lot of explaining. The email had to be from her attempted killer, and they might try again. Brian was tempted to call Detective Strahan and give him the details. Lainey had mentioned that Strahan was headed into Oregon to assist with the murder investigation.

Brian opened the tiny Velcro-sealed compartment under his seat. He pulled out the automatic Glock 26, removed the magazine, pushed it back into place, and engaged the release to ensure it was loaded. Lainey would go berserk if she discovered he owned a handgun, so he kept it in the car. He only removed it inside their attached garage when he needed to clean it. He'd practiced a few times at a local firing range to get used to its feel. He took out a spare magazine and double-checked that it was full. Each magazine contained twenty rounds – plenty if someone were to try to surprise him. Of course, nobody could know he'd be here at this time, but having the gun made him feel better equipped to deal with surprises. He changed from his trousers into light gray jogging shorts and a black zipped 4D top.

"Who's the real madman in this scenario?" He was ditching work, driving like a man possessed, to go into a forest to find a missing ring. "I wonder if Frodo Baggins had the same problem?" he asked. He secured the gun inside the front pocket of his jacket and walked swiftly into the forest.

Usually, he would be pumped, entering this environment, but the excitement was replaced by fear. He paused to stretch. Thoughts of Lainey chastising him were prominent. According to the police, whoever tried to kill Lainey had succeeded in Oregon. The killer was still out there. They could be here. It was improbable that they'd come back for a second bite, knowing Lainey would be watched and protected, but anything was possible.

Since Lainey was attacked, a perpetual emptiness enveloped Brian. Standing at the entrance to the trees … it toyed with him. A man who couldn't protect his wife was no man at all. Then again, Lainey wasn't the kind of woman who needed protection. He tapped a hand on the gun, reminding himself that he was prepared to kill to protect his own life. There was a fine line between the psychotic and those claiming self-defense. Brian's inactivity agitated him, and he marched at full speed into the redwoods. His senses were on high alert, as if the danger created an extra layer of sensory functionality. A part of Brian admitted that the gut-wrenching thrill was stupefyingly irresistible.

The earlier sunshine was hidden behind a thick layer of gray clouds, and without sunlight penetrating through the leaves, everything seemed shrouded in a hazy mystical effect. The density of the trees permeated the darkening of Brian's mood, and each noise from a passing bird, or scurrying animal, was magnified. His jumpy reactions annoyed him, as his resolve was easily pierced. "C'mon, c'mon," he repeated under his breath.

It was just over a mile along the trail before he came to the massive tree that once blocked the pathway. Huge chunks, cut by the chainsaws, were strewn along either side of the track and covered with layers of green moss. Brian checked up and down the trail; there was no sign or sound of anyone. He thought about going back to his car but said, "You have to do this."

If there was any chance to retrieve Lainey's beloved ring, he must try. His motives taunted him, telling him he was only doing it for self-elevation in his wife's eyes. He convinced himself he was doing something to give Lainey a much-needed boost. He needed it, too. It was a chance to break the cycle, feel like he had worth, and feel like he might still be a man, with the naïve belief that it could somehow return her to how she used to be.

Another check along the trail. Brian stepped into the thick of the trees, as shown in the video. He referenced the few seconds he had been able to record and took the first dozen steps as he lined up the trees and used an uprooted tree stump as a reference point. "Screw it." He pushed forward. Brian unzipped his pocket and took out the Glock. He placed his index finger down the gun's frame, with his middle finger ready on the trigger.

There was barely any breeze, and his ears picked up every distant sound. Each rustle or crack cautioned him to process the source and proximity. "No way I'm doing this again," he promised himself. A few more paces forward and bearing right, he approached the small clearing. He crouched low before walking any further, resting his back against a tree trunk, and waited. His eyes covered every gap through the trees. Brian looked along the forest floor just in case some sicko had placed some sort of trap there. As he lowered his line of sight, the raised earthen mound was only a few paces ahead. There was the small cross made of grass reeds. His stomach flipped, and his legs were shaky. His free hand locked into the dirt to steady himself.

"Oh shit." It was a good thing he was already close to the ground as his legs had given way. Suddenly, the adventure leaped from triumphant possibility to Brian now believing that he could die. Anxiety crushed him into the soft earth. He gathered himself to take stock and check once more in all directions. High above in the trees, the odd bird sounded, as did the crack of a tree limb in the distance.

He searched along the ground, taking an old branch four feet in length, and snapped away the skinny end to give himself something to poke around with. Paranoia convinced him a trap could spring and snap his ankle. He poked the stick ahead on the ground, moving the leaves before him. Slowly he progressed to the mound of earth. It was almost seven feet long, three feet wide, and twelve inches high.

He used the stick to move aside the makeshift cross. Someone had taken their time carefully crafting it. As he moved it, something shiny stuck out from underneath. Moisture had settled on its surface. He prodded it and pressed the stick into the soft soil around the material, revealing a see-through plastic bag. On closer inspection, it contained a paper inside. He prodded harder around it until the plastic protruded from the ground. He made a swift grab, but his fingers slipped with the wet material. "Shit! C'mon now." He reached again, pinching harder, and ripped the plastic from the soil. Moving a foot away from the mound, he found that it was a Ziploc bag containing a single piece of paper. He'd read somewhere about the KGB poisoning people with deadly kinds of ink on paper that would penetrate the pores of the skin. "If someone wanted you dead that badly, they could have found an easier way! Get a grip, Brian," he muttered.

He opened the thin plastic clips and removed the contents, but immediately the paper partially disintegrated in his fingers. It was thin rice paper, and the moisture inside the bag and on his fingers caused it to separate into five pieces. He placed them carefully on the soil, moved the parts closer together, and read, "Lainey's ring is under the soil. Dig carefully, and please be respectful."

The mound of earth was classically proportioned like a makeshift grave. "Be respectful?" The implication of the message scared him. A nearby sharp sound had him drop to one knee, and he aimed his gun in the direction of the noise. Nothing stirred between the trees. "Fuck, fuck."

Without taking his eyes from the view ahead of him, Brian took a small stone. He was reluctant to take his right hand off the Glock, but he needed his right arm to throw. A quick switch of hands, and he launched the stone in the direction of the noise. It clunked off the side of a tree trunk. The Glock was immediately returned to his favored right hand, and then he waited. It was a full minute, during which he stayed perfectly still, and nothing moved in the forest. "Fuck this."

Brian dug, placing the gun carefully within reach and using the stick as a makeshift earth mover. The soil quickly moved from the surface, but rainwater had compacted the earth once he got down four inches. He pulled at the damp earth with his fingers, keeping the soil well away from his gun. For a couple of minutes, he scrambled until he hit something slippery. He stopped, backed away, gun ready in his muddy hands, and waited. Zombies rising from the grave came to mind, and here, alone in the forest, anything seemed possible—no sign of anyone nearby or along the trail. The last thing he needed was to be found digging in the dirt, finding something awful, and having no reasonable explanation. Brian's gut told him to go home, but he couldn't. Not now.

He crawled back to the grave, jarred the stick into the hole, and exposed more of the slippery material – a thick plastic. He pulled frantically at the earth and soon revealed a sizeable blue vinyl bag with a heavy-duty black plastic zipper running vertically down the middle. "Ah shit, shit!" Brian had only seen a cadaver bag in the movies. He stopped again, too scared to continue.

"I have to know."

Lainey rechecked her cell phone. It was lunchtime, and no response from Brian on the text she'd sent him two hours ago or the email asking about pixelation. "Where is he?" she sighed.

"Who's that?" Veva asked without looking up from her screen.

"Brian."

"Do you want me to track his laptop?" Veva asked.

"You can do that?"

"Sure. It's a company-issued machine he's using. His name is attached to a unique ID. So I can see if he's online and where he's connected for Wi-Fi or a particular LAN. The network in the office is pretty basic. I took a look at it last week," Veva explained.

"Busy little bee, aren't you? See if you can locate him for me."

Veva switched from what she was doing and furiously typed away on her keyboard. "Just … one … second," she strung out the words.

"Could you see if Brian or anyone was watching porn on our work-issued laptops?"

"I could, but I know they don't." Veva briefly lifted her head. "I looked at that, too. Some folks watch YouTube on their lunch breaks, but nobody's doing anything bad … or good, depending on your point of view."

"That's good to know."

"The firewall works." Veva looked up again. "Do you think Brian is watching porn?"

Lainey's face turned red, and her skin felt glowing. "I don't know. Don't all men watch it these days?"

"I don't know?" Veva shrugged and went back to her search. "His laptop is on the LAN from his office and is physically connected to the port on his wall. It looks like he hasn't been active for a couple of hours. One of our techs, Phil, did a quick data search on his machine this morning. It must have been at Brian's request, as they took full control for a couple of minutes. I don't see any updates, so maybe he had an issue. Probably all that porn." Veva glanced at Lainey. "That was a joke. He can't – not on that machine, at least not from the office."

"Thanks," Lainey's response was hollow. It was unusual for Brian not to let her know if he was experiencing something unusual. "Okay, I need to run. You want to join me? We can run side by side."

"I have my running gear with me," Veva pointed at the sports bag by her desk.

Lainey was already in her leggings and running sneakers. "Get changed, and let's go. We can grab a quick bite afterward."

"I brought us a Mexican chicken stew with fresh salad. If you want some?" Veva was enthused as she took her bag and walked toward the door.

"Sounds great," Lainey replied with some amusement. "You don't have to go and hide to get changed."

Veva stalled in the doorway, clearly dying of embarrassment. "I, erm…"

"Run along, then," Lainey pointed to the nearest bathroom. "Not like I haven't seen it all before," she huffed.

"I'm just not…" Veva looked around to find the right words. "Not confident, like you."

"I'm the one who can't leave my house," Lainey reminded her. Veva's face dropped, and she looked sad. "I'm playing with you. Go on. Hurry up. We've got a full afternoon of meetings."

Within minutes, both women were on the adjacent treadmills, choosing to run the Mossy Ridge trail on the outskirts of Nashville, Tennessee. The five-mile loop had plenty of sharp twists and turns and challenging uphill climbs. They started out together, and, after the first mile, Veva had managed to get fifteen yards ahead of Lainey. It was more aggravating to Lainey that Veva held the gap between them. Each time Lainey got within ten yards, Veva accelerated and made the gap fifteen again. The race was firmly on, with both women entirely focused. Their three-dimensional avatars were accurate in the configurations of their actual physiques.

Three double-lensed cameras tracked their physical movement and fed it back into the system, instantly translating it to the avatar onscreen. Lainey's avatar was always in her signature pink leggings and sneakers. Veva's avatar was dressed all in black. They raced up, down, and around through the woodland and past the host of stone and wooden trail markers. The tension in the exercise room mounted, with no words exchanged … only the sound of sneakers meeting the treadmills and the accompanying heavy breathing.

Lainey hated to be beaten at anything by anyone. But, Veva was proving her speed and endurance matched her work ethic. Veva powered ahead, past the moss-laden trees and over the stream, as they blasted their way through the outskirts of Nashville. There was still over three miles to go, and Lainey was determined that they'd run every inch of it – the longer distance suited her years of highly developed strength. She snatched up her water bottle, taking only a sip to ensure there was no break in her stride pattern. Veva's high-handed action, with open palms, was constantly in her peripheral vision, and in front, on the 3D screen, Veva's black-haired avatar rushed between the high ferns and skipped up the steps cut into the hill. Lainey gained a few yards, going up the steps, and when it leveled out, coming through an open meadow, she gained a couple more yards. Ahead was another steady incline.

Lainey watched Veva closely as the gap remained at eight yards, and Lainey pressed onward. Soon they came into the dense trees where the sunlight on the screen showed a dozen different shades of green. It was an inspiring sight, even more so as Lainey sensed Veva was tiring. Her digital display showed two avatars ahead of them, and by the speed that they were catching up to them had to be a couple of folks walking. The data showed it was someone in Australia and another in New Zealand.

4D Fitness software allowed users from across the world to walk or run together as if they were there in person. Likely two friends or relatives walking together from the comfort of their own home but feeling as if together somewhere else on the planet.

Lainey seriously believed this software would continue to get better, cheaper, and increasingly interactive, where people wouldn't want to be without one. Veva and Lainey zipped past the hikers, each waving their hand to acknowledge them, and the hikers' avatars immediately responded.

The trail leveled out toward the last mile through ever-changing greenery, with Lainey only five yards behind Veva. Both women dripped in sweat, not exchanging a word in over forty minutes. Lainey's heart thudded like a drum in a marching band, and her thighs burned, but there was no way she would let up. Veva was barely holding on, but the last mile was where Lainey was at her best. She'd run the Tennessee track at least four dozen times, and the steep incline towards the end suited her muscular thighs. Veva hadn't taken on water. Lainey had sipped once every mile, her habit, and figured Veva would be dehydrated by now.

The steep inclines arrived, and the treadmills tilted high. Lainey dropped her head, clenched her fists, and hammered her arms through the air with an extra high lift in her knees as she powered up the hills. Within a few seconds, she'd caught Veva's avatar and, halfway up the steep incline, passed her and moved away so that by the time they came over the crest, winding down the twisting pathway, Lainey was twelve yards ahead. The countdown on the yardage ticked away as they raced toward the end. Veva made up six yards, but her pace dropped away in the last fifty yards, and Lainey finished twenty yards ahead of her.

Lainey punched the stop button, and the treadmill quickly wound to a halt. She leaned forward, both hands resting on her knees, gasping for air. Veva stepped off the back of her treadmill and lay flat on the carpet, with her chest heaving for oxygen. Lainey turned her head around and saw Veva lying flat out, staring up at her. They both started to laugh as they sucked in the air.

"You let me win," Lainey panted.

"No. You beat me."

Lainey wiped her face with a towel and tossed one to Veva. Her assistant mopped her sweaty brow and all around her neck.

"That was fun." Lainey staggered from the treadmill. She looked around at the screen. "That's my best time on that trail."

Veva raised her head and peered at her own time. "Me too! I can't believe you beat me."

"If I weren't your boss, it would've been a different story," Lainey suggested.

"No. I gave it everything. Half a minute better than my best ever – look," Veva pointed to her stats on screen.

Lainey reached down and helped Veva from the carpet. "C'mon. We need to shower and eat in less than fifteen minutes." Lainey pushed Veva out the door toward her ensuite bathroom.

"Oh, I don't need to…"

"Yes, you do," Lainey interrupted. "I'm not sitting in the office with you all stinky the rest of the day." Lainey hit the switch, and the overhead shower was already set to the temperature and water pressure she liked. "I'll go first." Lainey kicked off her sneakers and socks, stripped off her leggings, underwear, her top, and stepped inside the glass door under the stream of water.

Veva observed the vast stack of fluffy white towels in the rack, so there was no excuse. A small amount of steam rose through the glass, but the view was clear as she watched Lainey's hands move up and down her body with the washcloth, soaping every inch of her stunning figure. Veva, like most other women working in the tech business, had seen Lainey in magazines and online articles for the last few years, and now, here she was, first-hand, watching the toned curvy figure. Veva was embarrassed that her crotch was soaked in more than just sweat as Lainey's hands moved over her breasts and down over her thighs and soaped her glutes. As Veva was daydreaming, Lainey rinsed off and stepped out.

Veva froze.

Lainey reached around Veva and took a towel. "Go on. Get in."

Reluctantly, Veva stripped. She knew Lainey was looking and felt self-conscious. Lainey was one of those women who was open about her body and expected those around her to be the same. Nevertheless, it was an unspoken assurance that Lainey wanted the comparison.

Lainey made no pretense about looking. "Fresh towels galore, right there," Lainey said, and slowly walked into the bedroom.

Veva turned her back, entered the shower, cautiously soaped herself, and rinsed her body within thirty seconds. Before Lainey could walk back in, Veva was wrapped in a towel and using a smaller one to dab her face.

Lainey gave Veva a three-pack of the 4D Fitness invisible underwear. "Here, use these, so you don't have to put your sweaty cute little undies back on."

"Thank you," Veva removed a pair, giving the other two back to Lainey.

"Keep all of them. Great for running in," Lainey said. "They're not invasive like other underwear when you're running, and the panty line is virtually impossible to see unless someone has their face buried in your ass."

"If only," Veva grinned. She began to get dressed. Lainey did the same across the other side of the bedroom.

When Veva pulled on her clothes, Lainey commented, "My waxing lady is very reasonable. If you wanted the rest of your hair fully removed without too much pain," Lainey wafted her hand in front of her crotch to signal which hair removal she was referring to. "Unless your boyfriend likes you to have a little landing strip?"

"I don't have a boyfriend," Veva replied, her face glowing red as she turned her back to fasten her blouse.

"Why not?" Lainey asked, ignoring Veva's discomfort.

Veva shrugged. "I don't have time."

"Not buying it. Brian has lots of hunky, sexy male friends if you're interested?'

"Thanks, but I really don't have the time." Veva's reply was less than convincing.

Two minutes later, they were eating Veva's homemade chicken stew. There was no time to exchange any more talk of private parts or boyfriends. The dirty plates and cutlery were tossed in the sink as they rushed upstairs into the office and joined the live video conference. They exchanged knowing glances at each other with their wet hair pulled back in ponytails.

It was a punchy afternoon on the calls. Lainey was pleased with the progress. Veva's input gradually increased, and her suggestions were well thought out. Although not as fast as Lainey hoped, the team was slowly warming to her. Veva was a little quirky, albeit in a sweet way.

During their afternoon break, Lainey watched Veva walking at the back of the house as she ventured down the stepped terraces, disappearing into the trees. When she returned, Lainey asked, "Find anything cool down there? I haven't seen my garden for a year."

"Oh, my goodness, it's like something from a fairytale down by the little pond. And a bridge to the island and the old stone temple. Is it real?" Veva seriously enquired.

"No, but we modeled it after a folly we once saw in this place in England. I forget the place's name, but it does feel magical, especially in the summertime before the sun sets."

"Oh, I can imagine," Veva gushed. "I'd love to go there at sunset and play with the fairies and spirits of the forest."

Lainey waited for Veva to crack a joke, but none came. Instead, she remained with a child-like grin on her face. "If I ever get to leave the house, I'll go down there with you some time."

"I would love that. Are there any fish in the pond?"

"There's supposed to be, but Brian nor I have checked for a long time. I miss going down there."

"I'd like to be dressed all fancy and wait for a handsome prince to come along and save me from a dark magical spell," Veva dreamily said, staring across the infinity pool towards the trees.

"You like fantasy?"

"Yeah. If I had the nerve or time, I'd like to do that Cosplay stuff. It looks like so much fun."

"You are full of surprises," Lainey sighed.

Veva extended a hand and asked, "Can you step out?"

Lainey was inside the glass sliding door. Veva was outside, only three feet away. The rear courtyard was protected on three sides by the house. "I don't know?"

"You kicked my ass running earlier, and nobody kicks my ass. So I think you can stand here with me." Veva flexed her fingers to encourage Lainey. "Just for a few seconds."

Lainey saw there was a challenge underneath the genuine desire to help her. "Don't pull me, and if I say let go, then let go." She reached out and gripped Veva's fingers.

"I've got you," Veva earnestly replied. She squeezed Lainey's fingers, and Lainey stepped nervously onto the concrete.

Lainey's breathing became heavy, and she inhaled and exhaled as if she were exercising. Both her feet were on the patio. "That's enough." She blew sharp gasps from her lungs.

"You're doing great. If you can, just look at the gardens and the amazing colors of the flowers you guys have. Isn't it beautiful?" Veva moved closer to Lainey and slid her arm around her waist. "I won't let you go. You're perfectly safe."

"Thanks," Lainey gasped. She looked down at the terraced flower beds, and Veva was right. It was beautiful. She looked towards the trees, and her head felt light. "I can't," she whispered.

Veva helped her back through the door and sat her on the edge of the leather couch. "You did so well. Pretty soon, you'll be outside kicking nature's ass and mine."

"I doubt that."

"I'll get you some water." Veva had Lainey take some long breaths and sip the water before going upstairs into the office.

Lainey thanked Veva for her support and for being cool about it.

A couple of hours later, Lainey walked downstairs with Veva and stood in the reception area as she waved her assistant goodbye for the day. "Thank you for lunch and a productive day with some fun. I needed that."

"Me too," Veva readily agreed. "See you tomorrow."

"Yes. Check your passport; you'll need it," Lainey shouted before the front door locked itself.

Lainey watched Veva's BMW pull away as it swiftly descended towards the gate. She tightened her lips and pulled them to one side of her face as she thought about Veva proving herself more than worthy. "What have we signed up for?" Lainey wondered out loud.

She liked Veva. She had a pleasant way about her. The more they chatted at lunchtime, the more Lainey liked her. Veva was a good listener without being judgmental. Lainey's other friends couldn't wait to offer an opinion, even if they weren't asked for it. The thought made her pause; she thought Veva was fast becoming a friend and a colleague. "Huh. Who would have guessed?"

A mile away, on the coast road, Veva kept at a steady forty miles per hour in the inside lane. Her black trousers were pulled down to her knees, and her right hand was furiously exploring underneath the light material of the new panties Lainey had given her. Her crotch was moist, and inside her head, she fantasized that Lainey's fingers were placed inside the flimsy undies.

She imagined Lainey's firm voice, like the one she used on the conference calls, telling her that Veva must do as she was told or lose her job. Lainey's hand was rough, as it had yanked down her trousers, and her voice hoarsely whispered in Veva's ear how she was a naughty girl for being so wet.

The soft panties were easily pulled to the side, and Lainey rubbed hard at Veva's lips and insisted she tell her when she was going to climax. Veva shrieked higher and higher as she was right there, and the explosion of warmth shot through her crotch into her abdomen. The fantasy was so real that she imagined she could hear Lainey's voice in her ear, demanding to know how it felt. "It's still going," Veva gasped as her toes curled, and she had to focus on making sure she didn't crash her car.

The large truck on her left honked its horn at the sight of the woman rubbing herself. It only added to the excitement of being exposed as she confessed to the imaginary Lainey. "I came for you." Veva could hear Lainey telling her, "Good girl." Veva pulled her left leg as high as she could without tearing her work trousers as her body demanded movement of her limbs in the afterglow. "Oh, my God," she groaned as it continued.

Veva quickly became aware of her exposure, and although it was extraordinarily stimulating, she pulled up the black trousers and zipped the fly. The foot race against her boss was something else, but the extras had Veva itching to get home and explore more of the fantasy. She laughed to herself, thinking about how many millions of men would have willingly traded places with her today to see Lainey Stewart, naked and showering. She pressed her foot on the gas. There was much more fantasy left to play out. This was the fourth time in five days at the big house that Veva needed to let everything out. Lainey knew how to capture someone's attention without even trying, and Veva was already under her spell.

CHAPTER TEN

Brian packed away his things in the office and wearily made his way to his car. Thoughts of technical projects and brand awareness were distant echoes as he exited the building. His memory was scorched by what he'd witnessed in the forest. More so by what he'd done. He'd retrieved Lainey's engagement ring, but the cost to his conscience might never be recoverable. The thought of what he did after discovering the young woman in the body bag bothered him the most.

He should have called the police. Panic and disgust set in, but getting that damned ring, after all the effort, had become an obsession. He'd sat in the damp earth, staring at the dead girl for over five minutes. Something about her stillness – her peace – rendered him unable to do anything except stare at her. She was perfect in death. The fascination sickened him. Once he removed the ring from the dead girl's hands, he'd zipped the body bag back up and clumsily pushed the dirt over her.

After staggering back through the woods, Brian used the water tap next to the restrooms to clean away the dirt from his hands, and he picked at his fingernails to remove traces of the other awful things he'd touched. His body was weak, and the taste of vomit was stuck in his throat where he'd hurled out his breakfast. Thankfully, there were only two vehicles left in the lot besides his own. He sat inside the cold restroom, listening to the water steadily dripping from a leaky cistern onto the concrete floor.

It was the first time he had ever encountered a dead body. Brian felt he had to do something for that poor soul lying in the damp soil in the middle of the forest. But his DNA was all over it, and he couldn't produce any firm evidence to say why he was there and how he came to have Lainey's ring in his possession. He'd foolishly incriminated himself. His good intentions were meaningless, and his heroic attempt had been reckless.

When Lainey was first taken by her captor, the police questioned Brian as the prime suspect. He was the one who'd inherit the entire business empire, the house, the investments, and all the rest. So the media were extremely disappointed not to fry him when Lainey had been discovered, wandering in a silk nightgown through the woods in Humboldt Redwoods State Park near Weott. She had no idea how she had gotten there. The consensus was that Brian tried to kill Lainey and that he was the one who'd buried her in a shallow grave in the woods. Lainey had described her attacker's only noteworthy visible feature as two bright brown eyes, the same as his own. She'd clawed her way out of the body bag and eight inches of earth before stumbling into the arms of a retired couple who were walking with their grandkids for a woodland adventure. The Humboldt trail was the first offering on their 4D Fitness software and the trail they'd used as the prototype. It held significant sentimental value for Brian and Lainey, and that was all the more reason the police suspected him.

Brian could not risk being associated with another body in the woods. This time the girl was dead.

Before taking the ring, he noted that the deceased young woman was wearing a silk nightgown similar to the one Lainey was found wearing. Brian had inadvertently put himself at risk. He'd exposed Lainey, too, and the killer would come after her again. Thoughts smashed him like tidal waves over and over. He wasn't sure how long he'd sat in that stinking restroom, but Brian changed in his car, and somehow managed to get back in his office by two in the afternoon.

The rest of his day was a sorry daze.

Prizing the ring from the cold fingers of that dead girl, and not doing anything for her, was the worst of Brian's failures. He questioned the very fabric of his existence, where he had previously considered himself a decent human being. The ring was tainted, and he along with it. He placed the ring inside the Ziploc bag from the burial site. There was no way he could give it to Lainey. Not yet. How could he explain it without implicating himself? He'd been a classic fool!

He slouched from the head office into his car and sat in the driver's seat, staring blankly ahead. It was over a year since Lainey was drugged and almost killed, and the police had no witnesses, no suspects besides himself, and no other clues until now. "Fuck me," he groaned, resting his head on the wheel.

Fibers from his workout clothes were all over the burial site, along with his puke. He pulled out his cell and checked the weather forecast. There was light rain repeated over the next three days. That would help remove any traces of him. He decided to make a quick stop at the nearby grocery store to buy some trash bags to wrap his sneakers and workout clothes. Tomorrow he'd dispose of them and have his car detailed.

"You stupid fucker." He repeatedly slapped his palm against his forehead.

After getting the bags he needed, Brian wrapped his gray shorts, black top, and yellow striped running shoes in the plastic bag and headed home. The entire time he was in the store, he felt as if anyone giving him a cursory glance must know precisely what he'd done or, more accurately, what he'd failed to do. Brian would get rid of the clothing, use a payphone in a couple of days, and let the police know where the girl's body was. It was the least he could do for the unfortunate woman. Outside his house, he worked at picking off the price tag on the bunch of flowers he'd bought for Lainey. After several attempts, he removed the $9.99 sticker. "Somebody could make millions if they designed these fucking tags to come off in one go," he observed. If he couldn't give Lainey the ring, some grocery store flowers would have to suffice.

At home, he dropped his laptop bag on the counter. He passed Lainey the flowers, and she kissed his lips. It was good to see her with a genuine smile.

"How was your day?" she asked, sniffing the flowers.

"Long. I need a shower."

"Dinner will be ready in ten minutes."

As Brian walked along the landing, he stopped and listened. At first, he thought his ears were playing tricks on him like they'd done earlier in the day inside the forest. He paused and confirmed. Lainey was singing to herself. A song from the eighties. He recognized the tune and the words, but not the artist. He leaned on the rail.

"Send me an angel, whoo hoo woo, send me an angel, right now," she chimed.

That seemed like it was a good sign, with some normality returning. Brian left the doors open so he could hear Lainey's whereabouts. He took down an old pair of black and white running shoes he barely used from the top rack inside the massive walk-in closet. He stuffed the Ziploc bag inside the toe of the right running shoe and carefully placed them back on the top shelf. He had more than twenty different pairs of 4D running shoes. "Someday, I need to clear these out." Brian disliked excess, although their lifestyle afforded them plenty of luxuries. He shook his head at the number of unused possessions around him in the closet and sank to his knees, sobbing uncontrollably. From downstairs, he heard, "Send me an angel, right now, right now…"

The medical examiner covered the body with a white sheet.

Detective Strahan stayed beside the metal table, closed his eyes, and said a silent prayer. Detective Hurst walked away, removing her latex gloves and plastic goggles.

The police mortuary in Salem, Oregon, was bright with the stench of bleach ingrained into the tiled floors and walls. Detective Strahan finished his good wishes for the soul and followed Hurst to where they'd hung their jackets. The room was packed. All the eyes followed them across the room. Hurst was unusually quiet as she put on her jacket, adjusted her weapon holster, and headed out.

Once they were in the car, she exclaimed, "Those fuckers are itching to see us screw it up. No gratitude. You'd think they'd be happy to have us here, given that they shied away from taking on the case."

"I've had worse welcomes."

"By whom?"

"My ex-wife's family."

"No shit," Hurst cheerily replied.

"We need that toxicology report." Hurst had a bunch of papers in her hand containing the details of the deceased. "If they say anything stupid to me, I'm heading straight back to Albany."

"Why are you leading this case? No disrespect intended."

"They have four homicide detectives up here; one is retiring, one's on pregnancy leave, one is suspended, and the other is on the verge of quitting – out on stress leave. It's not like they asked me because of my sparkling personality or phenomenal track record. They were desperate, and I could use some good publicity," Hurst explained.

Strahan made no response to her comment but asked, "So, what do we know about Elizabeth Seguras?"

"She was declared missing four weeks ago. By the looks of it, she's been in the ground most of that time." Hurst opened the bunch of papers and browsed through them. "She's thirty-two, single, no kids, owns a Yoga studio." Hurst flicked through to the next page. "Correction - she owns four Yoga studios, with a fifth underway. Her record is clean, barring a minor traffic violation a few years back."

"She's a brunette."

"Yeah. Her vitals are – five-six, 120 pounds, hazel eyes, boobs were added in her early twenties, so appearances matter."

"Occupational hazard in the fitness business," Strahan suggested.

"She was doing well for herself. Broke up with her boyfriend a few months ago. We should visit him tomorrow. Her finances will come through tomorrow or the day afterward, but she paid cash for her Lexus and has a mortgage on a house in North Salem. So I'd guess she was doing nicely," Hurst concluded.

"Same as Lainey Stewart," Strahan added, rubbing a hand over his tired face.

"Our killer has a type. I've asked Salem PD not to let anyone into her house until we get there. Too late in the day for us to go there now. There was no sign of a break-in, so whoever it was, she let them in."

"Lainey didn't recall getting jumped. She's certain that never happened. No signs of bruising or restraints were used. Elizabeth Seguras is the same. So somebody was able to get close without using force."

"Both women work in fitness. A tenuous link." Hurst smacked her lips together, "I need a drink. There's a bar across from the motel. Are you coming?"

112

"Not for me. I need sleep and time to meditate."

"What do you do for fun, Strahan?"

"This. If you read all the reports on Lainey Stewart, then you'll know that when we ran her blood samples, we found traces of Digoxin. It was used with the intent to kill her. Little did the killer know Lainey had used her EpiPen earlier that night in the restaurant she'd dined in. Lainey had been bitten or stung by something and she injected herself when she went to the restroom. She guessed it was only an hour later when the killer took her. Whoever it was used some kind of roofie. Lainey was stripped, her nails were painted, then she was given the Digoxin, but there was enough epinephrine in her system to keep her airwaves and heart moving. She became unconscious, barely alive, and when Lainey came to, she was in the ground."

"Fucking crazy," Hurst observed.

"We never released details of what drugs were used by the killer or that Lainey took a shot from the pen. It was a pure fluke. The medics said Lainey should have died with the cocktail of drugs inside her. It's a good thing she was super fit, or her heart would have given out. Left her with a temporary murmur."

"Does she still have heart problems?"

"I don't know."

"You surprise me." She waited for Strahan to react to her insinuation.

"I'm sure we'll find Digoxin in Elizabeth's blood and some type of roofie," Strahan offered.

"It's the same person," Hurst assured. "The silk nightgowns are identical. We need to find where the killer sourced them. There's no label inside. Someone took the time and effort to make them. Some sort of retro nightwear. Classically sexy."

"Not on a dead body."

"Finally, we agree on something. And we have the calling card: 'Let them praise the name of the Lord. 2 of 7.' Whatever that means. Did you ever make any progress with the Biblical angle?"

"Nope." Strahan wasn't in the mood. The day was already too long. They checked into the motel, where they were given rooms next door to one another.

"Six-thirty in the morning, okay?" Hurst asked him.

"Sure. I'll text you before I knock."

"Sleep well, Strahan. You'll need it."

Strahan heard the door next to his slam shut in the frame as he finished in the shower. Looking out the window, he watched Detective Hurst make her way down the stairs and walk across the lot towards the bar. "She's something else." He closed his curtains, plugged in his earphones, and listened to a guided meditation. He woke up sometime after midnight when he heard a celebratory whoop and laughter coming from Hurst's room, followed by quiet again. He pushed the foam ear protectors into his earlobes and settled back under the covers. Hurst was right … he needed all the sleep he could get.

CHAPTER ELEVEN

There was no glorious victory parade for Brian Stewart. His misguided actions had led to him barely sleeping during the night. He put on his best façade with Lainey, and they had one of the least fractious nights together for some time. Internally, however, he was breaking apart. His woes surrounding their relationship were secondary, something he never imagined possible.

All he could focus on was the girl in the forest. Someone tried to leave his wife just like that poor soul. The killer had led Brian to the ring. The stupid ring! He should have called the police, but now he was in the thick of it. He'd read about killers keeping mementos from their victims, and his head ached, trying to figure out why the killer would give it back. Brian was terrified that it was an indication the trophy wasn't fully earned and only a temporary keepsake until the job was finalized.

His acceptance of the challenge had put his wife in the killer's sights again. Not only was he incapable of helping Lainey back to being her best, but now he had endangered her because of his shallow heroic fantasy. His selfish actions did not consider all the possibilities, which, ironically, was one of Lainey's recurring accusations about his work methodologies. "Oh God, what have I done?"

Detective Strahan woke with a jolt, and for a brief moment, the unfamiliar surroundings had him questioning whether he was dreaming or awake. A look around the most basic motel room reminded him that this was real, and he was in Salem. It was already six a.m. He quickly shaved and got dressed. After choosing a pair of dark blue trousers, and a green wool jacket, he spent a moment emptying his case and hanging up his spare clothes in the closet. A time-check, and then he headed next door. He had forgotten to text Detective Hurst and paused outside her door. He was about to message her when the door opened wide, and a woman in her early thirties glared at him.

"Hi," he said.

"Are you going to move?" The woman asked as she pulled a vape from her bra and sucked on it. She released a plume of fruity smoke into his face. Her facial makeup was heavy, with dark eyeliner poking from the corners of her eyes, and her long hair was dyed black with pink streaks. Her clothing was all black, including ripped fishnet stockings inside her shin-length black leather lace-up boots, with a matching short leather skirt to complete the gothic look.

Strahan stepped aside. "I was just texting Detective Hurst."

The young woman looked with dismay at Hurst. "Detective? You never mentioned that."

"You never asked," Hurst replied and launched a firm hand to the woman's buttocks, making a loud crack. "I'm usually the one asking questions. Go on now." Hurst gave her one-night lover a second spanking.

The young woman gave Hurst a friendly growl, straightened her skirt, and sidled past Detective Strahan, giving him the deadeye. Strahan returned it. She mockingly saluted him and walked away with an exaggerated shake of her hips.

"Had a good night, did you?"

"Something like that," Hurst replied. "Let me get my bag. I'm ready. You want me to drive?"

"I'll drive. I may have more energy than you," Strahan suggested.

"Orgasms are good stress relief. It would help if you tried it sometime. However, I wouldn't recommend it with her," Hurst pointed at her disappearing conquest. "She needs too much instruction, although she purrs like a kitten when you get going…"

"I get the picture," Strahan interrupted her. They stopped for coffee and a quick bite before driving out to Mehama. They exchanged notes on the police reports, but nothing showed itself as particularly helpful. From Mehama, they headed north to Shellburg Creek and walked the mile into the woodland area surrounding Stassel Falls. The clouds hung heavy overhead, but the rain stayed at bay. The ground was soaked, and Strahan's pants got drenched as they strayed from the well-trodden path, diverting into the trees.

Forensics operated underneath a couple of pop-up covers in the taped-off area between the trees. Detective Hurst said hi to a couple of cops she knew and introduced Strahan to the team.

Hurst knelt beside the shallow grave. "Soft earth. Nice and easy to dig. Was she firmly zipped in the body bag when you guys found her yesterday?" she asked the man in a white protective suit on his knees.

"Yeah. She was well preserved, too. The soil is dense and retained the water around the bag. Creates like an air pocket. She was as dry as a bone when we first opened it up at the lab."

"We saw her last night," Strahan said. "What have you got?"

"Someone used a small shovel as you'd find in any decent camping equipment store. From the cuts in the soil, I'd say it was the only tool used. Whoever was digging was very careful. We have nothing so far. No hairs, fibers, or anything to speak of. Behind us, there's a mixture of boot prints. The size nine's we believe belongs to the guy who found her. There are dog prints all over where his dog started digging. We also have size seven prints under the other tent. Faint and no distinguishing marks. Rains already wiped away any chance of being able to identify a brand."

"Thanks," Strahan said. He looked at the distance from the trail to where the body was buried.

"What are you thinking? About the same distance as the one Lainey Stewart crawled out of?" Hurst asked.

"Pretty much." Strahan moved around the hole in the ground. "The clearing in the trees is similar. A nice open area with light filtering through first thing in the morning. Same orientation."

"Does that mean anything?" Hurst enquired.

117

"Only that it's in keeping with taking care. There's some thought to it. Like I'm going to bury you in a sunny spot in the trees. Surrounded by beauty. A tranquil feel to it," Strahan suggested as he turned around 360 degrees.

"Like a mark of respect," Hurst added.

"Something like that. Why else take the time to do her nails and put on the silk nightdress? The card in her hand has to do with God's creation of angels. A Biblical reference, but nothing significant, as far we could tell."

"Significant to someone, I guess. It's a strange kind of respect after killing someone. There's some kind of ceremony here, but we need to find the reason. Not enough to suggest it may be solely religious or not so obvious." Hurst got off her soaked knees, wiping away the mud from her pants. She moved away from the forensic team and joined Strahan off to one side. "What else are you thinking?"

"The quote is from Psalm 148. It has no direct link to the number seven on the card. We couldn't find anything linking the number seven to angels. I think it's to do with creation of some sort."

"Meaning what?"

"Meaning it's personal to the killer. The number seven occurs many times in the Bible but never directly with angels. God created heaven and earth in seven days. Somebody who believes in God, or at least reads the Bible. It has to be something specific." He gave it some thought. "Everything else is kind of…"

"Too precise to be some loosey-goosey shit," Hurst suggested.

"Exactly that," Strahan agreed. "If Elizabeth Seguras is number two, as the card stated, we've still got five more people to save or bodies to find."

"We should assume they've already been targeted. There's a type," Hurst emphasized the words. "We should look at the significance of the number seven and see if we can find a link. It's pretty ballsy to leave a calling card."

"We contacted many printing sources to see if anyone had a record of making those cards with the small rose motif on the edges. We came up with nothing. We believe someone printed the cards at home based on the card and the ink. They're not amateurish."

Strahan walked among the trees surrounding the burial site, and Hurst followed. They both looked on the ground for signs of someone dropping something or leaving a clue of some description. "The flowers applied on the fingernails of Elizabeth Seguras were the same we found on Lainey Stewart, and they match the floral motif on the card."

"Are we ruling out Brian Stewart?"

Strahan stopped walking and gave Hurst some study. "No," he said with some reluctance. "He doesn't fit the profile, but he is involved in the fitness industry, and his wife was the intended first victim. It would be interesting to know if Elizabeth Seguras sold any 4D Fitness merchandise in her yoga studios."

"She did," Hurst replied. "I got one of my guys to look inside two of the Yoga studios last night. "We found some connection to 4D. They don't have any fancy treadmills, but they sell the leggings, vests, and hoodies."

"Thanks for sharing," Strahan caustically replied.

"It's the only surprise I have. It doesn't point directly at Brian Stewart, unless we find he was in those studios and personally sold the merchandise to Elizabeth."

"Hardly likely," Strahan said. "He and Lainey only do the top-level work. He travels abroad, meeting with vendors, suppliers, and whatnot." Strahan stopped and looked at the bark on a nearby tree that faced the burial site. He ran his fingers over the ancient wood. "Speaking of surprises, I asked my team to get a list of other young women who fit a similar profile to Elizabeth and Lainey who've been reported missing." He tapped his fingers against the tree's bark and looked up at the trunk.

"Did they find anything from the missing person reports?" Hurst asked.

"There's a couple similar, but one in particular – A young woman called Daphne Montclair from Santa Rosa. She's missing. She owns a company called Dynamo Fitness Wear. She started as an Instagram influencer and launched her own clothing brand."

"You think she could be number three?"

"I do. We should look at her when we get out of here. See if we can get details from the cops in Santa Rosa. She's not in the same league as Lainey Stewart."

"Who is?" Hurst interrupted.

"But Daphne was making some headway. She was young, fit, brunette, and catching lots of attention."

"The wrong kind, by the sounds of it. Have you spoken with anyone in Santa Rosa?"

"No. But I looked at her Instagram page. She's been missing for over a week. Her family and friends say it's out of character. No indication she took a vacation, and no sign of a struggle at her home."

"I wonder if she ever modeled 4D Fitness clothing on her Instagram?"

"She did. About a year ago. A lot of it."

"Sounds like we're all just full of surprises this morning. I'm not seeing anything useful here. You?"

Strahan pointed to the tree bark next to his shoulder. "If only these trees could talk," he said, shaking his head in response to her question.

"Can you ask your guides during one of your meditations?"

"Maybe you could fuck everyone in Salem, and we can narrow down our suspect list?"

"I knew I would get along with you," Hurst said. "Let's go back into town and visit Elizabeth's house. I call first dibs on looking through her panty drawer."

"Anybody ever told you that you have a sick mind?"

Detective Hurst pretended to give it some deep consideration, with her hand rubbing against her long chin. "I'm sure they have."

CHAPTER TWELVE

Brian made the anonymous payphone call to the police, alerting them of where to find the body in Prairie Creek. The three days had taken the edge off his guilt, although the residual greedily gnawed at him. He and Lainey had been embroiled in a couple more arguments and one where Lainey had thrown a glassware jug at him in the kitchen. She had profusely apologized, but Brian admitted he had deserved it. "There was no need for me to be so personal and selfish about things," he told her.

"I was demanding full honesty, and I wasn't open with you. I got taken in the moment, and it just happened. We should be celebrating. Finally, I might have some libido making an appearance," Lainey explained. "I was scared to suggest we use it between us in case…you know, I freaked out again."

Brian discovered the two triple-A batteries in the trash and found the empty packaging beside Lainey's bedside drawer in her trash can, and the only thing she had that used those size batteries was her vibrator. She told him she'd used it one night before he came home from work, and Brian felt betrayed. It took him two days to simmer down, despite their talking about it in bed that night.

"I don't ask you if you're jerking off to porn. I know you must be," Lainey casually remarked. "And I don't care, so long as it's not something weird."

"Weird like what?"

"Like people being whipped in dungeons all dressed in leather, or women giving blowjobs to strangers in parking lots at night."

"You seem to know an awful lot about whatever shit people are into these days," Brian had accused.

"Fuck you!" was the response, along with the flying glassware. Lainey hadn't lost her ability to blow a gasket when challenged. Thankfully, her aim was off by a couple of inches.

Brian figured it was a good thing he was traveling for a week. He wasn't thrilled about Veva coming along. Lainey sang the praises of their new director. Brian wondered if Veva would be reporting back to Lainey … not that he had anything to hide. Brian had never once strayed from his marital commitments, despite having a couple of very good offers. Most big foreign cities were filled with temptation. He was more concerned that Veva was dull. He longed to return to the times when he and Lainey had traveled, making deals, running the trails, and fooling around in hotels. Everything had been vibrant and uplifted by the possibilities they created together. Lainey was great in negotiations and could wrap distributors around her little finger. He longed for those days to return.

He removed his suitcase from the closet to prepare for his trip. The weather in Germany looked like it would be a mixture of sun and rain. Summer was just around the corner. Lainey assured him that she'd already provided Veva with all the latest GoPro equipment, the same as his and that Veva was more than capable of running with him. However, he wasn't thrilled about forcing conversations with someone who appeared socially challenged.

"Geez," he groaned and bent down to pick up his running socks.

Lainey caught his less than enthusiastic groan and asked, with a light and airy tone, "Aww, missing me already, are you?"

Brian eyed her with suspicion. His clothes were strewn on the bed as he sorted through a mixture of business and running wear. "I always miss you, even when…never mind," he sighed. "I'm not looking forward to this trip. All this stuff with that girl they found in Oregon and everything." He could not tell Lainey there was another body fifty miles away in Prairie Creek. The news would break in a couple of days. He'd be far away, and although Lainey was a tough customer, he wanted to be at home to offer support. There was no way he could make excuses or change all the European appointments. Lainey would see through it, and so would the cops. Brian was tired of being spotlighted as a potential murderer.

"I have my first therapy session on Wednesday. Dr. Peterson. They say he's the best."

"Let's hope so. Your health and happiness mean more to me than my own, even when I'm being a complete dick towards you."

"That's very romantic, in a strange way." Lainey half lay on the bed and peered inside his case. "I'm checking to see if you're packing condoms."

Brian cast his eyes upward and folded his socks into tight little balls.

"That was a joke."

"Traditionally, jokes make people laugh."

"Don't be so touchy, or I'll throw that lamp at you, and I won't miss this time. I come in peace." She rolled his socks tighter. "The German market could be massive if we get a good foothold. We need to be up and running; no pun intended before that place in Bremen gets their version on the market. German tech is always good."

"I agree. I wish you could see it with me," Brian couldn't prevent the words exiting his lips.

"I know, you lucky thing. The run at the Park Hotel through Bremen looks stunning. You can stay in that hotel for two nights in all those parks and around the lake! Five stars, and all that Gothic architecture to explore."

"And the talkative Veva for me to explain it all to," Brian complained.

"She's not that bad once you get under the surface," Lainey defended their new recruit. "She gets very chatty when you get into screen resolutions and our optometric scanners."

"I can hardly wait," he feigned a heavy sigh.

"She'll kick your ass around the track, especially on the flat. She's not great with gradients, but I'll bet she can beat you over the six miles in Bremen."

"I'll take that bet." Brian placed his underwear, three pairs of business slacks, four carefully folded collared shirts, and a light blue jacket inside the case.

"I like that jacket on you," Lainey observed as she straightened his stuff.

"Let's hope the Germans feel the same way." Brian placed some running shoes inside and stuffed the rolled socks deep into them.

"I need to clear out stuff from the closet when I get back."

123

"Leaving for good, are you?" Lainey prodded.

Brian ignored the barb. "I'll take a bunch of those spare running shoes to Goodwill, along with God knows how many training shirts, hoodies, and shorts. Too much shit in this house." He paused and clarified, "I mean, things we don't use."

"Are you having guilt over our material success again?"

"No. I just have too much stuff, and I'm not using half of it. They're all in brand-new condition. Someone could be making use of them."

"I should do the same."

Brian observed her. Lainey was being extra friendly, and rarely was she this compliant. "I know you've already said yes to this question, but are you sure you'll be okay here on your own?"

"Sure. I've got the nightly patrols, and with the new sensors in the grounds we've installed, you'd have to be like James Bond to get in here without me knowing about it."

"You can always have your mom come and stay."

"Definitely not," Lainey was quick to reply. "I've got enough on my plate without her telling me how I should go about my life. I know she means well, but it never ends well."

Brian checked the time. "I should get a move on. We need to be at San Francisco airport in seven hours."

"Three hours to spare with your driving." Lainey stretched out on the bed.

As soon as she turned her back, Brian made a childish face. She loved to take shots at his driving, despite his clean record.

Lainey's phone buzzed. "It's Veva. She's early. Bless her." Lainey pressed her phone, and the gates opened. "I'll make her welcome, seeing as one of us doesn't want to." She gave Brian a big smile and skipped from the room. As she passed through the doorway, she shouted back to him, "Stop making those faces at me; you could hurt my feelings."

Brian laughed to himself. Lainey always said she knew him better than he did and claimed she could read his mind. Given what he'd done in the last few days, he knew part of her claim was false. Before closing the case, he packed some casual shorts, jeans, a couple of t-shirts, and his toiletries. He released all the air from his lungs, closed his eyes for a few seconds, and tried to convince himself to make an effort with Veva. He heard the excited voices from downstairs, and the thought dissipated faster than a UFO sighting. "Ah fuck."

Strahan's captain had called and explained they had received an anonymous message about a body in Prairie Creek National Park. It had been decided to keep Detective Hurst on point for the multiple murder investigation, with Strahan in support. Strahan said they were visiting people across Salem in connection to Elizabeth Seguras, and they'd return to Northern California later tomorrow night.

"Get this mess cleaned up fast," were the captain's instructions.

Strahan pulled on jeans, a shirt, and an old leather jacket before wandering across the parking lot towards the bar. Detective Hurst was sitting in a booth in the far corner. With her was a young woman in her late twenties. Hurst saw him and immediately stopped whatever game she played with the young woman's fingers. The young woman turned her head to see why the fun had ceased and looked at the fair-haired detective.

"Didn't expect to see you in here," Hurst remarked.

"Hey, you said you weren't married?" The young woman complained, slurring her words. Her long brown hair was pulled over her shoulders, and her face was plain and pale. Her eyes were sharp, with a hint of silver sparkles around her cheekbones. She was dressed in a polo shirt, tight faded jeans, and cowboy boots. Her condition suggested she'd been in the bar way longer than Detective Hurst.

"I'm not married," Hurst replied.

"I'm her business partner," Strahan explained. He turned his furrowed gaze to Hurst. "We need to talk. Now."

125

"It can't wait?" Hurst asked with a sneaky glance at her female companion.

"No."

Hurst whispered something in the young woman's ear that made her giggle. "Go on now; I'll catch up with you shortly."

The young woman slid from the bench seat and stood in front of Strahan, giving him a dirty look for spoiling her fun. Then, she strode purposefully past with a loud 'tut' aimed at him.

"Sorry to spoil the party." Strahan slid in opposite Hurst. "I just got off the phone with my captain." Strahan paused as the waitress appeared at his shoulder and asked what he wanted. "I'll take a Miller, High-Life."

Hurst pulled her lips down as she expressed surprise at him ordering a drink. "I didn't think you…"

"I normally don't. When in Rome," he forced a smile. "We have another one. Prairie Creek Redwoods, just across the state line. It's fifty miles north of Eureka."

"Is it the missing girl from Santa Rosa?"

"It is. Daphne Montclair. Somebody drove 260 miles to bury her in a place they knew."

"Is it on their 4D Fitness website?"

"Yeah. Same as the others - a white vintage nightdress, a silk rose in her hands, with roses inlaid into her manicure."

"A floral manicure. You buy them in kits, mostly. You can find them anywhere. I've got our team researching the specific ones used and cross-referencing online purchases. It could take forever, and we may never know." Detective Hurst noted the heaviness in his brow, and the sharpness of his medium-blue eyes was extinguished. "You okay?"

"Not really. The captain told me she had a business calling card in one of her hands, but the others had their hands folded together. She didn't. The earth had recently been disturbed like someone dug her up and moved her around."

"Who found her?"

"We don't know. An anonymous call from a payphone in Eureka. We're checking nearby cameras on buildings, but nothing so far."

"Maybe whoever found her checked for a pulse?" Hurst offered.

"It's possible. It looks like she's been in the ground a week, so unlikely you'd check a wrist at that point."

"There's something else," Hurst pointed the end of her beer bottle towards him. Strahan's gaze was dull, and Hurst saw that he was bothered by much more than discovering a new body.

The waitress placed the beer in front of Strahan, and he waited until the server had gone before he continued. "It's the calling card in her hand that worries me more. Daphne Montclair is carrying 'four of seven.'"

"Ah, shit," Hurst exclaimed, slamming her bottle on the wooden table. "Means number three is already out there somewhere."

"Exactly. We've missed one, and number five is likely coming our way. In the meantime, we've got nothing, and we're sitting in some shithole, listening to jukebox country music.

Hurst looked around the bar. "Trust me, I've been in some shitholes, and this isn't one of them." Hurst tagged her bottle against his. "What else?"

"Prairie Creek isn't public knowledge yet. We have another day before it breaks. You think Salem will want to take this thing from you?"

"No way, despite the fact some old dyke with a sticky past is leading their case. They don't have anyone else."

"My captain said that as far as he's concerned, you have the first body in the ground, and it's still your lead."

"Is that a problem for you?" She observed every micro-movement in his face.

Strahan raised his bottle toward her. "It's all yours."

Hurst looked around the bar for a second time and briefly puckered her lips in disappointment. "Looks like I lost my date."

"Date. She looked more like your daughter."

Hurst gave a singular laugh. "I wasn't destined to be a mother. I tried, sort of, way back in the day. My sister passed away, and I took in my niece when

127

she was little. I was trying to work my way through the detective ranks, so I never had time to look after a little one. I had to send her to live with my other sister. What about you, Strahan, any kids?"

"No. My marriage was over and done pretty quickly, and we never had time to think about having a family. But, of course, I'm young, so you never know. What happened to the girl, your niece?"

"Oh, she was fine. I haven't seen her since she was eighteen. It's my only regret – that I couldn't make it work." Hurst's tone reflected a distant sadness as she focused on the bottle in her hands and twizzled it around in her long fingers. "So, we have a killer with a distinctive selection method. We'll need a team to profile women who fit that category."

"It's going to be a sizable list," Strahan suggested. "We need to tell Lainey Stewart. I'll call her tomorrow unless you want to?"

"No. You go ahead. You already have an established relationship. Best coming from you."

Strahan nodded his appreciation.

"I was thinking about the meaning of the angel thing. Before coming here, I looked online at some stuff, and I couldn't find anything useful. But, despite killing them, we have these angelic-looking young women that somebody took care of, and the burials weren't random. Another careful selection," Hurst summarized.

"I asked for some info from the team in Prairie Creek, and the forest location sounds the same as the others. There is a clearing in the trees, a body aligned with the head facing east to the rising sun. There's something there, like a new dawn, or something where the sun's rising is important."

Hurst suggested, "We'll be assigned some folks to assist now that we've got bodies in Oregon and California. But, unfortunately, the killer isn't leaving us any other clues." Hurst shuffled in her seat. "I don't like what our intel has given us." Hurst pushed her bottle to one side of the table. She leaned over and waited for him to meet her partway. "Our profile is all messed up. People tell us it's likely to be a white male, in his late thirties, with a strong build, who lives alone, and is into fitness. Do you like that?"

"That's all we have."

"That didn't answer my question." Hurst took Strahan's beer from his hand and drank half the contents. "It's Bullshit. Somebody is giving them specialist manicures with roses embedded and dressing them in silk nightgowns. There's no sexual assault, no trauma, nothing. There's no male serial killer with such a profile."

"Could it be a gay man?"

Hurst frowned at him and took another drink of his beer. "Homosexual killers rarely kill outside of their own demographic. How many straight white men give manicures and leave a body in pristine condition. Zero is the answer. This is something new," Hurst suggested, taking another sip of his beer and putting it back in his hand.

"You think a woman did this?"

"I have no idea who or what we're looking at," Hurst said. "I'm saying the standard profiles we've been given are useless. This could be either a man or a woman. Who knows? My point is that we should keep our options open and be cautious about what's pushed at us. This is different."

"How do you know?" he asked.

"I can feel it. Call it women's intuition or whatever you like, but I know I'm right."

Strahan looked over his shoulder at the dozen patrons scattered in the bar. "Doesn't look like you'll have much luck in here tonight."

"I was doing fine until you showed up, pretty boy." She snatched his beer again. "C'mon, let's get the fuck out of here. Tomorrow we'll visit Elizabeth's ex-boyfriend and put the squeeze on him."

Strahan left cash on the table, and they walked across the street to the motel together. Once they crossed the busy road, he stopped and looked at the darkened landscape.

"Aside from the motel, this looks like an idyllic green paradise," he gestured outward with both arms. "Hard to imagine why anyone would wish to spoil it by concealing dead women under the soil."

"Our killer doesn't see it that way. They believe they're adding to the beauty of the surroundings and laying their victims to rest in a paradise, befitting the beauty they once held in life. A reconnection with the land, or re-birth of some description?"

Her comment was frighteningly accurate as a summation of his thoughts. Thoughts that nobody wanted to say aloud. Strahan fixed his gaze on Hurst. In the dimmed light from the motel, she looked softer than before. He guessed that she may have polled many votes in a beauty pageant in her youth. He switched his gaze to the floor, realizing he'd spent too long staring.

"I know what you're thinking; my words make me sound like I could've killed those girls. But … the beautiful high-achieving women I like are covered in sweat and spooning in my bed. I don't waste time expending my energy burying good pussy in the ground. Our killer is ingenious. The planning and flawless execution require an incredibly detailed approach. I hate to tell you this, Strahan, but we could have seven bodies before we can get a break."

"We had Lainey Stewart over a year ago, and suddenly we found two in a week."

"Elizabeth Seguras was in the ground somewhere between 20 - 30 days. So technically, we have about an eleven-month gap before she was killed and only another three weeks until Daphne Montclair's life was taken."

"And Daphne is number four. So, somewhere between her and Elizabeth, we have number three waiting to be found. We'll need squads of police walking lines on all the trails 4D Fitness have available in their database. Chances are the missing girl is buried just off one of those trails," Strahan suggested.

"I'll make the call in the morning. My boss in Albany is an asshole. I'll ask Salem to initiate the help. Might be easier," Hurst pondered. She swiveled around on her heels, taking in the surroundings. "You're right; this is an idyllic paradise. But like the garden of Eden, it's full of fucking snakes." Hurst patted him on the shoulder and headed for her room. "Sleep well, Strahan."

"You do the same."

CHAPTER THIRTEEN

Brian lay star-shaped across the king-sized bed in his German hotel room and puffed air from his lungs. The journey had been easy enough but feeling obliged as the boss to make conversation had been exhausting. Veva had proven to be hard work. She was sweet and kind, but he started ninety percent of their conversations, and he had to continually push the talk along. So when Veva declared she wanted to listen to music on the plane, it was a relief.

He needed to get energized and kicked his legs outward, launching himself off the bed. He looked at the extensive water features from his window with a centralized ornate fountain spraying high into the air and thick trees beyond. Brian stepped out onto the large balcony. In the distance, people were strolling by the lake and throughout manicured gardens. The extensive gardens were as opulent as the stone-built hotel, with its magnificent central dome, tying together two massive wings that formed a u-shape. Everything was pristine and orderly.

He admired the German efficiency and the genuinely heartfelt welcome they'd received. It was late afternoon, and the sun pushed through low-level clouds, providing some warmth. Below his balcony, people were drinking coffee and beer at white metallic tables and chairs in the gardens. It looked tempting. A couple lounged in the hot tub next to the swimming pool on the next level below that.

"It's so beautiful, isn't it? Like being in a fairytale."

Brian hadn't noticed Veva leaning on the stone balustrade of her balcony. "I suppose." His response sounded tired. He turned his attention to the views.

"It's the kind of place where you'd expect to see horse-drawn carriages arriving for a grand ball – where magic and mystery will unfold."

"Exactly!" Veva agreed. "I'm going to run the Waldbuhne Loop. Want to join me?"

"Now?"

"Yes, while it's light and there's no rain. Heavy rain tomorrow. Bet I can beat you."

Brian could tell by her face that she was serious. "I'll meet you in the lobby in ten minutes."

He noticed that the loose-fitting black vest she wore revealed the side of her right breast and a shapely shoulder. Lainey had portrayed Veva as a fitness nut, and it certainly looked that way. Their eyes locked briefly before Brian looked away.

"Okay, the race is on," she cheerily replied and disappeared inside her room.

Brian shook his head. Their new tech girl was odd, but at least she'd started a conversation, even if it were goading him into running. Her challenge showed no fear. Lainey said Veva was competitive. He opened his case, got changed, and took the stairs three floors into the lobby. There were people everywhere, checking in, having snacks, or taking photographs. No sign of Veva allowed him to go outside and jog on the spot. The views over the gardens and the north side of Bremen were superb, causing Brian to wonder what it must be like living here. Everything he'd seen in Bremen suggested a social vibrancy.

Suddenly, there she was. "C'mon, Boss, are you ready?" Veva asked, springing up and down on the spot, raising her knees to her chest.

"I'm ready. Shall we?" Brian pointed the way down the grand stone steps toward the entrance driveway. Once Veva's sneakers hit the ground level, she was already running. Brian let her get ahead as he set his watch for the run. He sprinted after her. She moved at a pace he wasn't sure was sustainable. "Have you switched on your GoPro?" He pointed at her head.

She gave him the thumbs up and kept moving. Brian noticed Veva had no water bottle in her hands. The course was mostly flat, but even he wouldn't run six miles and without water. They ran side by side around the grounds, heading north to hit the main trail, and along the way, they passed swaths of people walking or riding bicycles.

Veva's running style was strong, along with the backs of her calves leading to two perfectly formed hamstrings and her rounded buttocks barely covered in tight Lycra spandex running shorts. Her midriff was bare, and her skin was milky white against a black sports bra, along with taut, muscular arms showing the seriousness of her workouts.

The competition was much less fierce than the rivalry shown between Lainey and Veva. Brian opened a thirty-yard lead and steadily maintained it all the way around. The app on his watch showed him the GoPro location of Veva behind him the whole way. When they arrived back at the hotel steps, Brian removed his headwear and waited for Veva. She stopped beside him, leaning on the stone wall and panting like a thirsty dog. Brian offered his water bottle, and she took a sip.

"I must be jet-lagged," she puffed.

"You should have drunk some water." Her head kept tapping against the stone. He leaned forward and unfastened the camera before she damaged it. "I'll download it with mine later tonight, and we can start fresh tomorrow."

"Now that I know the course, I'll give you a better race."

"How about we get the best footage and let the rest be what it is?"

"Sorry. I like to race," Veva gasped. Inside the lobby, she headed for the stairs. "I don't like elevators. Confined spaces scare me," she explained.

They huffed and puffed their way through the lobby and up the stairs. Their rooms were next to each other on the top floor. Brian found Veva much more talkative after their run and considered that she was just shy and needed time to come out of her shell. "I'm going for dinner in the main restaurant at six if you want to join me."

"Sounds good. I'll see you there," Veva agreed.

Lainey received word from Brian that they were safely in Bremen, and he sent her a couple of pictures from the hotel balcony. Lainey hmphed, sitting alone in their designer kitchen. She'd texted a couple of girlfriends to see if

133

they wanted to come over and have dinner, but none could make it. Lainey acknowledged a pang of jealousy and reminded herself it was her idea to send Veva. "How difficult can it be?" she asked as she looked out towards the pool and thought of stepping outside the door.

She put down her glass of homemade kombucha and marched to the sliding glass doors. Her fingers froze on the handle; she angrily snorted as if it were to blame for her imprisonment.

"You can do this," she encouraged herself. The door unlocked with a swift flick of her wrist, and Lainey dragged it open. The rush of fresh air was filled with scented hope. She tugged back the screen door and was about to step outside, but her heartbeat rocketed, and sweat gathered under her arms. Her limbs twitched. Lainey breathed heavily through her dry lips as though she were doing reps in the gym.

She dangled her right foot over the paving stone, but she could not set it down. So instead, she quickly pulled her leg back, slammed the screen, and locked the sliding glass door. "What the hell? I already did this," she reminded herself of when Veva had encouraged her.

She collapsed on the tiled floor, weeping, shaking, and overcome with uselessness and self-pity. So much for the once glorious pin-up girl of tech fitness who was named one of the top ten female CEOs to watch in 2019. It had been only a year since she was riding the crest of a mammoth wave, and now, she was, lying on the floor, drowning in sorrow as drool slipped from the corner of her mouth.

She remained in an embryonic bundle, with a heavy sobbing that held her to the ground. The thought of defeat pushed her upright, wiping the tears off her face and staring through the glass. "I'm not beaten," she shouted to the invisible forces.

She moaned and huffed, dragged herself to her feet, and stood tall. There was no way she'd taste any more of the salty humiliation, and there was no way she would ever give in. Other people might easily reach for a glass of wine or take out a tub of vanilla and raspberry ice cream from the freezer. Not Lainey.

She poured away the half glass of her favorite home-brewed ginger hibiscus kombucha, watching it ceremoniously spin down the drain. She wanted no distractions and complete control. She rinsed the glass under the tap, leaving it to drain on the other side of the sink—no Brian here to fuss about putting it back into place.

Lainey refused to wallow in her momentary misery. She needed something to fight back and sinking further into gloom was not an option. She opened her phone, selected her eighties playlist on her music app, and turned the volume up full blast as she took a cloth and cleaned the kitchen surfaces, including cabinet doors and fridge freezer. Her cleaning lady had done everything only days earlier, but she needed something to immediately occupy her mind and body. Cleaning was as good a release of toxic energy as anything. Lainey swayed her body in time with the music as she scrubbed away with the cloth.

She glanced out the back windows and snarled at the specter she imagined floating in the ether and laughing at her failed attempt to step into the world. "I'll be the one laughing," she defiantly declared into the open house.

Twenty minutes later, Lainey found herself cleaning out some space in the walk-in closet, as Brian had suggested. She kept the music blasting from her phone and sang along. It was a daunting task to pull out the unused items and organize the closet. She looked at her phone, thinking she'd need some dance music to get her in the mood. First, she stopped beside her laptop to check work-related email, a habit that always took precedence. Lainey scanned her inbox.

There were two emails back-to-back, and both had the headline: WATCH THIS ASAP. Lainey looked at the first email. The sender was unknown, but she never had spam or junk in her business inbox, so she clicked the link. It opened with a video that showed the bamboo forest trail of Arashiyama. She had just viewed it with Brian, and it was unmistakable.

The footage veered off the trail and showed some movement before a hooded figure came into view with its back to the camera. Someone wearing a blue hoodie, a pair of black jogging pants, and a pair of black and white sneakers. With the baggy clothing, it was impossible to tell if the figure was male or female, but the hooded figure knelt by a long patch of dark soil. A gloved hand took something from one of the pockets and placed an object at the head of the mound of earth.

"Are you fucking kidding me?" she whispered. Lainey paused and zoomed in, altering the pixels to give clarity. It showed a small cross made from grass, carefully tied together. "Oh my God. What am I looking at?" She asked the question aloud, but her instincts already knew the answer.

She began pacing up and down, thumping her right fist into her left palm. "You're fucking kidding me!" She could barely look at the screen. Lainey paused and ground her teeth together, forcing herself to look. The small mound of freshly raised earth was no different from what she'd clawed her way out of a year ago. "How's this even possible?"

Sitting on the end of her bed Lainey logged into her email on the laptop. She watched on the bigger screen as the figure slowly stood, walked back to the camera, and a gloved hand flashed in front of the screen. There was a pause, and then the view went back to the bamboo forest, moving at speed, showing that whoever filmed it was running.

She hit fast-forward and watched as the footage went quickly through the forest and toward the railroad tracks – the same path Brian had shown her. The same place he'd just returned from.

"Brian?" His name hung in the air. Lainey rewound and focused on the crouching figure, appearing to pray over the raised earth. Then, she noticed the white emblem on the upper arm of the dark blue hood. She paused and zoomed in on the white stitching. Lainey's hands clamped over her mouth.

"Oh no – nooo," she begged for it not to be true. She wished she'd never looked, but there was no denying the embroidered logo on the upper arm was 4D. Their logo. Brian was wearing one just like it only a few nights ago in the kitchen. Lainey ran into the closet and went to the far end, where Brian neatly kept all his stuff. She noted the various jackets and suits hanging in order. Three-quarters of the enormous closet was taken up with Lainey's clothes, but for a moment, the space felt it had no attachment to her or Brian. Lainey felt like she was prying into a stranger's belongings.

Lainey ran her hand over her dresses and the shoulders of her winter jackets to provide some familiarity. She came to the first of Brian's clothes, but she couldn't touch any of them. Instead, her eyes were drawn to the dark blue garment on its hanger. Lainey knew they sold two different styles of those hoodies, which were at least two seasons old. One had the 4D logo on the upper left chest and the other on the right upper sleeve. She couldn't recall which one Brian owned but hoped his contained the 4D logo on the chest. She remained frozen by the silence of the house.

An alien sensation crept over her at the thought of being discovered, rummaging inside her own closet space. After a few seconds, Lainey was done with her internal nonsense and extended her hand and lifted the hanger from the rack. The white 4D logo on the upper right arm shone brightly.

It fell from her hands and crumpled in a heap on the polished wooden surface. Lainey couldn't bring herself to reach down and pick it back up.

She rushed back to her laptop and followed the link in the second email. It showed the same weird ritualistic activity, but this time from the Prairie Creek Redwoods trail. The same thing as the Arashiyama video took place, with a blue-hooded figure kneeling by a pile of earth, placing a small cross at the head of what Lainey was sure was a burial site. She played around with the view and found a partial view of the 4D logo on the right upper sleeve. It must be the same person. The videos had times and dates on them. Lainey checked, and each matched when Brian was in Japan or at home in California.

Lainey looked at her inbox. The email message was gone. A quick check confirmed it had vanished.

Lainey paced up and down, checking her logic, gripping her stomach, and trying to retain her sanity. She ran the computations through her head. Brian was as devoted to her as any husband could be, and she knew his love for her was unquestionable. Sure, they argued and disagreed about work or home life, but who didn't. Surely Brian had nothing to do with the body found in Oregon. Brian hadn't been anywhere near Oregon. The video she'd seen was taken in Prairie Creek. Lainey recognized the trail with the fallen tree sawn in half. She decided to call Detective Strahan and find out when that unfortunate woman near Salem was killed. She watched the figure in the video again. Almost impossible to tell how big or small the person was from the footage. Brian had nothing to gain by killing anyone. He was broody and sulked a bit, but he'd never shown signs of murderous behavior.

Suddenly, Lainey found herself questioning whether she knew the man at all.

"I can settle this with one phone call," she told herself. She picked up her cell and dialed Detective Strahan. She would ask him if there were any updates and see what else she could discover. She tutted when she was directed to his voicemail. The closet would have to wait.

It was six-fifteen when Brian ordered his grilled chicken with lemon and asparagus. He also treated himself to a local German fruit-flavored beer. The two-foot-high beer glass he received was embarrassing. Casually looking around at other tables in the hotel's fine restaurant, he felt marginally better when he caught sight of several other men with similarly overly-tall beer glasses. There was no sign of Veva, which he figured was because she'd fallen asleep as jetlag had finally caught up with her.

Brian used two hands to lift his glass carefully and sipped at the elderberry beer. The taste was sharp and fresh, and his lips appreciatively smacked together. His peripheral vision noticed the diners to his right were nudging one another. He presumed they were watching his attempt not to spill the contents over himself. Then he glanced again and saw that the attention was fixed beyond him, towards the restaurant entrance. He looked in the same direction as the other people around him and became slack-jawed as Veva approached from the maître-d's station.

She wore a tight little black dress that hugged her skin. It was matched with black spiked heels, stockings, and flapper-style shiny black hair. In her right hand, she carried a tiny black clutch purse. Veva no longer walked with her head facing the ground and shying away from the world, but her stride was confident, her head upright, and the sleeveless dress showed off her molded arms and toned thighs.

Brian rose from his seat, dropped his napkin on the table, and closed his mouth. He pulled out the spare seat. Veva courteously smiled as she carefully sat down, ensuring she didn't expose herself in the dress that was barely two inches beyond her butt cheeks. He pushed her seat forward until she acknowledged she was close enough to the table.

"You look a little different from the person running around Bremen earlier," he remarked and instantly regretted admitting he had noticed.

"I hope I'm not overdressed. I took a peek in here earlier, and everyone was dressed nice, having afternoon cocktails."

"I'd say you chose well," was Brian's limited response.

"Good. Your wife said I should show off more of what I've got."

"She did?"

"Yeah." Veva pointed at the tall glass between them and asked, "What is that?"

"A hangover in the making," Brian suggested as his eyes studied her. "Elderberry beer. Brewed on the other side of the city. It's got quite a punch." His gaze flitted over her exposed thighs and caught the thick edge of her thigh-high hold-up stockings.

"May I?" Veva pointed. Brian gestured for her to go ahead. Veva stood up and lifted the glass to her ruby-colored lips, taking a large sip. Her hips were only a foot away from Brian's face, and he could see the faintest trace of the thong she wore under the tight-fitting material. She sat back down and added, "Sorry I was late. I couldn't figure out the damn shower controls. I don't think my shower works properly."

"No problem, unless you consider you're our lead technical director and developer."

"I'm no plumber." Veva politely replied and then, referencing the beer, said, "I'm going to have one of those."

Brian tilted his head to suggest that she might want to reconsider. "I just ordered the chicken. I didn't think you were going to join me."

The waiter came and handed Veva a menu. She ordered the same elderberry beer and the orange grilled salmon in a white wine sauce. She asked the waiter, "How much alcohol is in this?'

"It is 7.5%, madam."

"You might have to carry me upstairs after this," she told Brian.

"I'll ask a porter to put us both on a luggage cart."

"Okay, but no elevator for me. They'll have to lug me up the stairs."

They ate together, chatting about the footage they'd captured. Veva explained to Brian how she'd been able to capture the fountains on her run. They both agreed Bremen would be an excellent addition to the portfolio.

Brian checked his 4D app and said, "Looks like we have twenty-seven volunteers coming tomorrow with their own GoPro's to run the course. So that should give us what we need."

"So long as the weather holds out. Heavy rain from lunchtime onwards," Veva replied.

By the time they'd eaten and finished their massive drinks, both were quite buzzed – Veva in particular. They spent time sharing details from their phones on places they liked to run, leaning shoulder-to-shoulder to view the pictures.

"I'll bet I can drink a second one," Veva goaded.

"No way. I'm not much of a drinker." He'd already spent too much time ogling Veva's thighs, where the hem of her dress had risen enough that the white skin was exposed above the line of her stockings. A couple of times, she'd uncrossed her legs, and he'd glimpsed the flesh of her inner thighs less than an inch from her crotch.

"I think you're only saying that because you're scared I'll beat you on tomorrow's group run." Veva half-rolled her eyes as she laid down the challenge.

"Another one of these beers, and I won't make it to the run," he theorized.

"Knew you were scared."

"There must be two pints in that thing." Brian watched her nonchalantly shrug her shoulders. "Alright, you're on. You'd better not sleep in or call off in the morning."

"I won't," she insisted.

It took them another forty minutes to get down the second massive beer, and in between, they each also had two shots of local cinnamon-flavored schnapps. Their conversation had long since moved away from running or business-related matters. They talked about sports, travel, and environmental issues, and Veva laughingly explained how she had twice seen Lainey stripped bare in the shower last week.

"How did she look?" Brian asked.

"Pretty hot for a girl," Veva affirmed.

140

"What would Lainey say about you?"

"I think she'd say my body needed more work to compete with hers." Veva chuckled at her suggestion. Her dark hair flopped onto the edge of the table as she rolled forward and straightened in her seat.

The more they drank and moved around, the more Brian saw flashes of stocking tops and, on a couple of occasions, the silky black triangle at the front of her underwear. He told himself not to look, but it was impossible. Veva's body was tight. More than once, he became aware of the swelling in his crotch. He reminded himself that he was the boss, and he must set a decent example.

Brian's head buzzed. Veva relayed how she had twice raced against Lainey. His eyes repeatedly glanced at her legs and between them as she provided some actions to her story. Once she finished, Brian went back to safer territory. "Why don't you send me your footage from today, and I'll review what you have. Seeing as you managed to capture the whole of Bremen," he teased.

"Why don't I show you what I have, and then I can cut out what you don't want. That way, I can send you a more manageable file."

The thought of being alone with Veva twelve hours ago was highly unappealing, but the alcohol and her outfit were tempting enough for him to quickly agree. "Okay, but it's getting late, and I need some sleep." So he gave himself a get-out alibi.

"It's only eight p.m.," Veva pointed out. She wobbled as she stood. "I'm giving Bremen five out of five stars on my Yelp review, and the same for this beer."

"You leave Yelp reviews?"

"Everywhere I go. And I read other people's too, to get an idea of where I'm going or what to do when I get there. I love Yelp," Veva slurred. "I've been using it since I was fourteen. It's one of my few obsessions. Some well-chosen words can benefit someone else's journey, don't you think?"

"If you say so."

"I use it back home anywhere I go or whatever I do, and I love being connected with others who do the same."

"I'm glad you found your people," Brian mocked.

"Pessimist," Veva bumped shoulders with him and took hold of his arm. "Don't let me fall. I don't normally wear heels. I'm always in flats because of my height, but Lainey said I should wear heels."

"We must all do as Lainey says."

They exited the restaurant and took the stairs together, laughing at their lack of coordination. Veva let go of his arm and ran a couple of steps ahead of him. "I can beat you on the stairs, too," she shouted as she went ahead.

Brian ogled her rearview. Her dress had ridden up, barely covering her firm cheeks. From behind, the view was highly appealing. But, inside his head, Brian talked himself down. He must be polite, be a good boss, and be a good husband.

In Veva's room, Brian was immediately uncomfortable sitting on the edge of her bed as she grabbed her laptop and began downloading the video from her earlier run. She bent over the desk opposite the bed, declaring, "It will only take a minute."

Brian forced the air from his top lip down over his chin as he made up his mind to quickly view the trail run and then immediately head next door. This was more than he could stand, and the swelling had returned in his crotch. He quickly adjusted himself to make himself comfortable and decrease any chance his erection might be visible through his trousers.

"I'm pretty sure I captured the fountain, the pavilion, and the banks of beautiful rhododendrons. They have a special park just for that," she explained, turning her head, and catching Brian staring at her. Veva acted as if she didn't notice. "Here, let's take a good look." She sat next to him and placed the laptop on his thighs.

Brian saw that the download was almost complete, with the gauge climbing steadily from 60 to 70%. Veva's hand tapped at the keyboard and brought up a photographic file. Using the pad, she selected the one titled 'Bremen.'

"I took some pictures earlier. I couldn't help it." She walked him through the dozen pictures, mainly from the balcony next to his. A couple was of her taking selfies, with her smiling face in the foreground and her straight white teeth on full display.

"I didn't know you could smile like that."

"There are lots of things you don't know about me."

"Like what?" A question, if sober, he would have never asked.

"If I told you that, you'd never travel with me."

"So, you say," he dangled the carrot some more.

Veva placed one hand on the top of his thigh, only an inch from where his erection rested. "Brian, I couldn't risk you repeating my secrets. God forbid I show you. You are a happily married man, after all." Her smiling face was only inches from his.

In the dim light, and with the fuzziness in his head, he had to stop himself from kissing her plump lips. "Your secrets are safe with me." He kept up the innuendo.

"I'm a girl who likes particular things." Veva sounded increasingly tipsy. "There are things I like to do that make me…unusual, I guess," she insinuated as she moved her hand across his leg. Her slender fingers overlapped the bulge in his trousers, and she flexed the ends of her fingers to feel it. Veva leaned closer and gasped, "I like that." Her smile was gone, and she stroked his length.

"Not a good idea, Veva." Brian cleared his throat. He could have moved away, but the electricity in the air compelled him to stay. He was already too far in, but that sudden sexual aggression from her had sparked something in him, and the needy groan she emitted suggested Veva would go further. He should stop.

Veva's fingers played with his erection. Her other hand removed the laptop, placing it behind them on the bed. "You never asked me my secrets."

"I'm not so sure I should." He made no effort to stop her.

Veva's top lip angrily arched as she looked him square in the eye, increasing his interest. "Then maybe I'll just show you." Veva rubbed through his trousers, sliding to her knees, keeping her head close to his crotch as she knelt on the carpet. Her steely gaze never left him. "You have a nice cock," she purred, sticking out her lips and pouting an inch from his flies.

"Veva, this is not a good idea." Brian pushed his hands firmly into the mattress to keep himself upright as he looked down on her. He should push her away.

Veva narrowed her eyes, opened her mouth, and leaned slowly forward, softly touching her upper and lower teeth on either side of his erection through his trousers. Her mouth edged down to the tip, making soft groaning noises as she teased him. "If you want me to stop, then leave. If not, you should watch in that mirror," she pointed to the full-length mirror next to the bed.

Brian followed her finger to their reflection. He saw himself sitting rigidly on the bed and Veva on her knees. Her dress had inched up, revealing the tops of her firm thighs, and her stockings on full display.

"Oh fuck," he gasped at the sight. A fantasy unraveling that could easily unravel his entire world. *Leave the room.*

Veva looked at the reflection and hitched up the dress to the small of her back, revealing the tiny black thong and her solid rear. She placed two fingers between her legs and began to rub her lips.

"I'm soaking," she purred as her hips slowly rotated, pleasuring herself in front of him. From the reflection in the mirror, Brian could only see the black string that arched over her hip and dipped into her buttocks.

"Keep watching," she encouraged.

He looked down at her, and she turned her face upward, looking into his eyes. The small triangle at the back of her black underwear was only an inch long before it turned to a string that cut between her cheeks and out of sight. "Oh fuck," he gasped.

"I'll show you what I really like to do," Veva cooed as her other hand drifted from his bulge and unzipped him. With ease, she unbuckled his belt, unclipped the metal fastener of his trousers, and pulled his fly open. Her hand went inside and stroked him through his underwear. "Oh my God, it's so hard," she whispered with admiring satisfaction. "Yummy. I like to swallow. Every drop," she pouted and kissed the material over his erection. "It's pulsing." She teasingly moaned as if he were keeping it from her. "I want your juicy cock in my mouth." Veva nibbled on him.

"We shouldn't be doing this," he feebly said. Every part of him knew he should have never entered her room. Nevertheless, he dared himself to see if she might flirt. Now he was on the cusp of betraying Lainey, their marriage, their whole life together, and himself. Veva's touch was delightful, and the little noises of satisfaction signaled that she wanted to do it, and all the while, he hated himself because he wanted her to do it.

"Veva," he desperately strained.

She looked into his eyes, keeping her long, wet tongue slowly teasing the edge of his swollen penis. Her light green eyes were filled with desire. "Watch in the mirror," she forcefully whispered. She tugged down his shorts, and his erection sprang upward.

Veva wrapped one hand around the shaft and stroked it, placing her pouty lips right at the tip. She tilted her head slightly sideways, meeting his gaze in the mirror. She stopped playing with herself, and with her other hand, she gently rubbed his testicles. "Stand up," she said.

"Oh, my God," Brian groaned as he got to his feet.

"Keep watching," Veva commanded. First, she pulled his underwear and trousers down to his ankles. Then, opening her mouth slowly, she ran her tongue and lips with great precision from the tip of his erection to the base of his testicles. All the while, she stared at him in the mirror, and he reciprocated. Her tongue slithered all over his swelling around the tip, and her lips caressed his skin.

"I want every drop," she gushed, turned her head toward him, and wrapped her lips over his shaft, moving up and down while playing with his balls.

"Mmm," she moaned over and over. Veva removed her lips from his pulsing member, "I want you to fuck my mouth. Do it," she insisted, sliding her mouth back onto his throbbing cock. She placed one hand on his buttocks and pulled his hips forward, so he began to pump himself into her mouth.

Once he was in a rhythm, Veva pressed her hand firmer to his cheeks, demanding he pump faster. She made satisfied noises and pushed her lips up and down over the head of his increasingly uncontrollable thrusts.

Brian's guilt and self-loathing evaporated as he placed a hand on the back of her head and thrust his erection in and out of her willing mouth. In the mirror's reflection, her body was arched so that her tight butt cheeks were sticking out, and the sight and sound of her demanding moans had him pumping harder, which quickly brought him to the point of no return.

At first, he was silent, but he groaned aloud after less than a minute and could not stop himself from saying, "Yeah, that's it," as he upped the momentum. Finally, her full lips around his trembling shaft were too much, and he told Veva, "I'm gonna cum."

Her hand pulled harder into his buttocks, signaling she wanted it all. Veva's other hand felt his balls tighten, and her moaning increased. His entire body was quivering as he spurted inside her mouth and all over her tongue. She kept her lips over his shaft, and once he'd stopped thrusting, she eased off and moved to his tip, using just her tongue to lick the end of his swollen dick.

"Mmm. I told you I like particular things." Veva tipped her head back and opened her mouth, with her tongue hanging out, so he could see his release on her tongue. "Every last drop." Her hand squeezed gently on his dying erection, and her tongue lapped up the last droplets of his semen. She finished by putting him back into her mouth and taking all of him so deep that her nose touched his pubes. After swallowing him whole several times, Veva stood upright, and Brian fell backward onto the bed.

"Oh fuck." He placed his right arm over his eyes. He kept his eyes closed, partly in disbelief at what he'd done, what she'd done, and also to hide his embarrassment now that it was over. "Is there anything you want me to do?" he guiltily asked.

"You just did," Veva replied as she poured herself some water. "What happens in Bremen stays in Bremen." She offered Brian the glass, which he readily accepted. Veva wiped her lips with the back of her hand. "You don't have to worry about anything. Once I've finished, my lips are sealed."

"So you say."

"My word is good."

"You are full of surprises," he replied.

"Bet I beat you on the run tomorrow."

"I'm not sure if I should take any more bets with you?"

"So, you say," she playfully tossed his line back at him.

CHAPTER FOURTEEN

Arriving back in Eureka, Detective Strahan felt no relief at being home. His time in Oregon was helpful with Detective Hurst, but there was no new evidence to put them closer to the killer. He had learned plenty about his new colleague, who was something of a highly functioning hot mess. She was methodical, insightful, provocative, and willing to share, but Strahan wished she could be less generous with her opinions. He guessed Hurst needed a high level of cutting remarks and foul-mouthed denigrations to survive through the years in their profession.

Being a female was tough in homicide, and to be successful in the role for so many years was even more brutal. The more Hurst was herself, the more she was exposed to ridicule and unwanted glances. Yet, as she pushed back on people, she seemed to enjoy herself more. He admired her fearlessness, if not necessarily her saw-toothed approach. Although she'd shown with Lainey Stewart that she could produce a full charm offensive even if it were a rarity.

So far, they hadn't clashed. Strahan focused on the productive, not wishing to give the opposing frequency a chance to flourish. He envisioned the good moments that he and Hurst shared and hoped similar experiences would be in abundance.

The body found in Prairie Creek Redwoods was still under wraps. Strahan would personally visit with Lainey and explain. His motives were more than some simple policing concern. The moment he'd first met her, she had held him captive. There was much he admired about Lainey, including her toughness. Few people would have dug themselves from the ground and stumbled through the forest to live.

He received her message last night, asking for an update. He had deliberately ignored returning the call, as only a face-to-face would be appropriate. Unfortunately, it would be tomorrow before he could get to her and perform one of the less desirable parts of his job. No matter how directly or delicately he put the news, it would be ill-received, and no wonder. He recalled the police psychologists assuring him that most people in Lainey's position would have remained under the earth. Her survival instinct was unquestionable, but this news would hit hard.

The snort from the passenger seat alerted him that Detective Hurst had nodded off. Her breathing was peaceful, and with her eyes closed, she looked much different than what he'd been exposed to. Moreover, there was a softness in her sleep that never appeared in her waking existence. Nevertheless, Hurst proved as good a detective as her record suggested, although her personality was like some blustery natural disaster.

When they met outside their motel rooms earlier, Hurst kicked out the young gothic woman for a second time. Hurst explained, "They like a bit of experience. I'm like a lesbian quarterback, where I can lead them around the field until we score the winning touchdown if you know what I mean." Strahan disliked the fact he knew exactly what she meant. At least Detective Hurst's sexual appetite matched her hunger for solving homicides.

It was challenging working alongside Hurst. She was engaging, as well as a provocateur. She liked to make Strahan squirm. But, once she was satisfied that he could take all her prodding and give her some back, she opened up. Strahan figured it was her way of releasing the pressure all detectives had boiling within. His approach to dealing with the workload and the demands for results was the polar opposite of Hursts. All cops needed an escape. The shit they dealt with daily was enough to send most ordinary people hiding under their therapist's couch and never coming back out. He considered it a psychologist's dream to get Detective Hurst on their couch for a few sessions. Enough for a strong thesis – or even a bestseller.

As Strahan pulled into the parking lot beside Eureka Police Headquarters, the car sprang on its suspension. Hurst jolted in her seat and opened her dark eyes. "No welcome committee?" she mumbled as she loudly yawned.

"We'll check in with my boss, and then we can go visit Lainey Stewart."

"What's your thoughts on what we found in Prairie Creek?" Hurst asked.

"Whoever found her has something to hide. Why else cover the body with soil like it had never been disturbed? All we have is an anonymous male caller from a payphone in north Eureka."

"Could have been a guy walking with a lover and doesn't want his wife to know they were playing nooky in the woods," Hurst suggested.

"Shame there's no cameras in that parking lot," Strahan thought aloud. "Whoever found the body must have parked there. There's no other way in. We've put out alerts for information, but it's a long shot." As he struggled with parking the car, he added, "Our guys said the earth was slightly compacted from the last couple of days of rain. It looks like someone waited a couple of days before calling it in. Why wait? It doesn't make sense, even if you were cheating on your spouse."

"I hear you. Somebody with something to hide, in more ways than one."

Strahan gave Hurst a suspicious glance, expecting her to follow up with a smart-assed comment. He was deflated when she remained quiet.

"The lab reports came in while we were driving. They're in my email."

Before he could say anything else, Hurst had taken his cell from the center console and opened his phone. "Got anything in here I shouldn't see? Like some dick-pics you sent one night after some tequila?"

"No. Just read the email," he said, hiding his agitation.

"You need to get out there more. A handsome guy like you should have some interesting adventures." Hurst smiled to herself. "Here, let's see…" She browsed his inbox and found the lab report for Daphne Montclair. "Looks like our girl Daphne was loaded with Digoxin."

"I knew it."

"Liver shows there was some alcohol in her bloodstream around the time of death, but nothing major. There's PCP. That's new. Probably used to put her out before she was injected with the Digoxin."

"Phencyclidine? It seems like our killer must have run out of Rohypnol. I wonder if we can get a trace on the type of PCP used and use that to narrow down the source."

"I was thinking the same thing. If our killer is buying their drugs in Eureka or Salem, it would suggest they might be local to that area. Unlikely you'd drive a few hundred miles just to buy drugs and risk dealing with folks you don't know."

Strahan parked and looked at Hurst. "Anything else in my emails I should know about," he flatly asked.

Hurst ran a suggestive tongue over her lips, deliberately going back and forth, humming, before she turned the phone at an angle where he could no longer see what she was looking at. "Well," her tone was suddenly playful. "Your subscription to ashleymaddison.com renewed, so you might finally get laid."

"Not happening."

Hurst straightened in her seat with her eyes laser-focused on his emails. "Really, you might want to look at this one." She passed him the phone, with her finger pointing at the email on the top. "Are you used to getting Japanese spam?"

"No." He thought she was joking. He was surprised to see an email from the Kyoto Police Department from Detective Shinji Kagawa. "Is this one of your friends in Salem dicking around," he asked. The title of the email read: Regarding your flower girls, please contact me asap.

"I swear it's not." Hurst raised her hands in surrender. "I might mess with you to pass the time, but I'd never waste time on a case."

Strahan could tell by her deadpan expression that she was serious. He looked back at the phone. "Could be someone clowning around."

"Give me his name and details, and I'll Google him," Hurst offered, producing her phone.

Strahan read aloud the Kyoto address on the email. Hurst got busy with her phone. "Some English translations aren't precise, but the message is clear enough. We'd better hope this is a joke, or this case just went international."

"Why, what's he saying?"

"He says they've found a dead girl buried in the Arashiyama Bamboo Forest, on the outskirts of the beautiful shrine of the sacred Tenryuji. Whatever that means. The body has the trademark signatures we reported from Oregon. So, he'd like to speak with me. Which means you – the lead detective," Strahan added with a smile.

"May I?" Hurst asked for his phone again. They exchanged phones, with Hurst reading the email while Strahan searched for Detective Kagawa.

150

"This guy's real, and he works out of Kyoto in Japan. If somebody's playing with us, they've gone to a lot of trouble. I'd pay to watch you have this conversation." Strahan suddenly enjoyed himself.

"You're not out of it, Dr. Watson," Hurst reminded him. "Asian guys like me. Always think they can turn me straight."

"Is that so?"

"Yeah, it might be a cultural thing? I'm not sure. Always fun, though." Hurst continued to read the email.

Strahan changed his search to Kyoto's news. A quick scroll revealed the headline-making his gut turn over. "Hey, get a load of this. They found the body of a young woman buried in the forest outside Arashiyama."

"Are you shitting me?" Hurst snapped.

"No. A different Google search. Listen," Strahan raised a hand for her to simmer down. "Kumi Shinnabe was found buried within ten meters of the famous walking trail, north of the city of Kyoto. Blah blah blah," he scrolled through the media report. "She was found serenely placed inside a body bag, holding a silk rose in her hands, with her hands folded over her body."

"We'll ask your boss about calling internationally," Hurst sighed. "I wonder if the same calling card was used."

"Oh, hang on. Here we go – Kumi Shinnabe is a Japanese Instagram fitness celebrity. She is famous for her online workouts, lingerie modeling, and her own line of clothing and make-up." Strahan passed Hurst her phone back. "That's our link right there."

"We'd better find out if anyone from here has been to Japan recently. Does it say how long she'd been dead or missing?'

"Not in that report. You'll need to ask our new international partner, Detective Shinji Kagawa," Strahan couldn't restrain the delight in his delivery.

Hurst swatted him on the shoulder. "Fuck you, pretty boy."

Lainey received a brief update from Brian, saying they were preparing to meet the volunteer runners to get the footage they'd need in Bremen. She messaged him back, wishing him and Veva the best of luck.

She'd been up earlier than usual, had breakfast, and had already completed a run on the treadmill. Her first online meeting was two hours away. She decided to do something nice for Brian, and it would be something worthwhile.

After a panic attack the previous night, where Lainey was spiraled downwards by those damned videos, she'd reassured herself that Brian had nothing to do with any murdered girls or the attempt on her own life. She hadn't heard back from Detective Strahan, a minor annoyance, but it indicated that everything was fine. Thousands of people owned 4D Fitness wear – so what. She would discuss what she'd seen with Brian on his return and be done with it.

Honesty was the key and not her silly assumptions. Brian was out there, doing the face-to-face and all the traveling. Lainey knew it was exhausting. Brian never complained and got on with business.

Lainey knew Brian hated clutter and thought it would be nice to clear out his old clothes and footwear. Lainey would do the same with her stuff. They had enough 4D Fitness wear in their closet to supply a brick-and-mortar store. She picked out most of Brian's clothes for him, as he was useless with fashion. Next, she would go through his stuff and bag what he no longer used. Then, sometime soon, she would do the same, although sorting through her collection could take a couple of days.

Lainey took some trash bags from under the sink, half a dozen boxes, and a roll of tape from the hall closet. There was a natural spring in her step as she bounded upstairs. Brian hated clutter, so this was a win-win. She often teased Brian about taking him clothes shopping and how much he hated it – the irony that was no longer a possibility hit hard.

Lainey sharpened his appearance with tailored jackets and smart jeans with nice leather handmade boots and shoes. Until this last year, she'd also taken charge of his grooming on all parts of his body. She still trimmed the hair on his neck and sometimes did the little bits on the top of his shoulders, too. There was something very satisfying about grooming her man. During their failed attempt at lovemaking a few days earlier, Lainey noticed that the hairs in his pubic region were no longer trimmed down to how she liked them.

Something to think about, as her sexual energy was on an upturn, and she had used her vibrator again last night. Any sexual inclination was an improvement from months of zero interest.

Lainey readied the boxes and bags. The closet had thirty feet of rails, filled mostly with her clothes, and the opposing shoe racks at the far end. Her footwear took up half of Brian's space, and he had at least thirty-plus pairs of dress shoes, boots, and mostly running shoes. She liked that he wanted to donate the 4D running shoes to charity. She was grateful to have such an understanding husband.

Lainey began with his jackets, trousers, and collared shirts. She knew the ones he rotated for work or business trips and those not used for months or more. Removing each one with care, she tied together those that needed a nice strong hanger, using the string from the trash bag to secure the garments. She created three bundles of a dozen hanging items, and then she got started with his jeans, shorts, t-shirts, and sweatshirts. She made a point to remove the dark blue hooded top, like the one she'd seen in clips from the two running trails. Although satisfied there was no connection; it somehow felt tainted. It went into a box, along with eight other hooded zip tops and several sweatshirts.

After an hour, she'd made excellent progress. With all the space she'd created, Lainey toyed with the idea of treating herself to an online shopping spree. Instead, she preferred Brian's suggestion that they could create a small meditation space, where Lainey could put in a trickling fountain and whatever other bits and pieces she wanted. A sanctuary sounded appealing. She'd already looked at different configurations, and Brian had estimated, based on how much of her clothing she was prepared to part with, that the sanctuary space could be the full twelve-foot width of the space and around ten feet deep. It could be cordoned off and had natural light from the raised side window.

Lainey could choose her own subtle lighting, and as Brian suggested, "Fill it with cushions, more cushions, small statues, candles, a nice rug, and all that other kitschy stuff that women seem to like so much." Lainey liked to think she had excellent taste. She'd fill it with cool ornaments, places for incense, and a little water feature, with surround sound to get deep into a meditative state. When Lainey described what she intended, Brian joked, "Once it's completed, you'll never leave the house again." She knew he'd said it jokingly, but she let him apologize and explain himself anyway.

"Yes, I need a meditation space," she convinced herself, excited at the prospect of re-designing the back of the closet. She began on Brian's footwear. First, she picked out some pairs of shoes he hadn't worn for at least two years. She inspected the soles and the upper leather, noting the near-perfect condition. Several pairs of his running shoes followed, with Lainey checking the tread of each shoe. 4D Fitness running shoes started at a minimum of $100 a pair, and someone would be pleased to get a bargain. She took more pairs from higher up in the custom-built shoe rack and finally got to the pairs at the top, having to stretch to reach them. "These can all go," she muttered.

The black and white pair she took from the upper rack came from their collection three years ago. "Aah!" Something fell from the right shoe and bounced off her shoulder. It happened so fast; she had no time to figure out what it was or get out of the way. It was far too big to be a spider. She looked at the small, filthy plastic bag on the floor. Lainey crouched next to it but didn't want to pick it up. "What the hell?"

She could see it was a Ziploc bag, with the outside covered in dry mud, giving it a filthy, crusty appearance. She wondered why the usually tidy Brian would have a dirty bag inside one of his running shoes. She poked it with her finger, trying to feel it. A bit more prodding convinced Lainey it was okay to look closer. She picked up the bag and slowly spun it around in her fingers. She felt a solid object inside, something round and hard. "What's he up to now?" Lainey placed it on the floor and carefully unsealed the plastic edges. Peeling open the two sides she tipped the contents onto the wood floor.

The bag may have been filthy, but the gleaming silver band, with a dozen tiny inlaid diamonds and a large central diamond, was unmistakable. Lainey slumped backward onto her behind, using one hand to steady herself to prevent herself from toppling over. The spasm in her lower body released some urine, dampening the front of her leggings. She reached out an extended index finger and turned the ring over. She saw the inscription on the inside: 'For Lainey.'

A hundred questions simultaneously hit her. The answers were incalculable, but it was the worst answers that clamored for attention. Lainey quickly turned on her butt, rose to her feet, and ran into the restroom, where she hurled her breakfast down the toilet. She had the presence of mind to hold back her ponytail as her body lurched a second time, and more foul liquid spurted into the bowl. She gasped for air and spat residual lumps of her soured, half ingested scrambled eggs. The rest of her body was in shock.

She spun around, yanked down her leggings, and sat on the toilet, as her bowels now demanded to empty. She picked up the small metal trash can, holding it in her lap, feeling like she would hurl again.

Her diamond engagement ring was here! "Brian?" she found herself spluttering as she dry-retched into the trash can. The spasm in her bowels released more diarrhea as her bodily functions collapsed. She ran her tongue all-round the inside of her mouth and spat out the residue.

"What the fuck!" Lainey told herself, "Be quiet, be still." She wiped herself, washed her hands, removed her pee-soaked leggings, and rinsed her mouth under the tap. She put on clean underwear and leggings and went back into the closet, where she stared at the ring on the floor.

"Double check it's mine." She thought maybe Brian had a copy of the original made and planned the ring as a surprise. He was thoughtful that way. The explanation must be a simple one. Why hide it? And why in a muddy plastic bag? "It doesn't make sense," she argued.

She forced herself to stop procrastinating and look at the ring. Lainey knew there was a tiny mark on the underside of her engagement ring, where she had once trapped her fingers when replacing a dumbbell into the rack. Apart from severe bruising, she'd scratched the silver and permanently scuffed it. Lainey took the ring to the doorway of the upstairs patio. She opened the door to get the maximum light and give herself some fresh air. Lainey found herself holding out her hands into the light. She turned over the diamond ring and burst into tears when she saw the scuffed silver.

She stumbled forward to her knees, and her forehead touched the wicker covering underneath the patio furniture. "Why?" she screamed. Sticky spit hung from her mouth. Her question was multi-layered: why did Brian have it, why didn't he tell her, why was he doing this?

Her despair came to an abrupt halt, as was typical with Lainey when anger took over. "Who the hell are you?" she asked, holding the ring out before her into the morning light.

The extent of her angry distress took Lainey a few seconds to realize she'd stepped outside. She was actually out in the open air!

She curiously observed the cute patio set as if she'd never seen it before. Then she raised her head and took in the valley view. There was no distress registering from her body or panic in her mind. Instead, a residual pain of betrayal coursed through her veins that shielded Lainey from the anxiety of being outside the house. She touched the patio furniture with her fingers, enjoying the texture. Then, she stepped back into the bedroom, not wanting to push her luck.

The gut-wrenching questions made Lainey unsteady as she staggered around, considering whether Brian had been the one who tried to kill her and took her ring. "But why would he keep my ring?" she asked herself. It had no significant monetary value. Plus, her wedding ring was left behind, as was her necklace.

"Not you, Brian, please, no," she stammered. How else could he have it? There was no doubt it was hers. Their wedding anniversary was coming up in two days. Did he somehow recover her ring and held it as a special gift?

Lainey dropped her butt onto the bed and stared at the shiny object in her hand. She looked around for her phone, wondering if she should call Detective Strahan again. She had to use both hands to straighten herself. Lainey was pissed that Brian had dissolved her earlier happiness. "I'll fucking kill you!"

She picked up the dirty Ziploc, placed the ring back inside, stuffed it back into the shoe, and set the pair back onto the top shelf. She replaced the pair next to them to make it look like she hadn't touched them. Until she could get answers, the ring must remain where she had found it. If Brian had anything to do with her attempted murder, the last thing Lainey wanted to do was let him know of her discovery.

The more she considered it, the more baffling it became. Brian could have found easier ways to bump her off. Lainey believed Brian was devoted to her and would do anything to please her. She'd always had a slight upper hand in their relationship, but Brian was the one who worked harder at keeping her happy and maintaining the peace. He was already a millionaire, the same as she was; there was no need for him to consider killing her for money. They were set for life, and business was good, with him giving his all.

The discovery only raised more questions, and Lainey was tired of not having answers. No matter how she looked at it, and no matter how wrong it felt, there was still the possibility that Brian may have tried to kill her. Then again, it didn't explain the girl Hurst and Strahan had traveled to Oregon to investigate. "Oh, my God," she groaned.

She checked the time and saw that she needed to get to her first conference call. Once she was done with that, she'd call Brian in Germany. It would be early evening for him and a good time to talk.

"What am I going to say?" Those words that spilled from her lips were ones Lainey had never found herself asking until now.

CHAPTER FIFTEEN

Brian consolidated most of the video data they'd received from those who had come out to run in Bremen. Only fifteen people had showed up, mainly because the weather had threatened to rain all morning. He'd been cordial with Veva, although they'd barely had time to converse about anything. There was no way he could avoid her. She did not comment on the previous night or give any curious signs about their liaison. Veva did her part to organize the runners. It was quite a relief that Veva acted as if nothing had happened between them. Brian locked himself away in his room to assure some respite, but it did not alleviate his conscience.

His guilt was like a debilitating weight pushing down his neck and shoulders. Brian knew it served him right. Veva had beaten him on the run, as his body was groggy with the alcohol from the night before. He'd defeated himself in all manner of things. Veva ran like she'd not touched alcohol the night before and finished two minutes ahead of him. The first thing she did was publish it via the 4D online user's Facebook Group. When Brian staggered over the finishing line, Veva informed him, "I've already got eighteen likes for beating my boss on the run." Brian didn't find any of it likable. Insult to injury, and all of it self-inflicted.

He reapplied his focus on getting the videos uploaded into their system and having the tech group make adjustments before the presentation for German investors tomorrow. The initial presentation would be shown in a demonstration, but they would have enough Bremen footage to make a profound impression.

Alone in his room, Brian wrestled with his reckless actions. He was certain Lainey would call him, having found out what a useless lying piece of shit of a husband he was. Lainey was adamant that infidelity was unforgivable.

If Veva told his wife, then divorce was a formality … if Lainey didn't kill him first.

"Stupid, stupid," he hissed for at least the fiftieth time. He didn't ask Veva to dinner and instead chose to dine alone via room service. Having found Lainey's ring, leaving that poor girl's body in the ground, and climaxing in Veva's mouth, Brian frosted his shit-laden cake. He stopped what he was doing every few minutes as he drifted into a daze, with terrible flashbacks of the corpse in Prairie Creek Redwood Forest. It was swiftly followed by thoughts of Veva working her lips on him. Worst of all, he found the recollection of thrusting into Veva's face unbelievably exciting.

All these things slashed like razored edges into his psyche. Interchanging images of Veva's tight body were swamped by the pale dead girl's face with her lifeless eyes staring at him from the shallow grave. Trying to close the eyelids on a corpse was sickeningly difficult.

"Oh geez, get out of my head," he agonized. He could not fathom why Veva had become so sexually appealing when, previously, Brian never looked twice at the mousey director. He tried to rationalize that it must have been the alcohol and his yearning for sexual contact. Veva's openness fueled a fascination within him. Brian hated that she'd become a source of intrigue in any capacity. Mostly he hated himself.

"Fucking jerk." His self-summation was the only thing he'd gotten right these last few days.

The loud knock at his door caused him to jump. He walked to the door and peeked through the spyhole. Veva was standing outside, staring straight into his eyes. "Oh, no."

Brian had to be respectful and cautious to make sure he did nothing to upset her. He partially opened the door and smiled politely. "Hi."

"Don't worry; I come in peace."

She was wearing one of the long, white hotel bathrobes, with her bare legs sticking out of the bottom and nothing on her feet. "I'm trying to get the last of the data uploaded and run a quick analysis on it," he said, making an excuse to get rid of her.

"No need – I already finished it." She held up her laptop in one hand. "Thought we could run the analysis together before sending it over to the Eureka team. Don't worry! I haven't been drinking. I think we'll both be safe."

Brian's reluctance to be alone with her was quashed by his fear that rejecting her friendly approach could lead to trouble. Moreover, he was perfectly sober, which would be good enough to avoid further trouble. So he opened the door and stepped aside.

"One second, I need to pee," he said. He ducked into the bathroom and splashed cold water over his face. He stared at his hollow reflection. "Don't you fucking dare," he warned himself.

While he was there, Veva quickly opened Brian's black jacket and dropped something into the inside pocket. She straightened the jacket on its hanger and sat on the end of the bed. She opened her laptop and patiently waited.

Brian flushed the toilet and joined her in the room. "I'd offer you a drink, but…" he gave a resigned shrug and a fake grimace.

Veva understood. "I'm good, thanks; besides, we can't have me beating you on another run, can we?"

"Once was enough," he conceded.

Immediately a heavily woven atmosphere provided the potential for anything to happen. Brian wanted to keep it strictly about work and not have any more time with innuendos or conversations that could produce conflict.

"How did you compress all the files so quickly and pull them together?"

"That's one of the reasons why you guys hired me," Veva replied matter-of-factly. She took him through her work, and they spent an hour reviewing various points of interest they wanted the onsite Eureka team to focus on. Finally, Veva downloaded the final version onto the server, shut her laptop, and headed for the door. "Sleep well," she said wistfully.

"It's only seven p.m.," he responded. She said nothing and left his room.

Brian locked the door and breathed a massive sigh of relief. He wanted to raise the subject of the previous night, to at least confirm that their awful secret would remain so, but he was afraid to push it. Being in the hands of someone else and not knowing the outcome was a worrying new experience. The part of Brian that sickened him the most was the slight anticlimactic feeling that they did not have wild sex. His lustful desires showed him the adventurous Veva on her knees and him watching in the mirror. The flush of excitement in his groin added a further self-loathing.

His cell lit up with Lainey's picture. "Be cool," he told himself. "There's no way she knows."

Strahan sat quietly, listening to Detective Hurst argue with his captain. She insisted the case should remain firmly in the hands of her and Strahan. It wasn't like his captain suggested they hand control over to the Kyoto team, but Hurst pilloried everyone and everything as if threatened with giving up the case. It was a sign of her pride and desire to maintain a high success rate. As he listened to Hurst's continued argument, he played with his phone, scrolling through emails.

A message entitled: WATCH ME – FROM A FRIEND caught his eye. Strahan opened the message, and there was a video player attached. He pushed himself back into the couch in the captain's office, muted his phone, and pressed play. The scene showed someone in a dark, blue-hooded top, scratching in the dirt in the woods. It only lasted a few seconds and skipped to a similar scene, with the same person in a different woodland setting doing a similar thing. Both clips were only seconds long. There was a pause before a third clip showed the back of a man with short, dark brown hair, wearing gray shorts, black-hooded top, scratching in the dirt. Strahan almost leaped from his seat as he immediately recognized the woodland space as the crime scene they'd just visited at Prairie Creek. The last clip did not reveal the man's identity and was only seven seconds long. The third clip ended with the words: God and his Angels are merciful to all.

He watched it again.

Strahan stood. "Hurst, captain, sorry to break things up, just when you guys were getting along so well. You have to see this. It was in my email. We'll need to trace where it came from. It must be from the killer." He put his cell on the captain's desk and waited for them to huddle in close. Strahan pressed play.

Hurst exclaimed, "The prick is taunting us." She ended the link with the Japanese homicide team.

The captain picked up his phone. "I need someone in my office right now to trace an email," he barked and slammed down the phone.

Strahan eyeballed Hurst. "You remember when we were in Stassel Falls in Oregon, and you looked at me like I was crazy when I was feeling one of the trees near the burial site? I only looked at it because there was a slightly different texture. When I touched it with my fingers, a small part of the bark was smoother than the rest. I didn't think much of it at the time." Strahan rewound the video to the clip taken from Stassel Falls with the blue-hooded figure kneeling in the dirt. "See the camera's angle, in line with the direction of the burial, from head to toe? Whoever took the video had their camera secured to the tree. The same tree where I touched the bark."

"They had something wrapped around the tree trunk to hold the camera?" Hurst asked.

"I guess so. I didn't notice anything in Prairie Creek, but the angle would suggest something similar was used. We need to get back up there and take a look."

"What about visiting Lainey Stewart?" Hurst reminded him. "We need to go see her before the news breaks." Hurst pointed at his inbox. "You've just received another email from those assholes in Japan."

"Probably asking why the hell we cut them off," he suggested.

"Fuck those guys," Hurst twisted her face.

Strahan opened the email and paraphrased, "Detective Kagawa said they are sure it is the same killer or at least the same style. He wants us to contact him asap. Let's see what he attached." Strahan opened the PDF file, and the picture of a white business card with a rose floral motif and the words; "Let them praise the name of the Lord" were neatly typed across the middle. "It's printed in English, not Japanese." He passed his phone to Detective Hurst.

She snatched it from his hand. "Son of bitch. It has to be the same guy. It says: '3 of 7'."

Strahan cut in, "Lainey was 1 of 7. Elizabeth Seguras in Oregon was 2 of 7, Kumi Shinnabe, the girl in Japan, was 3 of 7, and Daphne Montclair in Prairie Creek was 4 of 7. Three more to find or prevent."

"Then what the hell are you standing around here for?" the captain asked. "Go on, get moving." He emphatically swept his arm toward the door.

"Can you tell us when we get the trace from Strahan's emails?" Hurst asked the captain

"Yeah, I'll get you both coffee and donuts, too," the captain scornfully replied. "Get out!"

"You're so sweet," Hurst called back at him from the middle of the office. She blew him a kiss over her shoulder once all eyes were on her. She did not see the one-fingered salute that he returned, nor did she care. "We'll see Mrs. Stewart and return to Prairie Creek. See if your tree-hugging theory rings true."

"If it does, we can be sure we're dealing with only one person, or there'd be no need to strap the camera to a tree."

"I know there isn't much content, but did you see anything that struck a chord?" Hurst asked.

"Not much. In the third video clip, we've got a single white male. In the first two, the person placed something in the dirt. Looks like a small cross of some description. We'll need to see it enhanced to be sure. We haven't found anything at our three sites. Maybe Detective Kagawa in Kyoto has something," Strahan theorized.

"A crappy attitude," Hurst snappily replied. They walked briskly from the Police headquarters. "I'll drive. You play with your phone on the way there and see if you can produce anything else."

"I'm going to email Kagawa and ask them not to go public with the floral business card. We should keep that piece back. I wonder if Miss Shinnabe had her nails manicured like the others?"

Lainey was about to hang up when Brian answered. "Hi, how's it all going over there? How are you?" she asked.

Brian cleared his throat, and his face turned purple with the rush of guilt-ridden heat coloring his cheeks. "Bremen is just like we expected, clean with beautiful parks, and every building along the trail has some kind of significance. It will all look good once we complete the edits."

"Nice. And how are you?"

Brian detected the subtle sharpness in her tone. "I'm okay, thanks—a little jetlag. Europe always gets me a little bit that way. And you?"

"As good as I can be," She skillfully hid the trepidation in her voice. "The Irish investors came back to us. I might need you to spend a couple of days in Dublin. Not a big market, but some possibilities." Lainey switched hands since her right hand was shaking. "Prague looks like they're going cold, so I'll let you know tomorrow. It could give you three days back. Veva can fly back here while you go to Ireland."

"Sure. Keep me posted."

"And how's our Veva doing?"

Brian guessed he would surely receive both barrels any minute and that Veva had called Lainey and confessed. "She's doing okay. She finished the data compression and said she would send it to the tech team. So they should have it any minute."

"She beat you on the run by quite some margin. Are you okay? I can't believe Veva took you like that."

Brian delayed his response, believing it was a baited question. "I um…I think I was just tired, and getting the runners organized was hard, with the language barrier, and even though the German people were amazing and so excited, it was like trying to corral a bunch of wild chickens."

"Don't let her beat you again. How's the food?" Lainey switched subjects.

"Food is good, service is great, and I know I've said it before, but it sucks traveling without you." Brian waited for the inevitable.

"Are you sure you're okay – you sound weird. Is there something you're not telling me?"

Brian's voice faltered, and he coughed hard. "I think…"

Lainey's phone showed the incoming call. "It's Detective Strahan calling me. I'd asked him to call me after they found a body in Oregon. Let me call you back, Bye."

Brian was only seconds away from telling her of his shameful actions. It wasn't Veva's fault. Sure, she'd dressed up sexy, and they were both drunk, but Brian knew he was fully responsible and could have easily walked away. A woman should be able to dress sexy and not be hit upon by the man she's having a business dinner with, especially her boss. The cliche was so disgusting it made him want to puke. The blame was his. They would have to release Veva from her duties and pay her off. No way Lainey would let her work in the business. Once Lainey was done with someone or something, there was no going back. Brian's sickness increased, thinking he'd have the same result.

Lainey listened as Detective Strahan explained that he and Detective Hurst were back in Eureka, and he was sorry they hadn't called her earlier. He asked if they could stop by, as it was the only chance they'd get to speak with her for the next few days.

"I can postpone my next call for an hour," Lainey offered.

"Good. We'll see you in ten minutes," Strahan replied.

Lainey went downstairs and decided to make a fresh batch of green tea. She knew Strahan liked his Yoga, organic foods, meditation, and all things Zen and guessed the tea would be appreciated. Lainey toyed with how she could work the story of the ring she'd discovered into the conversation without telling them she had it or how it came to be in her house.

Two miles northwest of the Park Hotel in Bremen, the tall apartment building on the Geihler Strasse was quiet. Anyone walking the stairs or down one of its long corridors could not detect a sound from any of the hundred-plus luxury apartments. Set back from the main road and on its own grounds,

165

the five-story building folded into a horseshoe configuration, with woods on one side and traditional terraced housing opposite. On the top floor of the newly refurbished apartment building, Marlene Durr was lying on her bed, her body immobilized, and her eyes were blinking hard at the circular pattern she had designed on her ceiling.

She hazily recalled drinking in a nearby wine bar what seemed only a short time ago. She couldn't understand why her unresponsive limbs ignored her command to get off the bed. The bedroom was silent, and the same inside her apartment. She tried shaking herself, guessing she must be asleep, trapped in some strange dream. She managed to move her neck and noted the time on her bedside clock read 9:48 p.m. She wasn't able to flex her fingers or wiggle her toes. She became scared out of her wits, noting the knee-length white silk chemise that covered her. Its lacy trim was something Marlene would never have purchased. She'd been stripped – but why? Her fingernails were freshly painted with a floral motif on her index fingers. Her hands were loosely folded over her abdomen.

The quiet was interrupted by the toilet flushing from the nearby bathroom. Marlene cranked her head in that direction. "Timo is that you?" she asked, her voice barely able to push the words from her lips. She didn't recall drinking heavily, but her speech was slurred and heavy. She'd been talking English with someone but couldn't recall why. Timo did not reply.

A voice hummed a tune as water trickled in the sink. "Timo, this is not funny," she struggled to convey. Her long-time boyfriend liked to play lame practical jokes on her, but surely even he wouldn't go to these lengths. Marlene began to cry as she realized the tone wasn't Timo's, and she'd not seen him since yesterday. Instead, she had dined alone in a neighborhood bistro. There was a stranger she'd met at the bar. They'd talked. There was a kindly face and playful mannerisms, but the exact features were blurry like an evening mist.

The water stopped running, and the humming became louder as the bathroom door opened. A darkened figure appeared. The only light source in the room was a solitary candle in the corner. Marlene saw the figure pull on black gloves. "No," she begged.

The hooded figure approached and sat beside her. The dim light shadowed most of the face, with only a pair of bright brown eyes visible. A gloved hand took hold of hers. The gaze was filled with a soft love, as though coming from her late mother or dear sister. "What do you…"

166

"Sssh," the figure interrupted. "Save your strength. It won't be long. I will sit with you and pray over you."

"Who are you?" Marlene asked, finding speech increasingly impossible.

"I'm an angel sent by God to take away your pain. Don't worry; you'll soon be an angel, too. I know everything. We both know your boyfriend is a cheat – that he uses you, uses drugs, and whores. Since your mom died, you've been alone, and your sister has abandoned you because of your career choices."

"No," Marlene protested, but she could not force her throat to say more.

"At first, I nearly missed the chance to help you. Your Instagram and YouTube showed a happy girl doing something she believed in. It's good to encourage other girls to work out and be fit. You're being rewarded for that. But, unfortunately, the other things I discovered on your Patreon account told me of your unhappiness." The figure sympathetically and lightly squeezed her hands.

"My life is good," Marlene choked on her words.

"No, it is not," the figure argued. "The sex acts you perform and what your boyfriend does with you on behalf of those who ask too much. This nice place that you've bought doesn't atone for the way you've degraded yourself for the pleasure of others. We both know Timo is out whoring with the money you made. Yet, you sit here silently suffering. Where is the goodness in that?"

"Please don't," Marlene sobbed. "We are to be married."

"He's not worthy of you. I'm setting you free from the pain." The figure bowed its head. "It is not for me to condemn you but to liberate you. I will ask the angels to welcome you for eternity. Let them praise the name of the Lord, for he commanded, and they were created."

The brown eyes suddenly burst open with excitement. "Listen! Do you hear them? They're calling you. Take care, my sweet girl."

CHAPTER SIXTEEN

Detective Hurst sat on the edge of the couch, holding Lainey's hand and, in her other hand, using a table mat to fan Lainey's face. "Just take it easy," Hurst gently encouraged as she fanned the shattered Lainey.

"I can't. I can't." Lainey blustered, unable to finish her thought, as her breath labored. The moment Strahan described finding the body in Prairie Creek, Lainey's legs had buckled, and she was left clinging to the countertop. He was the one who caught her before she slipped to the floor.

"In through your nose, slowly and deeply, and out through your mouth," Hurst encouraged. She demonstrated several times, pinching Lainey's fingers to let her know she was doing fine.

Detective Strahan looked on from the kitchen as he filled a glass with water. He took a large gulp from the glass and refilled it. Hurst's proximity to Lainey made him strangely uneasy. Detective Hurst sidled herself up against Lainey. His partner looked too comfortable, which was more than could be said for Lainey.

He came alongside the couch. Hurst took the glass from him and held it to Lainey's lips. "Nice and easy. Just sip it." She softly returned Lainey's head to the cushion. Lainey tried to sit upright, but Hurst forced her to remain still. "Not yet. Let's make sure your brain has enough oxygen. Just give it a minute, and then we'll get you on your feet."

"I have to be…you know," Lainey chuntered, chewing on her lip and her eyes darting around the room.

"I know. Just take it easy for one minute." Hurst took Lainey's hands together, "Here, let's do this," she said. Hurst moved Lainey's hands over her heart and kept them there. "That thudding in your chest needs to be a steady beat, or you might blackout. Let's focus back on breathing," she suggested.

Lainey nodded, closed her eyes, and breathed deeply through her nostrils as Hurst guided her.

Strahan noted Hurst was dangerously close to having her hands all over Lainey's ample chest. He considered his colleague's reputation drove his interpretation along with jealousy.

"Lainey, I'm going to call Brian," Strahan said.

"No. Don't. He's in Germany. It's after ten o'clock at night there; he'll be in bed. I'll call him tomorrow. There's nothing he can do."

Strahan observed there was no sign of Lainey's new employee. "Where's Veva? Is there someone we can call to sit with you? Your mom?"

"Definitely not! And Veva is in Germany with Brian. I'll be okay in a minute."

Hurst had Lainey sip some more water.

"Do you have kids?" Lainey asked Detective Hurst.

"No. I once had my late sister's kid. It was tough being a cop and raising a four-year-old. It didn't work out as I would have liked. That was over twenty years ago," Hurst explained.

"You seem like you know what you're doing." Lainey felt helpless, like a little girl.

"I think it's in our instincts as women to know what to do. Especially woman to woman."

"I can't have kids," Lainey said.

"But you'll always have a mother's love within you. As women, we know when to love and when to fight."

Hurst's comment got Strahan's further attention. Hurst sounded like she was laying the groundwork for making a move on Lainey. He sat on the arm of the nearby chair. "Are you sure there's no one you want here with you?"

"No, I'm good," Lainey insisted.

"Stay lying down. We also need to tell you that we may have another victim in Japan. We've yet to confirm that. Detective Strahan and I are going from here to conduct an online meeting with our international partners. We want you to be aware of it now so that if it turns out there's a connection, you won't have any further surprises."

"Where in Japan?" Lainey asked.

Hurst gave Strahan the nod to provide details.

"A place called Kyoto."

"Arashiyama," Lainey said.

"How did you know?" Hurst asked, placing her hand over Lainey's heart.

"We have a trail there in our database offering. I ran it myself on the treadmill last week. Oh, God, no," Lainey groaned, folding her knees towards her body.

"Hey, it's okay," Hurst whispered. "We'll find the person responsible."

Lainey had questions, but agony stunted her speech. In the recesses of her mind, she feared that she already knew who the killer was. The locations of the bodies alongside their digital running trails, finding her engagement ring, and Brian had just returned from Japan. Lainey's heart and stomach excruciatingly fluctuated.

Both detectives noted Lainey's painful reaction. Anyone who'd seen Lainey on the cover of a magazine or TV interview could easily be forgiven for thinking she was some rich go-getter who was truthfully rude. But, on the other hand, Strahan witnessed her compassion, and now detective Hurst saw Lainey's acute connection to these unfortunate young women.

There was something else, too. The way she rolled around, grunting as if stabbed in the gut and having to be held down by Detective Hurst. It was out of character. This was not the time nor place to push too hard. Lainey's temper was unpredictable, and she might kick them out of her house. She'd done it with therapists, reporters, and even her mom.

"Take it easy." Hurst had both hands on Lainey's shoulders. "Lainey, I need you to focus. You're perfectly safe. Detective Strahan and I will…"

"Safe!" Lainey yelled at the female detective hovering over her. "Nobody's fucking safe! Bodies are showing up everywhere." She pointed a finger toward the glass sliding doors. "I wouldn't be surprised if there's one buried in my yard. Are there any more?"

"Not that we know of." Hurst tried keeping her still.

"Lainey, we have a twenty-four-hour watch on your house. You're safe," Strahan added.

Lainey pushed a hand into Hurst's ribs, signaling her to move. "I am fine," she growled. Sitting upright, Lainey brushed past the detective. She drank half the water and slammed the glass on the coffee table. "Is there anything else I should know?" Her fierce gaze pinged between the detectives.

"Yes, there is," Hurst replied, standing upright. She straightened the sleeves on her jacket, covering up her skinny wrists. "What we've shared with you is in the strictest of confidence. Please keep it that way, or you'll have to answer to me," her tone was no longer friendly. "Make sure you check in with the patrols as we've asked, and if there's anything that you think might help us, let us know. It's a murder investigation, and neither you nor anyone else should impede it." Hurst stressed the last phrase with menace.

Lainey glared at the tall female who'd flipped from being like a caring big sister to her virtual accuser. "I'll do that." The firm tone was reciprocated.

"Good. I'd hate to waste your time, as well as ours. But, we're getting closer to catching this person, and we will." Hurst turned to Detective Strahan. "Okay, let's be on our way."

"Thank you, Lainey; we'll be in touch," Strahan said and followed his partner to the door.

"Detective Hurst," Lainey shouted after the detective. She waited for Hurst to turn around. "Thank you for your honesty."

Hurst nodded her head, and the detectives left the house.

Lainey drank more water and walked to the front window, watching them drive towards the gates. Nobody liked terrible news, but Lainey hated bad news dressed up as something controllable. She liked that Hurst was straightforward. "Cantankerous old bitch," Lainey appreciatively noted.

Strahan asked his partner, "Are you okay?"

"She's hiding something. You saw it, too. Our jobs are hard enough without our only witness jerking us around. We'll return," Hurst assured.

It was 6.30 a.m. when Brian knocked on Veva's door. He was surprised to find her already dressed in running clothes and ready to go. He was dressed in his exercise clothes and about to run the same circuit as they had the day before.

"Hi, I wanted to let you know that Prague fell through. Lainey emailed me. I'll be going on to Dublin tonight. They've changed your flight so you can go back to San Francisco this afternoon. You'll be home by mid-afternoon Pacific time."

"Aw. shame I wanted to see Dublin. I always wanted to do a tour of the Guinness factory. and see Trinity College – I'm a big fan of Oscar Wilde."

"Yeah, well, I wanted to let you know. I'm heading for a run."

"Mind if I join you? I'm about to do the same."

"Sure." Brian failed to disguise his hesitancy.

"Brian. What's done is already forgotten as far as I'm concerned. A moment of madness, great fun, but done all the same. Can we go forward as if it never happened? I don't want there to be any awkwardness between us."

"Works for me."

"Good. I'll get my GoPro."

They ran hard around the same circuit, with Brian finishing half a minute ahead of Veva. Their only contact was a high-five when they returned to the hotel before heading into separate rooms.

It gave some slight relief from the immediate pressure of discovery for Brian, but his conscience remained shattered. He was glad to be heading to Dublin on his own. Before getting in the shower and preparing for their next in-person meeting, Brian took a quick check of his emails. His mouth slipped open, and his tongue went dry as he noticed the same style of the capitalized and bold headline he'd seen last week. YOU SHOULD BE MORE CAREFUL.

Brian forgot all he was supposed to be doing as he opened the video link. This time he readied his cell and began to record, presuming the link and email would fizzle away like last time. He followed the link, this time to a server where the language surrounding the media player was all swirls, curls, and symbols, in some kind of Arabic. He pressed play, and the words appeared on screen; YOU KNOW THE PLACE.

The scene showed a small burial mound in a woodland. All of it looked familiar. After a few seconds of nothing, Brian came into view of the camera, stepping carefully forward, poking the stick into the ground before him. It showed him kneeling beside the corpse. A message appeared, telling him the video and email would disappear.

He staggered backward from the desk and fell onto the bed, grasping at the sheets to avoid slipping onto the carpet. He dropped onto his back on the bed and stared at the ceiling. "Oh, shit," he whimpered. He'd walked into a trap in Prairie Creek Redwoods. There must have been a covert camera in one of the trees, the one he'd leaned his back against. The video clearly showed his face.

The killer had trapped him. No one else knew where that girl was buried. He was done for if the killer sent the video to the police. "Ah, Jesus Christ! You stupid fool." His recent actions were regrettably pathetic. He'd cheated on his wife, taken a ring from the fingers of a dead girl that he left buried in the ground, and now he'd made himself the lead suspect in a murder case. Ten days ago, life was about bearable, but now he'd taken a bad situation and somehow transformed it into a living hell.

"You fucking idiot," he sighed. His heart rate was sky-high as his world disintegrated. Thoughts of life in prison circulated in his head. Brian was tall and athletic and a non-combative, middle-aged white male. Prison would be harsh on him in every respect. He'd seen those prison movies and was sure he'd be somebody's bride in a six-by-eight space. "How do I get out of this?"

The knock at his door startled him, and his body's instinct took over. He feared it might be the police coming to put him on a plane back to the US. A look through the spyhole showed Veva in her dressing gown. His head dropped to his chest. There was no way he could cope with her right now. She

173

knocked again, but harder this time. He tried to show a relaxed face as he partially opened the door.

"Brian, I'm sorry, but I swear, my shower is broken. I had problems with it before, but I was too lazy to report it. Can I use yours? I'll only be a minute. I know you need to be ready for the meeting as well."

He noticed Veva had her work clothes and a towel hanging over her arm. "I swear I'm not here for anything else if that's what you're worried about."

"No, that's not it. Everything is fine," he lied. "Go right ahead. We start the presentation in an hour."

"I'll be quick." Veva smiled. She pushed open the bathroom door and said, "Want to join me?"

"I err…"

"I'm joking. Don't worry," she laughed and closed the bathroom door.

A moment later, Brian heard the water rushing from the shower. He seated himself on the bed. He replayed the video from the recording on his cell phone. The email and video link on his laptop were already gone. It occurred to him that what he recorded was self-incriminating. He had no way to prove he'd pulled it from an unknown source. He deleted it into his trash items and left it there. At least if anyone took him in for questioning, he could easily remove it and make a call to his lawyer.

His cell rang. "Hey," he unenthusiastically responded.

"You'll never guess what I've just heard." Lainey's opening words were hostile.

"By whom?"

"By Detective Hurst and Strahan, that's who."

Brian waited, but Lainey kept quiet. He was sure news of him scratching in the dirt had come through, and likely he was being framed for murder.

"Well…" Lainey impatiently prompted him.

"Well, I don't know. They could have told you anything." The thought suddenly occurred to Brian that maybe it was good news, and all this shit could be left behind them. "They caught the person who tried to kill you."

"No. They couldn't catch their own shadows," she spat down the line. "Another body found here in California; Prairie Creek this time. Same pattern as whoever left me for dead, but this time they succeeded. And now they're speaking to someone in Kyoto about a body found in the woods."

"But we have running trails in those places," Brian stammered. "I just left Kyoto the other week." Finally, his leg strength completely deserted him, and he slid to the carpet.

"I know!" Lainey shouted. "Every one of these has something to do with us. Like somebody's playing with us."

"Playing with us," he repeated. "All the places where you can run in our system." His elongated thoughts were hollow.

"I know – that's what I'm telling you!" Lainey exasperatingly snapped.

Brian paused as he heard Veva singing in the shower. Her tone was light and high as she sang some old Frank Sinatra tune. He cupped his hands around the phone and turned his back to prevent the sound from getting to the speaker. "You think somebody is targeting us because of our business?" he asked. Brian was desperate to have Lainey do the talking so he could mute the phone on his end.

"What are you talking about? I was the first target, in case you'd forgotten!" she roared. "Are you still there?"

"Yes."

"Oh, the line sounded like it was dead. What are you doing?"

"About to get showered and prepare for the presentation. Why'd you ask?"

"You sound stressed," Lainey forced herself to quieten her voice.

"Of course I'm stressed! Dead bodies are showing up around our business. I worried about my wife, and we need to make an impression in an hour. This could be big or could be the end." Brian immediately muted the phone.

"Have you got the TV on in the background?"

"Yeah, let me turn it down," he said, unmuting and muting again as he switched on the TV and got some volume to where hopefully it drowned out any noise from Veva's singing. "Is that better?"

"I suppose. Brian, do you know how bad this will be for us? Journalists will put two and two together and ask why women are being killed and buried beside the running trails in our digital offering. How do I answer that?" Lainey violently shook with anger and was faced with the possibility that the man she loved, admired, and trusted could be a killer. An unthinkable thought.

"I don't have an answer. Could be some sicko who purchased from us and decided the locations were suitable. How would I know?"

"Do you know?" Lainey couldn't stop herself.

"Lainey, we've said some stupid shit to one another during this last year. There's a lot I'm ashamed of for what I've said or done, but you just beat everything. Really, Lainey, really?" Now it was Brian with the anger in his tone. "You of all people would ask me that. Bad enough, the police have asked, but…argh," he groaned like he was in agony.

Lainey held herself from screaming down the phone to tell him that she'd found the engagement ring. There was some residual loyalty to Brian, the man she knew, or thought she knew, that told her there's no way this could be him. They shared an uncomfortable silence—another of many spartan moments they'd shared in the last year.

Brian stared at the TV, and although the news was in German, he quickly recognized that the line of police cars, ambulances, and news media were by the boating lake just north of the hotel. It was only half a mile from his hotel room. An overhead shot from a helicopter showed a body being lifted into the back of an ambulance. The exact spot he and Veva had run past three times in three days. From somewhere, he found the strength to stand and look out the window. In the distance, he saw the army of blue flashing lights. He was instantly afraid. "Oh Christ," he exclaimed.

"That's it?" Lainey replied. "We have all this going on, and that's all you can say." She waited for a response. "Brian, are you there?"

It was clear from the early morning Bremen news that a woman's body had been recovered from the park area nearby. Brian recognized the other landmarks from the report, showing the music pavilion, the large stone fountain, and the petting zoo. "I'm here," he muttered.

"Say something then," Lainey demanded.

"You're not going to believe this. They just found another body."

"Where?"

"Here."

Veva came from the bathroom, wrapped in a towel with her wet hair clinging to the sides of her face. "Are you okay?" she asked, seeing the paleness of his face.

"Is that Veva?" Lainey barked down the phone.

"I need to call you back," Brian said.

"Brian!" Lainey heard the call drop. She immediately dialed him back, but he didn't pick up. It was almost eleven p.m. in California. Lainey was too wired to even think about going to sleep. She called Veva's cell, but nobody answered. Why the hell was Brian with Veva in his room so early? He was good at preparation, but he was pushing it if they were starting that early. Lainey texted him and told him to call her back immediately.

"I can see you're busy. I'll change in my room," Veva offered.

"I'll meet you in half an hour," Brian muttered, his thoughts far away.

"Sure. You know the place," Veva said and headed to her room.

Brian snapped from the undulating static in his head. The door slammed shut, and he shuddered from his eyelids to his feet. "You know the place," he slowly repeated Veva's words.

He was frozen to the spot. His ability to analyze a single thought was impossible. Multiple possibilities collided as he repeated, "You know the place."

He was aware Veva meant they should meet at the entrance to the lobby. The words were simple enough, as was the insinuation. Those simple words etched deep in his mind, but his instinct screamed that he should pay attention. Brian ignored the beeps and vibrations from his cell from Lainey, demanding that he call her back. "You know the place," he repeated.

Brian ignored the continuing texts and calls from Lainey. He faced multiple issues and threats. "Oh, fuck!" Brian had no words for his beloved wife.

CHAPTER SEVENTEEN

Strahan finished writing his notes and put aside his pen and pad. It was old-school stuff that worked. He read through the last paragraph. It was good to be back in the comfort of his bed. During their late afternoon conference call, he'd cut into the conversation a couple of times to help his partner out, who had become increasingly frustrated on the call with Detective Kagawa. The Japanese authorities were initially reluctant to share all the details of what they'd found until Strahan's captain stepped in and convinced the Kyoto team that it was in all their interests to have full transparency. He instructed Hurst to share everything they had. Hurst was less thrilled at going first, but she gave a sublimely detailed report without referencing any paperwork or digital sources. Strahan was impressed by her ability to faultlessly regurgitate information, although less so by her lack of patience in the delivery.

Strahan took off his reading glasses, yawned aloud, and rubbed his tired eyes as he nestled back into his pillows. He was about to switch off the light when the gentle tapping of knuckles rapped on his bedroom door.

"It's me. Are you awake?"

"Just about," Strahan replied.

Detective Hurst entered and stood on the other side of his bed. She was dressed only in a long white t-shirt covering half her thighs. Her legs were tanned, and Strahan was surprised that her slender legs had a strong muscle tone.

"If only you were a girl," were her first words, and then she continued, "I was thinking about what Kagawa told us, and it's bugging me." Hurst made herself comfortable, sitting next to him, and fluffed two of his spare pillows before relaxing.

"Specifically, what?" he frowned.

Hurst pulled the end of his duvet over her feet, and the glint in her eyes showed how much she enjoyed his discomfort. "Relax, pretty boy, you're not my type. I did some digging on my tablet on the three murdered girls. We know they're all into fitness, modeling, and the likes, but the fitness side is the only thing they have in common with Lainey Stewart."

"And your point is?"

"Lainey did plenty of magazine shoots before the attempted murder. She was well known and easy to find—the same as these other girls. Anyone with a computer can find them. But Lainey was the first. She was selected because she stood out. Most serial killers strike close to home."

"You mean her husband?"

"Brian Stewart doesn't fit the profile. We'll come back to him in a minute. He's not out of the picture, and we should look at the history of any digital device he uses. Elizabeth, Kumi, and Daphne were all YouTubers and Instagram chicks. Smoking hot. All three had Patreon or other private accounts, where for their paying audience, they'd do more than model gym clothes or lingerie – they were stripping out of it and getting jiggy with it."

"What's that mean exactly?"

"For the right monthly subscription payment, I found our girl Elizabeth would show you everything and how she uses toys on herself, with nothing left to the imagination. Kumi was going a little further and doing some roleplay sex. The guy in her videos is a little-known Japanese porn actor. Kagawa is working on him as we speak, but the porno guy hasn't ever set foot in the US, so he's not our killer."

"There's no way we have two killers working in tandem."

"We're looking at one person. Anyway, Daphne Montclair also went with full penetration on her paid access-only account. The three dead victims were putting themselves in the public eye. I'm definitely not saying they were asking for trouble. It doesn't take much to trigger a nutcase."

"Lainey wasn't doing that."

"True. But her media exposure was massive, and a lot of it with her tits half exposed and plenty of cameltoe. Look, nobody asks to get killed but there psychos everywhere. It's like an invitation to a madman – that's the sad truth of it," Hurst unnecessarily added.

"So, we look for common account holders on the other girl's respective websites," Strahan said.

"Yep. And we check to see if they have a 4D Fitness treadmill."

"You said to come back to Brian Stewart."

"Yeah. I had one of my guys in Salem take a look, and guess who was in Japan two weeks ago." Hurst patted his leg through the covers. "Brian Stewart just came back from Kyoto. And not only that, but the running trail he went to film was none other than Arashiyama, the same place Kumi Shinnabe's body was found." Hurst was about to explain further, but she stopped as her cell phone rang. "It's my boss. It can't be good at this time."

Strahan shuffled under the covers as she took the call. He thought that letting Hurst stay in his spare room may not have been a great idea.

"Hey, chief, what's up?" Hurst nonchalantly asked.

Strahan heard the voice at the other end but couldn't pick up the words.

"Yeah, he's right next to me, in bed," Hurst mischievously added. "We're a close team." She put her phone on speaker.

"Very funny," her chief said, his voice and patience sounding worn out. "When you two have finished your honeymoon, you might want to contact Dieter Matthaus in Bremen, Germany. We have another one. He's the senior detective on the case, and he speaks pretty good English." The chief explained what he knew and told Hurst and Strahan to get right on it.

The call was short but not sweet. Hurst looked at her partner and began to snort with an ironic laugh. "Remember where Lainey Stewart said her husband was traveling to earlier today?"

"Bremen, Germany," Strahan frowned heavily, reaching for his notebook. "I think she said that Brian left two days ago."

"Three days ago," Hurst corrected him. "Detective Matthaus' communication said their dead girl has the calling card "5 of 7" in her hands."

"It's too obvious," Strahan said, sitting upright. "A cautious killer doesn't suddenly lay a perfect trail and say, "Here I am." There's no point to it if you're Brian Stewart."

"I hear you. Why would a killer take all that time and effort to leave no traces of anything, only to do a 180 and leave a perfect trail of breadcrumbs to themselves? I agree, it makes no sense, but it does place Brian Stewart at the top of our list."

"Didn't know we had a list."

"Start writing one in that notepad of yours." Hurst removed herself from the bed and straightened her nightshirt. "Guess we'd better get down to HQ and make a call to Germany. Brian Stewart has no religious affiliation that we know of, right?"

"None. His parents were hippies, so he wasn't brought up around Christianity or anything like that."

"He's hiding something, and so is his wife. This whole case is like a gangbang with the lights out."

"And you would know how?" Strahan asked.

Hurst slyly smiled at him. "I still don't think Brian Stewart fits. But, then again, he's all we've got, and he's in all the right places." Hurst shrugged her skinny shoulders. "Let me get my panties on, and we can get moving. Have you got any coffee?"

Strahan remained under the covers while she loitered in the doorway. "Yeah, I'll make some."

Hurst gestured with her eyebrows, daring him to get out from under the sheets.

"After you," he nodded back, telling her to leave.

Hurst turned around and laughed her way back to the spare room, making sure Strahan heard it.

"I still have a reputation to manage," he called after her. All it did was make Hurst laugh louder.

Veva was very satisfied with her trip to Germany, although miffed that she didn't see Prague or Dublin. During the morning client demonstration, she pulled on her running shoes and gave a five-minute demo using the imported 4D treadmill that helped sell their offering to the investors. In addition, one of the German team placed a personal order for his wife during the morning break-out session.

Brian thanked her for the support and technical input she brought to the meeting. In a couple of weeks, the extent of their efforts would be written into a contract. Brian told her he was confident the money and orders would come.

Her travel back to the US had gone without problems, and by late afternoon, she was at San Francisco airport. When she switched on her phone, Veva found several texts from Lainey, asking her to call as soon as she landed. The message's content indicated Lainey was worried about Brian. Veva rushed down the causeway to get her next flight to Arcata airport. She called Lainey as she hurried along.

"There you are. Where are you?" Lainey's voice was slurred and stressed.

"I'm in San Fran, about to get my flight back to Eureka. Are you okay? You sound a bit…you know."

"I am…you know. All this death and despair bullshit, and Brian. Brian! I mean…I don't know what he's thinking," Lainey rambled. "One minute, Mr. Nice guy, and the next, anybody's guess. He's always been into unusual things. I don't know him anymore. I need you to come straight here."

"You mean now?"

"Yes, as soon as you land. I know you've had a long day and all that, but you've been with him for the last few days, and I need to know what he's been like or what he's said. It seems like he's determined not to speak to me." Lainey took another sip of her white wine. "He won't call me back. The bastard. When will you be here?" Lainey didn't give Veva a chance to decline.

"I'll be in Eureka in about an hour, and by the time I get in my car and come to you, it will be around six p.m.," Veva estimated.

"Thank you, Veva. I need your help, and you can tell me about the meeting you guys had earlier today. Brian's not answering my calls. Fucker." Lainey's voice trailed off. as if she was going to cry but pivoted immediately to anger. "I'm his wife. He's messing with the wrong woman."

"Okay, hang in there. I'll be there as soon as possible," Veva said, getting to her boarding gate. "I'm going straight on the plane, so I have to switch off my phone for a little while."

"Call me as soon as you land. I'm depending on you, Veva," Lainey slurred.

"Okay. Speak to you soon." Veva felt her boss's tension leap from the phone. The flight was half-empty, and Veva had a double seat to herself. She was tired, having only nodded off for half an hour on the flight back from Germany. She put in her earplugs, listened to calming music, and closed her eyes.

Lainey constantly checked the status of Veva's flight to see precisely when it touched down. She desperately needed someone to confer with, and Veva had proven trustworthy. More importantly, Veva would know if Brian had done anything out of character in the last few days. On her other screen, Lainey tried to get more details about the murder in Bremen. She'd left voicemails with Detective Strahan and Hurst, but neither called her back. "Screw you all," she scolded.

Lainey stumbled around in the kitchen, attempting to open another bottle, but she had difficulty locating what she'd done with the corkscrew. She remembered having her first drink upstairs in the bedroom, staring at the black and white running shoes that contained her engagement ring. "Aha," she said, thinking it must be in the bedroom. "Why's that fucker got my ring in his running shoes? Brian Stewart – bastard! What are you doing?"

As she walked from the kitchen, her phone rang, and she dashed to the counter to answer. "Veva, thank goodness, are you here?"

"On my way. Already in my car. I'll be with you in ten minutes."

"Good. I'm opening the wine if I can find the damn opener. It keeps hiding from me. Ha," Lainey laughed at her struggle. "I think Brian tried to kill me."

"I'm sure he didn't." Veva offered, hoping to appease her.

"I'll pour you a glass if I can find the fucking opener."

"I shouldn't, with all the travel. It'll go straight to my head. I get buzzed quickly."

"It doesn't matter. You can stay here the night," Lainey found herself volunteering. "Besides, we have lots to talk about—Brian and his stupid games, whatever he's doing. I have spare clothes, or whatever you'll need. It'll be like a girls' night out, except in." Lainey laughed again and muttered something that Veva couldn't make out. "Men! Unreliable."

"I'm on the 101, so I'll see you soon."

"Okay. Hurry up," Lainey said with desperation. "I'll meet you at the door."

The line went dead, and Veva looked disbelievingly at her cell. She knew Lainey couldn't go near the front door. Veva tried ignoring the flush of excitement that performed a slow scintillating dance between her legs and forcibly stopped herself from reaching down and completing what had started. Being alone with a drunken and distressed Lainey provided an opportunity.

The front gates opened wide before Veva pressed the intercom. She drove straight to the house. Veva collected her shoulder bag, leaving her small suitcase in the trunk.

The front door was also open, and to her surprise, Lainey was leaning on the wall outside, holding a glass of white wine in each hand. "Veva, at last, here you are my, techy dynamo. C'mon. Are you hungry? Do you need to shower? What do you need? I have food or snacks. Look, I'm outside," she happily declared.

"How much have you had?" Veva asked as Lainey squished her in a firm hug and almost spilled wine on her.

"Not enough. Stupid Brian."

"You're outside."

"I know, but don't tell anyone. You gave me courage, and I salute you for that." Lainey stumbled, almost falling over. She pushed a drink into Veva's hands. "Here. You might need this after you hear what I have to tell you. Remember, what happens in the big house stays in the big house."

"I'm good at keeping secrets," Veva earnestly replied.

"Me, too." Lainey put an arm around Veva's shoulder and guided her into the living room. "Are you sure I can't get you anything? What do you need?"

"I could use some food, but I can make it," Veva offered. Lainey swayed side to side. "At some point, I need to go home and take a bath. I hate that icky feeling from traveling."

"Me, too," Lainey agreed with her eyes wide and head-nodding like it was something much more terrible. "No, you can't go home; you need to stay here. We have the best bath in Eureka, with all the jets going to all the right places, if you know what I mean. It gives you that tingly feeling all over."

Veva froze, not knowing what to say, staring back at Lainey.

"It's okay. Just us girls. I've already seen your cute little Brazilian bush."

"It's not a bush," Veva giggled, turning bright red.

"You know what I mean. I insist you have to stay. We have far too much to cover for you to go home tonight. Eat first and have some wine. No – have wine or whatever."

"We'll see." Veva selected some items from the fridge. "When did you last eat something?"

"Lunchtime. This is my dinner." Lainey held up her wine glass.

"I'll fix you something, too."

Lainey told Veva everything Detective Hurst and Strahan had told her and that it must remain in confidence. She kept stressing to Veva how important it was for her not to repeat anything, or she'd get them both into trouble. "Bodies of young, beautiful women are buried everywhere. There could be a dozen in my backyard, by the infinity pool, and I'd never even know," Lainey rambled.

Over the next hour, she told Veva all about some of her own experiences when she was found stumbling through the Humboldt Forest near Weott. After a glass of wine, Veva was yawning like crazy. Lainey poured her a second, despite her muffled protests. She talked about Brian and everything he used to do when they first met and how this last year had taken much of the fight out of him. She acknowledged his dedication and hard work, but there were critical elements of him that no longer existed, and Lainey partly blamed herself for helping to push some of them away.

It was almost eight p.m., and Veva's eyes were heavy with jet lag, and the alcohol rendered her fuzzy. Lainey saw Veva's head dip a couple of times, and she sprang into action. She took Veva by the hand, ensuring they each had a full glass of wine, and dragged her upstairs.

"Let me do something nice for you," Lainey pleaded. "C'mon, we'll take a bath."

"Oh, I don't know if I…"

"Oh, shush," Lainey insisted, with her arm around Veva's waist. "Please. I never get to fuss over anyone, and you've been so kind coming here and listening to me throw up all this stuff at you all night. I know I've talked your ear off. But, please. You said you needed a bath. Stay here. You must be exhausted. Drink your wine."

"I am."

"You see. I'll run the bath for you. You'll love it."

"Only if we get in together," Veva said. "I'd feel weird on my own. And with all this wine in me, I could slip under the water and never come back up."

"I would never let that happen to you," Lainey replied with drunken determination. She guided Veva next to the massive tub set into the floor. Lainey ran the water and brought towels and bathrobes. "I'll wash your hair."

"I use just a regular old Garnier. It keeps my hair soft."

Lainey ran her hands through Veva's hair and kneaded her scalp. "You have lovely hair, always super shiny. Unless I'm on a video call, mine's usually a sweaty mess," she tugged at her ponytail. "Let me do your hair for you. I promise you that it'll be the softest and shiniest ever."

"I guess."

Lainey clapped her hands and went to fetch her shampoo and conditioner. When she returned, Veva was standing awkwardly by the tub. Lainey dipped her hand through the bubbles to check the temperature. "Okay, let's get in." Lainey started to pull off her clothes, struggling to wrestle herself from the sports bra. She began to snicker as it got stuck halfway between her shoulder and neck. "Veva, help me," she laughed. Veva inched forward and stretched it over Lainey's head. Lainey whipped down her leggings without hesitation, standing naked in front of Veva. "My tits are great, aren't they?" Lainey stuck out her perfectly rounded breasts. "Cost me twenty grand for these puppies. Worth every penny."

"Definitely," Veva agreed.

"Turn around," Lainey gestured for Veva to spin around. "Don't worry; I won't peek– too much." Lainey reached around Veva's front and unbuttoned Veva's blouse, pulling it from her shoulders and unfastening her bra, which Veva then dropped on the floor. Next, Lainey unfastened the clip on the front of Veva's black trousers, unzipped the fly, and pulled them down. Veva stepped out of them.

"Lainey, are you sure?"

"Oh, hush now," Lainey said. Veva pushed her fingers under the top of her underwear, but Lainey stopped her. "Nah ah," she hummed, removing Veva's hands. "Let me," Lainey drunkenly cooed in Veva's ear and slid her panties over her legs. "Okay, let's get in." They stepped slowly into the water together.

Veva gasped out loud as she stepped into the tub. "Wow, hot."

"Good for your skin. Wait until I put on the jets– you won't ever want to get out, and it'll give you ten orgasms in an hour," Lainey snickered, spilling wine into the tub.

Veva slowly rested herself on one side and extended her arms on the tiled neck rest. Lainey moved through the water and sat beside her. She filled her hands with hot water and carefully drizzled it over Veva's dark hair.

"Try not to get any in my eyes. I wear contacts."

"I'll be real careful, I promise." Lainey put her hand on Veva's hip and guided her off the built-in seat. "Here, sit between my legs so that I can do your hair properly." Veva nestled back and stopped as soon as the bare skin of her rear end touched Lainey's thighs under the water. "Come all the way back. I won't bite you." Lainey put a hand on Veva's waist and pulled her close so her back rested against her breasts. "There we go. Your hair will look and feel amazing when I'm done with it."

Lainey shampooed and conditioned Veva's hair for fifteen minutes as they chatted about their favorite places to run in California. The atmosphere was mellow, with Lainey constantly pressing her fingers into Veva's scalp and providing small neck rubs that made Veva purr with satisfaction and slowly rotated her head, easing the tension eased in her muscles. "Isn't this so relaxing? All these little noises. I bet you sound sexy as fuck when you climax." Lainey's statement was more of a question.

"Lainey!" Veva giggled like a naughty schoolgirl being encouraged to tell about a first kiss. "I'm verbal, is all I will say." She hummed as Lainey's hands kneaded her shoulders. "You have a nice touch. I should hire you for a full body massage."

"I can do that for you," Lainey said, eager to help. She lowered her hands and began to work on Veva's trapezoids. "I'll rinse your hair in a second." Next, she used the spray attachment to wet Veva's shoulders.

"It feels so good, especially in the warm water. You should let me do yours," Veva lightly suggested.

"I'm supposed to be pampering you," Lainey drawled. She reached back for the remote and dimmed the lights.

"Thank you," Veva sighed. "I want you to feel how good it is, too,"

"Okay. Let me finish your hair, and we'll swap places, but only for a little while. It's nice for me to spoil someone. Me and Brian barely…well, you know."

Veva covered her eyes as Lainey rinsed off the conditioner with the extended water sprayer to get out every last drop. "I'm sorry to hear that," Veva sympathized.

"We've tried, but I can't relax," Lainey explained. "With all this other crap going on, who knows how long it might be." Lainey continued to lament her lack of physical connection and how she longed for it but kept falling short. She told Veva that, despite her libido recently making an appearance and calling for the use of her vibrator, engaging with Brian was still impossible.

"What kind of vibrator do you have? I have a few," Veva confided like it was something illicit.

"A normal one, nothing unusual, I think. I'll show it to you, seeing as how you're the expert."

"I'm no expert," Veva shyly replied.

"You're our senior tech director, developer, assistant, or whatever – aren't you supposed to know about all this stuff?"

Veva laughed. "Not about vibrators, though."

"What kind do you have?"

"I'm not telling you," Veva replied with embarrassment.

"Now you have to tell me," Lainey insisted with her mouth against Veva's ear. "Us girls need to share what works. You can't keep those secrets to yourself." She finished the rinsing and used both hands to wring the excess water from Veva's hair. "My little miss prim-and-proper indeed. Do you have one of those massive dildos or double ones that go in your butt?"

"No!" Veva held her hands over her mouth to stop her cringed laughter from escaping.

"You sneak," Lainey pinched Veva under the water, making her giddily whoop. "You're not leaving until you spill all your sexy secrets."

"I don't have any."

"I know that's a lie," Lainey whispered provocatively in Veva's ear. She placed her hands on Veva's hips, guiding her from between her legs, and they swapped places. Lainey settled back and rested her head against Veva's shoulder. "I think I might be drunk," she said, closing her eyes.

Veva stiffly moved around on her butt, trying to get into a place where she could work on Lainey's neck and shoulders. "I can't get to your shoulders."

Lainey took Veva's hands and placed them on her clavicle. "Do the front."

"Erm, are you…"

"Stop fussing; it's okay," Lainey sighed. She moved Veva's hands onto her breasts, "If you're worried about brushing against these, we can get that out of the way."

"They're really firm," Veva said with admiring curiosity.

"They'd better be," Lainey moved their hands over her implants. "I'm thrilled with them. You can feel them; it's fine. No big deal."

Veva had to stop her body from arching as Lainey guided her hands over the perfect mounds. Veva felt Lainey's nipples instantly harden. "I've never felt

189

any before. Can I squeeze them, only to see what they feel like?" she quickly added.

"Knock yourself out." Lainey removed her own hands. "I love having my boobs touched. If you're not shy about it, you can massage those too. I don't mind. In fact, I like it."

Veva's cheeks were roasting, and she flexed her fingers all around Lainey's breasts, giving each a gentle rub and squeeze. "They're beautiful."

"Keep going. It feels dreamy."

Veva caressed every inch of Lainey's chest, moving her hands from her shoulders down her arms and diagonally up and over her breasts. With each motion, she focused more attention on the breasts and embraced the pert nipples under the palms of her hands. She continued with the slow circular movements, feeling Lainey's body softly rise as each time she moved from her neck and caressed her breasts, with Lainey letting out tiny, satisfied moans of pleasure. Her receptiveness was such that Veva was encouraged to run her hands underneath her breasts and over Lainey's rib cage, teasing at the top of her stomach.

"Oh, that's so good," Lainey uttered. She stretched out her body, opening herself up as Veva's delicate touches bristled her skin. Lainey nestled her back int Veva's front and tilted her head towards Veva. "I could have you do this full time."

"You're okay with it?" Veva checked.

"Are you kidding me? It's perfect. I'm in heaven right now."

"I haven't done this before, so I don't know what to do exactly," Veva said, dipping her head, so their eyes were only inches apart.

"You know me; I'm not prudish. Let your hands go wherever. If it doesn't feel divine - I'll let you know." Lainey stared into Veva's light green eyes and studied her face. "I can't believe you don't have a boyfriend. You're so cute."

Veva blushed and smiled.

"Are your lips natural? or have you had them done?" Lainey asked. Her words were slurred to the point that she was barely comprehensible.

"Natural." Veva pouted.

Lainey strained her neck upward and softly pressed her lips to Veva's. "Mmm. they're yummy."

"Oh, my," Veva quietly whispered. "I've never kissed a girl before."

"What?" Lainey exclaimed. "C'mon, really?'

"Really. I never had close girlfriends or anything when I was younger."

Lainey shifted her body around. "Me and my friends practiced with each other when we were younger. Girls have softer lips than guys." Lainey ran her fingertip over Veva's bottom lip. "You have to try."

"I don't know," Veva partially shied away. "I'd like to, but it might seem…"

"It's just you and me. Not like we have anything to hide from each other." Lainey pouted her great lips, pretending to sulk. "Just a little kiss," she teased.

"I'm not…" Veva held her bottom lip under her top row of teeth, maximizing her coyness.

"I'll be the boy," Lainey offered. She twisted around so they face one another. Lainey placed both hands on Veva's head, resting it on the towel. "Now you can't run away." Lainey pressed her lips to Veva's. At first, their lips only touched, without any movement. "Your lips are fucking amazing." Lainey blinked through droopy eyes. "Let's try it properly, and then you can say you've kissed a girl but never say who." She reapplied her lips to Veva and motioned as if kissing a lover. There was no response from Veva, who held perfectly still. "You don't do it like that. Give it to me," Lainey demanded. "Pretend I'm some sexy boy that you've had your eye on forever." She placed a soft hand on Veva's cheek and engaged her mouth-to-mouth.

Veva loosened her lips and followed Lainey's lead. Soon their sweet kiss rolled as their heads opposed, and the pressure of their lips increased against the others. They kissed for a full minute.

Veva asked, "Was that okay?" But, of course, she already knew the answer.

"It was better. What would you do if some hot boy were kissing you? Use one of your many vibrators, huh." Lainey prodded Veva's ribs and tossed her head back, laughing.

"No. Don't," Veva curled herself into a ball, trying to hide the broad smile on her face.

"I knew it," Lainey grabbed at Veva's torso. "C'mon, let's do it properly this time." She leaned forward and stopped, suddenly raising her index finger. "The jets. That'll get you in the mood." She leaned past Veva and grabbed the remote for the tub. "Get a load of this." Lainey flexed her eyebrows up and down. "I swear, once these get going, I've had at least a dozen full-on orgasms without ever touching myself."

"Lainey!" Veva snickered.

"It's perfectly natural." Lainey switched on the water jets that whooshed from all angles.

"Ooh!" Veva rose from the seat. "It tickles."

"In all the right places. Sit here," Lainey instructed, tapping her fingers to a specific spot. "This is the best place. It gets you all over." Lainey stood upright in the tub and wobbled left to right. "Head buzz," she laughed at her inability to stand straight.

Veva couldn't help but stare at Lainey's naked torso standing above the bubbles. "I wish I had your body."

Lainey unsteadily moved through the water and pushed herself closer to Veva. "One last kiss, and then you have to find a new boyfriend," she suggested. "Make it a good one. Pretend I have a massive, hard cock pressing against you."

"Lainey!"

"Shush. Let's have those lips." She put both arms over Veva's slender shoulders, and instantly they became locked again at the lips.

Veva was bolder and placed her hands on the small of Lainey's back, running her fingers over the top of her buttocks. Their lips were in sync, and Veva slipped her tongue inside Lainey's mouth, licking delicately at the insides of her lips.

"Mmm," Lainey responded as their tongues entwined with a heavy open-mouthed exchange. "You're going for it, you little slut," Lainey whispered as their lips unlocked and quickly found a second rhythm.

Veva seized the opportunity, and her fingers stroked at the top of Lainey's rounded athletic cheeks, gradually sliding down and caressing handfuls of her buttocks. She wondered if Lainey would pull away but instead found her kissing partner pushed closer, and Lainey began to let her hands wander from Veva's shoulders and down over her small pert breasts. The smooching increased in passion, with each making pleasurable groans and little noises of appreciation. Veva repeatedly pulled Lainey's cheeks apart and pushed them back together with her fingers gripped into the glutes.

Lainey broke her mouth away, and Veva instantly stopped. "You've done this before with a girl, haven't you?"

"No, you're my first."

Lainey swayed in the bubbles and drunkenly smiled at Veva. She ran her fingers down Veva's chest and played with her nipples. "They're like bullets. Does it feel good?"

Veva bit her lip as the shivers ran through her body. She nodded.

"One more kiss then," Lainey said. "Let's really go for it. Can you feel those jets going between your legs?"

"No," Veva replied, looking down.

Lainey sank her hand beneath the water and touched Veva's left butt cheek and slipped her hand lower. "Hold still a second." Lainey strained to keep her head above the surface. "Let me see where the jet is." She groped around until she located the source pushing through the tiles. "Aha, here," she flexed her fingers, tickling Veva's butt crack. "Move your butt, so you're right over this baby."

Veva shuffled three inches to her right until Lainey's fingers were in the middle of her butt. The water rushing into the tub instantly rippled under Veva's cheeks and out underneath her vagina, causing an instant tremor between her legs. "Oh, my God," Veva exclaimed.

"Don't worry. Let yourself go. I do. Amazing, isn't it?"

"I don't know if I can take it – it's so…" Veva rolled her eyes.

"You deserve some pleasure. Relax into it, and don't worry about anything else." Lainey threw her arms back around Veva's neck and pressed her chin into the side of Veva's face.

"I can't hold back," Veva's voice came in short breaths. "I don't think I…"

"Don't think, just let go." Lainey lowered her hands and toyed with Veva's nipples again. "Is this better?"

"Oh, yes," she whispered. "Lainey, it's so fucking good. I'm going to…soon." Veva dug her hands into Lainey's glutes once more.

"Yeah, grab my ass and go with it," Lainey hissed in Veva's ear as her fingers twisted and pulled at Veva's sharp nipples. Lainey slipped her tongue inside Veva's ear and licked all around it while whispering, "Tell me when you cum, I want to feel it with you. Come on, that's it."

"I will, I will," Veva gasped as her body moved up and down with the fast-rushing waters billowing between her legs and taking her higher. Veva's hands went lower over Lainey's cheeks and slowly gripped the insides where they met the back of her thighs.

"It's okay," Lainey whispered as she felt Veva's fingers only a fraction away from touching her privates. "Do what you want. I like it."

Veva inched the ends of her fingers inward until she felt the outer edges of Lainey's vaginal lips and the slight little bumps from her waxing. "Oh, I'm so close," she whimpered.

"Yes," Lainey encouraged through clenched teeth before slipping her tongue back into Veva's earlobe. "Go for it, Veva." Her hands rubbed at Veva's breasts, circling them around in time to the movement of her body.

Veva's body lurched up and down, and her moans became louder; her fingers touched the lips between Lainey's legs and met with no resistance, encouraging her to tease them and slide her fingers inside. Finally, her spasms rose to a point where she whined, "I'm coming," and her mouth gaped open with a long rasping groan. Lainey's body dropped lower, and Veva's fingertips stroked the insides of Lainey's tender pussy lips as she shuddered with the water jets that elongated her orgasm. "Ooowee," her shrill cry sounded as she gasped for air. Veva's body flopped loosely against the tiles. "Oh, my God," she groaned.

Lainey stopped her tongue action and moved herself to one side in the tub. She rested her shoulders against the tile and leaned her head back, staring with a broad smile at the ceiling. "That was beautiful. Told you those jets would get you."

"It's still going," Veva whispered. "Would you like me to do something for you?"

"No. I wanted you to enjoy yourself."

"Do you like that kind of…you know," Veva inquired.

"No. I'm not into chicks," Lainey said, closing her eyes and smiling. "We're all good here, in the big house," her voice trailed away, sounding like she was going to sleep.

"I've never done any of that before," Veva confessed.

"Well, now you have." Lainey cranked her head forward an inch and opened one eye. "I'd like you to stay the night. Can you do that for me? Just as friends." She inched out her hand, feeling for Veva's fingers.

"I can make up one of the spare bedrooms?" Veva held Lainey's hand.

"No. You can sleep with me. Just two girls snuggling as friends. I don't snore."

"Me neither."

"Then it's settled. It'll be a perfect night. Come and sit with me so that I can play with your hair," Lainey said. Veva sat close beside her, and they got comfortable. Lainey stroked Veva's hair and played with her scalp. "My little Veva. Full of surprises," Lainey hummed.

Veva rested her head on Lainey's shoulder, perfectly content in the afterglow.

CHAPTER EIGHTEEN

During their call with the German Police, Hurst described how Brian Stewart was their prime suspect. She'd asked the Bremen Police to find exactly which hotel he was staying at and get all copies of every security tape to monitor his activities. Within ten minutes of the call ending, detective Matthaus sent an email confirming Brian Stewart had stayed at the Park Hotel less than a mile from the burial site and less than two miles from where Marlene Durr resided. They pulled the hotel surveillance videos and swept Marlene's apartment for evidence. The German Police informed them that Brian Stewart had already flown to Ireland. Hurst and Strahan said they'd link back up with Matthaus in a few hours.

The two detectives returned to the Prairie Creek Redwoods.

Hurst crouched on her heels, with her long fingers resting in the soil beside the burial site. She looked ahead at the tree where Strahan suspected the video evidence came from. "We've received three short videos from three burial sites. Two with a guy in a blue hoodie and one with a guy in gray shorts and a black top. No face showing in any of them."

"Tech hasn't located the source from whoever sent them. It's from somewhere abroad, and the location keeps moving, like a software bug showing different IP addresses," Strahan added.

"The killer knows you're involved in the case and want us to dance to their tune. The guy in the black top looks like Brian Stewart from the back, but without the face, it's useless," Hurst made a clicking sound with her tongue as she thought aloud.

"We'll interview Brian when he returns to the US."

"Assuming the Germans don't have him extradited from Ireland and hold him. If that happens, we're in a whole other mess, with lawyers and whatnot." Hurst moved the beam of her flashlight around in the dark of the woods. "All these bodies were put in specific places with the intention that they'd eventually be found. Why? Facing east, taking in the sun. Like you'd place potted flowers in your yard." She looked as far into the trees as she could.

"I'm sure it's some sort of rebirthing, or, as you indicated, like planting a seedling. Each location is idyllic."

"It's as creepy as fuck in the dark," Hurst assured.

"Somebody who loves the forest knows that 4D Fitness has these places on their digital platform and targets brunettes who model gym wear or go a little further. A voyeur of some description." Strahan followed the line of Hurst's flashlight. He never said it, but Hurst was right about it being creepy. "The killer sees something in these women that we don't. The hair, the nails, the fitness, the modeling could apply to thousands of women, so why these particular ones?"

"Public profile is key, and what they're hiding from plain sight," Hurst said. She continued shining her flashlight around the trees. "Each woman has a concealed story."

"Who doesn't?" Strahan suggested.

Hurst ignored his comment. "We need to get Brian Stewart's shoe size. Forensic pulled sizes seven and eleven prints from here."

"Lainey Stewart wasn't getting naked on the internet."

Hurst focused her beam back onto the burial site. "No, but she's hiding shit from us. It's something the killer recognizes."

Strahan brushed his fingers through the damp soil. "We had size seven prints in Oregon. Given his height, Brian Stewart must be a size ten or bigger," Strahan said. "Let them praise the name of the Lord," he sighed as if the words caused him personal offense.

"We should ask a preacher that I know about that," Hurst said as they walked back down the trail to the parking lot.

"We know it doesn't appear anywhere in the Bible or in some other religious text– the creation of angels; killing to create."

"Listen, when I was younger, my late sister, a super Christian woman, God rest her soul, used to say stuff like that. She believed all humans were potential angels if they lived a good life or something like that. So it suggests the killer is a firm believer and sees these women as angels in the making. They are angelic. "Maybe our killer is growing them or giving them as an offering," Hurst theorized.

"Being a good Christian woman doesn't run in the family, then?" Strahan hinted.

"We only had room for one. I got all the good looks and personal charm." Hurst sounded pleased with herself.

"Your Thanksgiving gatherings must be a riot."

"I wouldn't know. I haven't been invited to one since my sister passed away. I couldn't look after my niece, so I was seen as a bad aunt and a horrible human being. It's a terrible thing to give up on a little child, especially one you love. Such a sweet little thing she was. My remaining sister rarely speaks to me unless she has to. My mom eventually took the little one. After that, my mom barely spoke to me; she said I gave up too easily, which was a sin."

"What was her name? The kid."

"Ginny. My other sister, Lucy, had her for a while, but Lucy got pregnant with her fourth, and so Ginny had to go live with Grandma Priscilla when she was seven. Poor thing got bounced around through no fault of her own. Time was not my friend, and neither was my family," Hurst explained.

"Angels in the making," Strahan repeated her words. They walked and talked through the pitch dark to the car. As they drove away, Strahan looked back into the forest and remarked, "We can see where someone strapped a camera to the tree to get the footage. You've got a firm conviction if you came out here to bury a body in the middle of the night. This is a mission."

"Yes, with a means to completing that mission," Hurst agreed. "I know, I keep prattling on about Brian Stewart, but there's a distinct lack of aggression in this case. He's a former personal trainer, for God's sake. All that training and shouting in someone's ear. Everything we've seen is very gentle and done with tender psychotic compassion. Most men usually rape and butcher. This isn't even close. It's like these girls were laid to rest by their mom."

Strahan pulled the car to a screeching halt and glared intently at Detective Hurst. "We need to watch those three videos again. I think you've hit on something!" He pulled out his cell and opened his email. "What the hell. It's not there. I didn't delete it."

"Maybe tech services pulled it to do their thing," Hurst suggested.

"I'll call them now." Strahan put the phone to his ear. "Killing with kindness," he muttered as they waited for the call to connect. "Luis, it's Strahan. I don't have that email with those videos in my inbox. Can you put it back? We need to view them." He paused while he listened to the explanation from the other end. Strahan ended the call. The tiredness showed on his face. "Guess what?"

"Please tell me they didn't accidentally delete them."

"Even better. The email removed itself and vanished into nowhere. It was designed that way."

"So, we lost it."

"No. Luis copied them straight away before it vanished. We can't get a trace of where it came from and never will. We'll go back to my office. Luis is sending us the videos." He set the car in motion again.

"A killer and a technical whiz. Great!" Hurst sarcastically remarked as she drummed her impatient fingers on her thighs. "Brian Stewart is their head of technical, isn't he?"

"On paper he is, as well as sales and marketing. However, I'm not sure how savvy he is with computers."

"Savvier than either you or me, I'm sure." Hurst pulled her jacket tight around her torso and shivered in her seat while making an audible groan to emphasize the cold in her bones. She stared into the night as if she hated it. "I can't wait for retirement."

"I'm sure there are plenty of cops looking forward to your retirement."

"You're still my favorite, pretty boy. Get me something to eat, will you? I'm frickin' starving."

An hour later, they were eating burgers in Strahan's office. Luis provided them with a thumb drive that contained copies of the three videos. Hurst plugged it into her laptop, and they sat side-by-side, watching each one in turn.

"We should send copies to our partners in Japan and Germany," Strahan said. "Kagawa said the forest has significance in terms of growth and re-birth."

"He also said that I was a rancid, skinny bitch," Hurst reminded her partner.

"I kind of like that guy."

Hurst punched a greasy fist to his upper arm. "You send them copies." She took another bite from her double burger. "Listen, you don't go to all the trouble of being ultra-careful not to get caught and suddenly hand yourself over on video. This is a decoy."

"Maybe," Strahan said as they watched them a second time. He used the mousepad to switch to the third video taken in Prairie Creek. "Watch closely. Why remove the hooded top and dress differently than the others? Look," he paused the video and pointed at the outstretched arm. "The hands aren't covered. In the first two, the hands have black gloves on."

"Go back." They watched the first two again and the third one in slow motion. "Can we get a close-up on that left hand in this one?" Hurst asked.

"Yeah. Luis already installed the software."

"Do you know how to use it?"

"We'll find out," Strahan countered with confidence. He ignored the grunt from Hurst and pulled up the menu to use the zoom feature. "Here we go."

"All you had to do was click two buttons and use the pad – I'm impressed," Hurst mocked. "There," she exclaimed, moving forward in her chair. "See the left hand and the wedding band. Can you get in closer so we can make it out?"

Strahan gave her the dead eye and enhanced the view.

"Looks like a gold band, with something flat on top. What is that?" Hurst thought aloud.

"I'll ask Luis to see what he can do with it. Some kind of small logo, I'd guess."

"Good catch with the gloves," Hurst acknowledged. "It means whoever it is in the third video didn't take the time to try to hide their DNA, even though we can't get anything from the soil."

"We need to check with forensics and see if anyone ran the body bag for fingerprints. It's only a few seconds, but they look like they're digging the soil out, not filling it in," Strahan noted.

"You're right. And with bare hands. No tool was used. Even if you forgot something and returned, you'd take your camping shovel. We know our killer is highly organized. Can you put one of the other two videos besides this one? Let's look at something else."

"I can." Strahan split the screen view and pulled up a shot of the hooded figure from Strassel Falls in Oregon.

After closely observing the comparison, they estimated that the person in Prairie Creek was broader in the shoulders and waist, and the size of the head was bigger. After plenty of debate, Detective Hurst and Strahan were certain the videos showed two different people.

"Our killer must be the one in the hoodie and gloves. Otherwise, there's no point in covering up. The Prairie Creek video is to keep us dancing to the killer's beat," Hurst theorized. "If you wanted to throw us for a loop, it means you're getting nervous because you know we're getting close."

"Who knows we're close?" Strahan pondered.

"Me, you, and both our bosses. The next in line would be Lainey Stewart and her husband. No way a husband and wife aren't talking about this," Hurst tossed her burger wrapper in the trash. "Who is Lainey closest to, outside her husband? Are there any jealous girlfriends or business rivals?"

"She has a couple of close friends from high school here in Eureka. One of them works for her as an administrator of some description. But she's married with three kids. No way she has time to travel around the globe killing young women. There haven't been any threats or falling out with anyone that we know of, and even if we did, it doesn't explain the other murdered women," Strahan explained.

"But Lainey was first. She was the one with the highest profile by quite some margin." Hurst wagged her finger at the images paused on the split-screen. "If I'd selected seven young women for murder, and the first one got away, and she was the one I wanted before all the others, then I'd make damn sure I came back and finished the job." Hurst leaped from her seat and pulled on her jacket.

"Where are you going?" Strahan asked.

"The bar near your house closes in an hour, and I need a drink. You want to join me."

"No."

"Any objection if I return to your place with some company?"

"Lots of objections."

"Who's going to take care of this?" Hurst asked, grabbing her crotch.

"A taxidermist, most likely."

Hurst laughed at his reply. "Don't worry, pretty boy, I won't make you try. Besides, you'd become addicted to how sweet I taste and start following me around with an incurable older pussy addiction," Hurst winked at him.

"I think HR would be interested in this conversation."

"You like my harassment, I can tell. Nobody else will make you a better offer."

"I'll come and have that beer with you if you'll shut the fuck up."

"I love it when you get feisty. It makes me moist. I'll buy you a caffeine-free diet beer to keep your conscience clean."

On their way from police headquarters, Hurst said, "First thing tomorrow, we'll have Detectives Kagawa and Matthaus pull all records of US citizens who were in those areas about the time of the murders. We know Brian Stewart is one of them. Who else knows his schedule?"

"4D Fitness blog all their upcoming travels and potential connections. Wherever they go, they want people to know, so they can get volunteer runners to film the trails. Anyone with a computer could easily figure out his schedule. I'll email our foreign partners while we have a drink. That way, we might have the data tomorrow morning."

"Thanks," Hurst said. "Don't get upset if I flirt with the waitress."

"When are you retiring?"

When Lainey awoke, she flicked open her eyes, trying to adjust to the morning light. Immediately, she was aware of the arm across her waist and the slender hand resting on her own. She'd forgotten Veva had spent the night in her bed. They were snuggled close; Lainey could hear Veva's light breath and feel the warm exhale between her shoulder blades. She looked under the covers and was surprised to find she was butt naked.

Lainey usually liked to sleep in her undies and a t-shirt, but the immediate magnitude of her headache gave away the explanation. It was over three years since Lainey was drunk, and she had gone for it last night.

Slowly she released her fingers from Veva, which caused her sleeping companion to stir and turn to face the opposite way. Lainey listened as Veva stayed in slumber. It was only five minutes after six in the morning. Too early to get up, and the pain in her head was not encouraging her even to try. She recalled they'd frolicked in the tub, but nothing too intrusive, although a hazy recollection that Veva had climaxed using the jets in the tub. Some harmless drunken girls' fun.

She slipped from under the comforter and tip-toed to the bathroom, desperately needing to pee. She remembered Veva had insisted that Lainey drink a full glass of water before going to bed, as it would help with a hangover. A theory she contested. Lainey held her head in both hands while sitting on the toilet and repeatedly groaned as she stared at her toes. She noticed her feet were perfectly manicured and the nails neatly painted. She partially recalled Veva kneeling at her feet, but the memory seemed more of a dream than reality. Her toes looked great. On her way back through the bedroom, she stopped and pulled on some cotton underwear and a t-shirt. She set her alarm for seven-thirty and settled her thumping head on the pillow.

"Do I need to get up yet?" Veva faintly asked.

"No. I've set the alarm. I'm hungover."

"Me, too. Terrible isn't it. But we had a fun night."

"I can't recall half of it."

"I can. I'll make breakfast when we have to get up," Veva yawned.

Lainey rolled over and took a long look at Veva's naked body. It felt weird, but Lainey was used to weirdness and shrugged it off.

The alarm from her cell made Lainey's head pop from the pillow, and for a moment, she was dazed. She switched off the buzzing and checked the time. It seemed impossible that over an hour had passed when it felt more like only a minute. Her head was still throbbing, and her stomach was queasy. "Geez," she snorted and dropped back into her pillow. "We have a meeting at nine." Lainey waited for a response, but nothing came back. Finally, she turned her head to find the other side of the bed was empty. "Veva?" She expected a reply from the bathroom, but silence greeted her.

Swinging her legs onto the carpet made Lainey feel sick. She required a few deep breaths to stand upright and staggered toward the wardrobe to pull on a robe and push her feet into her slippers. "Oh, God, never again."

She stumbled onto the upper hallway and called, "Veva?" Several items were neatly placed on the end of the kitchen counter and partly covered by a hand towel. Her voice echoed in the large space and came back to her. She looked inside the office and headed downstairs. The smell would typically have made Lainey ravenous, but in her condition, whatever had been toasted or grilled made the revolutions in her gut spin like a circus act performing tricks.

"Hey," Lainey speculatively called out.

Still no response. As she came around the bottom of the staircase, Veva's shoes were arranged at the end of the hallway. The back sliding door was partially open, and the fresh air crept into the living space. The coolness of the breeze felt good on Lainey's face. She walked toward the opening and looked outside. In the distance, she saw Veva walking barefoot, coming towards the house, already dressed in her business casual clothes and her hair shining brightly against the morning sun. She waited for Veva to get within a few feet of the door, and they exchanged a small handwave.

"It's stunning down by the folly this morning. You should see how the light comes through the trees and illuminates the water's edge. I can't believe you don't have unicorns grazing down there," Veva enthused.

"Aren't you hungover?"

"My head's thicker than mud." Veva stopped outside on the stone patio, less than twelve inches from Lainey. "How are you feeling?"

"Rough." Lainey poked her head in line with the open door. "The air is divine. I wish I could …" she gestured to the world outside the confines of her home.

"You can do anything. You're Lainey Stewart." Veva extended her hand. "Stand here with me."

Lainey stared at the open-palmed invitation. Her eyes looked beyond Veva and down the hill into the woodland.

Veva flexed her fingers to beckon Lainey forward. "You're braver than anyone I know. C'mon."

Lainey slowly extended her hand, "Don't pull me, okay?"

"I won't. I promise," Veva quietly confirmed. She watched with a childlike fascination as Lainey pushed one foot onto the stone, followed by the other. "That's it; see how amazing it is right here. I've got you. I bet you can take a few more steps." Veva turned her body and gently led the way. "God gave us this to enjoy it. The colors, the smells, and the birds singing in the garden. I know you can do this."

Lainey gripped her hand tight to Veva's. "It is nice," her words were strained. "I can't go any…"

"It's okay. You're doing great. We'll stay here." Veva pointed her spare hand towards the gothic folly beyond the meadow. "I would love for us to have lunch one day down there or walk around the pond together. We'd be like two blissful angels, walking on white clouds. It has special magic there, like a place where heaven and earth touch, and we get to share it."

"Not today. I can't, but I would like to." Lainey's body shivered. "It is beautiful. I used to read books, sitting under the stone-arch."

"One day for sure. I bet we get to talk with God."

Lainey glanced at Veva, unsure what to make of her fanciful ideas. "Two more steps," she pointed forward, feeling like she could push herself. They stayed locked together and slowly stepped further from the house. Lainey exhaled in long, controlled breaths. Four further cautious steps, and she halted.

"That's enough." Her head dithered on her neck as her nerves produced a slight tremor.

For the first time in forever, she could see down to the gardens without looking from an upstairs window. The instant euphoria enticed her to go further, but she knew this was as much as she could stand. "Do you see beauty through your eyes or through God? I'm curious, given the way you describe things."

"I love God. I see all of his creation through my heart. My eyes are just a simple receiving mechanism. God has granted us the privilege of interconnecting our internal components so we can appreciate nature." Veva looked down at Lainey's feet in her fluffy slippers. "Step out of those, and let your skin touch the earth. It will nourish you and give you what you need."

Without questioning Veva's words, Lainey slipped off the slippers and felt the cold of the stone on her bare feet. "Ooh. Your feet must be freezing, walking barefoot in the dew."

"They are, but my whole body is energized through it."

"You sound like those hippies who want to live in the trees."

"No. I like my home comforts too much, but I do love nature. When the weather gets warmer, I like to lay in the grass and let the earth talk to me."

"What does it say?"

"How lucky I am to be alive. Life is complicated enough and hard to appreciate. Truly appreciate," Veva emphasized.

"You think we don't show enough gratitude for what we have?"

"Gratitude for having things that mean nothing is easy – cars, clothes, jewelry, and flatscreen TVs. To be grateful for mother earth, the universe, being alive, and living a meaningful life is beyond the comprehension of those who appear as if they have everything."

"You mean like me?"

"Are you happy? Were you truly happy before the thing that happened to you?" Veva's gaze was steadfast into Lainey's. Her intensity was like they were competing on the treadmill.

"I don't know if I've ever been truly happy. There were times when I thought I was. Happiness comes and goes."

"I'm happy all the time. It doesn't mean I don't make mistakes and have urges for things I know can be destructive, but I use God as a guide to help me make difficult decisions. Then, I get through, and I'm truly happy," Veva explained.

"Was last night a mistake?" Lainey asked.

"No. I had a great time here with you. I would gladly do it all again. Don't worry; my discretion is assured. You already know that."

"I never thought it would be anything else," Lainey said with certainty. "Does your God consider it a sin?"

"In some respects, it could be damaging to other people if they found out. God gave us free will and these bodies to enjoy. I intend to atone for any sins and make sure I do my best to live with meaning and good grace. If I can help someone else be delivered into God's love, and be at peace, then all the better. We must act as we believe God intended for us and live with the consequences."

Lainey studied her new friend and colleague. "You're quite a curious person, aren't you?" There was no reply as Veva gave one of her customary polite smiles. Lainey used her spare hand to run her fingers through Veva's hair. "I told you your hair would be amazing. It's softer and shinier than ever."

Veva touched the sides. "I know. Thank you. Never looked or felt better."

"A bit like my toenails," Lainey pointed at her freezing feet.

"I can do your hands, too, if you like."

Lainey gestured with a flick of her head. "Let's go inside. We need to get the day going."

"I made French toast with strawberries, avocado, greens, and a drizzle of fresh lemon. You'll love it," Veva said.

"Not sure I can stomach anything this morning."

"I guarantee it will revive you, along with an iced green tea. You'll see. We'll have you ready for anything." Veva squeezed Lainey's hand and led them into the house. "I would never let any harm come to you."

Lainey cocked her head to one side like the words were an echo of something she once heard. She went to the breakfast counter and forced down some French toast. She allowed Veva to cater to her. There was something nice about letting go and having someone take care of her.

Once they'd finished eating and Lainey had freshened up for work, they settled in the office with a few minutes to spare before the first video conference of the day. It was only now that Lainey checked her cell and realized she'd not had any communication from Brian. His lack of thought dented her feelings, and she knew he was brooding. There was still so much he needed to answer to, and part of her was afraid of what she might find. He would be in Dublin by now, presenting to the potential Irish partners. He should have called or texted instead of sulking.

No way Lainey was going to apologize. Not after all the mounting information that pointed in the same terrible direction. There was no time to give it further consideration as Veva dialed into the conference and brought up the view of their team in the head office. Lainey waved and said good morning as they waited for the stragglers to join.

She glanced once more at her phone. "C'mon, Brian, where are you?"

CHAPTER NINETEEN

The initial meeting with the Irish investors went well. Brian was confident that the small Irish market was doable. He canceled his other scheduled meetings and personally called the investors. Brian had not relayed the updates to Lainey or his administrative assistant in the head office at Eureka. He deliberately left the meetings populated on his calendar. Brian needed to take care of more pressing concerns in California.

Brian used his personal credit card to book himself a business class seat out of Dublin and return home immediately. Brian figured he'd be home by late afternoon if all went as planned, including a two-hour layover in New York.

Sitting in Dublin airport, he fidgeted with his phone, going around in dizzying circles as to whether he should call Lainey. He was beyond pissed that she dared infer his link to the killings. It grated his core, and even though he'd cheated on her, Brian felt there was a level of loyalty that had been broken. He intended to confess his indiscretion and demand Lainey explain her outburst. Each time their relationship seemed like a peaceful, steady cadence was achieved, something would explode and bring everything into question, leaving them both hanging by a thread. Despite his anger and incredible stupidity, he loved Lainey with a ferocious determination.

Brian had no choice but to do all he could to fix what remained of their marriage. She deserved a faithful and devoted husband, and he wanted the return of his once vibrant and passionate wife, or at the very least, some portion of that. If Lainey could be half of what she was before the incident, she was light years ahead of any woman he'd ever met or would be likely to meet. Brian needed to be at his very best every day just to keep up with the formidable Lainey. He thrived on the challenge, which made him a much better man, except for his mistake in Bremen. Brian decided it all needed to come out to clear the air. The outcome would take of itself.

Other things were revolving in his mind. He'd suddenly been lured into the forest, the videos, the cheating, and becoming the chief suspect all falling within the two weeks that coincided with Veva's arrival on the scene. Brian wasn't a conspiracy theorist, but he was convinced they were linked.

The announcement came over the speakers to begin boarding his first flight to New York. He switched off his cell and decided he would call Lainey once he arrived back in the US. He would not tell her that he was coming home early or why. Giving Lainey eighteen hours' notice would leave him at a severe disadvantage. He wanted something akin to a level playing field. Lainey would blow higher than a volcanic eruption when she discovered his drunken frolic. An almighty fight was inevitable.

The two of them wanted the same things, but circumstances hideously conspired to ensure they were coming from places of hurt for various reasons, and both were stubborn, and they would not back down if they felt threatened or wronged. Brian was aware that no matter what the outcome, nobody was going to win, and for them to reach any mutual agreement was going to be virtually impossible. If he'd learned one thing from his marriage, it was that nobody wins an argument between a husband and wife. Anybody who was ever foolish enough to claim victory was destined for divorce.

There were things Brian needed Veva to explain. Brian knew a few words she'd uttered were a tenuous link at best, but he had realized that they were precise, word for word, on the email that directed him to retrieve Lainey's engagement ring. The more he thought about it, the more it bothered him; 'You know the place.'

He'd considered how Veva was a technical whiz and more than capable of sending him the emails and videos that would suddenly vanish. She knew all of their running trails. The German beer had loosened her tongue in more ways than one. Veva hadn't displayed anything to suggest she was capable of such terrible crimes, but the timelines, the places, and the events lined up. At the very least, Brian considered she was looking to blackmail him. Brian was angry with himself for so easily incriminating himself in every way possible.

The next group began boarding, and Brian shuffled forward. He couldn't believe that this woman they'd invited into their home was connected to his impending downfall. Perhaps his anger was getting in the way, and he just needed Veva as a scapegoat for his reckless actions.

He had a pen and notepad in his bag, with which he intended to sketch out his thoughts based on what Veva had told him. She must have some sort of ulterior motive. An affair with an employee would be the kind of headline that would send the company's reputation plunging. So at each turn, he was going to get hammered.

"Pen and paper."

"Excuse me," a confused flight attendant asked.

"Sorry. Nothing. I was talking to myself." He made his way into his seat.

"Enjoy your flight," came the slightly caustic response from the young man. Brian lamely smiled.

Brian noted how events had unfolded with the pad in his lap and his pen working vigorously. It was two hours into his flight when he finally stopped scribbling. A dozen pages of notes showed nothing was sure, but many things were not to his liking. If Veva was simply someone looking to blackmail him, she had all she needed.

The engagement ring was the sticking point. If Veva was behind that, then she knew the killer or, fortuitously, found the burial place of a dead girl. That was far-fetched. Brian produced his phone, paid the ridiculous $12 fee, and connected to the Wi-Fi on the plane. He began searching Veva Unwin's background to find out who she was.

Going back through her previous employment in Silicon Valley was easy. Finding anything else of use proved less than forthcoming. Brian was more competent than most regarding technology and using the internet, but he couldn't find Veva's college information. Veva had said she was raised in Oregon, but nothing checked out.

"You know the place," he whispered Veva's words. Words that initially presented intrigue and now a creeping terror. Beyond working in Silicon Valley, her past was a mystery. Brian convinced himself that the way Veva presented herself was solely to bring his world crashing to a miserable end. He wouldn't stop searching until he had answers. Veva was from the area where these girls were killed and not too far from where Lainey was once buried alive. Veva had been in Bremen! He had to be careful his imagination wasn't

211

running away from him and that he was trying to shift blame for his circumstances onto someone else.

His next search would be in birth registrations and check out Veva's origins. Brian wondered, "Who have we invited into our business? Our home." He reminded himself not to shift his misfortunes to someone else. "Get a grip."

Detective Hurst sipped at the coffee. "It's good," she gestured by raising the mug as she poured over the latest reports from Kyoto and Bremen.

"Anything stand out?"

"Not yet."

Strahan continued stirring the eggs in the pan, contemplating the surreal nature of his present situation. Hurst was sitting at his small kitchen table, with her glasses perched on the end of her nose, while he cooked their breakfast. Her dark jeans made her long legs appear skinnier than ever. Her V-necked yellow sweater showed the protruding clavicle bones leading to her slender neck. Her hair was its usual unruly mess, sticking in all directions and in at least four different colors. He dished the eggs onto two plates, each with two grilled slices of bacon, and put them on the table.

"You'll make somebody a lovely husband one day," Hurst muttered without shifting her gaze from the laptop. "I like this Kagawa guy. He's right to the point like he's angry all the time. Bet he's a firecracker in the sack."

"You seem to spend a lot of time thinking about those things."

"Good to know who you're dealing with and how they operate," Hurst replied. "We know it's the same person doing the killing. Toxicology showed the Digoxin is an exact match to the ones here."

"Have they sent over the lists of US citizens in those areas yet?"

"Let me see." Hurst switched back to her email. "Not yet."

"Let me know as soon as they come through, and I'll cross-reference them through Excel. Then, any name that appears in Germany and Japan will be easy to find."

"You cook breakfast, make good coffee, and you can make spreadsheets. I should marry you myself. Do you like to eat …"

"Not happening," Strahan cut her off. "I'm not your type."

"Not yet," Hurst goaded him. She pushed her laptop away. "Thanks for breakfast and for putting me up."

"No problem. I was thinking last night about the videos. We know everything points to Brian Stewart, yet none of it is solid. Whoever sent those clips, especially the third one, could have easily sent us something with his face in them. The more I've looked at the first two videos, the more I'm certain it's not Brian Stewart. He's too big."

"You think the person in the blue hoodie is our killer?"

"I do."

"Why take the videos in the first place? Just to frame Brian Stewart?"

"Possibly. But I think it's more than that. There are personal mementos of something sacred. A kindness shown to these young women. Everything is carefully done, no pain, no mutilation, no penetration… only the opposite. Bodies clean, nails polished and painted, hair neat. Not that you could resonate with that," he motioned his eyes to her head. He noted the wry smile on Hurst's lips. "Somebody loved these women enough to kill them."

"Putting them out of their misery. A mercy killing," Hurst offered.

"Exactly. We're dealing with a strange level of murderous compassion and one I haven't come across before."

Hurst finally looked up with a curious frown. "You've never been in love, have you? But you were married."

"I was married, but love had nothing to do with it. Infatuation and too many hormones were blinding the truth."

"Detective Strahan, you get more interesting each day. We need to get a couple of beers down you and hear those stories."

"Nobody needs to hear those stories," Strahan assured. He glanced at his laptop sitting on the edge of the table. "Detective Matthaus sent us the list. It's here."

Hurst looked in her email. "He only sent it to you then. Must be all those raging hormones of yours, and that he plain forgot I'm leading this investigation."

"I'll forward it to you. Maybe it was something to do with the fact that you told him the last time we tried working with Germany and Japan, we were forced to drop an atomic bomb to make ourselves heard."

"He wouldn't listen. He just kept on talking," Hurst explained.

"You should have it any second. I'll pull it into an excel file and wait for the Kyoto list. Why don't you read the names from the bottom of the list, and I'll start from the top? See if any names we recognize pop up," Strahan suggested.

"Sounds good." Hurst already had her eyes focused on the document. "Brian Stewart stands out."

"Thought we were starting at either end."

Hurst flipped her middle finger at him as she shoveled the eggs and bacon into her mouth. The kitchen fell silent for a couple of minutes as both detectives looked over the extensive list.

"Veva Unwin," Hurst said. "She went with Brian Stewart to Bremen, but her name isn't on the list. She's their new technical director or whatever. What do we know about her?"

"Nothing much. 4D Fitness hired her a couple of weeks ago. Lainey said she comes with a large technical pedigree and has already made noticeable changes to their software. She wasn't in the picture when all this started over a year ago. But, she was in the house when we were there last week."

"When she ran upstairs, I only saw the back of her. Straight black hair," Hurst gestured with hands on each side of her head.

"Yeah, that's her."

Hurst stopped looking at the list. "We have Lainey, who survived a year ago, and then, suddenly, four murdered women in the ground, all discovered within ten days of each other, and the oldest we believe was killed about four weeks ago. So if Lainey were your first attempt, and you found out you bungled it without knowing why, you'd get scared and wait a while to make sure you had your techniques worked out."

"None of these women appeared to have put up any kind of struggle. On the contrary, they willingly went to their deaths."

"If you're a female and minor celebrity with a well-known media presence, you'd be inclined to trust a woman's approach," Hurst theorized.

"Unless that woman was you," Strahan noted.

"Touché, pretty boy.

"We're looking at a female suspect." Hurst took a large gulp of coffee. "We think these women all went missing when they were out, either shopping or going for a bite to eat at night by themselves. No texts or communication indicating they ever intended to meet someone. Not the kind of girls who took strange men home. But a woman chatting with you, there's little threat in that."

"I'll have one of our guys pull everything they can on Veva Unwin. I haven't had a good look at her. But she doesn't look like a serial killer."

"Who does?" Hurst curtly responded. "We need that list from Japan. I'll email Kagawa."

"I'll do it," Strahan hurriedly replied. He tilted his head to suggest to Hurst that she knew exactly why it was better coming from him. She gave a solitary nod to affirm.

"I'll ask one of our team to run the list of names from Germany and see if anyone has any priors," Hurst said.

CHAPTER TWENTY

Lainey yawned when they broke for lunch and watched as Veva cut up the chicken breasts into small pieces and sprinkled them over the fresh salad.

"We look like we live together," Lainey observed. "Does it feel weird that you stayed here last night, and now we're having meetings and then lunch together?"

"No. It feels…" Veva looked up for inspiration. "Natural."

"Thank goodness there's only one more call this afternoon, and we can wrap up early. I think I'll take a nap and run tonight. I'm never drinking again."

"Do you want me to stay here while you rest?"

"No, it's okay. You should go home and unpack from your trip."

"It's no trouble. I'd be happy to stay over," Veva cheerily offered as she dressed the salad with balsamic vinegar.

The sincerity of Veva's tone struck Lainey. There was a domestic bliss on her face, making her look like she'd always been here. Lainey was grateful for the offer but wanted to curtail any of Veva's fanciful notions. "Thanks for offering, but there's no need. Not sure I can cope with company two nights in a row."

"No problem. I hope last night didn't preclude me from being invited back." Veva was unable to hide her disappointment.

"Not at all. It was good to have a girl's night. I've missed that. I had a nice time," Lainey explained, not wishing to dent Veva's enthusiasm.

"I had the best time ever," Veva cutely smiled.

"What? Like ever?"

Veva nodded. "Didn't you? It was like our souls connected."

"It was more like I had two bottles of wine. Look, it was fun, but a one-off thing. Nothing else."

Veva was suddenly dejected and stopped working on their lunch preparations. Her eyes burned toward Lainey as though betrayed. "Nothing else?"

"Don't get in a huff. We'll do it again sometime, but with much less alcohol."

"You sound cold, as though you don't even like me."

"I never said I liked you," Lainey qualified. "We had a fun night, drank too much, and got a bit carried away. That's how things sometimes go, especially in this house," Lainey explained, as though the four walls had some behavioral influence.

"It's good to know where we stand."

"I agree," Lainey added. "Look, I'm glad you're here, and I obviously trust you or we wouldn't be having this conversation."

Veva smiled without any of her usual warmth. They began to eat. The conversation was much less fluid than any of their previous ones. Lainey tried to keep her tone light but remained firmly in the driving seat. She didn't want to hurt Veva's feelings, nor did she want her to expect more than Lainey was willing to give. Over the next thirty minutes, Lainey could see Veva's cool attitude and reluctance to be her typical jovial self.

"Let's go and get ready for this last meeting, and then we can call it a day," Lainey suggested.

"Are you still feeling tired?"

"Yeah, a bit. After a quick power nap and a run, I'll be fine."

"Why don't you go upstairs into the office, and I'll make some fresh green iced tea for us,"

"That would be great." Lainey pointed at the plates and cutlery, "Just leave those in the sink. I'll do them later."

"You don't want them in the dishwasher?"

217

"No. I only use that if we have dinner guests. That hasn't happened for ages. I hand wash everything. My mom did it that way, and I got into the habit." Lainey explained.

"Me too. My grandma was the same way."

Lainey went upstairs into the office and prepared her notes for the call at 1:30 p.m. She was glad to finish in an hour, and then Veva could leave right away. Lainey could take her nap and finish running by five. If Brian hadn't call by then, she would give him absolute hell. Never in all their time together, and no matter what difficulties they had, he'd never failed to communicate with her on any given day.

A few minutes later, Veva passed Lainey a tall glass of iced tea. "This should help get you through," Veva said.

"I hope so." Lainey took a couple of sips. "What did you use? It's good."

"I used your organic green tea with mint and added a drop or two of fresh lemon juice. It gives it a real zest." Veva explained.

"Thanks. I love it."

"It'll take you to places you've never been before," Veva assured.

Brian's internet search had mixed results. Eleven years ago, at the age of eighteen, Veva Unwin legally changed her name. Her resume carried her current name. He'd been unable to dive any deeper with his online search to access her original name. There was a requirement to physically sign documents to get what he wanted. It made Brian think she had something to hide, like a juvenile record.

Brian fully intended to ask Veva in person. His demand for answers would risk his exposure, but he was so wracked with guilt that he would confess all to Lainey.

Brian's notations on Veva contained a level of bias, despite his best effort to write down basic facts. He didn't like anything he'd compiled, and less so his part in the proceedings. He was fully complicit, as if he'd manipulated himself. He reviewed his notes a second time, showing a solid case that Veva had come into their organization to put herself in a position for personal gain. When Lainey first said yes to hiring Veva, Brian had cautioned that there was something odd that a person of her qualifications and talent would want to come to work for 4D Fitness. It was a technical and monetary step down for Veva, even though it was quite a coup for Lainey and Brian. He had asked Veva why she would turn down her pick of organizations and come to work for them. No matter how sophisticated 4D improved their package and software, it would pale into insignificance compared to what she'd done previously in advanced biomechanics and artificial intelligence. Her response had been, "I believe I can help make the 4D Fitness name unforgettable." A boast that now worried him more than ever.

Brian was convinced Veva sniffed out quick monetary opportunities by holding him and Lainey into a deal to keep quiet about her sexual liaison during that night in Bremen. One stupid night, a few beers, and her in that sexy dress was all it took. Veva had to be motivated by something more significant than job satisfaction or brand development. Brian felt he was onto something.

Flying over the Atlantic meant he was chasing time back into the US eastern time zone and into Pacific time. The internet connection was increasingly spotty, and Brian was annoyed at paying for something that continually resulted in his searches spinning in circles as the connection came and went. He wasn't going to argue over a few dollars, but he would write a review of how crappy the service was. He was four hours into the eight-hour flight and was tired. A quick nap seemed inviting, but Brian did not want to stop. His initial findings were enough to spur him into continuing.

He plugged in his laptop as the useless internet connectivity quickly drained the battery power. Veva's background, since her name change, had checked out. He couldn't find anything before she was eighteen.

"What next?" he tapped impatient fingers on the edge of his laptop. He rested his eyelids, thinking he'd take just a moment to work out his next steps.

He awoke with a bump. His arms gripped either side of the seat, unsure if he was dreaming or experiencing turbulence. Brian detested being jostled in the air, and he always felt so helpless. It was a reminder that nature is always one step ahead of anything man could design. His stomach tightened in a knot as he waited. The passenger next to him was bundled in a blanket and fast asleep. Brian looked around; most of the front cabin was semi-dark, and people were sleeping. Thankfully, there was no more turbulence. He'd produced quite enough of that for himself.

His laptop was still sitting on his thighs and now fully charged. He must have been out for over an hour. He pressed the button on the screen in front of him and selected the in-flight status. Only two and half hours left until touching down in New York. He yawned and stretched out his arms.

Carefully Brian squeezed past his sleeping neighbor to use the restroom. But unfortunately, the soap dispenser had no soap left, and he used the last hand towel to dry his hands. "This is not getting a good review," he said to himself, "A useless internet connection and depleted supplies in the restroom. Not good."

The thought struck him like he was wired with electricity. "Reviews." That was his next step. Veva had told him in Bremen that she reviewed everything, everywhere she went. He couldn't recall from what age she said, but he knew it was in her teenage years. "Now, I'll find out what you're up to." Her sentiment about reviews being useful had some validity. Veva's admission of her obsession (as she'd called it) would give him a clearer picture. He hoped it would cement his theory that she was a corporate parasite and using Brian as an avenue to advance her financial standing. Even so, he knew he was solely accountable for his reprehensible actions. Brian never wanted to find the bad in anyone, but for Veva, he was willing to make an exception.

Back in his seat, he had to wait a couple of minutes for the lousy internet to re-connect before commencing his search. As soon as it was working, he tapped into Yelp and searched recent reviews for the Park Hotel in Bremen, thinking that was a logical place to start. It only took him a few minutes to find Veva's review of the hotel, complete with pictures taken from her balcony over the grounds and other snapshots of the features around the park. It was a comprehensive review on how to get from one place to another, descriptions of how amazing and helpful the hotel staff was, and how beautiful the city was. Her review was equally as articulate as her work.

Brian scoffed at the Yelp name she used; Veva the Diva. "Really?" He shook his head. Most of the time, she scurried around like some barely noticeable mouse. "Diva, my ass." She'd even reviewed the locally brewed beer they'd had, which had led to his difficulties. So, he tracked backward; he searched through the reviews she'd posted and found she reviewed things regularly from 2006 until today. Brian calculated that if she was twenty-nine now, she must have started at age 14.

"Shit!" He complained as the useless connection dropped out again. He was agitated enough to press the button that summoned the flight attendant.

"Can I help you, Sir?" The young man asked.

"The internet keeps dropping out. Is it just me, or has anyone else said anything?"

"I'm so sorry. It's the same for everyone. I'll make sure you get a refund. I've told the captain, and he's alerted the maintenance crew to take a look when we land."

"There's nothing you can do to boost it?"

"I'm sorry, we can't. And I know it is getting worse. Sorry." The attendant made a long sad face.

"Thanks, anyway." Brian waited over two minutes for it to come back, which seemed way longer. Brian read Veva's early reviews in Albany, Oregon, where she'd reviewed just about every store in town, every park, and all the city utilities. She wasn't kidding when she said she liked giving reviews. He could see where she'd lived when she was a teenager, although the details did little to complete his picture of who he thought she might be.

He went back to his original search and worked backward from Germany, observing the circles she moved in. She reviewed her first day of orientation at 4D Fitness and gave it five stars, saying how friendly the people were and the profound level of detail to help her make a positive start, including the honor of meeting Lainey Stewart. It seemed a little over the top, but Brian wasn't complaining about good press.

He slowly combed backward through the prior weeks that showed Veva running trails while she was unemployed. She'd been all over Oregon and northern California. The internet connection fell out again, causing him to smash his fist onto the screen. "C'mon! Jesus!"

He looked around and found a couple of agitated fellow passengers who shared his angst. Each relayed a knowing roll of their eyes and looks of disgust.

"C'mon," he encouraged. His fellow internet users were angrily looking at their devices and pressing buttons on the screens to see if they could magically alter the outcome. Finally, the symbol on the bottom right of his laptop switched from a globe to five bars. Brian immediately got back to his research.

There were reviews of cafés, even gas stations. He checked the following review twice to make sure he read it correctly. It was by Veva the Diva, and it was her review of the Arashiyama running trail in Kyoto. "Are you kidding me?" Brian almost slithered out of his seat. Veva wrote a perfect description of the shrine, the lake, and the bamboo forest, including the run along the old railway line. However, she had not mentioned she'd been there, which immediately made him suspicious. The date of her review made his entire body jump, and the laptop slipped between his legs to the floor. He had to squeeze forward as the passenger in front had their seat fully reclined, making it difficult to retrieve the laptop. He placed the machine on his thighs and focused back on the screen.

The internet failed again, and all he could see was a message telling him there was no connection and to try again shortly. "C'mon, you motherfucker!" he hissed at the technology.

He thought he'd made a mistake, but the glance showed Veva was in Kyoto a few days before his arrival. They were both there at the same time. He needed that damn internet connection to be sure.

"C'mon, you bastard," he growled at the screen. His imagination worked overtime. He tried his phone, but it had no connection. Veva was with him in Bremen when that girl was killed in the parkland forest. She was in Kyoto, too. Lainey had just told him Detective Strahan informed her they were investigating a link to a murder there. The others were all relatively local in the northwest of the US, on the doorstep of where they lived. His life was blowing up all around him, and the common denominator, as far as he could tell, was Veva. "Where's the internet connection?" he asked.

Brian sifted through his copious notes. He dropped the notepad as another thought took over and shook him through to his bones.

"Lainey!"

Brian checked the calendar on his phone. Despite no signal to his device, he could see the scheduled meetings and where each participant had logged into previous online calls. Veva and Lainey were together. It meant Lainey was in the house with Veva. "Oh, fuck."

Still no damned connectivity. If Brian was right, even though it was a stretch, without any actual evidence, the level of coincidence was too high for it to be anything else. Fear bred on fear, and within a minute, Brian convinced himself that Veva was the one who'd tried to kill Lainey and murdered those other young women. "That's why she came to work for us." Veva was highly paid in Silicon Valley and came to 4D Fitness as their costliest employee by some margin. She didn't come for fame or the challenge. "She came for Lainey,"

His voice faltered, and he began to weep. Veva couldn't care less about money or blackmail or any other bullshit story of which he'd convinced himself. She came to finish what she'd started.

He pushed aside his useless laptop and fiddled with his cell phone. He could pay the fee and make a call home. He'd tell Lainey to call Strahan and get Veva out of the house. Looking at the time, it was early afternoon at home. Nobody was expecting him to be home for another two days. He tried again with his phone, following the instructions to connect so he could make a call. After five minutes of getting nothing, Brian summoned the flight attendant again.

"Hey, I have an emergency, and I need to make a call, but I can't get a connection."

"I'm sorry, sir, let me go to see what I can do." The attendant disappeared up front, and Brian watched him in discussion with a colleague. The attendants began to open various panels and make internal calls back and forth to what he assumed were the pilots. Brian was aware that the pilots had ultimate control of all aircraft communications.

Ten minutes went by before he climbed from his seat and went up front. "Guys, I need to communicate with my wife on the ground. Is there any resolution in sight?"

"Not yet, sir; please retake your seat. We're doing all we can. The captain is rebooting the entire system. Unfortunately, nobody can watch any movies or connect to the internet for a few moments." The attendant waited impatiently for Brian to walk away.

"Please, can you give me an update? I have to get a message to my wife. An emergency."

"As soon as we can, sir."

Brian retreated to his seat, cursing under his breath. He ignored the concerned looks from the passengers scrutinizing him. He immediately returned to watching the screen in front of him. Every second of the reboot was agonizing! From the middle and rear of the plane, there was a slight noise of relief as those watching movies or shows were able to return to whatever they were viewing. The screen in front showed all of the usual options, but the internet connection to his laptop failed to initiate. Brian returned to where the flight attendants gathered.

The attendants saw him coming, and one held out a hand, telling him not to approach any further. "Sir, we're unable to get our Wi-Fi systems back online. So you'll have to wait until we touch down in New York to make a call or use the internet. I'm sorry, but the captain has said there's nothing else we can do."

"I need to speak with the captain," he demanded.

"Sir, I respectfully ask you to retake your seat and comply with our requests. If you fail to do so, we'll have to alert the ground authorities, and you'll be escorted from the plane."

"What? I only asked to speak with the captain. I have a real emergency," he pleaded.

"We appreciate that, sir, but we need all passengers to be in their seats."

"This is crazy. You can't pass on a message and have the pilot contact someone for me?"

"I'll ask, but I already know the answer. Now please take your seat, sir."

Brian threw his hands in the air. "This is ridiculous," he grimaced as he walked away. There were still over ninety minutes before they touched down. But, at least he was near the front and would be one of the first to disembark.

Brian sat nervously watching and hoping for the internet to work, but it never became operable. He should have called Lainey over a day ago. "Stupid bastard," he cursed his stubbornness.

CHAPTER TWENTY ONE

It was mid-afternoon, on a bright sunny spring day in northern California, when Detectives Hurst and Strahan returned to Eureka. They'd been called away earlier in the morning when an eyewitness claimed they spotted someone acting suspiciously in the parking lot of Prairie Creek Redwoods National Park the previous week. Hurst and Strahan made the hour drive north to Klamath Glen RV Park. It was only twenty miles from the Oregon state line and set in rugged forested terrain. The only distinctive feature was the Klamath River, which flowed through the Yurok Reservation and eventually out into the North Pacific Ocean. The man who came forward lived in the RV park. He was working illegally in the park. Hurst assured him his testimony would not be used against him in any prejudicial way.

The witness was Eleonso Zamora. A former small-time criminal with priors for burglary, theft, and assault. For most of his adult life, he worked in the farmlands of California. Once he was released from jail (the last time), he'd moved further north to keep himself out of trouble. Eleonso lived quietly and had worked in the RV park for the last four years. His tiny camper van wasn't big enough for Hurst, Strahan, and him to fit inside, so they sat in the open air by his makeshift fire in the dry dirt and listened to his story.

He told them how he drove to Prairie Creek on his day off work and went for a hike in the redwoods. He stopped to take a leak on his way back and saw a tall man in a black top doing something in the woods. Eleonso noticed the guy was busy, like he was digging or moving something around. Eleonso didn't want any trouble, so he made his way back to the lot and moved his van off to one side, behind the entranceway's trees. He opened a can of chili con-carne and used his little stove to heat it. While eating, the same man arrived back in the lot and got into what Eleonso described as some fancy rich guy's car.

Most people there drove an old truck or four-by-four. Strahan used his phone to show Eleonso pictures of a Jaguar I-Pace, and he confirmed it was the same type of car he'd seen. He noticed the man had gotten changed inside his car into business clothes, put his shorts, top, and sneakers into the trunk, and left in a hurry. Eleonso claimed he didn't think much about it, as many people do crazy things in the woods. A few days later, when he heard the news that a young woman's body was found there, he decided he should say something. He didn't believe he could identify the man's face, but he was tall and fit, and Eleonso guessed the man was in his mid-thirties.

Hurst pulled up a picture on the internet of Brian Stewart and asked if Eleonso could identify him. But he could not positively say for certain.

They updated the captain, as well as conferencing Hurst's boss in Salem. They would bring Brian Stewart in for questioning when he returned from his business trip. The evidence was against Brian. He had visited Bremen, Kyoto, and now a car just like his, and a man fitting his description, was seen near the grave of Daphne Montclair.

Detective Hurst sat in the comfy chair inside Strahan's office. "I don't like it any more than you do, but he's got his hands in everything," she said, trying to straighten her unruly hair. "If we don't pursue it, and it turns out he's our man, you'll be hooking the bait lines on my boat – where we'll both be living."

"As if I needed more incentive to get this closed out."

"Let's get back to the lists of names we got from Matthaus in Bremen. Anything from Kagawa yet?"

Strahan glimpsed at his emails. "Not yet. I'll ask again."

"Tell him to pull his finger out; we just need the names. After that, he can poke around with them as much as he likes." Hurst snorted.

Strahan pulled up the list from Germany and began. He got through about seventy names, all of which meant nothing, until he got the one that stuck out, simply by the first name and the surname that went with it.

"You said you had a niece called Genevieve. Is she Genevieve Hurst?"

"Yeah, Ginny – my niece. Why?" Detective Hurst had her head buried close to her screen.

"There's a Genevieve Hurst on the list from Detective Matthaus in Bremen." Strahan opened the link to her name. "She flew into Bremen from San Francisco earlier this week."

Hurst popped up her head. "What day? Was it Sunday, by any chance?"

"It was."

"Same day Brian Stewart flew there from San Francisco," Hurst replied. "Whereabouts was she staying?"

Strahan searched deeper. "Just hang on…" He arrived at the data. "She stayed in the Park Hotel in Bremen. Same as Brian Stewart. Is it your niece?"

"Could be. I haven't had contact with her since she was a teenager. There can't be too many Genevieve Hurst's coming out of the northwest." Her reply sounded like the words caused her some pain. "But no Genevieve Hurst is working at 4D Fitness."

"Where does she work?"

"I've no idea. Last I heard, she was somewhere near San Jose, working for a big tech company. I don't know which one." Hurst stopped what she was doing and stared at Strahan. "My sister … the one who died years ago? Remember I said she always used to say things like, 'Let them praise the name of the Lord, etc.' My mom – Genevieve's grandma - could barely string a sentence together without involving scripture or calling in Jesus."

"Did Genevieve go to church and believe in all that?"

"She went to church alright. Hell, I even took her when I had her. My sister, the one who died, believed she was called to serve God, and if you did something exceptional here on earth when you died, you'd be rewarded with the hands of angels waiting to welcome you. A celestial vision to carry you into the kingdom of heaven, placing you alongside God. I mentioned it the other day, but it was more a family story than anything else. Before she passed away from cancer, I used to visit, and little Ginny would tell me she was helping her mommy go in peace and that she'd join her one day," Hurst explained.

Strahan felt his stomach roll over, and he noted the glistening in his colleagues' dark eyes. "Do you think it could be…"

"It could be anything," Hurst cut him off. "Find out if she's been anywhere else on our search list. I'll search where she lives and where she's working. She's always been super-smart, if not a little strange."

Strahan buried his head back into the data sent by the German Police. "I'll ask Detective Matthaus if there's any surveillance video from the Park Hotel in Bremen showing her coming and going."

"Matthaus said they would pull all of it. Let's call him."

"It's probably midnight over there," Strahan observed.

"I don't give a shit. He can wake up." Hurst used the desk phone and called Detective Matthaus. A few seconds later, the ring tone sounded over the speaker. It was only two rings before Matthaus groggily answered.

"Detective Matthaus, this is Hurst and Strahan here in California. We wanted to ask you about the video footage from the hotel."

"You know it is the early hours of the morning?"

"I know. We have a potential lead. We need your help. Wouldn't ask if it wasn't urgent," Hurst said.

They heard a woman's angry voice in the background, followed by Matthaus heavily sighing. "Hang on." He argued in German with the female and groaned again. The slamming of a door sounded before he spoke again. "Now, I do not disturb my wife anymore. There is nothing that we can use on the tapes. The camera on the hotel's front doors doesn't work, so we have nothing from there. The only shot we have is from the main lobby. It shows somebody in tracksuit bottoms and dark blue hooded top, with the hood raised, exiting the hotel around eight p.m. on the night Marlene went missing."

"Can you see anything else? A shot from the parking lot or somewhere nearby?" Hurst asked.

"We've tried, and there is nothing. We know Marlene told a friend she was going out to eat locally in Bremen. She never paid for a meal with her credit cards, and there was no cash in her purse. We believe the killer paid for her food. We're still searching local bars and cafés to see where she might have gone. Nothing so far."

"Can you send us the footage from the hotel?" Hurst asked.

"Sure. You can see somebody five-foot-seven to five-nine in a hooded sweatshirt leaving the hotel and returning at three a.m. Somebody with black hair," he explained.

"I thought you said the hood was raised?" Strahan interjected.

"It is, but a small amount of black hair is sticking out from the side. The hair is shoulder length. Not enough to make any identification possible. I am sending you the link to the file; it's too big to send," Matthaus said.

"Is it a man or woman in the video? The one who leaves the hotel and comes back at 3 a.m." Hurst asked

"We cannot tell, but it is likely a woman by the shoulders and the movement. Do you think the killer is female?" he asked, as though it came as no surprise.

"We do. Do you know something we don't?"

"No. The files and evidence show these girls were treated too kindly for it to be a man. The nightdress and the nails are too precise for a man, unless the killer is a professional, erm…"

"They call them 'nail technicians' these days," Hurst helped him.

"Ah, yes. I do not have the English for this. You should have the link any moment."

"From Marlene Durr's autopsy, and based on her last meal, can you narrow it down to where she may have been for dinner?' Strahan asked.

"Unfortunately, not. A small trace of red wine, some chicken, and vegetables. Every bar and restaurant within ten miles of her life serve the same foods. There is one other thing I learned only yesterday. I have yet to share it, as I was not certain it had any relevance. One of Marlene's dear friends, the one she contacted the night she was killed, told me that, although Marlene lived with her boyfriend, she liked the company of other women when she could get the chance. Does that make sense for you?"

"She liked pussy," Hurst replied.

"Ah, yes. Your American pussy," Matthaus quietly laughed. "I have seen this in the movies. When you look at the hotel video, you will see the black hair when the person steps down into the main lobby. However, the view on the return shows nothing of any use. What else can I do to assist you before I get back into bed with my unhappy wife?"

"Try to find more video of this character in the blue hood. It might be the person we're looking for."

"We still do not have the missing ring, taken from Marlene's hand, or the photograph taken from the apartment. If your suspect has these, you likely have the right person," Matthaus advised. "Her fiancé wants the ring back. It's worth a lot of money."

"He sounds like quite a catch," Hurst sneered.

"Ah, a good joke, I think. The details of it are in the report. The ring is unique. You have the description. A red ruby, surrounded by diamonds."

"A guy who used her for porno films, with a romantic heart," Hurst implied the opposite meaning.

"He is, as you would say, an asshole, no?"

"Correct."

"I must be back to bed, or I will need to find a ring for another wife. Goodnight," Matthaus concluded.

"Thank you for your time, and sorry we got you out of bed," Strahan added, seeing Hurst was itching to get off the call. "Apologies to your wife, too."

"Goodnight, my American colleagues."

Hurst cut the call. "Let's get that link on the screen."

"He only sent it to me." Strahan hid the smirk that desperately wanted to spread across his lips.

"Those German guys like your fair hair and chiseled jawline. Reminds them of the good old days," she coldly cast her aspersion.

Strahan moved his laptop onto the desk and faced it toward them. "Let's see what they have." He clicked on the link, and it took them to the interface where Strahan logged in with the credentials Detective Matthaus had provided. "The German database is superb."

He selected the case name of Marlene Durr, and the system confirmed they had permission to access the files and any associated evidence. Strahan looked down the comprehensive list of entries. The system was translated into English, although some of the phrases were awkward. "Park Hotel surveillance. Here we are."

Inside was a list of interviews with staff members and folders containing dozens of pictures from around the hotel. Strahan ignored the huffing and puffing that came from Hurst as they had to wade through a mountain of data to find the exact folder. "Ah, here we go," Strahan added extra cheer to his discovery to annoy his colleague. "Das video file."

The video showed precisely what Detective Matthaus had described. Strahan paused the video, with the long strands of black hair protruding from the edge of the hood. "I'm no expert in hairstyles, but that jet-black color, and the way it has a slight curl towards the underneath the jaw, looks like Veva Unwin. She went with Brian Stewart to Bremen."

"I only got a quick look at her from the back when she ran up the stairs that one time. So I can't say for sure."

"I can," Strahan replied. "Let's take a look at something I bet nobody bothered to check."

"And what's that?"

"Her feet."

"I didn't have you down as one of those guys," Hurst jibed.

"I don't think I am one of those guys. We have access to enhancement software."

"If you're thinking you can measure a size seven footprint from a video, good luck trying to make that stick in court."

"I am thinking that, and let's see if we can view the state of the footwear. When they found the body, it was covered in mud. The parkland didn't drain after the downpour." Strahan whizzed through the video until they found the part where the same figure returned to the hotel at 3 a.m.

"Why wouldn't you use the elevator? I'll send Matthaus a note. I bet the elevator only operates if you scan your card to a reader. Each scan registers a unique ID. If you worked in tech and at a high level, you'd know the stairs are the only way to avoid detection." Strahan paused on the figure approaching the stairs and used the software to focus on the sneakers.

"Anybody could have dirty footwear. So it doesn't prove anything." Hurst sounded bored.

"Maybe not, but it would suggest someone was in the mud, and why would you be in the mud at three in the morning? By itself, it's not proof of anything unless we could get our hands on the sneakers and show they contained soil samples from the park." He pointed as the image sharpened. "See there on the edges of the sneakers? Mud everywhere. Whoever this is, they've been busy in the mud in the early hours. And look there, the hooded top has the embroidered 4D logo."

Hurst split her focus between Strahan's updates and typing on her keyboard. She showed him her screen. "Genevieve Hurst legally changed her name in 2010. She's now Veva Unwin! The same Veva Unwin who works at 4D Fitness. Unwin was our great grandmother's maiden name."

"Oh, fuck!" Strahan's face dropped, and his complexion turned pale.

Hurst added, "Looks like Genevieve got into some trouble in a domestic argument with a former girlfriend in 2009. She was charged with assault and threatening behavior. Charges were eventually dropped. She changed her name the following year and moved away from Albany to San Jose. This is my niece. Jesus Christ, Strahan, I might have created all of this. I was the one who couldn't take care of her."

"You were a young Detective - you didn't stand a chance."

"Shit. It must be her. Genevieve – Veva. Little Ginny. She must have two different passports– one with her old name and one with the new one."

"We'll figure that out later. If we're right about this, then it isn't on you. You didn't tell anyone to murder young women and bury them in the woods. We have an immediate bigger problem."

"What?"

"Veva Unwin has been working out of Lainey and Brian's house. We've seen her there. She may be about to finish what she failed to accomplish a year ago. It's not a coincidence that she's working at 4D Fitness."

Hurst briskly walked alongside him to the car, already with her phone to her ear. "It's ringing," she said and put the call on speaker. The ringtone switched to voicemail. "Hi, you've reached Lainey Stewart. I can't take your call right now, but if you leave your name and number and a quick message, I'll call you back as soon as I can."

Hurst jabbed Strahan's arm, and they ran to the car.

When Brian landed in New York, he called Lainey and left her a dozen text messages to call him straight back. He emailed her three times without a response. No doubt she was angry at him for not contacting her, and she was simply giving him the same treatment. He hoped so. It was better than the other possibilities. He called her again when he arrived in San Francisco. If she was blanking him, then he thoroughly deserved it. He was only a few minutes from touching down in Eureka and a ten-minute drive to the house.

The small aircraft he was flying in had no creature comforts, like Wi-Fi, so he could not call Detective Strahan. He should have done that from New York and San Francisco, but he had no evidence and felt stupid. The longer the journey progressed and the closer he got to home, the more paranoia crept over him. He wanted to ask the detective if he wouldn't mind checking in on Lainey to make sure she was okay. Brian had many circumstantial touchpoints suggesting Veva could be crooked, but none were viable evidence of any kind. It wasn't like Strahan liked him anyway. Brian saw the envy. Lots of men looked at Brian that way for being married to Lainey.

Brian left Lainey three voicemails. He told her that he'd received an anonymous message from someone claiming to know where her engagement ring was, and Brian had found it, thinking he could do something nice for her, only to realize how stupid his actions were. He let her know he had the ring and would explain further when he got home. Brian did not tell her it was hidden in their walk-in closet, and there was no way he would admit prizing it from the cold fingers of a dead girl. He apologized for not being in touch and for being an asshole. Brian had to come clean with Lainey about his actions. Brian had more than enough to be ashamed of.

The plane wheels bounced on the tarmac, and he guessed by the time he picked up his case and made it to his car, he was twenty-five minutes from home. He sent a couple of texts to Lainey with no reply. It was almost five in the afternoon, and she should have responded to something. He reminded himself it was her prideful rage that kept her from replying. Lainey would undoubtedly unleash on him the second he walked through the door.

CHAPTER TWENTY-TWO

Lainey opened her eyes, and it took her a moment to adjust to the light overhead. The sound of a light breeze rustling the overhead leafy branches accompanied the birds twittering back and forth in the foliage. The air was a pleasant median temperature, and she could see shafts of brilliant sunlight cutting through the canopy that sprinkled spots of light over her body. Her eyes blinked hard, wondering why she was outside and why her legs were bare from below her knees.

She closed her eyes, telling herself to wake up. She must have dozed off when their last call had ended. Having recently ventured outside, she had no fear of being in the open air. There was a strange sense of calm to the peculiar scenario, where she would have awoken in a state of panic only a few weeks ago. Lainey shook herself and opened her eyes again.

She was lying in a slight indentation in the ground, and bushes and trees surrounded her, and across, on the other side of the pond, she could make out the gothic folly, with its stone arches and crooked pillars. She realized her immobilized body was adorned in a white silk nightdress. "It can't be," she told herself. She resisted the dread-filled sensation shooting through her body. "There's just no way," she said aloud. The sound of the material underneath her body made her aware of the slippery man-made material that lined the hole. It had a distinct rustling sound and an all too familiar feel.

From somewhere behind her and out of sight, she heard a soft voice singing a familiar hymn. Lainey recognized the words from services she'd attended in her childhood but could not pinpoint the song. "Veva?" she called out, sure that her voice was singing. "Veva?" she repeated, with an increased spike in volume that demanded a response.

"I'll be right with you. Just relax."

"Veva, what have you done?" Lainey asked the questions like a disappointed mother talking to a guilty child.

Veva did not respond and continued singing the hymn.

Lainey was familiar with this feeling, where her body and mind were alive, but their internal connection was somehow broken. She gritted her teeth and attempted to move. Spit flew from her angry lips.

"Veva!" She called again. Lainey knew what was happening but not why. There was no sense in berating Veva; instead, she needed to attempt to reason with her. Her instinct was to curse and scream at the flapper-headed lunatic who'd put her in the ground. Lainey's hazy recollection from her previous scrape with death was of someone with brilliant medium brown eyes and not the light green of Veva's. It made Lainey think there may be an accomplice nearby who was helping. The effort not to scream was agonizing. She told herself to stay calm. If she did anything to upset Veva, there was no way out. They were flirting and kissing only twenty-four hours ago. Lainey's only regret was that she hadn't seen what else was coming.

Since this morning, however, Veva had been cold after Lainey had made apparent their little fling was exactly that. Veva wanted more, and there was an element of desperation. Nevertheless, there was a connection between them, and if she was right, Lainey intended to use it.

"Veva, my sweet, can you come here, please? I need you."

The singing got closer, and Veva's head appeared two feet above her own. Lainey noticed that Veva was wearing a matching white silk nightgown that revealed her pale shoulders and arms.

"Isn't it beautiful? I told you we should come here together." Veva lightly uttered the words as though they were sitting on the grass, enjoying a champagne picnic. "You look divine," Veva ran her hand on the left side of Lainey's face and slightly adjusted her hair.

"Veva, I think we should sit out by the folly and watch the sunset together. It's the most spectacular sight on earth. We said we would, didn't we?"

Veva looked across the pond to where the sun's low angle had penetrated the trees and illuminated the fallen temple. Her face lit up as strong as the rays of sunbeams as she marveled at the spectacle. "You're right; it is the most

236

beautiful sight. You and I will see something else, something where we can embrace it and savor it for all eternity." She looked down at Lainey with an eager expectation.

"And where might that be?" Lainey had to know.

"To meet with God, of course. I've been waiting for this moment since I was little. My mommy told me the day would come. So we're taking the journey together."

"But we were just getting to know one another and enjoy each other's company in all kinds of special ways." Lainey did her best to smile sweetly.

"Our time has already been special together. I wouldn't swap it for the world. But now, we'll be like two souls, combined into one, going forward together," Veva almost sang the words, and her state of happiness was enough for her to sway her body from side to side.

"Veva, I'd love for us to do that, but I want to enjoy more of you in this life. Think about how amazing last night was and how much more we could explore this life together. I know you felt it as much as I did."

"I did. Right through my heart and into my soul. The first time I saw you interviewed on Fitness Fanatics Podcast, I knew that we'd fall in love and we were meant to be together."

Lainey's gut heaved with every word penetrating her ears, like knitting needles shoved into her brain. "You see. God wants us to finish this journey here before thinking about the next phase."

"No. You're wrong," Veva wagged a finger, and her facial expression lost its innocence. "You were mean to me this morning. After all we've been through and the sacrifices I've made to get you into God's hands. You said you didn't even like me. I know you lied, but even so, it was mean. I'm relieving us both from the tawdriness and limitations of these blood-fueled vessels. It's too easy to be cruel or to suffer unnecessarily. You should be grateful we're about to be done with it," Veva explained, like she was presenting a PowerPoint.

"What have you given me? I don't feel good," Lainey complained, hoping to garner some pity.

"A roofie. You barely made it through the last conference call. I was worried that I might have to cut the thing short as you started to slur your words. It'll wear off soon. We'll have already passed peacefully over to the

237

other side by then." Veva shuffled forward on her knees and took hold of Lainey's hands. "Can you hear that sound?"

Lainey had to swallow hard and concentrate in order not to burst into tears. "I hear nature in all its glory," she said, sounding like she was fully connected with Veva. "It's like the birds call us to enjoy the sunset and live our lives as God intended."

Veva squeezed Lainey's hands. "That very poetic and slippery of you, my love. There's no delaying or avoiding God's intention. I was put here on this earth to deliver you into salvation. The same as I did with our other sisters."

"Veva, what have you done?" Lainey wanted to add more, but the trembling in her lip prevented her from continuing.

"I've listened to my calling and done as I was asked. I haven't told you about how mommy died, have I?"

"No. Please do. I want to hear all of it," Lainey pleaded to buy herself time and to provide an opportunity to reason her way out of this predicament.

"She was sick for a very long time. Cancer. Ever since I can remember, she was sick. She was barely able to leave her room most days. Her two sisters and my grandma would come over to clean, cook, and take care of me, or at least as best they could. I used to curl up on mommy's bed when she was asleep, and I'd shut my eyes and ask God to please make sure she would wake up. She slept so quietly, so peacefully. It was like she was practicing for death. I was terrified she would leave me behind, so I'd snuggle up with her, even though I wasn't supposed to. She was the most loving person, with a kindness that seeped from her pores. It was hard, watching her suffer."

Veva steadied herself and took an extra tight grip on Lainey's hands. She sniffed hard and shook her head, trying to stop the tears from rolling off her face. "She taught me all about compassion and love. Mommy said you had to look beyond the surface of what people showed to the world and find the real pain underneath before you could judge what someone is like."

"Can you show me that?" Lainey asked.

Veva smiled down upon her dear friend, and the love was evident in her expression. "I'm doing it right now. I won't let you suffer anymore." Veva leaned into the hole in the ground and kissed Lainey on the lips. "I love you too much to let anything bad happen to you."

Veva used her index finger to wipe away Lainey's tears. "There, there, it's okay. This is a time for happiness. We're going to fall asleep together, side by side, and we'll hear the sound of the angels calling for us."

"I don't hear anything."

"You will. I've heard them before." Veva looked at the surrounding trees and bushes that formed a barrier around the folly. "This is the perfect place, Lainey." Veva released herself from Lainey's hands and carefully placed a finger into her eyeballs. Lainey watched helplessly as Veva removed something from each eye and flicked away the residue.

"That's better. I hate wearing contacts. This is my real color. Do you like it?"

Lainey spluttered and tried to move her body but was unable to register a twitch in her limbs. Staring into the bright brown eyes was a sight Lainey could never forget. The nicely formed eyebrows above, and the love in Veva's gaze, were the same as in her nightmares.

The endearing smile and true love on Veva's face were misguided. Instead, Veva delivered a destructive love. "Veva, please. If you love me, then don't do this."

Veva placed a finger over her lips, calling for quiet. "Let me tell you all about mommy. I can't wait for you to meet her."

"And guess who just touched down on US soil?" Strahan said with fake surprise.

"Enlighten me." Hurst was unamused by the question as she climbed into the driver's seat.

"Brian Stewart. He wasn't supposed to be back for another two days. I just got an alert from our new system. Finally, something works. Things are getting more complicated by the hour. Did you hear back from Lainey?"

"Not yet. I can't believe this could be my Ginny unless she and Brian Stewart are in this together somehow. It has to be one or both of them."

"You said you haven't seen her for years, and her childhood was traumatic in terms of being bounced around after her mom died. So a lot could have taken place between now and then."

"I could be part of the problem," Hurst grimaced.

"We need to get to the house."

Hurst started the car. "Call for backup and have them on silent approach. The last thing we need to do is spook anyone. Christ knows who's doing what in that house."

"We've got enough to hold Veva for questioning. And Brian Stewart!" Strahan said as Hurst backed the car from its parking space and spun around. He dialed Lainey's cell as they exited the parking lot. "Still no answer. I don't know who to arrest first."

"We'll arrest all of them. Veva's the one we want," Hurst added with some certainty. "The timelines fit. She has…" Hurst paused. "She might have a deranged motive."

"Brain Stewart would solely inherit all of 4D Fitness – I'd say that's motive enough."

"True. But you wouldn't go with the theatrics of burying her in the woods dressed like she's on her honeymoon. Plus, he'd know about her use of Epinephrine. He would have made sure that the original dosage of Digoxin was enough to take her out. He's in the thick of this, but I don't think he's our man."

"I'll tell our backup to shoot everyone on sight except me and you," Strahan replied.

"If my instincts are right, I may just shoot myself. I should have seen this sooner."

"We could all say that. I've been wrestling with this case for over a year."

They were quickly followed by three police vehicles as they pulled onto the street. Strahan told their backup absolutely no sirens. Hurst called Lainey but got the same result as Strahan.

240

They raced through the small town of Eureka and went south down the 101 freeway until reaching the exit. As they came around the corner of the tight road, there was a scattering of large houses, and in the distance, the Stewart residence was sitting proudly on the hill.

"From here, it looks like a great place to live," Hurst observed.

"You wouldn't want to live in it?"

"Too much to clean. Besides the modern open style, with its sleek lines and everything minimal, it feels cold. I could never be warm in a house like that."

"I'd guess Lainey and Brian might agree with you."

CHAPTER TWENTY-THREE

Brian was at the mercy of his imaginary darkness. He no longer believed Lainey ignored his calls but envisioned something quite terrible. He should have called her from Bremen. He should have called Detective Strahan. He tried to reason that it was only since he left Germany that he had first realized Veva was up to something. He should have known that the minute she took him in her mouth, a bigger game was being played. He'd cursed himself to the point where he'd run out of expletives. The more he reflected, the more the ugly details joined together. Brian knew it took excellent planning and technical skills to pull off positioning a motion sensor camera in Prairie Creek Forest that trapped him as he searched for Lainey's ring.

Veva had those skills in abundance and could program emails that vanished without a trace. She'd had access to the murdered women in Europe and Japan and those closer to home. And she had access to 4D's entire system. On top of that, she wasn't even using her real name any longer. He cried aloud, a visceral scream that burned his throat. It took somebody with a particular level of cunning to murder in such a precise manner. Admirable, in some perverse way. He had allowed that woman into their home and gladly accommodated her, thinking it good for Lainey to have company in the house! He viewed it like the devil knocking at the front door, and he'd opened it wide with welcoming arms.

He zoomed past the other cars on the freeway, going as fast as he dared without bringing himself to disaster. He leaned forward and reached underneath the front seat. There, in the tiny hidden compartment, he pulled out the Glock 26 and a spare magazine. Driving close to a hundred miles per hour with only one hand on the wheel wasn't easy. He stuffed the spare magazine in the side pocket of his jacket, keeping the gun between his legs. It seemed crazy that any part of his life could have come to this point, and yet, at this exact moment, his actions seemed perfectly appropriate. If Lainey were in danger, Brian would do anything to protect her.

Anything.

He increased his speed. If a traffic cop came after him, Brian wasn't stopping. A ticket and some jail time paled insignificantly compared to what he believed were at stake. Brian tossed around whether or not he could put a bullet in someone if necessary. All he wanted to do was get Veva out of the house.

Brian screeched the car off the exit ramp around the corner and blasted towards home. He could see their house in the distance—something of a homage to someone who'd been successful, at least in business. It displayed a magnificence, and yet Brian knew that the inner walls were stained with the permanence of desperation. The road climbed, turned left and right, with fields on either side, and the two lines of trees led to the gated entrance. He needed all his driving skills to avoid smashing into the four vehicles in the gateway as he skidded the car around them. He pressed the switch inside his car, and the massive gates began to open.

The car next to him wound down the window. Brian recognized Detective Strahan but not the female sitting next to him.

It was Hurst who spoke first. "Brian, we need to talk with you and Lainey. I'm Detective…"

"Lainey's in trouble!" Before Hurst could say another word, Brian sped through the gates, leaving them in a cloud of dust. Inside the gateway, an officer manually tried to operate the gate system. The scene informed Brian that Lainey had not answered the call from the intercom.

Brian scraped either side of his car on the walls and bushes lining the way. As he came around the final bend, his worst fears were confirmed, seeing Veva's white BMW parked by the flower beds. Lainey's car was in its usual place, shining pristinely in the early evening sun.

Behind him was the rushing sound of the tires from the police cars coming up the road. He didn't have time to consider any options. Instead, he took the gun in his right hand and rushed towards the house.

Hurst and Strahan skidded to a halt. "Brian, stop!" Strahan shouted.

243

Brian ignored them and ran through the front door. Once inside the entranceway, he was beyond their line of fire. He rushed into the central part of the house. "Lainey. Lainey!" His cry was urgent and angry. "Lainey!" There was no sign of her or Veva on the ground floor. He ran up the stairs and into the exercise room. Nobody was on the treadmills or using the gym. He ran along the landing. From below, Strahan and Hurst, with two officers behind them, had weapons drawn and pointed them at him.

"Hold it, Brian. Hold it!" Strahan screamed at him.

Hearing Strahan shouting made Brian halt, and the sight of four guns trained on him had him slowly raise both hands and display his Glock that hung loosely in his fingers. "I need to find Lainey! She's in danger," he yelled back at them.

"We know. I need you to drop the gun. Now!" Strahan edged further up the stairs.

"Drop it and walk away, Brian," Hurst echoed.

Brian held his right arm outward and let the gun drop over the banister, and it clanged onto the tiled floor below. "We need to find Lainey," he called again. He ducked behind the upper solid wooden rail and hurried into the master bedroom.

Strahan rushed ahead with Hurst right behind him. "Brian, we need to see your hands."

"For fucks sake!" Hurst growled as they arrived on the landing.

"Brian, we're coming in. We just want to get everyone out of there safely," Strahan shouted.

"She's not here. I'm coming out. Don't shoot!" Brian shouted. He cautiously stepped from the doorway so they could see him. Both hands were half-heartedly raised above his head. "I just flew in from abroad. Veva was in Germany and Kyoto," he exclaimed.

"We know," Hurst held a cautionary hand to let Brian know he should remain still. Brian waited as Strahan stepped forward and quickly frisked him.

"Turn around," Strahan said,

"No." Brian glared at the Detective. "I haven't murdered anyone. She has Lainey! We need to find them." He noticed the sliding door was open at the back of the living room. He pointed. "There. Lainey can't leave the house. You know this," he pleaded with Strahan. "She's out there with that fucking maniac."

Hurst gave Strahan the nod, letting him know handcuffs weren't necessary. "If you sneeze the wrong way, I'll shoot you," Hurst told Brian.

He could tell by the Detective's eyes that she meant every word. "I just want my wife."

"Where would they go?" Hurst asked.

"I'm not sure. We're on twelve acres."

"Where's the most secluded spot you have? Somewhere tranquil, like a place you'd want to make love on a blanket," Hurst said.

"The folly," Brian replied, his eyes opening wide. "We have a gothic folly."

"Lead the way." Hurst ushered him ahead. She alerted three officers to search every room in the house and garage and the rest to follow them down the terraced gardens.

Brian spun around and ran back toward the bedroom. "The EpiPen," he cried out and momentarily disappeared from view. Then, a moment later, he pushed through them as he showed them the small plastic device in his hand. "Follow me." He stuffed it in his pocket.

They rushed outside, across the stone patio, around the swimming pool, down four flights of steps, and headed into the line of trees. A narrow dirt path wound through the trees and opened into a small meadow. "It's over here." Brian ran much faster than the trailing group and was quickly fifty paces ahead of them.

Hurst was lagging, her body unused to such physical exercise. She radioed for a paramedic team as she struggled to talk and run simultaneously.

Veva was curled next to Lainey in the shallow grave. Both wore a white silk chemise with nails perfectly manicured and inlaid floral design. Tears of joy rolled off Veva's cheeks as she stared at Lainey and then upward at the beautiful evening sky. "They're waiting for us," Veva sniffled. Lainey was sobbing too, but not for the same reasons.

Lainey was heartbroken to hear how poor little Genevieve had to watch her mommy slowly disintegrate, and she listened to how her mom believed the angels would rescue her from the torment of the gnawing tumorous cancer. Lainey's tears weren't for the loneliness of a lost little girl who nobody had the time to love or care for, nor was it for the sorrowful stories Veva believed would grant her passage to the kingdom of heaven. Lainey sobbed because she found herself strangely loving the pitiful creature who injected them both with Digoxin and had laid down next to her so that they could die together. There was no remorse on Lainey's part, only a deep sadness that Veva had such a warped perspective on merciful righteousness. Veva's story was sad enough, but the fact that she casually talked about murdering those other girls made it all the more despairing. All of them were preventable. Innocent beauty caught in Veva's delusion.

"Forgive me, Lainey. I've done it because I love you and want the best for you," Veva continued to cry. "Don't be mad at me."

Lainey could barely move her head to look at the forlorn Veva. "I forgive you for all of it. I only wished you'd talked to me. Maybe it was me who could have helped you." Lainey wanted to move her arms to take hold of Veva, but her body was unresponsive.

Veva saw Lainey's body struggle and snuggled closer, so their faces were only two inches apart. Her slender hands grasped Lainey. "I can feel my body fading, too. Don't be afraid. I failed you once before. I won't make the same mistake again."

"Oh, Veva, we could have had a different outcome." Lainey cast her eyes sideways, looked up at the trees, and listened to the birds singing. "You're right; it's beautiful here."

Veva tried to respond, but the massive amount of Digoxin she'd taken quickly took hold. Her mouth hung open, and no sound came from her lips as her eyes blinked rapidly, not understanding why she was lost for words. Drool dripped from the corner of her mouth and settled on the silk strap over her shoulder. She tried desperately to tell Lainey how radiant she looked and that she was sure that the angels would be awe-struck by her beauty.

Every detail of Lainey's face showed an expressive level of meaning, and although she was teary, she held a powerful gaze that swelled Veva's heart with admirable love. There was much more she wanted to say, but her throat constricted as the first wave of the drugs plowed through her system. Finally, Veva settled herself in her mind and knew that there was a final opportunity to assure Lainey all was well if she relaxed.

Lainey gave thought to the other women who'd been in this situation. Their lives were cut cruelly short by the misguided Veva. She said a prayer for those who were foolishly killed with kindness. She also said a few words for herself.

The heaving sensation in her chest felt increasingly like her heart was about to give out. Lainey asked aloud, "Brian, please forgive me for any transgressions." There were many, and he'd given as good as he'd received. His desire not to lay down and be a doormat was always something she had loved about him. She loved many things about him, not least that he could put up with her.

Lainey hadn't set out to be so particular and critical of things and people around her, but somehow it had developed within her. The more success she'd come by, the more she'd pushed everyone else away, with Brian being the only exception. Through thick and thin, he'd stuck by her, supported her, loved her, and been her champion and confidante. She wished she could see his face one more time and say something nice to him. God knows he deserved it.

The choking from Veva caused Lainey to break from her thoughts. The smile she offered to her fading companion was lopsided. Veva managed to smile back and release frothy white drool. Death was imminent, but the ridiculousness of their situation forced a strained laugh from Lainey's throat. She asked to come to the folly with Veva, and it seemed like it would be amazing to get outside in the air and the sun to experience its majesty. This was not the way she envisioned it would be.

She noticed Veva held a small card in her fingers with a floral motif on the edges. Detective Hurst and Strahan told her Marlene Durr in Bremen was 5 of 7, and Lainey presumed that she and Veva were 6 and 7. A fateful ending, with her body telling her the end was coming soon. "I love you, Veva," Lainey said. One last act of kindness seemed a fitting way to end.

CHAPTER TWENTY-FOUR

Brian sprinted through the sun-drenched meadow and into the scattered shade of the fallen arches. The toppled columns looked like an ancient place of worship had been ransacked by invaders. Brian's bursting lungs and pounding feet shattered the pond's tranquility. He slid to a halt in the dirt. "Lainey!" he bellowed.

The silence was only a few short seconds, but each second produced an irregular sickened beat in his heart.

"Brian?" The reply was faint. The tone was unmistakably Lainey's. In the quiet surroundings and the flush of energy rattling his body, Brian was uncertain which direction it came from.

"Lainey, where are you?" he called, his voice breaking apart in desperation.

"Here." The single word was strained and ahead to his right. There was nothing but greenery, shrubs, and ferns leading to taller trees. He sprinted forward and stumbled upon the darkened patch of earth, almost toppling into the hole. The earth had been scraped inward by hand into the double resting place. At the opposite end was a gap of two feet between the soil and green grass. Brian skipped around the darkened soil for fear of stepping on Lainey. None of it appeared real, like something from a terrible dream. He dropped to his knees, and staring back at him was Lainey's face, with Veva's head nestled against her. The whites of their necks and shoulders were visible, with thin silk straps over their shoulders. The open-mouthed horror on his wife's face was in stark contrast to the serenity of Veva's.

"Lainey, I've got you." He raked frantically at the soil around her. Suddenly he stopped and reached inside his pocket. There was nothing there.

248

He tried the other pocket. His fingers scrambled, knowing he put it there. "The pen," he groaned. "Hang on!" He turned and began to retrace his steps around the pond. He saw Detective Strahan running toward him and holding something in his hand, like passing a baton in a relay sprint final.

"You dropped it," Strahan shouted, sweat pouring down his face. He passed it to Brian, who turned and ran back to the partially covered bodies in the ground.

Brian slid to his knees beside Lainey and dragged away more earth. He pulled out enough soil to yank up the silk nightgown, giving him access to the top of her thigh. He brushed his hands on her skin to remove any residual dirt before he removed the blue safety cap, firmly gripped the body of the plastic pen, and jabbed the orange tip into the top of her thigh. He held it there, knowing three seconds was the dosage but counted to five before withdrawing it. Lainey didn't flinch, looking at him through teary eyes as though mesmerized at seeing his face. There was no cry of pain as the needle pierced her skin or the force with which he applied it. Brian withdrew the EpiPen and cast it to one side as he resumed clawing at the earth. Seconds later, Detective Strahan joined him and began dragging his hands at the soil that covered Lainey's legs.

The two men burrowed like crazed dogs who'd discovered a pile of fresh bones. Dirt flew in the air as they feverishly raked their fingers repeatedly. The dark blue material of the double-sized body bag was gradually revealed. Strahan parted the material to reveal the whole of Lainey's silken-covered body. Her thighs and genitalia were displayed where Brian had yanked up the nightdress to deliver the adrenalin shot. Strahan pulled down the silk to her knees to preserve some modesty. He beckoned Brian to move to the left, and he carefully planted his feet, ensuring he didn't accidentally step on Veva.

"On three," Strahan said. He and Brian placed their hands under Lainey's body. "One, two, three." They lifted in unison and picked Lainey from the grave, carrying her a few feet to one side, and laid her down in the lush grass.

"Lainey, I'm sorry," Brian wailed as he cupped a hand underneath her head.

She did not respond. Her body was limp, as though the tissue and muscles held no life.

Brian removed his jacket and placed it under her head. "Lainey, can you hear me?"

Her eyes opened, and she blinked hard three times. Her mouth fell open, and her tongue flopped around aimlessly inside her mouth as she tried to speak.

"It's okay," Brian softly assured her. The grim expression on his face suggested he had no idea if it would ever be okay. He knelt beside her and moved some stray hairs from her face. "I should never have left you."

Strahan radioed to their team, "Make sure that driveway is clear and guide the paramedics around to the back of the house and down the hill. Get as close to us down here as you can." He looked to Brian, "Keep talking to her and keep her awake."

Strahan spun around and jumped into the grave. Detective Hurst arrived, falling on her knees, and gasping for air as she stared in disbelief into the hole. "The pen," she pointed for Strahan to retrieve the plastic object in the grass.

Strahan picked it up and looked at the fill level on the side of the pen. He shook his head at Hurst, and she immediately understood.

Hurst shuffled close to Veva's side and sucked in large gasps of air as she tried to gain some composure. The soft brown eyes looking back at her from the attractive dark-haired young woman in the ground were familiar. The face had changed a little since Hurst last saw her as a teenager, but the eyes belonged to the little girl she once read bedtime stories to, with only the glow of a single candle, just as little Ginny liked it.

Hurst reached forward, took hold of the clawed fingers, and held them in hers. At first, the Detective couldn't speak, and tears swelled in her eyes. The memories and feelings of that beautiful little girl she used to snuggle with rushed through their connected hands like water running fluidly from an open tap, and words were impossible.

Veva's gaze signified their recognition. She made a strangled sound and coughed hard to clear her throat. "Aunt Carm, I'm sorry I wasn't a good girl, and you had to give me away. I've been good since then," her voice was faint, and the veins bulged from her neck.

"You were always a good girl," Hurst managed to blurt as snot and tears flowed. "It was my fault. I didn't know how to take care of you. What have you done, Ginny?" Hurst shook her head.

"I've helped people like mommy said I should."

"Oh, my sweet Ginny," Hurst sobbed. She wiped her face and growled, angry at herself for letting it get to her. Hurst looked into those beautiful brown eyes, seeing her unfortunate niece, a little girl who needed her help.

"I'll be with mommy soon," Veva gurgled and stared at the sky. "Angels." Veva's heart thudded as the increased pressure took hold.

Hurst found herself stuck between the world of being a detective and a loving aunt. "Lay still now, Ginny. Don't be afraid. I failed you once before. I won't make the same mistake again."

Veva's face cracked into a smile at the precious words. Happy tears leaked from the corners of her eyes. It was a special time having her aunt watching over her. "They're here…" Her stare went beyond her aunt into the branches of the trees.

Hurst looked over her shoulder, expecting to see one of her colleagues, but there were only the slender shafts of the fading light poking through the leafy branches. There was no way to fully comprehend what was going through the tortured mind of her niece, but she found herself saying. "They're as beautiful as your mommy said they would be. Are you ready to go with them?"

Veva coughed out thick frothy saliva and made a strangulated grunt.

Hurst tightened her grip on Ginny's hands. "I want you to close your eyes and take long deep breaths. I will pray that God will welcome you into heaven, and your mommy will be there, too." She brushed her hand over Ginny's eyes for her to close her long eyelashes. "Ginny, I want you to pray with me that the other girls you helped will be there, too. Elizabeth Seguras, Kumi Shinnabe, Daphne Montclair, and Marlene Durr." Hurst figured she owed it to their memories.

Veva's eyes popped open. They widened like they were about to burst from their sockets. Her gasp was cut short.

"Ginny?" Hurst gave her a mild shake. She shook her again, but there was nothing. The final breath was gone.

Hurst looked around, hoping that none of her colleagues heard the exchange. Instead, her focus switched to Brian Stewart, cradling his wife and wailing uncontrollably.

Strahan caught Hurst's attention, and he gave her a thumbs up to signal Lainey was alive. Hurst returned a thumbs down to signal Veva was gone.

In the distance, the first shrill piercing sirens filled the air. Hurst said a silent prayer over her niece's body and folded Ginny's arms over her chest. She looked like she was quietly sleeping in the woodland as the birds ceaselessly chirped their evening song. Hurst cleaned her face, not wishing to have any of the officers see her distress. The card with the floral pattern had slipped from Veva's fingers and lay next to her. Hurst left it where it was.

She stood on shaky legs and gazed down at the body in the ground. "If your mom could see you now, she'd slap the snot out of you," Hurst concluded. "No wonder I never had kids. Who in their right mind wants to deal with this shit." She wrestled herself back into detective mode. "Hey! Make sure that driveway is clear!" She called to the officers.

Strahan left the Stewarts to hold onto one another and stood beside his colleague. "Looks like we were just in time."

Hurst muttered her agreement, but her face showed dissatisfaction with the entire thing. She looked over the pond into the distance, where the sun was setting on the horizon. "Nice evening for it."

Strahan looked in the same direction and then at her. "Are you okay?"

"I'm not sure," Hurst observed the chaos around them. "Who's gonna be okay after all this?"

CHAPTER TWENTY-FIVE

Lainey Stewart was taken to Saint Joseph's General in Eureka and kept overnight for observation. Brian stayed in the room with Lainey. A heavy police presence was stationed within the hospital. The media were eager to feast on the sensational story of the fitness entrepreneur who had escaped death for a second time at the hands of the same killer.

Detective Hurst and Strahan made their reports and went to the hospital to visit Lainey and Brian. There was little conversation as Lainey was sedated, and Brian was spitting threats of violence on those who failed to protect his wife.

Hurst and Strahan left to inspect the apartment of Veva Unwin.

"Even I need a beer after all this," Strahan admitted.

Hurst didn't argue. "You can buy the first round … and the second."

The two weary detectives asked the police officers to get out of the way as they looked through Veva's apartment. Neither detective was in a celebratory mood. Catching a killer, in any circumstance, was typically something to be excited about, but both of them recognized that Veva's story touched a personal nerve in Hurst.

Strahan repeatedly apologized for not looking sooner into Veva. "We could have already gotten this done," Strahan complained as he inspected the stack of papers on the table. "I had the chance, and we might have saved some of those lives in between."

"Once it got moving, its pace was impossible to manage," Hurst said as she fiddled with her cellphone. "There was nothing obvious as to why you should – we should. It wasn't until we had a few other bits of luck fall our way that she came to light. I doubt it would have made much difference. By the time the introduction was made, likely, she'd already killed Elizabeth Seguras in Oregon and Kumi Shinnabe in Kyoto. You had no evidence from the first attempt on Lainey. Forget it. It's done."

"It doesn't make it any easier," Strahan admitted.

"There's something else," Hurst said as she looked at the side cabinet adorned with framed photographs. She pointed for them to look together.

"What's that?"

"Veva carried the calling card that read "7 of 7", and Lainey was number 6." Hurst gestured at the framed photographs of the women on the side cabinet. Marlene Durr's photograph is in Veva's suitcase, not yet unpacked from Germany."

"And what of it?" Strahan asked.

"She was precise in everything she did. There's still no ring. There are no hidden compartments in her stuff where we could have missed it. I'm sure she took Marlene's ring."

"She could have ditched it or lost it."

"I doubt that. Everything had a purpose. The emails sent to us purposefully led us away so that she could finish with her Angel's fantasy."

Strahan gave her a curious stare. "The ring aside, it looks to me like we have closure."

"I'm not feeling closure. Normally, if things fall into line, I get all tingly across here," Hurst said, running a hand over her chest. "I don't feel a thing."

Strahan stared blankly at her, not sure if she was being serious or not. He caught the attention of the forensic team scouring the apartment. "Give us a moment, will you."

The team dutifully left the apartment. Strahan waited until it was only Hurst and himself. "Tomorrow, we'll speak with Lainey. After that, we'll have to backtrack and see what comes up if we missed anything. There's no other picture on this cabinet or anything we've found."

"Exactly." Hurst looked around the apartment and shook her head.

"Now, I need that drink."

"Wow! I turned you into an alcoholic – I'm so proud. Am I going to be safe staying in your house tonight?" Hurst jabbed at him.

"You could stay in my house and be safe from me for the rest of your life."

"Have you ever thought about it?" Hurst flickered two suggestive eyebrows up and down.

"Never. Please don't put that in my vortex."

"We need to find that damned ring." Hurst looked at her phone.

"Lainey might know something about it."

Hurst grunted a partial agreement. She pulled on her latex gloves and carefully picked up the first picture from the top of the cabinet. "That's my sister, Veva's mom before she died," Hurst pointed at the attractive brunette. "A good woman."

Strahan browsed through the cabinet drawers. Behind him, Detective Hurst cursed and muttered as she searched. "That fucking ring," she hissed. "Veva never went home after coming back from Bremen. We know she spent the night at Lainey's."

"Marlene's boyfriend had recently proposed to her. He could have it and be looking for a fraudulent insurance claim."

"No. Veva liked her little trophies. We haven't turned up Marlene's or Lainey's ring. I'll ask Matthaus to see if we can get a photograph of what that ring looked like," Hurst said.

"In the report, Marlene's ring is described as an antique. A white gold band with an oval-shaped red ruby centered on either side with four inlaid diamonds. It sounds like that was worth a few bucks," Strahan suggested.

"Marlene's Patreon account was doing very nicely on the back of her performances with her fiancé. But there's only the photo in Veva's possession." Hurst stressed the point. She continued to look around. "Everyone gave up a framed photograph. But Veva had a design for the rings. I know it."

Strahan looked at the picture frames on the cabinet. "Is this an altar to the girls or something else?"

"Looks more like a family gathering than a shrine. Veva had a deeply misguided view of the world. You might notice that Veva didn't include a photograph of herself with the others."

"Maybe she considered herself unworthy?" Strahan speculated.

"She considered that she was on a mission from God. That's fucked up."

"If all we have left open are the two missing rings. I'm not going to lose any sleep over it." Strahan sounded exhausted.

"Veva believed wholeheartedly in what she was doing. She had those rings with a purpose in mind. Maybe we'll never know the answer," Hurst surmised.

"I know I've already said it, but that beer sounds better with every passing hour."

"I always knew I would like you," Hurst replied.

The following day, Lainey and Brian entered their house. Lainey was happy to be out of the hospital, but that's where her happiness ended. Their designer paradise had lost its appeal, and the space was tainted. There were too many fights, negative thoughts, and other fractious events under its grasp. Brian put her bags on the kitchen counter and brewed coffee.

"I'll make you a bullet-proof one," he said, knowing it was her favorite. "If you feel any fluctuations, I'm taking you straight back to the hospital."

"Thanks." Her body was still convulsing with all the drugs she'd taken to balance her cardiac rhythms. "Brian, do you want to live here?"

He frowned, unsure about the basis of her question. "You mean me or us?"

"Us."

He looked around at the grand structure and glanced at the extensive views, front and back. "It's spectacular, but I don't care. Where you go, I go. I can live anywhere unless it snows six months of the year– then we would need to renegotiate."

Lainey leaned herself on the breakfast counter and slid her rear onto a tall stool. "I want to sell the house and build something new."

"Why?"

Lainey tilted her head. "Look at it. We constructed this sleek, stylish, artful, symmetrical world of sharp lines and smooth contours. We built perfection. We don't belong here anymore."

Brian nodded his understanding. "Perhaps nobody belongs here."

"We'll stay in Eureka. We matter here." A small burst of energy came over her, and she walked briskly toward the rear sliding door, opened it, and stepped outside onto the stone patio.

Brian stopped preparing the coffee and ran to the back door, wondering what she was doing. He followed her outside to assess her reaction.

Lainey had her back to him as she looked down over the gardens. "It's beautiful here, but I won't miss it."

Brian put his arms around her and held her tight. "I love you, Lainey, no matter what or where." He quickly released his grip and took a step back. "There are some things I have to tell you about what happened in Bremen. I did some things I'm not proud of."

"With Veva?" she asked, as though she already knew what he was holding back.

"Yes, with Veva."

"Then I guess we have a lot to discuss." She softly kissed his lips. "We've both done things we're not proud of."

Brian narrowed his focus as he calculated her inference.

"There's something I want you to do for me," Lainey said and headed inside the house. She walked up the stairs, and Brian followed. In their bedroom, Lainey placed soft fingers on his chest signaling Brian to stay in the middle of the room while she went inside the master closet. A moment later, she returned and placed the small dirt-covered plastic bag in the palm of his hand.

There was no need for him to inspect the contents. "There's a long story attached to that and one where I've been about as foolish as possible. I took this from the hands of a dead girl in Prairie Creek Redwoods," he confessed as his voice broke. "The anonymous email said it would be there. I didn't know what else I'd find."

"Veva knew what you'd find," Lainey said. "She knew you'd go looking. So what were you going to do with it?"

"At first, I thought you'd be glad to have it back, but then I wasn't sure. And I didn't know how to explain how I came to find it. That poor girl. I was the one who called the police a few days later from a call box in Eureka and told them where to find the body. It was Daphne Montclair."

"I know it wasn't you, although I had my doubts for a while. Veva told me the names of the others she killed, including Daphne."

"You knew I had it. Why didn't you say something? You must have thought…"

"It occurred to me, on more than one occasion, but I know you would never harm me. Not intentionally."

Brian's weary face and dark rings underneath his eyes melted together as his lips pushed out, and his hands covered his face to hide his distress. He stayed hidden, covering the shame that poured from him. The worst was yet to come when he must explain himself and what took place with Veva. Lainey stood by and said nothing. It took him a minute before he was able to compose himself. "Lainey, I'm sorry if I ever hurt you."

"We both have things to be sorry about," she replied. She opened Brian's fingers and pulled them away from his face. She tipped her engagement ring into the palm of his hand and discarded the dirty bag in the trash. "This used to mean everything to me. Too often, I've forgotten what it stood for. Now I don't want to remember." She squeezed Brian's hand and closed his fingers around it. "I want you to do something for me without question."

"Anything."

"Take it down to the pond by the folly, and throw it in. Don't think about it. Don't ask; just throw it in. When you've done that, we'll make our peace.

The house can go on the market next week. We'll rent something until we know what we want."

He put his hand inside his black jacket and took out a silver band with a red ruby, centered amongst four diamonds. "I discovered this in my pocket when we were in the hospital last night. I didn't say anything to the police. I'll toss this one too. I'm in enough shit already."

"Yes, you are."

"I can't prove it, but I know Veva put it there when we were in Bremen. Something to frame me and have the cops keep me in jail, while she…you know."

Lainey touched her hand to the side of his face and smiled. "When you come back to the house, come upstairs, and get into bed with me. I want to feel my husband on my skin."

Brian curled his fingers around the rings. The fire that burned in Lainey's eyes left no doubt that she meant business. Brian dutifully turned, went down the stairs, and headed outside.

"A new start," Lainey called after him.

He took both rings down the stepped terraces and through the gardens towards the folly. Before disappearing into the tree line, Brian looked back at the upstairs of their house, where Lainey watched from the upstairs window. She waved to him, and he returned it. Once he went through the trees and across the meadow, he was out of sight. Brian walked along the dirt track, cutting through the bushes, and he entered the walkway that looped around the edge of the murky pond.

At the edge of the water, he removed Lainey's engagement ring. It shone brilliantly, causing him to stare. "A new start," he repeated Lainey's words. He took out the second engagement ring, once belonging to Marlene Durr. The red ruby, set with the four diamonds, dazzled in the palm of his hand. He placed it next to Lainey's ring.

Without further thought, Brian cast them both into the middle of the pond. He watched the two small circular ripples grow bigger across the top of the water. The memories they once held faded to nothing.

The surface settled, and the water smoothly reflected its tranquil surroundings. The gothic folly held onto the secrets below.

My ask to you dear Reader.

I am sure that you enjoyed this thought provoking and intriguing story. I would ask that you take sixty seconds of your time to leave a five star review that makes a huge difference for me.

Anything less than that and I ask that you keep your opinions to yourself.

In any event, I love you; Deal with it.

Thank you.

ABOUT THE AUTHOR

Vincent Redgrave is the author of The Angel Seedlings, The Third Coming, A Texas Sunrise and The Sideliners. He is also the proud recipient of the 'can do better' school report award – a title he's held since he can't recall.

Vincent has fifteen other works of varying genres, time periods, and settings soon to be released. Each story is complete and under numerous iterations.

In the meantime, Vincent is likely hard at work on a novel or dancing to the beat of a rattlesnake's tail under a blue Arizona sky.

Check out my other titles at:

https://www.amazon.com/author/vincentredgrave

https://vincentredgrave.com

Follow me on Facebook: Vincent Redgrave Author | Facebook

Reading a novel by Vincent Redgrave is like white water rafting in your favorite armchair. You know you're going to get wet and sustain a few bruises, but you can be reasonably confident about staying in the boat.

Coming soon:

Eternally Anonymous:

The prolific serial pedophile killer, known as the Demon Dentist, returns after a twelve month absence. The killer's pace rises to new heights, but the killer is collapsing under the burden of his mission. Nunez and rookie partner, detective Cam Sterling, have everyone breathing down their necks, including the dubious support of FBI profiler, Agent Harper. The killer, Nunez and Sterling are all battling personal issues. Unexpected events pull the central characters into an entangled finale, where everyone is faced with dire moral decisions, and nothing is as it seems.

Long Road to Vienna:

Twins, Livia and Luka are sold by their desperate father into the hands of Mr. and Mrs. Luknar. Everyone in the Austro-Hungarian valley dislikes the Luknars, and for good reason. Livia and Luka must use all their wits, guile, and determination in order to survive. Servant girl, Jirina, takes them under her wing, but soon the Luknars, along with invading Cossacks, and other dreadful people spin their insufferable world into a nightmare. Luka and Livia establish unbreakable bonds with a local wolf-pack - useful allies in the fight for life. The sanctuary of Vienna seems like an impossible dream, and dreams are misleading.

Printed in Great Britain
by Amazon